The Post Generation

by Howard Manning

AF265284

Copyright © 2019 Howard Manning
All rights reserved

ISBN: 978-0-9957293-9-1

To my grandchildren

Poppy, Iris, Jack, Harry and Kit

It's a beautiful world –

please take care of it!

Contents

People

In order of appearance; ages and places are as of 12 April in the year
of Phraya.

On holiday on Salay in the Far Isles:
Steven Lynn, 45, engineer.
Margaret (Maggie) Lynn, 43, nutritionist.
Peter Lynn, 15.
Julia Lynn, 13.

On holiday on their boat Eolia, berthed at Glendonan on Estra in the
Far Isles:
Charles Lenton, 50, businessman.
Olivia Lenton, 49, lawyer.
Philip Lenton, 20, electronics student.
Katherine Blair, 20, biochemistry student; Philip's girlfriend.
Henry Lenton, 18, schoolboy.

At home in London:
Bruce Lenton, 47, epidemiologist.
Alexandra Eades, 47, sociologist, Bruce's second wife.
Jessica Eades, 15, Alexandra's eldest daughter.
Benjamin Lenton, 14, Bruce's son.
Isabella (Bella), 10, Bruce and Alexandra's daughter.

At home on Mansay in the Far Isles:
Rory Scott, 36, fish farmer.
Lucy Scott, 34, general practitioner.
Alison (Ali) Scott, 6.
Calum Scott, 4.

At home in Edinburgh:
Alan Petrie, 30, joiner.

At home on their smallholding in Morrie:
Alice Petrie, 28, smallholder; Alan's sister.
Ruth Paterson, 27, smallholder; Alice's partner.

At home on their farm in Morrie:
David Tanner, 41, farmer.
Deborah Tanner, 40, farmer.
Samuel (Sam) Tanner, 12.
Rose Tanner, 10.
William (Billie) Tanner, 8.

Andrew Wilson, leader of the humanist group.

Alastair Dunbar, leader of the engineers.

Rhona Anderson, leader of the chemists.

Gregory Clark, leader of the rapeseed farmers.

Glen Buchanan, member of the westsiders.

Peggy Fraser, leader of the cereal group.

Raymond Barber, leader of the animal husbandry group.

Gordon Lyle, leader of the doctors.

Liam Brodie, member of the westsiders.

Gavin Baird, leader of the westsiders.

Richie Carr, leader of the northers.

Keith Johnston, leader of the electronics group.

Patricia (Trish) Carter; meets Henry Lenton.

Adam Middleton, leader of the electronics group in London.

Shona Macfarlane; meets Samuel Tanner.

Fergus Sutherland; meets Rose Tanner.

Donald Grant; meets Isabella Lenton.

Graeme Melville.
Anthea Melville
Their daughter Kyla Melville; meets Calum Scott.

Ramsay Macrae, a doctor.
His son Cameron Macrae; meets Alison Scott.

Anne Holmes; meets William Tanner.

Children born after Phraya:

Stewart Paterson, Ruth's son.

Jocelyn Blair, Katherine and Philip's daughter.

Flora Paterson, Ruth's daughter.

Thomas (Tom) Eades, Jessica and Peter's son.

Marcus Carter, Patricia and Henry's son.

Sarah Eades, Jessica and Peter's first daughter.

Craig Macfarlane, Shona and Samuel's first son.

Victoria Lynn, Julia and Benjamin's daughter.

Eleanor Carter, Patricia and Henry's daughter.

Fiona Macfarlane, Shona and Samuel's daughter.

Mary Eades, Jessica and Peter's second daughter.

Rachel Tanner, Rose and Fergus's first daughter.

Douglas (Dougie) Lenton, Isabella and Donald's first son.

Robert Lynn, Julia and Benjamin's son.

Roy Macfarlane, Shona and Samuel's second son.

Celia Tanner, Rose and Fergus's second daughter.

Dylan Holmes, Anne and William's first son.

James Lenton, Isabella and Donald's second son.

Louise Holmes, Anne and William's daughter.

Jeannie Scott, Alison and Cameron's first daughter.

Una Scott, Alison and Cameron's second daughter.

Max Holmes, Anne and William's second son.

James Scott, Alison and Cameron's son.

An unnamed girl, Kyla and Calum's daughter.

Places

References to people apply to 12 April in the year of Phraya.

The Far Isles, a chain of islands off the west coast of Scotland. From south to north:

Beag Salay, the southernmost island, small and uninhabited.

Salay, a small uninhabited island near the southern end of the Far Isles. The Lynns holiday on it.

Two further small islands, then:

Mansay, a small lightly populated island. Home to the Scotts. Joined by a causeway to:

Pennay, a sizeable island. Ferries sail from Bailecas, the main town at the south of the island, to Caladion on the mainland; and from the north of the island to Estra.

Estra, a large island. The Lenton's boat Eolia is berthed at Glendonan, its largest town. Caoloch is a small village on its east coast. Estra is joined by a causeway to:

Iseala, a sizeable island. Joined by a causeway to:

Nestra, a large island. Ferries sail from Lochmoran, the main town at the north of the island, to the island of Dubheilean near the mainland.

Other islands, at the northern end of the Far Isles, are further from the Dubheilean and the mainland.

Dubheilean, a large island between the Far Isles and the mainland. Connected to the mainland by a bridge.

The Near Isles, islands off the west coast of Scotland but not as far out as the Far Isles.

Letheilean, a sparsely populated peninsula on the west coast of the mainland, south of Dubheilean. Local ferries sail from Tirglas, the largest village in the peninsula, to Innisdu, a town on the nearby island of Eilard. The Achar Hotel is in a remote part of Letheilean.

Eilard, an island just south of Letheilean. Ferries sail from its largest town Innisdu to Tirglas in Letheilean, and from its eastern end to Caladion on the mainland.

Caladion, a port on the west coast of the mainland, east of Eilard. Home to Lucy's parents and brother.

Port Monard, a town in the west of the mainland, on the way to Letheilean.

Morrie, a village at the northern edge of the arable part of central Scotland. Home to the Tanners' farm, and to Alice Petrie's and Ruth Paterson's smallholding.

Part 1 Islands

Chapter 1 Intimations

On Saturday 12 April the Lynn family disembarked from a chartered boat to begin a fortnight's holiday on the uninhabited Scottish island of Salay. Steven, an engineer, robust, red-headed and inclined to privacy, was looking forward to the seclusion and peace of this lump of rock near the southern end of the Far Isles. Margaret, a nutritionist, brunette, sporty but fearful, was rather apprehensive about the remoteness. Their teenage children soon informed them this wasn't a good place for a stay of any length; they too were concerned about isolation. Julia observed, 'Dad, there's no mobile reception!' Steven replied, 'Maybe at the top of the hill? A little solitude will be good for you.' Peter wanted to know: 'No broadband either – what am I going to do for two weeks?'

The family was soon distracted; the weather was clear, and from the island's high point they could see the first few links in the chain of islands stretching northwards. In the distance, on the right, the spectacular mountains of Dubheilean were also visible; the mainland lay just beyond. To the south there was only the dot of Beag Salay, and westwards it was water all the way to Canada. Salay itself, four kilometres by three of wilderness that scarcely looked as if it could have been inhabited until 1912, would be their home for the holiday. Luckily one ruinous building, once the schoolhouse, had been restored recently, and they were going to stay in it by special permission. Although the accommodation was comfortable enough, Margaret wouldn't have fancied it in the winter, and the weather was still too cool for the summer campers. Much of the island was a scene of the usual battle between bracken and heather; what on earth did the islanders eat at any time of the year?

While the children were busy with the vain pursuit of a signal, Margaret sought clarification: 'Steve, it's nice to have a proper break from phone and email, but without them we can't get hold of anyone in an emergency?' 'Sorry, Maggie, I was told the mobiles would work. I'm sure everything will be alright, and the boat is coming down from Pennay on the 26th to pick us up. In any case from 1 May it does day trips routinely. Your sister knows where we are, and work colleagues. We've got a radio for the news.' The last remark was a reference to the announcement earlier that day that a new influenza virus had emerged; Margaret liked to keep up with these things.

***

On the same day the Lenton family arrived at Glendonan, a small port on the island of Estra to the north, beyond Pennay. They made their way to the berth of their yacht Eolia. Charles, tall and portly, was a successful businessman; and Olivia was a lawyer. They were English but had moved to Edinburgh many years earlier and attained a position in life which enabled them to devote some of their time to exploring the islands. They planned to spend the next two weeks sailing northwards along the west coasts of Estra, Iseala and Nestra, and back down the eastern side.

On this occasion they were to be accompanied by their son Philip and his girlfriend Katherine Blair. When they arrived later in the day, he outlined their plans. 'I can only stay until the Easter weekend, if that's alright; then I've got to head for Strathclyde for the start of term on the 21st. Katherine has to go back as well. We'll stay aboard past Iseala, disembark and fly back.' His younger brother Henry had come with them; 'Me too, I suppose I shouldn't get expelled from school in my last term.'

Olivia, slim with hair allowed to grey to match her husband's, was in charge of practicalities. 'Let's load the boat with plenty of food, because there are limited opportunities for shopping on the west coast of Estra.' Eolia itself was Charles's domain, however. 'I hope we're going to sail for the most part, but with the Atlantic on the port side we better fill up with diesel in case we need to motor.'

Katherine, tall slender and fair, was slightly worried as she had never been on a small boat. She tried to demonstrate that she had done her homework: 'At least if we're driven ashore it seems to be mostly beaches rather than rocks.' Henry, well-built with lank brown locks, over-confident and inexperienced with girls, was meeting her for the first time; he thought he could have some fun. 'But then the great white sharks might get us while we're wading ashore.' Philip, lean and as dark as his parents had been, was a gentler soul than his brother; he reassured her: 'Don't worry, dad's been sailing for decades.' Henry continued, 'No trouble, if you punch them on the nose they leave you alone.' 'Just ignore him, Kat,' said Olivia, 'A teenage boy is a work in progress.'

***

The day after their arrival the Lynns conducted a proper exploration of Salay. On the east side the remains of a village, once occupied by more than a hundred hardy souls, lay near the only beach. Everywhere else cliffs, sea stacks and a natural arch guarded the island, and provided safe homes for an impressive population of birds. Even in the lee of the island the swell attacked relentlessly.

Julia, thirteen years old, mousy and gentle, expressed surprise: 'Look, rabbits, how did they get here?' Her brother, even redder than his father and impish despite his fifteen years, seized the opportunity to tease his sister for becoming a vegetarian. 'Yummy, let's have stew tonight.' Margaret remonstrated, 'Must you, Peter?' Steven ignored the sensitivities: 'I think the rabbits have been here since they were introduced by the islanders. There were sheep too, even after the island was abandoned, but they were taken off because it was too hard to land at the beach.'

They looked across the strait to Beag Salay; once again their father was a fount of knowledge. 'That was also inhabited, for longer than Salay because of the lighthouse, but it was automated in 1980.' Their mother, looking with a professional eye at its steep slopes, muttered, 'It looks even less promising than this place for growing an adequate range of food.'

****

Bruce Lenton, Charles's brother, worked in a medical research unit in London, specialising in the modelling of epidemics. His receding and greying hair seemed to bear witness to deep thought. On 14 April he started to pay attention to the Phraya virus, named after the river in Bangkok where it had spread from chickens to people. Hospitals and researchers were starting to collate data on its incubation time, transmission and fatality rate.

His second wife Alexandra, an academic in sociology, slim, almost thin, was dyed fair; she had little use for mathematics, preferring precise verbal analysis with its greater relevance to people's lives. That evening Bruce remarked to her, 'This new virus is another avian escapee; it doesn't look very nice.' She spent a moment pondering the idea of an insentient life form abandoning one host in order to be unpleasant to another; but she was used to his prognostications and thought no more about it.

Over the next few days Bruce developed his model and grew concerned. By the 18th he was convinced that Phraya was in another category from SARS or even Ebola. Alexandra noticed he was more stooped than usual, and insisted, 'Out with it.' 'This disease is really serious, it's going to spread all over the world and cause a huge number of deaths.' She detected a different tone from Bruce's other warnings. 'How can you be sure?'

'For a start, the victims seem to remain well for a week before they become ill. That allows them to fly to other continents, drive to small towns and go to crowded places like restaurants. By the time each person is sick enough to stop mingling with other people, he has infected a certain number of others – this is a key parameter in any model, and I think the value is eight.' His voice rose a little as he gave this number, and Alexandra noticed, but it seemed no worse than any other he might have mentioned. She could feel some technicalities looming; 'OK but stick to plain English please. What does that mean?' Bruce continued, 'The next cohort starts their own symptomless period, and does the same thing. The number of cases grows exponentially until such time as the publicity produces a change in behaviour.'

'Most of this is true of the common cold. Presumably this is more serious?' 'I'm afraid so. The other key parameter is the proportion of people who die of the disease, and that's not clear yet. My concern is that it doesn't have to be all that high to produce a threatening result. Only a few hundred have died worldwide so far, but depending on the parameters this virus looks set to kill hundreds of thousands, maybe millions.'

'What can people do?' Alexandra certainly knew the significance of these numbers, and now she was taking the matter seriously. 'This is why I'm concerned. There's no treatment yet, and it may take months to develop anything effective. In the meantime, only being isolated helps. Most people will continue to travel and mix, and governments won't prevent this until it's too late. As a result, the epidemic will run its course, causing a number of deaths which depends on the characteristics of the disease. Of course a properly organised virus doesn't want to kill its host, but both evolved in times when people didn't move around so much. Let's hope Phraya isn't much more dangerous than most viruses, but I think it is.'

'What do you suggest?' Bruce thought for a while. 'Let's get away from here. We could go up to Charles's house in Edinburgh; he's on his boat, so he won't mind. Then we can go somewhere further afield as required, maybe join him? Alexandra was incredulous and protested: 'Seems an extreme step on the basis of a computer model!' 'Perhaps, but we could tell colleagues that we've been called away by a family situation and that we propose to work remotely?'

On the following day Alexandra wrote in her diary, "19 April. The virus has spread to cities worldwide, infecting many thousands and killing hundreds. The word pandemic has been used for the first time in a news report, but this has been criticised as a wild exaggeration."

***

Lucy Scott, a family doctor on Pennay, was not expecting the virus to put in an appearance any time soon. Small, fair and slightly over-weight, but self-confident and capable, she was worried only about her young children. That evening she had to admit to her husband Rory, 'I had a patient today who might have the Phraya virus. There isn't a test yet, so I can't be sure.' He was surprised: 'Seems unlikely that the bug could have got from Thailand to the Scottish mainland to the Far Isles so soon?' He went off to bathe Alison, six years old, who was apt to screech when he washed her long fair curls; and Calum, four with a shorter brown mop, who was less trouble.

Lucy turned to the web to investigate the virus; she saw that it had reached most countries, and countless cities and towns, so even if it wasn't on Pennay yet it was only a matter of time. Apparently the virus was highly contagious and resulted in serious illness. She looked for any advice that might have been generated for medical professionals, but found none. She began to consider how to protect her children and her patients. Rehearsing the usual precautions – hand-washing, covering your face when sneezing, and staying away from others when feeling ill – she doubted that they would be sufficient. She was glad their house was one of only a few on Mansay, a small island connected to Pennay by a causeway.

Rory recited to the children at bedtime, 'Diddle diddle dumpling, my son John,' but was interrupted: 'I'm not John, I'm Calum.' 'And I'm not your son, I'm a girl.' He continued, 'Went to bed with his trousers on. One shoe off, and the other shoe on, diddle diddle dumpling, my son John.' He left to a chorus, 'I'm wearing pyjamas, not trousers.' 'And we haven't got any shoes on.'

Lucy summarised her research: 'Very little is known about the virus except that it's quite aggressive.' Rory, built like his wife but darker haired, outdoorsy and practical, replied insouciantly, 'I expect they're watching it, and will keep the profession informed on the appropriate action.' She sighed, 'I suppose so, and as usual those at the sharp end will be the last to hear.'

***

By now the Eolia had sailed past the beaches of Iseala, and the Lentons had mobile reception again. 'It's Bruce, glad I've reached you.' Charles guessed immediately why he was calling: 'We've heard about the virus; they seem to be making quite a fuss about it.' No time was wasted on small talk: 'Yes, I've been looking into it and I have to say it's the most serious epidemic I've seen. I judge it's going to spread everywhere and may kill millions. I don't want to be in London. I have persuaded Alexandra that we should take a break, and I'm hoping we can use your house.'

Charles had seen his brother over-react in the past: 'Are you sure it's that bad?' Impatient at having to explain again, Bruce gave him the same account as Alexandra, and got a similar reaction. 'By all means take a break in my place, but if the virus is as sinister as you're saying, is Edinburgh any better than London?' He replied, 'I'll watch the epidemic from there, and move further north if it seems necessary;' and ended by saying, 'things will be clearer in a few days. Will you at least ask your children to stay on the boat rather than going back to university and school?'

Charles reported the conversation to Olivia privately, and she was inclined to give Bruce the benefit of the doubt, on the precautionary principle rather than because she really believed him. 'I don't want to get calls from Philip and Henry in a few days' time saying they're not well, or are surrounded by ill people; let's at least tell them.' The upshot was that they all decided to stay aboard for the time being.

***

On Salay, Steven was aware that his wife was concerned by the news of the epidemic. 'Maggie, I've got a confession to make: our radio doesn't have a mains cable, and we don't have that many batteries. If we want to follow the news, we must switch the set off when we've heard each bulletin.' She didn't react but a corner of her mind started to consider the resources of their temporary home; at any rate they had brought plenty of food. The island was charming, but she was looking forward to the boat taking them off it in a week's time.

Steven insisted that they should enjoy their holiday. He found an old fishing rod, Margaret suggested mussels as bait and Peter managed to catch some flounder. They didn't feel they should cut down the island's only tree for firewood, so they cooked them indoors. Julia, true to her principles, wouldn't eat them. Instead she found wild celery and sorrel, checked with her mother and was allowed to experiment. Peter, seeking revenge, refused to touch them.

***

On 20 April Rory Scott took the children to school and nursery on Pennay, established that no-one was ill and reported this to Lucy. His duty done, he continued to the industrial estate where his fish farming business was based. He wasn't going to let a tiny bug disturb his work; he was more concerned about the lice that were giving farmed salmon a bad name. He was planning to accompany a member of his staff on a boat trip to one of several cages off the island, but first he had to inspect the smoking equipment in which the business had recently invested. He wanted to make sure that the processing of the fish was optimised for the high fat content of farmed salmon.

Lucy monitored the patients who presented at her surgery, saw no further cases of Phraya and began to wonder if it was a false alarm. It was her duty to follow these foreign diseases, but they usually posed little challenge in developed countries.

***

In London Bruce Lenton, better informed than most, or more neurotic – he wasn't sure himself – was stocking up with food, fuel and equipment including a diesel generator. At the other end of the country Olivia, slightly embarrassed at being so influenced by her brother-in-law's twitchiness, was likewise filling the Eolia with supplies.

***

Alan Petrie, a joiner in Edinburgh, had heard the news too. Although well-built and competent he was a pessimistic type, with a penchant for preparation. He spent a lot of time on the internet, trying to determine whether this virus was more serious than others which had given rise to exaggerated news and then evaporated without causing significant trouble. He found some of the same reports as Lucy but lacked the medical knowledge to interpret them properly. Nevertheless, he was worried by the information he had uncovered; on 21 April, even without the Lentons' privileged knowledge, he decided that he should stock his house with much more food than normal. He bought a lot of tins, sugar, flour and other dry basics; and some luxuries like chocolate.

In the towns and cities, others of Alan's mindset were also hoarding food; the news started to reflect this, and began to create a run on the shops everywhere, but he was well ahead of them. Even though he knew that this kind of thinking creates real difficulties without true cause, and was faintly ashamed, he continued anyway. Soon his shelves were groaning, and the shops were struggling to re-fill theirs.

Having prepared, he turned his mind to business. He had quotations to prepare for three jobs, and followed his normal procedure of entering all necessary materials onto a spreadsheet. Multiplying by prices, adding labour and including a small amount of contingency led to totals which seemed reasonable. He was always surprised by the fact that many of his rivals simply made up the numbers. As for the virus, Alan knew that most people would be less concerned than he was about distant threats, and would want their wardrobes built as usual.

***

On 22 April Rory Scott went shopping in Bailecas, the main town on Pennay. This was routine, as he was neither forewarned nor anxious, but he found that already the town was emptying of essentials, and the retailers were complaining that deliveries weren't arriving from the mainland. At suppertime, Alison complained. 'Daddy, you promised we would have sausages.' Lucy explained, 'There weren't any left in the shop, Ali, but we can have some of daddy's special fish.' Calum piped up, 'I like sausages better. Why can't daddy grow them in the sea instead of yukky fish?' Alison teased, 'They can't swim, silly, so they have to grow on land.' Rory remonstrated, 'Ali, don't confuse him. Anyway, I'm not sure you know yourself how they're made.' 'Yes I do, they start off as tiny sausages in their mummy's tummy …' Lucy said, 'Bedtime I think.'

***

The same day, the Lentons set off from London for Edinburgh. Bruce had failed to persuade his mother to accompany them, and Alexandra hadn't even tried with her mother and sisters. Their youngest child Isabella, at ten still a podgy girl, was innocent of the reason for the trip. 'This is great, going on holiday is much better than school.' The other children were old enough to know that something was up. Jessica, Alexandra's fair and pretty daughter of fifteen, was cramped despite being slim: 'We can hardly move; why are we taking all this stuff?' Benjamin, Bruce's fourteen-year-old son, also thin but growing, sat with his feet splayed either side of a generator, occupying more space than seemed fair to his sisters. 'Yes, I know what this is for, but surely they have electricity even in Scotland?' Alexandra tried to divert the conversation: 'Let's discuss this later, we don't want to bore Bella.'

On arrival in Edinburgh, they could feel the darkening mood. The following day Bruce ran his model, using the latest data from his contacts, and concluded that the coming pandemic would trigger worldwide chaos. When he and Alexandra were alone, he explained his thinking. 'The superficial emptying of shops is just the beginning. When this causes widespread alarm, people will divert their energies from their normal activities, and the supply chain will slow down. The shops will remain empty, worsening the panic.'

Alexandra resisted: 'There have been shortages before, and people understand that they are soon corrected. A few years ago, someone stood in a street and shouted, "The sugar is running out." Soon it was, but nobody was seriously inconvenienced. It's not as if this virus is really compromising the world's ability to function, at least not anywhere except Bangkok, or Thailand at most?' 'In the past, crises have been limited geographically, and the ability of the system to withstand a local challenge has been buttressed by normality elsewhere. In this case Phraya has probably already reached every corner of the world.'

'Maybe so, but there's still no fundamental reason for things to break down. The vast majority of people are still healthy. Your model can't know how people will respond. I think you're far too pessimistic.' 'Indeed, people have nothing to fear except fear itself. The question is, will they behave well under such a challenge? I may be influenced by my tendency to assume the worst, but I doubt it.' Alexandra fell silent. Her intellectual life was predicated on a world where cooperation between people was as important as their conflicts; she didn't want to believe that this was under threat.

Once Isabella was in bed, Bruce gave the older children a moderated version of his prognosis, and announced, 'I think we've got to get out of the city, and go somewhere away from other people. Alexandra suggested: 'How about that hotel on Letheilean where Charles took us a few years ago?' 'I can't be sure I'm right, and I hope I'm not, but a stay at the end of such a long road will at least keep us out of harm's way. If the virus fizzles out, we'll drive for two days to get home, tell some fibs at work and you'll be able to tease me for years.'

That night Alexandra made a prophetic entry in her diary: "Off to Letheilean, so beautiful it's like another world." The next day Bruce bought a large roof box for his car and started to fill it with equipment for an indefinite stay in the wilderness.

***

The Eolia, still with five on board, made its way around the tip of Nestra. Olivia wanted to stock up on food and fuel yet again, just in case, so on 25 April they docked at Lochmoran in the northeast. They found the port thronged with passengers keen to get onto the ferry to Dubheilean, and over the bridge to the mainland. The shops were full too, with everyone complaining over inadequate supplies, and some snatching and shouting.

Chapter 2 Crisis

Alexandra's diary expressed her concern: "26 April. The day Phraya really begins for most people? An enormous number of people are ill – estimates vary from hundreds of thousands to many millions worldwide – and there have been thousands of casualties. Media reports are contradictory, the internet is a maelstrom of rumour and misinformation, and mobile networks have become badly overloaded. It's impossible to determine the seriousness of the crisis, but I suspect the numbers are much larger than those given out. However, two things are clear: the virus is spreading rapidly, and those affected are mostly in the third world. Developed nations closed their airspace today to both international and internal flights."

"I don't know what the future holds, but I fear the world is ill prepared for Bruce's scenario. He seems unruffled, even intrigued, but despite his model I don't think he can have any more idea than anyone else how this will play out. As for me, I'm simply scared."

***

On Salay the Lynns' access to the news was restricted to the BBC news on the radio, which was calm and reassuring; and Far Isles Radio, less so. They were extremely concerned, and were thankful that the boat would be taking them off the island that day. They were ready well in advance of the agreed time, and waited long afterwards, but no boat! 'The weather is rough,' Steven rationalised, 'so they may have to come tomorrow.' Margaret bit her lip, and they had a tense supper. He was wondering whether they could get off the island without external help, she regretted agreeing to come to a speck of land with no means of outward communication, and Peter and Julia watched them failing to discuss the matter.

***

Lucy had been telling Rory for a couple of days that Phraya was in a different class from earlier epidemics. 'I'm afraid you were right,' he admitted, 'this disease must be really serious. They wouldn't ground the planes without a very good reason.' She was relieved that at last he was engaging. 'Yes, there's no treatment, and perhaps more of the victims succumb than with other viruses.' They discussed the medical details and concluded that reliable information was impossible to obtain. She concluded, 'The only thing to do is keep out of the way. The virus has probably arrived on Pennay, but may not have reached Mansay, because there's so little traffic along the causeway. I think we ought to keep the kids away from school. Maybe you could look after

Ali and Calum at home – I suppose I should keep trying to help my patients?'

***

Hearing the news and watching the reaction to it in Edinburgh, Alexandra finally began to wonder if her husband might be right. 'If your predictions were to prove accurate, it would be horrifying, I wouldn't want to witness the way people behave.' Bruce replied, 'Well, that's why we're going to Letheilean, to try to stay out of the way while the world goes through whatever hiatus the virus produces. It doesn't look a very promising start.' She wanted to know, 'In your scenario, who and what would be left afterwards, would it be worth living?' He was a little callous: 'I'd have thought it would be interesting to a sociologist to see what kind of world emerges?'

Alexandra was quiet for a long time. 'Are you enjoying all this?' she said frostily. 'I'm not causing it, I just saw it coming sooner than others.' 'Yes, but how do you feel about it?' He asserted unconvincingly, 'It horrifies me, and like you I'd like to avoid witnessing what's to come,' and continued more honestly, 'but I have to say that if it happens it will be a riveting experience.' Alexandra was stricken. 'It may not be so enthralling for my family; God, I wish I'd tried to persuade them to escape when we did!' She called repeatedly but couldn't get through.

After a long struggle Bruce reached his brother on his mobile: 'Thank goodness! I haven't been able to make contact. Where are you?' Charles replied, 'In Lochmoran on Nestra. We tried to buy supplies there yesterday, and it was tense. The shops are emptying, and shipments aren't getting through. A lot of people are trying to get off the island. Presumably you're in Edinburgh by now; what's it like?'

Bruce ignored the question and moved on swiftly: 'Charles, listen carefully. I was right about Phraya. The flow of data on it is drying up, but I've gathered what I can and put it into the model. It now shows the virus infecting half the population of the world, and hundreds of millions of deaths. If anything remotely like this happens, there will be a complete breakdown of law and order. That will kill more people than the virus.'

'Good grief!' Charles spluttered, 'Are you sure?'

Bruce continued, 'Edinburgh is showing the same signs of incipient panic as the islands. We are going to leave soon, with as much food and equipment as we can carry, and will try to get to the Achar Hotel in Letheilean.' 'Yes, I suppose that's a good place to sit out an emergency, if you have enough supplies. But is it really necessary?' 'Charles, let's agree to meet there if you can get away from the Far Isles …' At this point the call failed, and they were unable to reach each other again.

***

Charles relayed the conversation to his family, in appalled silence. Philip spoke first: 'I'm not sure I believe uncle Bruce's dire predictions, but Lochmoran seems potentially nasty. Perhaps we shouldn't be docking each night in port? Let's just keep out of the way and watch what happens from a safe distance?' The others agreed, and they scoured their map for quieter anchorages. Before they left Olivia called her parents in Edinburgh, although she wasn't at all sure what to recommend; but that didn't matter as they simply didn't believe Bruce. Katherine did rather better with her parents, who undertook to leave Glasgow with her sister if things took a turn for the worse.

***

Later that day the Lentons left Edinburgh for Letheilean, an underpopulated peninsula projecting from the west coast of Scotland towards the islands. Just outside the city Jessica asked, 'Why are there so many army vehicles around?' Bruce replied, 'I read that the government is planning to control the movement of people; hopefully we've escaped in time to be allowed through.' Alexandra was no lover of the state: 'Oh splendid, military rule!'

Benjamin had been studying a map online. 'It's a long way, about five and a half hours by road, but we can use the ferry just south of Port Monard to avoid a long drive round the lochs. Then it's only four hours.' Bruce thought otherwise: 'Yes, but we can't be sure that the ferry will be running, and it might be worthwhile going through the town to stock up; it's the biggest on the west coast, and it will be useful to know the state of affairs there.'

At every opportunity they filled up with diesel, but were allowed only ten litres each time. Once the tank was full, Bruce insisted on finding an out-of-the-way spot to syphon some fuel into plastic containers. Jessica was concerned; 'Wow, you are expecting trouble, dad.' He still wasn't willing to expose his children to his full vision. 'Well, my model of the epidemic shows enough people getting ill to cause quite a lot of trouble. We want to avoid running out of fuel in the middle of nowhere.'

When they reached Port Monard they found the shops almost empty of food; even so, they risked the queues and threatening atmosphere to buy what they could. Alexandra didn't like the behaviour she observed. 'I don't think we should come back here until things calm down. It isn't safe and may get much worse.' She got through to her family at last, and tried to persuade them to leave London, with the same result as Olivia.

Late in the afternoon they reached the Achar Hotel. Despite the fact that Letheilean seemed calm, Bruce insisted on hiding their food and equipment in several different places. He was pleased: 'Well, we've reduced the number of people around us from a metropolis to a handful.' Benjamin, numerate like his father, said, 'That's a million times better.' Isabella wasn't so sure; 'No it isn't, there's no-one to play with here.'

***

On 27 April the Lynns waited all day for a boat to take them off Salay. Steven remained outwardly confident: 'The weather still isn't very good.' Margaret argued, 'It doesn't seem impossible to land at the beach. They could at least come nearby and shout to us that they'll come back.' 'They wouldn't do that. We were told that you just have to wait until they can land. The weather is getting better.' Margaret went off to cheer herself up by reassuring Julia, who sensed her mother's anxiety and reversed the roles. 'Don't worry mum, Dad will have a backup plan.' Margaret allowed her mask to slip. 'Sure, just as he did with the mobiles.'

***

Alan Petrie had never thought of himself as a survivalist, and hadn't made it his business to prepare ahead of any previous emergency. Now, however, the situation in Edinburgh was getting out of control and he was extremely worried. It was astonishing how the reporting of a medical threat, though genuine, led to over-reactions in other seemingly unrelated areas of life. He wasn't guilty of this himself, he just found it easy to imagine a mess snowballing into a major disaster. He started to download information of relevance to worst possible scenarios. A plan was already forming in the back of his mind, and he switched from buying food, which was becoming difficult, to purchasing equipment, still readily available. He acquired portable cooking equipment, water purifying tablets and an extensive medical kit.

Alan phoned his sister Alice who, with her partner Ruth Paterson, ran a market garden in Morrie at the northern extreme of the arable land in central Scotland. They got on fine, but he tended to call only when he had something to convey. 'How are you, Alan?' She sounded more relaxed than he felt. 'People are panic buying food here, what's it like in the countryside?' She didn't share his pessimism, but took a dim view of orthodoxy: 'It's not so bad here, but it's starting. The government is saying that if everyone stays calm things will be alright, and they're probably right, but people are like sheep!' He told her about his preparations: 'Maybe, but I saw this coming sooner than other people. I bought loads of food before anyone else felt the need.' She didn't approve but made no comment. 'What are you going to do?' 'I'm not going anywhere, because I've got jobs to do if and when things calm down, so I've been buying kit and preparing to hunker down.'

Alan spent the evening on the internet, looking up 'prepper' web sites; there was a world of neurosis out there. He drew the line at guns and knives, but maybe the rest of it made sense?

***

After a night at anchor, the Lentons took the Eolia close enough to Lochmoran to get reception. Olivia wanted to call her friend Deborah Tanner who, with her husband David, ran a large farm just south of Alice and Ruth's smallholding. Eventually she got through: 'How are you?' she asked. 'OK, but I can't believe what's on the news. Out here we're not seeing much of the turmoil that seems to be kicking off in cities.'

'Debbie, I have to tell you something terrible. You may recall that Bruce, Charles's brother, is a professional in the area of epidemics. He knows more than the public about the Phraya virus, and has a model of how it's going to progress. He predicts it will infect billions of people and kill hundreds of millions.' She paused, to allow Deborah an incredulous, 'What?'

'I know, it's hard to believe, and I don't necessarily, but so far the things Bruce has predicted have happened. I just thought I should let you know what he says; if he's right about how the serious the virus is, the world isn't going to stay peaceful and organised while that many people fall ill. He has already decamped from London to Edinburgh, and by now is probably further on; he proposes to avoid the danger by staying at a remote hotel at Achar in Letheilean. If things get too bad in the islands, we may try to go there.'

Deborah, struggling to absorb the enormity of it all, could only say, 'Surely the government is trying to develop treatments?' 'Bruce thinks that medical systems will break down before they've achieved a cure, and that everything else will fail too. You may want to consider joining us on the peninsula, at least for a while, if the troubles reach you?'

***

The Tanners had to wait until the evening before they could discuss this conversation. David, of middling height and thickset, already greying and receding at 41, was the horticulturalist. Deborah, a year younger, shorter and curvier with brown hair of practical length, was a highly organised woman who ran the administration of the farm. They had three children: at twelve Samuel already wanted to be a farmer like his father; Rose, at ten still girlish; and William, only eight but thuggish. They put them to bed and sat down to talk.

David's reaction to the bombshell was disbelief. 'There have been scares like this before, and they came to nothing much. Perhaps the authorities know something which hasn't been made public, and that explains the air travel ban. Even so, by now all the medical researchers in the world will be on Phraya's case; they'll sort it out soon and then everyone will be back on planes to Bangkok. In the meantime, how's a bird flu going to get onto the farm?' Deborah didn't know enough about medicine to argue, and caved in immediately: 'I suppose you're right, this is my friend's husband's brother's opinion, so it's fourth hand information obtained in a snatched phone conversation.' They left it at that.

***

On 28 April the weather was better, but the boat didn't come for the Lynns. Local radio told them that things were getting bad on the islands. Margaret said it first: 'What if the boat can't pick us up, or doesn't even try?' Steven did his best: 'Your sister will have expected you to call her the day before yesterday, and will be onto the boat company.' 'She isn't very effective at that kind of thing.' Steven tried again: 'Maybe the boat has broken down, and the owner reckons any day will do.' When she intoned, 'I wish I'd checked about the reception, we could have brought a satellite phone or something,' he thought it best not to argue. Instead he was pondering how he could make amends for his lapse.

***

In the morning of 29 April Lucy saw that food shops on Pennay were emptying completely, amid rows and violence. No supplies had been delivered in recent days, and everyone was desperate to get off the island. The ferries to Caladion on the mainland, and northwards to Estra, were fully booked for vehicles, and by lunchtime the terminal was mobbed by a crowd demanding passage on foot.

The staff from Rory's fish farm called to inform him they were leaving. When Lucy came back from work and heard this, she said, 'I'm not surprised. Bailecas is a madhouse, and there's nothing in the shops.' Rory had been thinking about food: 'I wish my lads the best of luck, but I think their absence might be to our advantage because I can go to the cages without anyone knowing. If I feed the salmon, I can keep them alive for quite a while. I can operate the smoker to give us a source of food for even longer.'

The children were starting to notice the changes. Alison asked, 'Why can't I go to school? We have ham for lunch.' Calum was single-minded: 'You always make us eat Daddy's fish. I like sausages best.' Lucy resorted to bribery: 'If you eat your supper you can have a little bit of ice-cream afterwards,' and added under her breath, 'while it lasts.' Rory seized the opportunity, 'As you're getting a treat, Ali, you have to lean your head back when I wash your hair. Then you won't get shampoo in your eyes.' Calum took advantage: 'I'm good when you wash me, daddy.' Alison was chagrined, but found an argument: 'That's because you're a boy, so you've got short hair, and daddy doesn't have to use much shampoo.' 'Poo to you too.' Lucy tried to tell him off, but had to laugh when Rory pointed out, 'The last word as usual, and with a rhyme what's more.'

***

The Lynns were busy and missed the local radio coverage of the situation on Pennay. Steven and Margaret still weren't talking productively about the situation the family faced; instead the tension emerged in bickering when they were together, so the family divided. The boys were considering the prospects of escaping from Salay – not at all promising – and Steven wondered privately about the lighthouse on Beag Salay. Meanwhile the girls were making an inventory of the food resources of the island. Margaret could see possibilities for protein and fat, from fish and birds, but there weren't any obvious sources of carbohydrates.

***

The Lentons had spent several days just offshore from Lochmoran, watching the port and listening to the radio. On 1 May Far Isles Radio signed off, suggesting to its remaining listeners that they should try to leave the islands. Many had already done so; those with cars had travelled onwards, but foot passengers had got no further than their disembarkation ports. Nevertheless, the family observed an attempted exodus from Nestra. Perhaps the government was organising food on the mainland? The ferries were insisting on sticking to the regulation number of passengers, and serious violence broke out in Lochmoran.

The question was whether to try to sail to Dubheilean, in order to reach the mainland; they were at the closest point, and the journey was within Eolia's capability. Katherine pleaded that they make the attempt: 'I'm worried about my sister and parents in Glasgow, and I don't think I'm going to reach them on the phone.' Philip pointed out, 'Kat, we have no idea of the state of affairs over there.' Olivia tried to analyse: 'Far Isles Radio was giving us local information, and seemed to be telling the truth. On the other hand, the BBC has nothing to say about the islands and is clearly under government control. It's a whitewash, and that isn't encouraging as regards the situation on the mainland.'

Charles said regretfully, 'It begins to look as if Bruce may have been right about the virus causing a general breakdown of law and order.' Olivia agreed, 'Yes, I'm afraid so. I think we must stay in the islands for a while.' 'In that case, we ought to move southwards, away from likely points of departure. Lochmoran can only get worse.'

***

The staff from Lucy's surgery took the local radio's advice and, with considerable difficulty, left Pennay. She decided that her role as a doctor to the local people would have to be suspended for the time being. However, she wanted to be in a position to resume it if and when things settled down. She went to the pharmacy, removed as much medical equipment and supplies as she could, and took them home.

That evening she asked Rory, 'Should we go too? I think tomorrow could be our last chance before the ferries grind to a halt.' He replied, 'The only ways we can get off the island are via Dubheilean and directly to the mainland. I hear both routes are chaos with all the foot passengers piling up.' 'Oh no, Caladion! If my family has stayed at home, they'll be caught up in it; I'll try to warn them. It's even getting too dangerous to go to Pennay. I think we should stick to Mansay and hold out until things calm down; we'll have it to ourselves.' After many attempts she reached her brother on the phone. 'We don't know what's going to happen, but we've decided to stay at home and ride it out. Maybe you should get out of the port? Good luck, promise me you'll look after mum and dad.'

At last Rory admitted to himself that something momentous was taking place, and that he couldn't predict the outcome. He was relieved that his immediate family were safe, at least for the moment, and his mind turned to others. He tried to get through to his brother and parents, but failed; the mobile networks were collapsing.

Chapter 3 Escape

The Lynns were clinging to their last remaining hope, that boat trips might start on the first day of May as normal, but they peered northwards in vain. When they caught the local radio signoff, they knew there would be no rescue. Margaret took a frontal approach: 'Steve, you've got to face up to it: we will never be picked up.' This time he was ready with some thoughts. 'Well, there isn't a boat on this island, and the nearest inhabited one, Mansay, is twelve kilometres away, so we must build something.' 'And how are we going to do that?'

'I've been looking for materials to use. There's a lot of wood around the schoolhouse, but very few tools, so no way to join timber, or to seal it. I imagine there would be more kit on Beag Salay, because of the lighthouse. There might even be a boat.' The children had been listening, and their parents saw no point in sheltering them from the discussion. Julia was quicker than her mother: 'Dad, how do we get there?'

'I'll swim, it's only a kilometre.'

***

The day after the radio signoff, Rory went to the fish farm premises to see what he could find. He was relieved to see that the boat was still there; although people were keen to reach the mainland, nobody was crazy enough to attempt the seventy-kilometre crossing in a small open boat. The supply of petrol was undisturbed too – his staff had been forced to abandon their cars – so Rory was able to run the outboard motor. He took the boat to the nearest cage and came back with a generous supply of fish. He set the smoker going, detached the outboard, hid it and the fuel, and returned to Mansay to tell Lucy the good news. 'That's great, Rory, but from now on you can feed the kids and I'll bathe them.'

***

On 3 May Alan Petrie, following developments in Edinburgh, was alarmed to hear a government announcement through BBC radio and television. The number of people suffering from the Phraya virus was not given, and deaths were not mentioned; instead the crisis was described as serious but manageable. In order to control the epidemic, roadblocks were being set up on all major highways, and travel was to be permitted only for authorised purposes. People were urged to continue with their jobs if they were deemed essential. Food distribution was to be organised by the army. The prime minister appealed for calm but didn't sound as if he believed the arrangements would hold.

Alan realised that things were extremely serious, and that he would now have to remain in the city. He put into operation a plan he had been developing for days: to build a hideaway consisting of a bedroom at the back of the house and its ensuite bathroom. He disguised the door from the hall into the bedroom, by attaching to it a bookcase on castor wheels, and reinforced the door with bolts on the inside. Blackout curtains on the window completed the security arrangements; his main aim was not to create a fortress but to avoid discovery.

He envisaged a long stay in the two rooms, and anticipated that the utilities might fail in due course. Therefore he built a lid for the bath, to store water and keep it fresh. He made provision for the accumulation of waste in large plastic boxes, with tight-fitting lids, in a wardrobe; and arranged ventilation to the exterior. Finally he installed in the bedroom a camping stove and a gas-powered fridge/freezer bought for this purpose, and moved all his food from the kitchen. For the time being he continued to occupy the whole house, but made it look as if he wasn't there. He went out as little as possible and kept away from others.

***

While Alan was arranging to stay in one place, the Lynns were working on their escape from another. Steven had made a basic raft and a makeshift paddle, and had observed the tides. The weather was calm, and there was nothing for it; he embraced his family, clutched a bundle of food and spare clothes wrapped tightly in several plastic bags, and started the crossing to Beag Salay. Julia was tearful, so Margaret took her to the schoolhouse, leaving Peter to observe his father's journey through binoculars.

Steven had misjudged the feasibility of propelling a blunt, half-submerged craft, armed only with a plank of wood; he made very little headway. He had also underestimated the extent of the spray generated by the impact of the modest swell. Soon he was soaking and extremely cold; he began to doubt that he would make it. Eventually he remembered that swimmers feel colder out of the water than in it, and made a difficult decision. Peter watched in horror as his father slipped from the raft and swam away from it.

Steven convinced himself that he was better off immersed, and set a steady stroke. He made faster progress but Beag Salay remained obstinately in the middle distance. He lost feeling in his fingers, and then his toes, but he worked hard enough to prevent the numbness from spreading. Pausing to look backwards, he saw that Salay was receding, and he suspected that the landing place ahead might be growing. His mind began to wander, but he focussed on a group of rocks which he fancied looked like a map of the Far Isles. After an hour he reached a patch of choppy water and wondered dully whether this indicated that the seabed was close. Sticking his legs down produced disappointment, so he forced himself to make a final effort.

Suddenly he grazed his foot on something, and was grateful; he picked his way carefully through the waves and dragged himself clear of the rocks. He waved in the direction of Salay, knowing that Peter would be watching, but couldn't make out any acknowledgement. He was now exposed to the air and was soon shivering violently. His fingers were lifeless, but he held the parcel with his palms and used his teeth to tear it open. He was relieved to find that the clothes were dry. He thawed his hands sufficiently to allow himself to get changed, and with warmth came clarity of mind. He set off to investigate the lighthouse.

Steven found the light-keeper's cottage and workshop in a semi-ruinous state. There was a boat, but it had been left outdoors and was rotten. Still, there was much more to be found than on Salay, so he was glad he had risked the crossing. He spent the remainder of the day building a much better raft; he knew he would have to get it back to Salay. It had a pointed end to help it plough through the water; sides to deflect the spray; and crude oars. However, he was under no illusion that it was really a boat.

Peter had watched the first raft drift away, but had eventually seen his father emerge at the landing place. Margaret and the children, cheered and energised, busied themselves; food was running short, and they didn't know how long it would take to build a boat. They visited the cliffs and collected puffin eggs and, with rather more difficulty, those of razorbills. After a struggle to learn how to use the spinning lures they had found with the rods, they caught some young pollack. Julia even harvested seaweed and tried to make it palatable. They treated it as a savoury by frying it to crispness, and as a pudding by adding plenty of sugar. Peter, aware of a pressure to behave like a man in his father's absence, tasted the results and avoided teasing his sister.

That evening Margaret struggled with her feelings. She was still cross with Steven for bringing them to Salay with no means of communication. However, she recognised that whatever had prevented the boat from coming might have done so even if they had been able to call for help. She admired Steven's courage in making the trip to Beag Salay, but was worried. She was almost fonder of him when he was away, and not simply because they would be in even worse trouble if he failed to return. Julia saw the conflicted look on her face. 'He'll be OK, mum.'

The next day Steven searched the lighthouse for boat-building materials and tools. He loaded the new raft carefully, starting with timber and other things that wouldn't suffer from immersion in seawater. He placed screws and tools on top, covered to protect them as far as possible. He set off on the same slack tide as the previous day, and found that although the raft floated very low, it was reasonably manoeuvrable. Peter spotted him approaching slowly, and fetched the others. In the late afternoon Steven reached Salay to a rapturous welcome. Now all they had to do was build a boat capable of reaching Mansay!

***

On Letheilean, the inhabitants of the peninsula soon discerned that the government was hardly likely to provide food for a hundred or so people in such a remote place. There were rumours that there might be supplies in Innisdu, a sizeable town on the nearby island of Eilard. However, the ferry needed to get there from Tirglas, the small local port, was no longer running; and few trusted the much longer ferry needed to enable their escape from the island to Caladion. It seemed a better idea to stick to the mainland, so most people set off in cars, in defiance of the roadblocks. The owners of the hotel also departed to try to reach relatives, leaving the Lentons to take care of their property.

Bruce ran his model one last time and concluded, 'We're going to have to remain in Letheilean for a long time, irrespective of the difficulties.' Alexandra said, 'We've got the place to ourselves now, but might the locals come back?' Although his computer couldn't predict social behaviour, Bruce was dubious: 'I doubt it, I'm afraid I believe they're heading into a maelstrom.' Alexandra did her best to cling to her faith in human nature: 'Perhaps the government will get a grip, or people will see sense?' Remembering Alexandra's anger when he expounded the worst version of his theory, Bruce left her to her optimism.

***

Until the barriers were set up, David Tanner had been trying to operate his farm on the assumption that normality would return in due course. Now he had his doubts. Deborah took a break to visit her friends Alice Petrie and Ruth Paterson on their neighbouring smallholding. She explained the difficulties of running the farm: 'You're lucky, this place is hidden away. The government's food programme is hopeless, people are flooding out of the cities – the barriers don't stop them – and they see us from the main road. They seem to imagine a farm is a source of food, but all they're finding is the uneatable early shoots of our crops.' Alice hadn't realised things were so bad out there. 'Yes, I'd heard from Alan that people are panicking in Edinburgh, and he said he was preparing, but he always sees the worst case.'

'Look, I should tell you about something I heard from my friend Olivia Lenton. Her brother-in-law studies epidemics, and he said early on that this would be serious. Apparently he predicted hundreds of millions of deaths,' – Ruth gasped – 'but Olivia didn't really believe him, and David certainly doesn't. Just thought I better tell you.'

Alice clasped her cropped head, but was calm: 'That's incredible, but maybe Alan wasn't being so pessimistic? Unfortunately rumour and insecurity are breeding a genuine crisis. I guess all we can do is react to what we see round here?' 'We are certainly getting unwanted attention on our farm,' Deborah replied, 'and I'm worried about the children; some people seem desperate.'

Ruth gave her a matronly hug and made an offer: 'If you like, I'll look after the children here, while you and David try to defend your place.' Deborah was relieved: 'That's so kind, thank you.' 'You're welcome, they'll relieve my broodiness.' Alice ignored this, adding, 'If things gets too bad, you can all move here and we'll work the market garden. We've got crops coming up, and animals which we can feed for a while yet. Your farm may have to be restarted when the world recovers its senses.'

***

The Scotts were not alone in losing their staff; they could see that by now most people had ceased to do their jobs. Commercial radio, television and online news services stopped, and newspapers were no longer printed. Internet, email and mobile phones staggered on, but for many islanders the only information source, trusted to a diminishing extent, was BBC radio and television controlled by whatever was left of central government.

On 5 May ferries stopped running to Pennay. Those remaining tried to leave by means of smaller craft, aiming at the mainland via Nestra and Dubheilean. Then the electricity cut out, and all means of communication failed. The result was complete panic: people fought over food, boats and fuel, and Phraya claimed its first victims by conflict rather than disease. The Scotts watched Bailecas from Mansay, which they had to themselves. They had a petrol generator, so they were able to keep their fridge and freezer going. In the evening they operated a few lights, with the windows blacked out to hide their presence, and they could still listen to the radio. They resolved to keep away from Pennay.

***

On 6 May Alan observed scenes of such violence in Edinburgh that he decided that he should occupy his hideaway permanently. He moved everything useful into the bedroom, arranged the rest of the house to look as if it had been invaded, and left the front door unlocked. He blocked the overflow of the bath and filled it to the top; he figured its 250-litre capacity, used for drinking and minimal washing, would last ten weeks, and he had food for that length of time.

He managed to reach Alice one more time. She told him that serious disturbance was starting in the countryside too, and ended the conversation, 'I hope you manage to stay out of harm's way. If you get a chance later, you could make a run for Morrie. We'd love to have you here.'

***

While the Lentons were sailing down the east coasts of Nestra and Iseala, they saw a flotilla of small boats leaving the islands. They concluded that the ferries had stopped sailing and thought it wise to avoid panicky people. On 7 May they saw Iseala go dark as the electricity failed on the remaining Far Isles.

Philip fiddled with the radio but couldn't find any stations other than the BBC. Olivia listened to its output, trying to peer through the official coverage to what it really meant. 'I don't think the government has a grip on the situation. I imagine that it's every man for himself in the cities.' Charles noted the nautical reference and indulged in a little weak humour: 'Maybe so, but we're not going to abandon ship.' They were still close to Dubheilean, so they decided to continue down Estra to escape the troubles.

***

On 9 May FM radio transmissions to the islands stopped. The Lynns' radio didn't have AM, so now they were completely in the dark, but in any case all that mattered was the boat they were building. Steven, helped by Peter, had spent the last few days cutting planks of wood and steam-bending them into shapes suitable for a rough hull. They were planning to fix them together with screws, but Peter was worried. 'They're steel dad, won't they rust, especially in sea-water?' Steven was impressed, 'Yes, but they should last long enough for one journey. The real problem is how to seal the joins.'

Margaret had a suggestion: 'In the old days, didn't they make pitch by burning wood? I think you get the fire going and then partly cover it so the pitch doesn't burn away too.' They dug a pit, put a metal cooking pan in the bottom and had a go. By the next morning they had a small pool of black gloop which they warmed over another fire and poured into a test joint. It looked as if it might slow the ingress of water sufficiently. Over the next fortnight much of the schoolhouse's furniture was sacrificed to stone age technology.

***

When the electricity failed on Letheilean, the Lentons went to look at Tirglas in the dark; there was no torchlight, so they concluded that everyone had left. They returned the next day to confirm this, and the village was silent. The peace was shattered when Isabella screamed, 'Rats!' The others followed her gaze and saw them swarming around a house. Bruce advanced cautiously, peered in through a window, recoiled and told the others, 'Stay here, I'll investigate.' He tucked his trousers into his socks and put on high boots. He tried the door and, finding it unlocked, went in with his arms covering his face and neck. A few moments later he came out looking drawn; 'I'm afraid there are dead people.'

Alexandra was appalled, and led the children away. Bruce warned, 'It looks as if the victims died of the virus rather than by injury. We must keep away from the bodies for the time being, in case of infection.' She saw immediately the significance of their find. 'If the virus has come this far it must be everywhere.' 'Yes, I'm afraid so, worldwide. Essentially the entire human population is at risk. We better go back to Achar for now.'

Jessica wasn't fazed by the discovery of the bodies. 'First let's look in the empty houses to see what's in them.' They found some food and various useful things, including packets of seeds and a book on foraging for wild food. Alexandra struggled to be practical: 'This is horrible, let's get out, but I suppose when it's safe we could explore properly and maybe even move here.'

In private Alexandra, no longer able to sustain her optimism, poured her most honest thoughts into her diary: "As a holiday this experience would be wonderfully peaceful, but the fates of countless people are echoing through my head. How many will die of the virus, of starvation, through lack of medical care, by conflict? How many are suffering alone, or in despair? Will people retain the ability to help others, to sympathise, even to distinguish right from wrong? Are religious people losing their faith, and their power of forgiveness? If humanity fails Phraya's test, civilisation may fall entirely. When the worst is over, will there even be anyone left? Will they understand what's happened, will the history be written?" Alexandra paused, and suddenly it all came closer to home: "God, what's going to happen to my mother and sisters?"

***

By 12 May the Eolia had reached Caoloch, a small village in a deep indentation of the east coast of Estra. The Lentons had almost completed their originally planned trip, but were reluctant to approach their home port of Glendonan. It seemed likely that there would be people there, frantic and probably violent, and the family was keen to avoid encountering any departing boats. Caoloch was dark by night, so they thought it was deserted. In the morning they approached cautiously and found no-one; the houses looked as if they had been abandoned in a hurry, presumably to catch a ferry. They found food and supplies; this was the place to wait and watch.

***

Over the past few days a stream of people had been arriving at the Tanner farm, seeking food and finding nothing – David and Deborah had moved everything edible to Alice and Ruth's smallholding, and were staying there overnight with their children. They became resigned to giving up any attempt to work their farm.

Deborah regretted their earlier snap judgement: 'I think we should go to Letheilean as Olivia suggested, and aim to return later.' 'At the moment it's doubtful that we can even get there.' 'Yes, it would be far too dangerous, let's prepare by loading the van with fuel and equipment and hide it at the smallholding.'

Alice and Ruth agreed that Letheilean, if they could reach it, might be a suitable place to evade the turmoil. In the meantime, they were anxious about the possibility that hungry people might find their way to the market garden at any time. They tried to keep the Tanner children busy and quiet: Rose helped Ruth with the fertilisation and weeding of the crops, while Samuel and Alice fed the animals and did their best to entertain William. He had a curious mind and asked later, 'What happens to the animals when they grow up?' Deborah thought it best to avoid details: 'When they get too big, we send them away.' He wasn't so easily fobbed off, 'And then what?' She braced herself for further explanation, but Samuel intervened, 'They are killed to make meat.' She expected trouble but was relieved to hear the reaction: 'Wow! Can I eat some of it?'

***

On 13 May Alan noted that TV transmissions had ended; only the radio remained to indicate, by its propaganda, that a rump of government persisted. Three days later this stopped too when the mains failed in Edinburgh. The lack of official information made no difference to him, as he preferred to judge the situation by looking carefully out of the front window. The absence of gas and water were more inconvenient, but he had prepared much earlier. He had a considerable supply of bottled gas for cooking food. Also a petrol generator, which he had installed in the wardrobe surrounded by a lot of sound deadening; however, he hesitated to use it in case the noise gave him away. Another blow was the discovery one morning that his van had been stolen. He risked emerging from hiding long enough to move his bicycle from the garage into the bedroom, and settled back into a tedious but safe existence.

*** *

On 15 May Philip and Henry Lenton walked inland from Caoloch to inspect the main road running through Estra, Iseala and Nestra. The boys had been selected as the fastest runners, and it had been agreed that they would not engage anyone in conversation. As it happened, they encountered no-one, and observed that the road only carried traffic going northwards. When they returned Charles reasoned, 'Perhaps people are trying to get closer to Dubheilean, or they may simply be fleeing conflict in Glendonan.' Olivia judged, 'It's still too dangerous to go to there.' Katherine finessed: 'Yes, I agree that we shouldn't take the boat, but perhaps we can monitor the port on foot, from a distance?' This was agreed and over the next few days the boys explored cautiously.

*** *

On 16 May BBC radio transmissions stopped. Lucy remarked, 'So much for modern communications,' and Rory lamented, 'for an unknowable period of time.' They had been keeping clear of Pennay for the past ten days, but now he suggested, 'We're not going to find out what's happening unless we go to Bailecas; I wonder if it's safe to have a look? She was concerned, but had the same idea as Katherine: 'Perhaps you could drive across the causeway, park the car out of sight, walk up the hill and look down on the town?'

Rory carried out this plan and saw very few people. He retreated and described to Lucy what he had seen, 'Some people seemed ill, and others were behaving oddly, like zombies.' She chided him for his overactive imagination, 'Even the Phraya virus doesn't have that effect on people. They might have been delirious, or shell-shocked by conflict, or simply starving. We've certainly got to keep Ali and Calum out of there.'

***

By this time Alexandra had recovered from the shock of the bodies, and was focussed on survival: 'Let's move to Tirglas. It's more fertile for growing food and nearer the sea for fishing. Here we're just eating our way through a fixed food supply.' Bruce cautioned, 'I agree, but we'll have to stay in houses which weren't visited by the virus.' Jessica pointed out: 'We ought to leave a note for uncle Charles in case he comes to the hotel.'

The family made the move. Letheilean was mostly rough land, fit only for forestry and sheep, but Tirglas was low-lying and had been cleared over the centuries for crofting. Alexandra thought it promising; 'Surely this place can support a family, provided we learn how to grow food?' There was no mains water, but they found a stream. 'Yuk, the water is brown!' 'It's alright, Bella, it's just peat, it's actually good for you.'

Bruce had a plan for handling the bodies. 'The virus can't survive outside its host, and not for long after death. We'll be OK if we keep clear of the victims until we can bury them later.' He and Jessica nervously excluded the rats and carefully wrapped the corpses, while Alexandra and Benjamin kept Isabella out of the way.

Over the next few days they planted the seeds they had found earlier. Alexandra confided to her diary, "I never thought we'd be doing such things out of necessity. I hope it works, because we've got no idea what we're doing." The girls were sent on a tour of the safe houses, and returned with a surprising amount of food; Jessica thought, 'The people must have left in quite a hurry.' Benjamin found a boat in the harbour with some fuel, searched the houses until he found the key for the motor, and triumphantly appointed himself captain.

***

On 20 May Alan's house in Edinburgh was entered for the first time. He stayed in his hideaway and remained absolutely silent. The visitors were disappointed as he had planned: 'There's bugger all here.' 'Yeah, let's try somewhere else.' Alan didn't emerge until it was dark, and was cautious. He saw cars abandoned where they had run out of fuel, a fire in the distance, a body lying in a pool of blood in the street. Now he knew the crisis had crossed a terrible line. When he heard a gang of young men shouting, he returned to his house, determined to stay in hiding for a lot longer. He had a great deal of time on his hands, and spent it reading the survival books he had downloaded. He had been embarrassed at the time but was pleased to have them now.

***

The following day Bruce and Benjamin took the boat across the strait between Letheilean and Eilard. They looked at Innisdu from a safe distance and saw abandoned cars, burned buildings, people moving about – and boats in motion, so they returned to Tirglas. Alexandra was not in favour of repeating this experiment: 'I imagine there will be groups of survivors in all towns, but they may not be the nicest people.' Bruce concurred: 'Indeed, we must stay in Letheilean for the time being. Perhaps Innisdu will be safe later, and may be useful, but we have enough to survive here at this stage.' Benjamin still wanted to make use of his boat, 'But we can go fishing if we keep close to Tirglas?' Isabella pleaded, 'Yes, can I come, I can swim fifty metres, please daddy.'

***

On 24 May Rory made a further trip to Bailecas. This time he saw no-one, but he wasn't confident that the town was empty, and didn't want to risk an encounter. He returned to Mansay and reported to Lucy. She asked, 'How long do you think we can survive like this?' 'Well, we have some food here; also I can keep the fish farm going a while longer, and preserve by smoking. There may be more food in Bailecas, given the panic as everyone left, if the stragglers didn't ransack all the houses.'

Alison and Calum missed their friends but had replaced them with a succession of imaginary characters. She was a master playwright, and he was happy playing the roles assigned to him. On one occasion she was a doctor, and he was ill with what he called 'a vilus'; he had a 'deadful headache, and my feet hurt too.' She took his temperature, treated him with an 'antirobotic' and he got better. Lucy sighed, 'They're such a welcome relief from the world of adults gone mad. I wonder how long we can preserve their innocence.'

***

By now Salay's new boat was approaching completion. Steven had tested it at the beach on a calm day, and had patched the few leaks revealed by the trial. Peter had carved four oars, and it proved possible to propel the boat at a modest speed. They had erected a mast, and Margaret and Julia had made sails. None of it inspired confidence.

Margaret had been studying the map: 'There are two islands between us and Mansay. They both have beaches on their eastern sides where we might land and rest.' Steven had been watching the tides: 'I reckon we should set off when the tide is flowing towards the mainland, but about to slacken. That way we avoid the risk of being carried into the Atlantic. We might not make it to Canada.' 'Very funny, carry on.' 'We'll end up east of the intermediate islands, and if it takes us a long time to reach the first one, the tide will turn and carry us to it.'

On 25 May the weather was calm, so the family loaded the boat with as much food, water, clothing and equipment as possible and waited for the tide. At mid-day they set off with barely a backward glance at their holiday home. Margaret muttered, 'I bet there's no reception on Mansay either.'

The boat floated high and leaked only slightly; and the waves produced only a small amount of spray. The children bailed with cups to limit the water in the bilge to a small puddle. Steven rowed, accompanied by each of the others in turn, and they made a reasonable pace. He was so pleased that he began to lecture the family: 'This is why seafarers, even in ancient times, built boats rather than rafts.' They were able to proceed in roughly the planned direction, except that the wind was taking them too far eastwards, so they furled the sail. Now Margaret indulged in a little mockery: 'When the wind direction is unfavourable, rowing is hard work, so that explains why the Greeks had slaves?'

After a while the jokes dried up. Nothing was going wrong, but the pace dropped as everyone became tired. They knew there was no choice but to keep going as long as it took – several hours – but they persisted. Eventually they made it to the first island, dragged the boat up the beach and collapsed for a night under the shelter of the sail. Margaret recovered her good humour: 'I hope the weather cooperates tomorrow, this hotel isn't up to much.'

The Lynns slept fitfully on the comfortable but chilly sand, and were woken by seagulls in the early light. The weather was kind again, and Steven was keen to take advantage. Margaret fed everyone as best she could, and they set off. The journey was a repeat of the previous day's, this time with a south-westerly wind helping. They reached the second island early enough that they decided to press on to Mansay. In the late afternoon they reached a beach on its southern coast. Margaret was overjoyed, and was all for finding some accommodation, but Steven cautioned: 'I think we should stay with the boat tonight and explore when we're fresh tomorrow. We know very little about what's been going on outside Salay; and have no idea of the mood of the inhabitants, if any.' Peter joked, 'OK, but I want a full Scottish breakfast in the morning.' Julia joined in, 'No black pudding, though.'

Chapter 4 Union

On 27 May Rory spotted the Lynn family walking across Mansay, and drew Lucy's attention to them. They looked so bedraggled that she felt they weren't a threat: 'I don't think they're from here. It might be best if I approach them? You could stay out of sight with the kids, and watch?'

Lucy stopped a few paces short of the newcomers, and was carefully non-confrontational: 'Hi, can I help you?' Margaret instinctively advanced on her own and the women shook hands. 'Yes please. We were dropped on Salay six weeks ago, supposedly for two weeks' holiday. We heard radio reports about the virus, and presume it accounts for the boat not collecting us, but we have no idea what's been going on. We've just escaped in a home-made boat and could do with food and shelter.'

Lucy was impressed; 'You made it here from Salay? Did you have a motor?' Margaret shook her head, 'No, we rowed.' On hearing this Lucy set aside her recent suspicion of strangers; 'You must be exhausted. Can I meet your family?' She greeted Steven, Peter and Julia and said, 'Excuse me a moment, let me fetch my husband.' She went out of sight, leaving the Lynns grateful to have met someone helpful – and well-fed.

Lucy had a quick discussion with Rory. He was cautious: 'It sounds like they're telling the truth, and we'll know when we see this boat of theirs.' Lucy, on the other hand, was already looking forward to a partnership: 'They sound capable, and we could do with more people to help with the kids.'

The families introduced themselves and went to the Scotts' house. While they ate Steven asked, 'What on earth has been happening?' Rory summarised: 'We're not really sure, but we probably know more than you. The usual supplies of food and fuel from the mainland failed, the ferries stopped running and most people have abandoned the islands. There has been chaos and fighting on Pennay, and it's more or less empty. As far as we know the situation on the mainland is dire, and there doesn't seem to be a government any more.'

Margaret, blank with exhaustion, didn't absorb the full significance immediately and merely remarked, 'Goodness, that's awful. It certainly explains why the boat didn't come.' Lucy continued, 'Even though I'm a doctor, I don't know much about the virus except that it has probably spread everywhere in the world, and is nasty. However, I doubt the virus has killed as many people as the collapse triggered by it.' As the Scotts gave details, Margaret became pale, and Peter and Julia were quiet. Steven, on the other hand, seemed to accept the new world order, or lack of it, with equanimity: 'Well perhaps this is a chance to build a better world.' Margaret gave him a quizzical look and tried to comfort her children.

Later Julia confided in Peter: 'Even though we've managed to get off Salay, I don't think mum's any happier.' He replied, 'It's not surprising, awful things were happening while we were trapped.' She was puzzled; 'But dad seems OK with it all.' He had an unwelcome insight: 'They're not the same, are they? I think what has upset her most is him not being bothered about the news.' 'Well, I'm with her, it's horrible.' 'Me too. Maybe he is just trying to show how tough he is, and he's secretly worried?' Neither of them really believed this.

When she got a chance, Julia approached her mother; 'What do you think dad really thinks about all this?' By now Margaret was upset enough to be more direct than she would normally. 'Your father isn't really a people person. Even work colleagues are – were – a challenge for him; he regarded them as part of the problem. I don't think he minds that millions may have lost their lives.' 'But what about those close to him?' 'Well, he loves us in his way, and he is fantastic when he's solving problems for us. Of course he doesn't have any other family, but I don't think he's thought about mine.'

***

Meanwhile the Lentons were trying to embrace the challenge of survival on Letheilean. They had found fishing rods and were now having modest success with them. They had seen red deer and hares as well as sheep, and had faced up to the theoretical possibility that they might have to kill and eat them. Benjamin made a bow and arrows but found them much harder to use than he imagined. It was also difficult to get within range of the animals, but he persevered and eventually shot a lamb. Jessica, who aspired to become a doctor, decided that she would overcome her squeamishness and process the carcass. Bruce and Alexandra were impressed by their children's efforts. Fruit and vegetables were much more of a problem, so Alexandra suggested, 'Let's not tell Bella how lamb had been brought to the table.'

***

The Scotts were happy to form a stronger unit with the Lynns; however, they were aware that food would now be eaten more than twice as fast. Rory judged that Bailecas might now be safe, so on 29 May he and Steven set off to investigate. They found no-one, and no boats of any size; Rory explained: 'For the last four weeks everyone has been trying to get to the mainland, but it's a long way in a small boat. The shortest crossing is from Nestra, so I guess people have been taking their boats northwards. Perhaps we can follow when it's safe.'

Over the next few days they searched Bailecas and the rest of Pennay systematically. They broke into houses and found most empty, but they also confirmed the fate of the sufferers Rory had seen from a distance. Steven broke a window and immediately smelled the evidence; 'I think someone has died in here.' Rory warned, 'We probably shouldn't go near the bodies.' Nevertheless, Steven felt oddly impelled to enter the house and see for himself what Phraya had done; and Rory followed, unsure why he was doing so. Neither man had seen a dead person before, and although they weren't surprised, they were deeply shocked.

The sudden exodus of foot passengers meant that most of the island's cars remained, many with fuel in them. Rory and Steven were surprised to find a considerable amount of food as well; apparently people had been too fearful of the virus to enter houses containing bodies. Lucy judged that it would be safe if they wore gloves and facemask, and disinfected all tins and packages taken from affected houses.

Later Julia, opening a can of baked beans, asked a simple question: 'I'm glad we're not hungry right now, but where will the food come from when the tins run out?' Margaret answered, 'We have to get to arable land.' Steven argued, 'Yes, eventually, but I think the people who have got away from the islands will cause mayhem on the mainland for a long time. We need to find a way to continue here for a while.' Rory pointed out that the islands offered some resources: 'We can catch fish in the open sea even if the farmed ones die.' Steven wondered, 'I suppose we could grow vegetables for Julia, even on the machair?' They continued to discuss the possibilities but were unable to draw firm conclusions.

****

By the beginning of June there were fewer people moving around central Scotland, but they were desperate and dangerous. The Tanners made careful trips to their farm and discovered it was relatively undisturbed because the crops were still immature. David looked at their life's work sadly but saw hope for the future; 'Although this season is a write-off, we could resume next year when law and order are re-established.' Deborah was more immediately focussed: 'For the moment there's no choice; we have to stay at Alice and Ruth's place, and escape the havoc as soon as we can.' They transferred all their equipment to the smallholding, carefully shutting and locking the gates along the lane, and grateful for the trees which hid their destination.

***

On 6 June people came into Alan's house again. 'Empty, the westsider gang must have turned it over.' 'They've driven the northers away, looks like they're coming out on top.' 'We better keep clear of both lots – no use staying here and getting into a turf war.' Alan was pleased that his house was so unattractive, and grateful for the visit; it showed that it would be premature to try to leave Edinburgh. All he could do was make plans, realise he had too little idea of the conditions outside, tear them up, start again and go round in circles … at least he was still alive, so doing nothing very carefully seemed to be the right strategy. He checked that no-one was around, started the generator to charge his computer, and went back to his books.

***

As part of his plan to move north, Rory wanted to have a look at Glendonan at the southern end of Estra. On 7 June, he and Steven took the motorboat there and peered at the marina from a distance. Rory observed, 'There are still some boats; maybe there's no fuel for them? I imagine all the cars have been taken northwards via the causeways to Iseala and on to Nestra.' They saw a few people, and Steven was cautious: 'I don't want to bring my kids here until it looks less threatening.'

***

At the same time Philip and Henry, on foot to the north of Glendonan, made similar observations. Food was running short on the Eolia, so they risked the disapproval of the rest of the family and approached the outskirts of the town. They entered isolated houses and found that while most had bare cupboards others, seemingly abandoned in a panic, yielded some food.

***

On 12 June Bruce judged that the bodies on Letheilean, though extremely unpleasant by then, were no longer hazardous as regards the Phraya virus. With Benjamin's and Jessica's help he buried them, and afterwards Alexandra brought Isabella along for a few words of ceremonial. She caught the mood: 'Mummy, are we going to die too?' Alexandra decided that a change was required. 'No Bella, we're going to get organised.'

Alexandra set the family to work. They explored all the buildings in Tirglas, gathered everything useful in one place and surveyed it dolefully. Jessica stated the obvious: 'There isn't that much food, we found most of it last time.' Alexandra had been thinking about the long term: 'Yes, but we're catching fish and lambs, the seedlings are coming on and there will be wild food in the summer and autumn. The real problem is the winter. We better produce more than we eat while the going is good, and learn how to preserve it.'

Bruce proved unexpectedly resourceful on the practical aspects of 'depriving micro-organisms of nourishment in order that we can eat unspoiled food.' For the moment they had fuel for the generator he had bought before most people saw the need; so they could keep food in fridges and freezers. For the longer term he tried drying, salting and smoking fish and meat; he experimented with boiling foraged wild plants and sealing the resulting mess in jars; and started to consider what equipment would be needed to make alcohol by fermentation. Benjamin became better with his bow, and Jessica at butchery. Alexandra boasted to her diary, "We are acquiring better practical skills than I would have thought possible."

***

By now invasions of the Tanners' farm were becoming rare. Deborah raised once more the subject of moving on: 'I wonder if it's safe to go Letheilean yet?' David suggested, 'Why don't we go and look at the route?' Reluctantly Alice accompanied him on a cautious investigation of the main road to the west; they found little traffic, and many cars abandoned. He said, 'I've got a Landrover with a winch, which would be able to clear any cars blocking the road. We could take it to Letheilean as well as the van.'

When they got back, Deborah argued, 'Maybe we should make a run for it?' Alice countered, 'There were people on foot who looked in a bad way; we might get stopped and then who knows what would happen?' 'Yes, but the alternative is dangerous too; the same people might find us here and that would be bound to lead to trouble.' In the end they decided to stay put until there were fewer people wandering the roads.

***

By 15 June the Lentons were sufficiently low on both food and fuel that they were ready to risk taking the Eolia to its berth.

Rory and Steven had chosen the same day to make a further trip to Estra to see what was happening in Glendonan. They hadn't seen any activity, so they had gone ashore to explore.

As the Eolia sailed slowly towards the marina, Rory spotted them. 'Look out, someone's coming.' Steven suggested, 'Why don't we get back in your boat and go out to meet them?' 'OK, we can outrun them if they seem unfriendly.'

Katherine, who was nervously watching the marina, saw them first. 'There are two men in a boat, and it's coming towards us.' Philip said, 'Let's talk to them. We can't escape anyway, and there are more of us.' When Rory's boat was within hailing distance, Charles called, 'Good day, what's the situation in port?' Rory replied, 'We're not from here ourselves, we've just come over from Pennay. We haven't seen anyone else yet. How have you been managing?' Olivia summarised, 'We started here in mid-April, before the virus went critical, and have sailed round Estra, Iseala and Nestra. We saw Lochmoran turn nasty as people tried to flee at the end of the month, and since then we've kept offshore. We have been hiding in Caoloch for the past five weeks, watching Glendonan and struggling for food and fuel.'

Steven provided a similar account: I was stranded on Salay with my wife and kids. We escaped by building a boat, and met Rory and his family on Mansay.' Charles acknowledged a fellow sailor; 'Very impressive!' Rory continued, 'We stayed out of the way while Bailecas emptied – we think people came here on their way to Dubheilean, or even headed directly for the mainland. We've been surviving on the resources of Pennay, and recently we've been watching Glendonan too.'

Charles suggested, 'You seem OK, and we're harmless! How about docking and continuing our chat on shore?' Both boats went back to the marina and the Lentons introduced themselves. Steven was reluctant to stay long, 'As recently as a week ago, there were people here, and if anyone remains they may not be peaceable. On Pennay a few people hung on after most had gone; when we returned there were signs of unpleasantness, but we're pretty sure it's now empty. Our intention is to search here for useful stuff and then go back to our families.'

Rory was thinking ahead: 'Why don't you come with us? We're better off working together; we've got a supply of food, including fish from my farm, and you've got a bigger boat. Mansay is safe, and we can always come back here for supplies if necessary.' Rory and Steven went off to enter a few buildings, leaving the Lentons to consider the proposal.

The world had changed, and Olivia appreciated that knowledge of business and the law wouldn't be paramount in the immediate future. 'They seem impressively competent, whereas our skills – apart from sailing – aren't particularly applicable. Maybe we should go with them.' The others were inclined to agree, and Philip and Henry were sent off to help Rory and Steven with their window-breaking. They found that Glendonan had been almost cleared of food and fuel, and that settled it – the Lentons were convinced that Pennay was a better prospect.

The following day both boats returned to Mansay and the Lentons met the rest of the Lynn and Scott families. Over the next few days they all got on well and decided to stick together. When Charles explained Bruce's predictions, he found it easier to persuade his audience than on previous occasions, and this triggered a discussion on where they should be for the best chance of survival. Margaret pointed out the practicalities of staying in the islands: 'The difficulty is that the food will run out, apart from fish. We need to grow vegetables, gather fruit and other wild plants, and eventually do serious farming. The islands are too windy – and as a result invaded by sand and salt – for all that.' Rory countered, 'Yes, but I think we all agree that Dubheilean and Caladion are likely be crowded with island escapees who can't get any further.' Katherine admitted, 'Although I'd love to get closer to my family, it's just too hazardous.'

At this point Charles mentioned the half-arrangement that the two branches of the Lenton family might meet in Letheilean. 'The peninsula has a very small population, and tiny roads, so it offers a safe way back to civilisation.' Olivia muttered, 'If it persists.' Rory's ears pricked up, and he started to work the conversation towards what he had been thinking since he saw the Eolia. 'I think we could aim for Letheilean directly, despite the long crossing, if we use both boats.'

The families checked that Pennay was still safe and spent several days collecting everything they would need for a long sea trip. The Lentons were particularly relieved to find plenty of fuel, as it wouldn't be necessary to sail everywhere.

***

By late June there were only a few desperadoes on the roads around the Tanner farm, and the question of moving arose again. Alice argued, 'We ought to wait until the crops mature.' Deborah objected, 'But the season doesn't end until September; we'll have to abandon some produce.' After some debate, Alice at last revealed her real reason for staying: 'I don't want to leave until Alan gets here.' She was implacable, and won the argument because Ruth wouldn't go without her and the Tanners were relying on them for help with the children. Instead they continued to tend crops which were close to readiness for harvest. They also prepared for departure by butchering the animals and preserving the meat. William rather alarmed his parents by his interest in the process.

***

On 22 June Alan ventured outside for the first time in a month, under cover of darkness, and found Edinburgh abandoned. He saw no-one alive, but felt sure there must be other survivors, so he was extremely cautious. He entered a few houses and found no food; here even the homes of the dead had been ransacked. It was evident from the state of countless bodies that most people had died some time ago, but fresher corpses and remnants of meals indicated that some people had been alive recently. Alan decided to return to his hiding place, but to keep a watch on the situation. He checked his bike again and repacked the rucksack that he intended to take with him.

***

For the past week the families on Mansay had been preparing for the journey to Letheilean. Early on 25 June they set off in fair weather, with Eolia full of people and equipment, Rory's boat manned by him and Steven, and a precautionary line between them. The crossing went smoothly, apart from the intermittent need to pump water from Rory's boat. However, it was a long journey, and they were grateful for Scotland's eighteen-hour days around the solstice. They made their way to a beach just along the coast from Letheilean's lighthouse, and got what sleep they could.

The next day Steven and Philip walked the three kilometres to the Achar Hotel, and saw that it was deserted, but found the note left for them by Bruce. They returned to the others with the good news, and they all took to the boats to motor round the coast to Tirglas.

***

Benjamin was fishing from his boat when he spotted two more approaching. He returned to Tirglas to fetch the rest of the family, and they watched apprehensively from a hiding place. Suddenly Bruce exclaimed, 'My God, isn't that the Eolia?' The first gathering was a bewildering mixture of joyous reunion, tears at the absence of loved ones, horror at the events of the past months and blankness at the prospect of what lay ahead. The Lentons already established in Letheilean showed the islanders what they had achieved, and it struck some of them as worthy but unequal to the task. They did their best to disguise their reactions, but Alexandra noticed. Olivia, wanting to prevent any criticism, suggested that everyone should rest for the night and look to the future in the morning.

Part 2 Peninsula

Chapter 5 Survival

In the morning of 28 June Olivia asked Jessica, Benjamin, Peter and Julia to look after Isabella, Alison and Calum. She gathered the adults and made a start: 'I would like to have a meeting, and am willing to chair it if that would be helpful.' She paused, and met no opposition; 'OK, I think we should discuss things separately, and try not to muddle them. The immediate challenge is how to survive, especially through the winter, and where we can best do so. Later we can consider our long-term strategy, and how to interact with other survivors.' Alexandra began to take notes, and Olivia continued, 'But perhaps we ought to start with what we think has happened to the world?'

Bruce apologised, 'May I go first? I know it's absurd, but I feel vaguely responsible because my model predicted all this. Certainly it appears to have played a role in bringing us together here. I should explain what it said.' Lucy objected, 'By all means, but we can't know how the pandemic actually played out.' Bruce resumed, 'You're right, but we can get something from the model combined with what little actual information we've got. For what it's worth, it predicted that the virus would infect a large proportion of the world's population and cause hundreds of millions of deaths. However, we've seen many people alive, long after the virus would have spread everywhere, so billions will have survived the disease and acquired immunity. As a result, the virus is probably dying away naturally. Soon even the bodies won't be dangerous from the point of view of Phraya.'

Rory interrupted: 'Does all this matter now? It seems the virus was just the trigger for the real crisis. The news reports made people panic, so they emptied the shops. Then everyone stopped doing normal things like growing food, driving lorries, making electricity and so on. Pretty soon the world really was in trouble, regardless of the virus.'

Katherine, thinking of her family, added 'Certainly everyone fled from the islands, because no supplies were getting there. But I wonder what has been happening in places like Glasgow?' Alexandra said, 'I agree this is what matters, but we just don't know. We witnessed the onset of a breakdown in Edinburgh and Port Monard, you saw the continuation in Lochmoran, Glendonan and Bailecas, and we've looked at Innisdu – all unpleasant. We know that all utilities have failed on the islands, and here. Most damning of all, there is the collapse of communications, even centralised broadcasting. This suggests that things aren't working anywhere.'

Katherine pleaded, 'So are any of our loved ones alive?' Philip tried to console her. 'Your folks promised they'd get out of the city if things got bad, so they probably escaped.' Charles added, 'We've all come through this, in different ways, so there must be survivors having conversations like this all over the country.' Alexandra cautioned, 'However, given the violence that we've seen in towns, surely it isn't sensible to go closer to centres of population at the moment.' Philip resumed, 'You told your parents that we might come to Letheilean, so they will be heading to the Achar Hotel,' – Katherine didn't look convinced, but he pressed on – 'so we better stay put for the time being?'

Olivia reinforced this. 'While mobile phones still worked, I was in contact with my friend Deborah Tanner, who runs a farm in Morrie, and I also mentioned Letheilean. If we stay here, and they make it, we'll gain some farming expertise.' The debate continued for a while, but it was impossible to determine the situation closer to the cities, and it seemed too dangerous to go and find out. Olivia summarised, 'It seems we have a consensus that we should stay here for now. Let's talk about how we're going to manage in the short term.'

Margaret returned to the theme of the discussion on Mansay: 'The most important consideration is food, obviously. We've been relying far too much on pre-Phraya supplies, so our main task, post, to establish a supply that matches the needs of eighteen people. Indeed, if we're to stay here for a long time, we need to generate a surplus and stockpile food for the winter.' Bruce said defensively, 'We've made a start on preservation, but we haven't got all that much fresh food in the first place.'

Silence, as this sank in. Olivia tried to elicit further analysis: 'OK, let's stick to immediate problem for a moment. What can we eat right now?' Rory offered, 'I've got a supply of farmed fish; we can easily catch more, in the summer at any rate. I can prolong its usefulness by smoking it.' Henry enthused, 'I'd like to have a go with Benjamin's bow.' He had been listening from a hiding place, and blew his cover: 'Great, I'll make you another one.' Peter was no smarter; 'And one for me.' Isabella wasn't going to be left out, 'It's not fair, girls are allowed them too.' Alison added, 'Even little girls,' and finally Calum staked his claim, 'And little boys.' Lucy appealed to the older girls, 'Jessica and Julia, could you please take these silly children away, and Ali and Calum too while you're at it.' Laughter all round, and Olivia announced, 'Time for a break. Does anyone know how to grow coffee in northern Scotland?'

When the meeting resumed Benjamin and Peter were allowed to attend, on condition that later they would relieve the girls of childminding duty. Margaret said, 'OK, we can catch enough fish and game for protein and fat. What about carbohydrate, sugars and vitamins?' Steven translated, 'She means fruit and veg.' Bruce had been reading the book on foraging, and spouted, 'Even if we can't grow enough food from seed, there are wild berries, nuts, shoots and leaves of various herbs, and mushrooms.' Philip interjected, 'Does anyone know anything about them? We don't want to kill ourselves.' Henry was gung-ho, 'I'll test them, I've got the constitution of a bear.' Olivia was having none of it; 'Not while I'm your mother.' Lucy advised: 'I propose that for each unfamiliar food we get someone to eat a tiny amount, wait a couple of hours, then eat rather more, and if they're OK the next day the rest of us can tuck in. It looks like we've got a volunteer. With mushrooms we could use a more cautious version of the same procedure, increasing the amount in three stages.'

Margaret observed, 'The foods mentioned so far don't provide bulk starch for lasting energy.' Bruce had an answer: 'There's also seaweed.' Alison had crept back and couldn't restrain herself: 'Yuk, I'm not eating seaweed!' Isabella joined in, 'It's not even food,' and Calum assured the meeting, 'No, it's poo.' Lucy looked pained; 'Sorry about that. Evidently the girls are no better than the boys at controlling the little ones.' Julia was chagrined, so Henry suggested, 'Oh, why not let them all stay, the rules have changed, perhaps forever, and we're only talking about food at the moment.'

'If I may continue,' said Bruce, 'Wild foods will be available in the summer and autumn. I've tried several preservation methods on various plants, and have prevented them from going off, but I have to admit that the results haven't always been palatable.' The discussion continued for some time, and eventually Olivia summarised, 'OK, let's assume for the moment that we have enough food, both for now and for the winter, here in Tirglas. Margaret, would you be willing to coordinate food production?' She replied, 'I'll try, but my expertise is based on the availability of a wide range of foods, and plenty of it.' Olivia thanked her and moved on: 'Can we turn our attention to the longer term? Julia, please, we don't want to upset the little ones.'

'Assuming we plan a return to civilisation,' – Philip emphasised the last word and paused to let the muttering die down – 'then hadn't we better wait until it has had a chance to re-establish itself?' The families tried to analyse whether this would take place, and if so how and when, but found it impossible to make any progress. Steven argued, 'We need to use modern technology if we're to avoid a primitive life, and that can only happen in the industrial areas. We just don't know enough about the situation there; perhaps we can scout cautiously before the winter, to see what's going on?' This was agreed in principle, and the meeting broke up.

***

While those on Letheilean wondered about life in the cities, Alan went out to explore Edinburgh more widely. It was an almost moonless night, and he used his torch sparingly. He took his bicycle, in order to be able to escape unwanted attention, but wasn't challenged. Indeed he saw no-one alive, just bodies. The city belonged to the rats, preyed on by the few cats and dogs that could hunt well enough to survive without their former owners. There were few vehicles, and weeds had started to sprout on the roads. It began to rain softly.

Most houses had been ransacked, so he tried buildings where food wouldn't be expected, but these sprang nasty surprises as often as pleasant ones. In any case, he hadn't yet run out of supplies, so he returned to his home; he intended to remain there until shortages forced him to risk abandoning his sanctuary.

***

In the days after Olivia's meeting, everyone sprang into action. Rory put Steven to work on the construction of a smokehouse, and they started to cut and dry timber for the winter. Benjamin and Henry produced bows and arrows, and learned to use them; Jessica butchered the kills. Charles and Peter fished, and Bruce preserved the meat and fish. Olivia, Alexandra, Philip and Katherine tended the vegetables, foraged for wild plants and tried to cook them. Julia helped Lucy with the younger children. Margaret ran around fretting about whether their efforts to feed themselves would prove adequate.

***

By 6 July the Tanner farm hadn't been disturbed for some days, but Deborah remained nervous that the smallholding would be discovered. David and Alice made a further foray along the road to the west, and saw no-one moving about. Instead they discovered that some of the people they had seen last time, wandering aimlessly, hadn't made it. David turned to her, intending to say something, but saw that she was stony-faced. They drove back in silence.

Once more Deborah raised the subject of making the trip to join the Lentons: 'I hate to say this, Alice, but wouldn't Alan have got here by now, if … he's …' She tailed off awkwardly and waited for the stiff response: 'He's very organised and self-sufficient, I believe he has survived and will make the journey as soon as it's feasible.' David found a compromise, 'Alice, let's wait a fortnight, and then accept the situation and leave.' She agreed tearfully, and they resumed their preparations.

***

Meanwhile, on Letheilean a debate arose about the benefits and risks of visiting Innisdu. Steven argued, 'It's a sizeable town, there must be all kinds of useful stuff there.' Alexandra said, 'When Bruce went a few weeks ago it looked threatening, and we've kept away since.' Rory pointed out, 'We're going to need more fuel, for fishing and eventually for a road trip. I'm aware that one can grow crops to make fuel, but I doubt Margaret would want to waste potential food.' It was agreed that some of the men would go and explore cautiously.

Margaret caught Alexandra alone, and asked her, 'Have you noticed how our husbands seem almost to be enjoying this situation?' Alexandra recognised a fellow sufferer: 'Yes, when Bruce was working on his model, he became caught up in the scenario, and forgot to be appalled.' Margaret, again revealing a little more than she intended, said 'When we got off Salay, I suspect Steven was pleased to find the world contained fewer people for him to handle.'

The next day Rory took Steven, Bruce and Henry to Innisdu in his boat. It looked like Bailecas, abandoned, with many cars remaining but few boats. Rory theorised: 'Parts of Eilard are quite close to the mainland, so most people would have been able to escape by boat even after the ferries stopped.' There were signs of survivors, and the men were keen to avoid them. They entered a few houses and found that they had not been cleaned out. Steven was triumphant: 'As I predicted! When it's safe we should come back and stock up.' After collecting some food and fuel, they returned to Tirglas.

***

By 8 July Alan's water was running low, so he decided he would soon have to leave. His original planning hadn't envisaged a bicycle journey, but he could see advantages: he would use tracks and paths to keep out of sight of other travellers. He knew he would have to risk some tarmac, but planned to retreat off road if challenged. Another advantage of two wheels was that it would be easy to get round any obstructions caused by abandoned cars. He intended to travel at night, hiding the bike and sleeping by day. He found a cycle shop and helped himself to spare tyres, puncture repair kits, lights, batteries, panniers and other equipment. He felt like a thief, but did anyone own these things now? He was minded to leave payment, and even looked at the cash in his wallet. He hesitated and eventually decided he had better keep it in case anyone was stupid enough to accept it in exchange for something useful later. Back at home he consulted maps for a route to Morrie.

Late in the evening of 12 July Alan set off. The bike was crammed with gear, but he also wore his rucksack as insurance, in case he had to abandon his wheels in a hurry. As he rode out of the city, now illuminated by strong moonlight, he saw the full extent of the devastation. It was as if all the people had been removed in an instant by supernatural forces, leaving cars akimbo, rubbish in the streets, burnt and flooded buildings; but the people had not simply disappeared, and the smell of decomposition indicated their fate. His torch picked out the eyes of animals, but he also saw other lights in the distance, presumably belonging to survivors?

Alan made his way without difficulty through the suburbs, equally blighted, and into the countryside. He had decided to avoid the bridges across the river estuary, so his route took him westwards past the refinery, still smoking after a fire which must have lasted many weeks. Progress was slow because of his circuitous route on dark paths, and he was unfit after months of immolation. At dawn he picked an isolated house and settled down to rest for the day. He was tired but sleep was slow coming; he felt uncomfortable being in someone else's home. What had become of the owners? Were they alive? The bedroom was silent on the subject.

***

On Letheilean the first harvest was under way. It shouldn't have been, but Alison had pulled out a carrot, declared it too small, pulled up another with the same result, and so on until Katherine caught her. Margaret was for replanting them, but Philip suggested that a few tiny carrots, along with the first radishes and young spinach leaves, might serve to cheer up the families. Margaret relented and that evening, as Julia struggled with a plateful of meat and seaweed with a miniscule helping of fresh produce, there was much hilarity at the expense of would-be vegetarians.

***

On the second night of his journey Alan was forced to use a road, and almost ran into some people. He swerved to avoid them, but they pursued him, shouting furiously, 'Hey, wait! Got anything to eat?' He accelerated away and was glad to escape. After that he switched off his lights while he was on roads, and redoubled his efforts to stick to paths, no matter however inconvenient. He persevered, and by the time he stopped at daybreak he was well on his way to Morrie.

***

Early on 15 July Alice checked the lane to the market garden, as she had on every other morning for weeks. In the distance she saw a bicycle approaching slowly; she screamed, 'Alan, thank God!' When he was closer, he grinned weakly, 'I'd like bacon, two eggs, toast made with fresh brown bread and four cups of tea, please.' They hugged and she wouldn't let go for a long time.

While Alan ate, Alice crowed, 'Deborah, I told you he'd come. Now we can go to Letheilean.' He asked, 'Where's that?' She realised there was a lot to talk about: 'I'll explain later, after you've had a sleep.' However, the children wouldn't give him any peace. Samuel inspected his bike, and was incredulous: 'Have you come from Edinburgh?' William said, 'Is that a thousand miles?' – this was the largest distance he could imagine – and Rose wanted to know, 'Why didn't you come in a car?' David interrupted, 'He's tired, he'll tell us all about it when he wakes up.' William wasn't satisfied; 'He should have slept in the night like a good boy.'

The following day Deborah told Alan about her conversation with Olivia. She was still concerned about the possibility of invasion if they remained in Morrie. 'Our land is in the open, and even Alice's smallholding is vulnerable to local survivors.' He replied, 'Yes, I've run across some of them, and I'm in no hurry to do that again.' She continued, 'Letheilean isn't much of a prospect for farming, but it will have some suitable ground. At least it looks like a safe place to wait until it's feasible to come back to the farm.'

Alan was pleased at the opportunity to go further from the madness, in good company, and assured her, 'I'm happy to join forces with you, and you might have some use for my skills. But how can you be sure that Olivia and her family will be there?' 'Charles has a decent boat, so they will have managed to away from the islands. What's not so clear is whether they know how to grow food – they're corporate types – so they may be struggling, and I'd like to help.'

Once the decision was made, they set to work: Alice and Ruth harvested those crops that were sufficiently mature, and tried to nurture seedlings for replanting later. Alan helped David load the van and Landrover; although they had more than enough fuel for the journey Alan insisted on putting his bike on the roof. Deborah tried to get the children to help or, in William's case, not to hinder.

Two days later Alan, Alice, Ruth and the Tanner family set off for Letheilean. They had worked out a route which used small roads for the most part, and avoided Port Monard. They saw a few other vehicles travelling on the roads but were not troubled by them. People on foot seemed more in need of help, but the Tanners were not willing to expose their children to the hazards of uncontrollable encounters with them.

The journey was slow at first, because they were often forced to remove vehicles that were obstructing the road. Rose asked, 'Why have people left their cars all over the place?' David replied, 'They ran out of petrol.' William was puzzled; 'Why didn't they get more from the garage?' Samuel answered, 'I think there's none left.' 'But why not?' Deborah thought it best to avoid this conversation; 'Everything has gone a bit crazy, we don't really understand it ourselves, and we are going away while it gets sorted out.'

They stopped for a first night in a house in the middle of nowhere, and were undisturbed. Alan tried to express his feelings: 'Isn't this odd, eating in someone else's kitchen?' Alice was unmoved; 'I'm sure they wouldn't mind.' Deborah agreed, 'Yes, plenty of people have come uninvited into our farm in the past few weeks, everything has changed.' Alan replied, 'It's just that I've been holed up in two rooms for months, while gangsters checked out the rest of my house. It's taking me some time to get used to the new rules.'

The next day they continued as far as the vicinity of Port Monard, and picked a house far from any others. While the children were settled down for a second night, David and Alan went to explore the town. They ran across survivors who shouted, 'Stop, we'll have that car.' David demonstrated that his Landrover had an unexpected turn of speed. Alan remarked, 'We're doing the right thing, driving away from all this. I don't know what the coming months and years will bring, but Letheilean sounds like a good place to face the future.'

Chapter 6 Team

On 20 July, Steven saw a battered van and Landrover trundling towards Tirglas. He fetched Olivia to check that these were the people she was hoping to see. 'Deborah, thank goodness, I'm so glad you made it, give me a hug! These must be your friends from the smallholding?' The implication was jokingly corrected: 'Yes, I'm Alice, this is my partner Ruth and my brother Alan. It may not be as big as the Tanners' farm, but our little market garden has fed us all for the past two months.' Deborah glanced apologetically at Alice; 'Indeed, it has been a haven, whereas the farm has been entirely useless.' She turned back to Olivia, 'So you made it over the water, and I see Bruce's family are here, but who are the others?' For the rest of the day, people introduced themselves and exchanged stories of survival and escape.

The next day Olivia organised a meeting of the twenty-six inhabitants of Letheilean. By this time Julia had grown into the role of childminder; she and Samuel undertook to keep Isabella, Rose, William, Alison and Calum out of the way. The other teenagers insisted on attending. Olivia asked those who had just arrived, 'What have you left behind?' Alan provided an update on the situation in Edinburgh: 'I'm sorry, this won't be nice. There were very few people, and almost all them were dead. The place was silent, apart from the squeaking of the rats – eating the victims I'm afraid – and the barking of the dogs that were preying on them.' There was a collective intake of breath.

Deborah's summary of the state of affairs outside the city sounded little better: 'There is no electricity, gas or water; radio, TV, and the internet have failed; shops are closed, money is meaningless. There is no government; no army or police; the rule of law is suspended. If the violence has diminished, it's probably only because so few people are left that they have been able to find enough food.'

Bruce asked, 'How many people have survived in Edinburgh?' Alan hesitated; 'It's hard to tell, but I went into a lot of houses and found no-one alive; just bodies, mainly indoors but also outside. I only saw people moving about in ones and twos. I think the population of the city may be no more than a few hundred.' David wondered, 'Perhaps that's because most people fled?' Bruce pressed him: 'OK, how many in the countryside?' He also found it impossible to say. 'The towns and villages were as deserted as the city sounds. There was no-one – alive anyway – in the houses we entered. The roads were almost empty of cars, but there were a few people wandering around. Maybe there are groups hiding to keep away from the violence?' Bruce frowned, and concluded, 'Sounds as if only one person in a thousand has made it.'

Everyone was so stunned that Olivia was forced to end the silence: 'I know it's awful, but let's try to carry on.'

Margaret turned to her usual subject. 'There is probably enough food to sustain a tiny fraction of the normal population for quite a while, but not indefinitely. Was there any sign of people in inhabited areas thinking about what happens when the food runs out?' David replied, 'I don't think so. Existing crops, planted before Phraya, are maturing as well as can be expected without attention from farmers. Otherwise little food is being grown, and it's hard to see how agriculture will be restarted without a complete restoration of order.' Alan added, 'That won't be easy until there's a trusted food supply, so it's catch-22.'

Alexandra, who had been muttering since Bruce spoke, suddenly woke up. 'It's not just a matter of numbers, it's an apocalypse.' Another awkward pause. Henry, who had been studying prehistory, remarked, 'There were several occasions in the stone age when natural disasters reduced the population of the world to a few tens of thousands, and it always bounced back.' Alice pointed out sharply, 'Yes, but all that happened was that the numbers recovered, but without any cultural change. I think Alexandra is concerned about whether we can rebuild a civilised world?' Philip tried to lower the tension. 'Perhaps we should try to visualise how things could go well, at least over the next few years?'

This was the discussion Steven had tried to start at the previous meeting. 'I think it's essential that technology is re-established. Otherwise all we can hope for is a hunter-gatherer existence.' David corrected him: 'We wouldn't have to go back that far. The world may be in chaos, but we haven't completely forgotten about agriculture.' 'True, but we're threatened with a return to subsistence farming. If we can re-establish mechanised agriculture, the necessary food can be grown by a fraction of the people, and the rest can work on starting other industries.' Lucy said, 'We'll also need a medical system, or people will die of trivial complaints.' Alexandra added, 'What about cultural pursuits. Life wouldn't be worth living, even with plenty of food and good teeth, if we couldn't hear Mozart.' When the laughter died down, Olivia saw that she hadn't been entirely joking, and tried to pick up on her theme, 'It's true that life consists of more than just surviving. We'll also need law and order,' and Charles added, 'and a financial system.' Philip looked worried; 'Restarting the world sounds complicated! If you think about it, in the pre-Phraya world everything depended on everything else; no wonder it has collapsed so completely. Post, we'll need to begin with fundamentals and slowly build up a more complete society.'

Alan confessed, 'Being a pessimistic type, I took this crisis quite seriously early on, while the internet still worked. I took the opportunity to download a huge amount of material on what to do when, as the preppers say, "it's the end of the world as we know it". Some of it is crazy, and much of it emphasises defending yourself against violence – quite useful, when you think what happened – but there's also practical information on how to move forwards after a collapse. The first things to tackle might be basics like farming, transport, fuel and electricity.'

Olivia wanted to focus much more narrowly: 'We can't solve the entire future of mankind now. Before the recent arrivals, we had decided that we had better stay here through the winter. Everything you've told us reinforces that conclusion – does anyone think otherwise?' The question was almost rhetorical, but gazes turned to Steven; 'I admit the situation doesn't look good in the industrial areas. All I've been saying is that we can't expect to make a good life here, in isolation.' Margaret was surprised; 'You like seclusion so much that you chose Salay for a holiday!' Everyone smiled, but Steven ploughed on: 'I'm not looking forward to tackling the crazy people that Alan ran across. I just meant that eventually we've got to go where engineering is possible.'

Olivia brought the meeting to a close. 'I suggest we stick to the original plan, keeping an eye on the rest of the world if it's safe to do so. We're in a much better position now that we've got farmers and a van full of equipment. Deborah, would you please join Margaret in steering our efforts on food production and preservation?'

Afterwards Jessica spoke to Benjamin: 'Mum certainly didn't like that discussion much.' He replied, 'Do you think it was just because dad was using numbers as usual? You know how she hates that.' 'No, I think she doesn't like what they mean in this case. What about the other nine hundred and ninety-nine people?' He was shocked. 'Yes, he didn't seem to be thinking about them, but I suppose she was.'

For the next few days those already established in Letheilean got to know the newcomers. Margaret was much more optimistic now that her knowledge of food was reinforced by expertise on how to grow it. Olivia felt that Deborah's friendship and ordered mind would ease the burden of her leadership. As for the children: Isabella, who had been on her own between the teenagers and the little ones, was over the moon at the arrival of Rose and her brothers. Samuel wasn't yet interested in girls; instead he aspired to join the lads. Calum, precocious at four, recognised in eight-year-old William a boy not entirely out of reach, and followed him around all the time.

Unresolved issues from the meeting continued to be debated in smaller groups. Alexandra sought out Henry; 'I think Alice put you down somewhat the other day, but she was right about my concerns. The question is whether Bruce's "one person in a thousand" can do more than merely grow enough food and reproduce. I meant it when I spoke of music. The team here seems better equipped for physical survival than for the propagation of culture. You're different.'

'Yes, there's plenty for farmers, joiners and doctors to do, but it's not so clear what use can be made of my parents' skills, and your subject has been changed completely. As for me, my studies have been cut off before they start. History doesn't look so useful as a guide to the future any more. But I'm happy to help if I can.'

Katherine was also struck by the starkness of Bruce's conclusion, and unburdened herself to Philip. 'If he's right, my family won't be alive; you and yours are the only people I know in the world.' He conceded that his previous encouragement might have been hollow; 'I'm so sorry, Kat, but you may be right. Perhaps we can make a family of our own?'

***

Steven and Rory, practical as always, reckoned that in order to cope with the winter they would have to obtain resources from Innisdu. It was agreed that they would mount another expedition; Rory urged, 'Let's go in my boat, not too loaded up so we can get away if need be.' 'OK, but let's take a generator; we may need to use power tools.' On 28 July they set off with Alan and David, who were keen to see what the town offered. They moored and left Rory to guard his boat and inspect the few that remained in the harbour.

The others went into the town and soon came across someone wandering the streets alone. David was polite: 'Hello, are you OK? Are there many people here?' The man looked at them with fright in his eyes, 'Just me, I keep to myself. What do you want?' David replied, 'We're just after a bit of fuel. Have you found any?' He looked puzzled; 'What do I want with fuel? Have you got anything to eat?' Steven gave him some food. He grabbed it, wolfed it down, and pointed, 'There's a petrol station over there. Watch out for the others.' David said, 'I thought you said you were alone. Is there anyone else here?' The man was reluctant to be drawn; 'I keep to myself.' Alan tugged at the others and said, 'OK, thanks mate, good luck to you.' They moved on, leaving the man to shuffle away in the opposite direction.

They went back to Rory, who said, 'The remaining boats look as if they would need repair work.' They decided to hide his on the outskirts of town and explore the industrial estate. They found a pump, with which they were able to extract fuel from the underground tanks of a garage. They broke into a storage facility that hadn't been breached, and found pizza flour, tinned tomatoes, olives, oil and red wine. Steven celebrated, 'Thank God for Italian restaurants! Margaret will be pleased.'

They discovered a garden centre, also undisturbed; David was surprised. 'This must mean that the people here are living off existing food, or there are very few of them, or they're all in the same state as that poor man we met. At any rate, it seems no-one is trying to grow anything.' They took seeds and other small items. There was even a petrol rotavator, but Rory said, 'We can't take that now, David, we'll come back with the Eolia and really stock up.'

Back in Tirglas that evening, after pizzas cooked in the smokehouse and eaten in the open air, the team tried to discuss Innisdu. David observed, 'There was so much equipment, we could really get set up for growing food. Maybe we should move there?' Lucy was against this: 'No, it's just too dangerous. I think towns and cities have traumatised people. Look at that man you met.' Philip empathised, 'Poor thing, perhaps we should have rescued him?' 'Alice was inclined to be judgemental: 'There must be thousands like him; unfortunately, those who don't cope aren't going to make it. We can't take them on.' Philip glanced at her and lamented, 'But he may have suffered dreadfully'. Olivia tried to steer a discussion on the dangers and duties of handling those less fortunate, but everyone had become tipsy on the red wine, and the debate reflected this. Eventually Henry brought it to an end by extemporising: 'I keep to myself. Watch out for the others. But no man is an island, entire of itself. Every man is a piece of the continent, a part of the main.' Olivia urged him, 'Put a sock in it, my boy.'

Alexandra disagreed, 'No, let's have some of the world before Phraya. Actually, this is relevant – can you remember it all, Henry?' He resumed, 'If a clod be washed away by the sea, Europe is the less, as well as if a promontory were, as well as if a manor of thy friend's or of thine own were.' Margaret interrupted, 'Clearly a reference to Letheilean, and I'm so glad I'm not on Salay any more.' More laughter and drinking, then a hush while Henry finished: 'Any man's death diminishes me, because I am involved in mankind, and therefore never send to know for whom the bell tolls; it tolls for thee.'

By now some were in tears; David, trying to lift the mood, waved his last piece of pizza, 'There you are, Margaret, some carbohydrate at last!' She smiled, raised her glass and there was a chorus of 'Cheers!' Lucy moaned, 'Oh, such lovely food! What does everyone miss?' Rory offered, 'Avocadoes, only just ripe, with real mayonnaise and fresh prawns.' Bruce countered with, 'Camembert, so warm it heals the wound when a piece is cut out, or better still Mont d'Or.' Ruth remembered, 'Watermelon, my mother used to say it was tastelessly delicious.' Philip, who knew little poetry but didn't want people thinking that only Henry was cultured: 'Do I dare to eat a peach?' Deborah muttered to Margaret, 'Only if we can grow it.'

That night Alexandra wrote in her diary, "We are so coarsened, I wonder if we're losing our powers of empathy? At some point, when the worst is over, people will have to start helping each other if trust is to grow again. Then society can be healed."

In the cool light of the morning, it was clear to all that they shouldn't move to Innisdu, but merely visit for its resources. Accordingly, David directed the planting of the recently acquired seeds in Tirglas, in the expectation of a late harvest. At the same time, the earlier batch of seeds was starting to yield results: the carrots spared by Alison were now maturing, along with more radishes, rocket and turnip tops. However, for some time the main supply of food would have to come from the wild: hunting and fishing continued, and were complemented by bilberries, raspberries, tiny strawberries, elderberry flowers, pignuts and chanterelles.

***

Isabella said to Rose one day, 'Where did you live before things went wrong?' She replied, 'Morrie, it's a little village about a hundred miles away. We lived on a farm, but we had to go and stay on Alice and Ruth's smallholding. Then we came here; it was scary. Dad says he's hoping we can go back when things are sorted out. What about you?' 'We lived in London, it's more than five hundred miles. We went to Edinburgh first, and it was horrible, then we came here.' 'When do you think we'll be able to go home?' 'Dad says it might be years. I don't like it here, but it's better now you've come.'

On 15 Aug it was Alison's seventh birthday. Alice rummaged through the remaining produce from the market garden, and selected a present which met with approval: 'Ham! Wow, thanks, scrummy.' A memory flitted across her face, 'We used to have it at school. When can I go back?' Lucy tried to explain: 'Perhaps not for a long time, Ali, there isn't a school here.' She wanted to know, 'Why not?' Rory said, 'Something very bad happened a while ago, and the world is all confused.' She sensed his tone and settled into her mother's lap. Julia took Calum to play games somewhere else.

Rory sighed and made a start: 'A nasty bug made a lot of people ill, so they couldn't do their work. Then the ferries stopped bringing things to our island, so soon there wasn't enough to eat. I'm afraid a lot of people ...' Lucy intervened, '... left the island, so then the school had to close.' He took the hint, 'Now we've come to this peaceful place.' Alison still didn't understand. 'But why can't we go somewhere with a school that's open?' Her mother continued, 'All the schools have stopped, everywhere. We are going to stay here for a while, until the world is sorted out. We'll grow food ourselves, and we'll teach you how to help.' She seemed satisfied, but another thought crossed her mind; 'What about my old friends?' Her father ended, 'You can be friends with the other kids here, it will be fun.'

Later, when they had recovered from this conversation, Lucy and Rory spoke to David and Deborah. 'We need to arrange proper schooling for the kids, not just childcare.' Deborah said, 'Yes, mine are turning feral. Alexandra has been talking about this, not just for Bella but for her older ones too. I'll get her.' When she arrived, Lucy made an offer: 'I'm happy to run a school for the children up to Sam's age. Julia is very good with the little ones, so she can help.' Alexandra replied, 'That would be wonderful. For my part, I will ensure that Jessica, Ben, Peter and Julia are educated too, rather than just be turned into under-age workers.'

Alison was less affected by Rory's explanation of closed schools than he and Lucy feared. She recounted to William the highlight of her birthday: 'Alice made ham, it was yummy.' He informed her, 'I bet you don't know how it's made. They kill a pig, and cut up the meat, and make it juicy, then it's ham!' She was dubious. 'Sounds horrid, but ham is nice, so that can't be right.' 'It is so, you can ask Alice if you don't believe me.'

Alexandra wanted to talk privately with Bruce. 'You predicted annihilation, and now you've enumerated the tiny remnant of the population. What do you think about the new situation?' He responded carefully: 'I never wanted Phraya to wreak havoc, I just put its characteristics into my model, and added my judgement of human nature.' She pounced: 'Which wasn't very favourable.' 'Indeed, I was dubious of people's capacity to deal calmly with such a challenge, and unfortunately I was right. It's not as if I've been running around taking food by force myself.'

Alexandra conceded, 'No, we haven't had to, and who can say they would have been better behaved in the thick of it. But my question stands, what do you feel now?' Bruce decided to risk honesty: 'The outcome is ghastly, but we must deal with it, and I'm finding the process surprisingly bearable. I said once that re-building the world might be interesting anthropologically, and you didn't like that, but it seems better to face the situation actively rather than experience it passively, like a nightmare?' This time she was regretful rather than angry. 'I suppose so, but I'm worried that mankind might not build a satisfactory post-Phraya world. Mere survival won't restore the full richness of human culture.' 'Well, you can be its guardian.'

***

The team continued to prepare for winter in Letheilean. Steven and Bruce attempted to calculate how much wood to cut for heating and cooking until spring. No-one wanted to burn furniture, so Benjamin and Henry searched for more axes and saws, and all the men took turns felling trees and splitting logs. Alan directed the building of a wood drying shed, with a roof to keep off rain, a slatted side facing the prevailing wind and a more open side in the lee. Margaret tried to supply lumberjack calories.

In September a bigger expedition was mounted to Innisdu, with Steven in Rory's boat and Charles taking Alan, David and Henry on Eolia. Although they were six strong, they had no desire to meet anyone on this trip. They made a quick visit to the harbour, chose two of the larger boats and towed them away for later repair.

The first priority was a visit to the garden centre, so David could have his rotavator, along with much else. Next they located another petrol station and pumped out its tanks. The Italian store was still undiscovered by anyone else; Charles wondered, 'Perhaps this means no-one is alive now?' Steven was firm: 'We can't worry about that. Margaret won't be amused if we don't bring back a big supply of food. We could leave a little for the poor guy we met last time, and any others who are capable of helping themselves?'

In the evening they chose a large isolated house in which to spend the night. Alan, who had experience from his time in Edinburgh, spotted an empty tin of beans in the bin, and was immediately alert. 'The remnants haven't gone off yet. There are still survivors, they may be nearby, we have to move.' They selected another house, hid everything and set a watch through the night. For the whole of the next day the men entered industrial premises and houses, and encountered no-one, but shared a sense of being watched. They found wood-burning stoves, oil lamps, more generators, car batteries – and broke into a cabinet to acquire a rifle and ammunition.

That evening Charles picked a third house, for safety; but when he broke in, he soon regretted the choice: 'Oh no, a body!' Alan was unsympathetic: 'I suppose you spent the whole of the crisis on your boat, so you haven't seen this.' 'No, but I knew I had to face it eventually.' David put an arm on his shoulder; 'I was shocked too, it wasn't part of our previous lives, but you'll get used to it.' After an unrestful night in yet another house, they loaded the four boats and made their way slowly back to Tirglas.

Steven was triumphant about the successful trip, but something nagged at Margaret. When they were alone, she remarked, 'I'd rather we'd bought all that stuff, in the old way.' 'I don't understand what you mean. Who would we have paid?' She tried to explain what was bothering her: 'Of course, but it doesn't seem right to be pillaging like this.' 'The people who owned the things we took are probably dead. In a way their possessions now belong to all the survivors. We've just got to take what we need and be grateful it's available. What matters is that we are winning.'

'This isn't a game! I'm concerned for the people who are still alive but aren't quite making it. Before Phraya we wouldn't have taken things just because we're better organised, or simply stronger. There was support for the less fortunate. I just don't like our heartlessness, damn it!'

Steven was angry, so he spoke carefully. 'I'm just doing my best in a terrible situation. I feel accused, but of what crime?' He waited, and after a while Margaret found the truth: 'I think it's quite simple. You like the post world better than the pre, and I can't share that.' He tried to mollify her: 'You may be right, but I suppose people who make things happen will be needed. By the way, you're certainly contributing, even without enjoying the process. As for plunder, I agree that when the world is put to rights, we'll have to make things or pay for what others have made.'

***

William was nine on 28 September. David gave him a model aeroplane that he had found in Innisdu. 'Thanks, dad! Can I paint it blue, because then the enemy won't see the plane when it flies over the sea and attacks?' David thought he had done well to get the colours shown on the box. 'Sorry, Billie, there aren't any shops here. I'll try to find some blue another time.' His son was willing to wait: 'You can get some when we go back home.' Samuel understood more than William, and put it rather harshly: 'Billie, there won't be shops there, or anywhere else either.' Now William was confused; 'Then where did you buy the plane, dad?' David could see he was in trouble; 'I visited a house, where a young boy like you lived before … he has gone away now, so I borrowed the aeroplane and some of his paints. I'm sure he would have been happy to make your birthday nice.' Rose sensed what he was saying and started to cry.

Deborah decided the best way to comfort her younger children was to explain. 'I'm afraid Sam might be right. You remember there was a horrible bug which made people ill; unfortunately, some people died. Most people got better, but they stopped doing their jobs, so there wasn't much food in the shops. Everyone was frightened and some of them began to fight. I'm afraid quite a lot more people died from hunger and warfare. We moved here to get away from all these troubles; we're growing food and we're going to be alright. When it's safe, we'll go home, and I hope everything will be better organised. Eventually there will be shops again, and' – here she paused to exchange nervous glances with David, who finished – 'they will even sell blue paint!'

When the kids were in bed, they compared notes with Lucy and Rory; he said, 'These birthdays certainly raise tricky issues. Our kids are innocent, but it's harder for you because yours span such a range of understanding.' Deborah moaned, 'We promised that we'll go home to a functioning society, but I don't think so.' David tentatively rehearsed Steven's argument: 'If the survivors can re-establish food security, without exhausting their resources, then society can move forwards in other areas.' Lucy pointed out, 'For that to happen, people are going to have to cooperate, trust one another, and help the unfortunate. Otherwise those who aren't coping are going to unravel the efforts of those who are. Technology alone won't suffice, we're going to have to re-ignite the human spirit too.'

Next day Rose asked Samuel, 'Do you think the shops will open again?' He was a little guilty at having upset her and William, but had to admit, 'I'm sorry Rose, I don't know. I've been listening to the grown-ups, and they don't seem to be sure either. Mum and dad want to go back to the farm so they can grow food, because that's the most important thing. Then gradually all the other stuff will get organised. It's going to take a long time, so we've just got to have as much fun as we can while we're waiting. At least we don't have to go to boring old proper school.'

***

The work continued on Letheilean. The autumn harvest, both wild and planted, was in full flow; as hoped, a surplus was being generated and preserved for the winter. Seeds were collected and dried for the next spring, and others were sown for overwintering. With the gun they could at least try to hunt deer, but it became clear that it wasn't easy.

The team were living in reasonable comfort, in several houses heated by wood-burning stoves. Water was carried by hand from a stream and boiled for safety. Cooking was communal, and everyone ate together. Washing involved adding boiling water to cold in baths; or filling a tank at high level to feed a feeble shower. Nor was there mains drainage; luckily septic tanks were the norm in rural areas. Clothes were washed by hand and dried on rails over the stoves.

Alexandra sat by a window, looking at the sea where no ferries sailed and the sky empty of airplanes, and reflected: "The world order is shattered, but we are coping physically and organisationally, and there are even signs of psychological healing and social bonding. It's tempting for the oldest of us to contemplate living out our lives in this arcadia, but it wouldn't be fair on the young ones. In any case the technocrats won't have it, and they're right that we can't make a stable and civilised society without an industrial backbone to support the cultural cranium. There's also the mystery of what Phraya has done; at the simplest level, some will insist on discovering the fate of their loved ones – though if Bruce is right yet again, they will be tragically disappointed."

The practicalities of country life continued. Alice had spotted an escaped ram and wanted to ensure that it serviced the sheep. 'Leaving him in the open isn't going to be reliable. We need to capture him.' Alan asked, 'How are we going to do that without a dog?' 'At this time of year he'll come to the ewes, so if we pen them we should be able to catch him while his mind isn't on evading us.'

Henry read the smaller children an autumn poem:

'In the other gardens
And all up the vale,
From the autumn bonfires
See the smoke trail!

Pleasant summer over
And all the summer flowers,
The red fire blazes,
The grey smoke towers.

Sing a song of seasons!
Something bright in all!
Flowers in the summer,
Fires in the fall!'

Chapter 7 Reconnaissance

In October, after the harvest, minds began to turn to a possible move in the spring. Steven urged, 'I think we should look at the route to Edinburgh, before the winter makes travel difficult.' Alan objected: 'Hold on, I don't think we can go anywhere near the city until we're sure it's in a much better state than when I left. Certainly we can't make a decision to move there.' Ruth concurred, 'Yes, even in rural Morrie people's behaviour was really alarming.' Alexandra pointed out: 'First we'd have to get past Port Monard, which was still hazardous when you came through. That was only three months ago, and I doubt it's safe yet.' Deborah suggested a staged approach. 'Let's explore the route as far as there, go on to Morrie if all is well, and even further if it's prudent.'

Steven reluctantly accepted this plan for exploration, but insisted on asking, 'OK, but where are we aiming to settle in the spring?' Margaret said simply, 'Arable land, wherever we can farm it safely.' Alice added, 'With rougher land for sheep pasture, and deer.' Rory suggested, 'And water, for fish?' Ruth concluded, 'That does sound like Morrie, and no-one else can claim ownership of the farm and the smallholding – if that even means anything.'

Charles tried to take this as an opportunity to introduce another subject, not properly addressed in previous discussions: 'I fear it may be some time before the idea of property is relevant, but it's essential to peace and prosperity.' Deborah asked, 'How does this link with the choice of where we settle?' He continued, 'It's a question of how we interact with other survivors. If we find that Morrie is calm enough for a move in the spring, we could farm it for a year,' – here Steven groaned, but Charles surprised him – 'and from there it isn't far to Edinburgh, so we could monitor the situation there.' Steven looked pleased but said nothing and waited to see where he was heading. 'Then, if we find the survivors there are peaceable, and are making use of the industrial resources, perhaps something like economics will develop? Eventually a government may re-emerge.' He was looking far ahead, and everyone was bewildered, so Olivia drew the conversation back to the near term. 'OK, let's agree that a small team – perhaps Steven, Rory, Alan and David – will explore as Deborah suggests; and come back unharmed.'

Lucy, as the mother of the smallest children, was particularly anxious that Rory was going on another expedition. He offered some encouragement: 'The road out of Letheilean is tiny and unpopulated. I'll avoid trouble and come back on my own if the trip looks hazardous.'

***

On 15 October the men set off in the Landrover and had an uneventful journey to Port Monard. They were aware of the presence of survivors, apparently as traumatised as those in Innisdu, and steered clear of them. Swarms of rats indicated that most of the inhabitants had remained in the town; Alan remarked, 'They probably avoided going towards the cities, because they were afraid of the violence.' Rory replied, 'Equally there was no point going into the wilderness, where they could expect nothing to eat.' Yet as far as they could see, none of the resources of the town were being used systematically. At any rate no crops were growing, and the garden centre was locked, so David took most of the seeds.

They went to a garage and found several cars mid-repair, along with their keys. David suggested, 'We could do with another car, for the team's eventual journey away from Letheilean. Can we fix one?' Steven replied, 'Let's try one of the diesels, we should avoid petrol.' Alan asked, 'Why? What's going to happen about fuel in the long run?' Steven explained, 'Diesel is OK for a year, maybe two or three if it's filtered and treated. Petrol goes off more quickly. There's no chance of making fossil fuel in the foreseeable future. Eventually someone will have to grow crops suitable for making biodiesel, but most engines won't run well on it unless it's mixed with normal diesel. That's a challenge for the future, just now we're OK.' Alan found a car with a tow bar and, after struggling for the whole of the next day, they got it working.

In the meantime David had found a trailer. Rory suggested, 'We don't want to continue with two cars. Why don't I return in the new one, loaded up with goodies from here, and you three continue in the Landrover? They spent a few hours searching the outskirts of the town for fuel and machinery, and he set off.

***

When Rory arrived in Tirglas Lucy was relieved to see him, but Calum was more thrilled with the trailer. 'Daddy, can your car pull five like my toy one?' Alison was scathing: 'No silly, trains can pull lots of carriages, cars can only do one.' 'What about aeroplanes? 'Now you're being diculous.' Calum was fed up with Alison rejecting his ideas, so he addressed his next question to his father. 'What about boats, daddy?' 'They don't usually pull other boats, but they could.' 'See, Ali, you're the one who's diclus.'

That evening Rory talked to Lucy about the future. 'If we go to Morrie, I won't be able to farm fish.' Lucy replied, 'Well, not in the sea perhaps. Can fish be raised in fresh water?' 'Yes, but the problem is what to feed them. Salmon are carnivores, and they're normally fed fishmeal, which comes from the sea.' 'That would be difficult in the future, even if we were near the coast. The trawlers won't be operating.' He was silent, so she continued, 'Can they survive on a vegetarian diet?' 'Maybe that's not so crazy …'

Charles was also pondering the future. 'Olivia, you're doing a valuable job leading the team; I've been thinking about possible roles for me. You recall I mentioned economics the other day?' 'Yes, I wondered what you meant.' 'Well, if Steven's mechanisation of agriculture enables a minority of the people to produce enough food, then the majority can specialise in other things, but only if they know that they can eat. I imagine that at first they will barter their services for food, but that could be standardised, and eventually represented by money. I'd like to re-invent economics by organising all this. If we move to Edinburgh, you could work towards establishing a government.'

***

Steven, David and Alan, continuing their journey beyond Port Monard, found that the road was in much the same part-blocked state as in July. As they neared Morrie, Steven observed, 'We're in farmland now, and I don't think the crops are being looked after. Makes me think the survivors aren't very organised.' Alan pondered this. 'If I were living here, I'd grow food away from the main roads. Why don't we go up one of the minor tracks into the hills and look from higher up?' When they did so, binoculars revealed various small-scale gardens hidden among trees. They approached a few, pausing at a safe distance from each one, but no-one seemed keen to talk. They persisted, found a particularly well concealed allotment and waited until they were spotted. A man emerged from a house and looked at them enquiringly.

David adopted a friendly tone. 'Hello, how are you doing?' 'We're fine. I haven't had the pleasure of meeting you – have you come from elsewhere?' David was encouraged by the man's tone; 'I'm a farmer, from round here actually, but my family and a few friends left for the west coast when things went wrong. We met some other people there; there are twenty-six of us, including kids, growing food, fishing and hunting. We've come to have a look if the situation is better here now; we intend to stay away for the winter, but may move back in the spring. My name is David Tanner, and these are Steven Lynn and Alan Petrie.'

The man relaxed; 'I'm Andrew Wilson. We stayed here throughout, and have just about managed in a similar manner. Welcome to our little oasis of peace.' Alan asked, 'I came from Edinburgh, which was horrendous; I hid for two months before escaping. Do you know how it is now?' 'I've met some people who say the city itself is still uninhabitable: unburied bodies, disease, survivors behaving like wounded animals.' Steven joined in; 'What about the surrounding areas? I think the industrial resources of the city will be crucial for rebuilding society. Do you think it's safe to go there yet?' 'The suburbs may be emerging from the worst of it. Perhaps you can go there in due course, but I just wouldn't risk it now. No-one's in charge, except the gangs.'

David drew the conversation back to the Morrie area: 'What about here; has the violence subsided? Are people cooperating?' 'Even small towns are still in a shocking state, but it's better in the countryside. Admittedly the dead haven't been dealt with, but at least the living are moving forwards. There are various groups operating like us, but separately. They don't steal each other's crops, but I wouldn't say they're quite cooperating yet. We have taken in a few individuals who weren't faring well.' 'OK, thank you, perhaps we'll meet if and when we return. Best of luck to you and yours.'

They continued to the Tanner farm at Morrie. It was deserted and undamaged, though untended, and David's heart sank at the overgrown crops. Alan pointed out: 'At least no harm has been done other than a wasted harvest. The farm can be started again in the spring?' Ever the horticulturalist, he began to see the positive side. 'We could gather at least a fraction of the seeds, hide them and take some back. Later we could plough all this in, if the tractor hasn't been stolen.' The farmhouse had been entered and a few things taken; the verdict was, 'Could have been much worse.' They went on to the smallholding, and found it intact, and all the farm equipment in place. Steven was particularly pleased to see the tractor, and it was all the others could do to restrain him from starting it up. They stayed overnight.

The next day they sought out further groups of survivors, who all confirmed that the team had done well to escape to Letheilean. The consensus was that although violence was occasionally still taking place, it was becoming less frequent. Someone mentioned Andrew Wilson's group as an example of good people helping the less fortunate.

Steven raised the question of continuing towards Edinburgh. Alan's view was, 'I don't think we can go any further now. Towns and cities are still bad news.' David agreed; 'Yes, things seem to be mending faster outside them. Clean water is available, food can be grown or caught, there's plenty of room. I think we should go back to Letheilean and suggest a move to Morrie in the spring.' On the way they stopped once more in Port Monard, and arrived back in Tirglas on 19 October.

***

Olivia allowed the reconnaissance team time to tell their stories, and called a meeting for the following day to analyse their observations. 'Let's begin with the positive side of things in Morrie.' David started: 'The farm and smallholding haven't been destroyed.' Alan continued, 'All the people we met properly were peaceful, even if they reported trouble elsewhere.' Deborah jumped in boldly, 'Don't those two facts already lead to the conclusion that we can move to Morrie, perhaps even now?' Alexandra was cautious, 'Yes to the move, but we must stick to the idea of waiting until the spring. The winter may prove beyond the capacity of some people, and things may turn awkward. Here we're on our own, but there we'd be exposed to panic among others.'

Olivia said, 'That takes us to the negative side of things. Any objections to the plan of moving to Morrie in the spring?' No-one was surprised when Steven pointed out, 'Things weren't set up for more than a subsistence way of life.' Deborah wondered, 'It's not obvious whether that's a good thing for us or bad.' Alice answered, 'Perhaps it's a promising sign. We know of several groups of people who are managing in the area, despite not being highly organised, and I think we're at least as well placed for farming as they are?' Margaret countered, 'But it's a competition without rules. If others fail because they get things wrong, probably in the winter, they'll cause trouble as Alexandra said. Don't we want everyone to be succeeding?' Charles agreed; 'Yes, I think the uncertainty itself argues for caution. Let's wait until spring.'

Steven was impatient. 'I think my point has been misunderstood. I'd like to get mechanised farming going for the good of all survivors. The problem with Morrie, as far as I'm concerned, is that there isn't enough equipment and expertise there to get the whole system going. I'd like to have gone closer to Edinburgh to see if anyone's got a grip, but I recognise the danger that it may still be mayhem there. My plea is: when we move to Morrie, let's mount a similar expedition to the city and at least find out what's going on.'

When David and Deborah were alone, he was upbeat about the possibilities for the farm. 'We can start again, plant heritage seeds, fertilise naturally, operate organically, use renewable energy, and re-position ourselves for the new world.' 'Slow down,' Deborah interrupted regretfully, 'I hate to dampen your enthusiasm, but I fear post will be more different from pre than you think. For a start, what does "re-position" even mean in the circumstances?' 'It …' His face fell; 'I see what you mean.'

Deborah wore her analytical expression. 'Assuming Morrie is still calm after the winter tests everyone's preparations, the first task will be to reproduce in Morrie what we're doing here, preferably on a bigger scale. That will need fuel for the tractor. Then there are challenges like growing our own true seed, making the fertiliser you take for granted, avoiding pests and weeds without chemicals, harvesting in a timely manner.' 'OK, no need to rub it in. Some of this may take a while to emerge, and most technology depends on the appropriate equipment being in place first. I suppose that's what Steven is pointing out.' Deborah was unstoppable; 'Then there's Charles's economic question: are we growing for ourselves, or will there be markets, even by barter?'

***

On the 5th of November there were no fireworks, but the team had hot soup around a bonfire. Charles reminisced, 'Just like the old days, apart from the rockets shooting horizontally when the bottles fell over.' Lucy asked, 'What else do we miss?' Philip answered, 'The internet, or at least information.' Ruth offered, 'Proper hot showers.' Henry opted for, 'Cinema, theatre, concerts, musicals. The roar of the greasepaint, the smell of the crowd.' Alexandra simply wanted, 'My piano.' Rory said, 'Contrails making saltires in the sky.' At this silence fell.

Katherine voiced what everyone was thinking, 'I miss my parents, and my little sister.' Margaret lamented, 'On Salay I didn't get a chance to call mine.' Alexandra was guilty: 'Early on, when I had the chance, I didn't even try to persuade my sisters and mother to escape.' Each person said something about family or friends, and at last eyes turned to Alan and Alice. She said, 'It's not the same for us.' He explained, 'Our parents had a child, Alexa, before me, but she died at two months. They didn't take it well, and gave us both names beginning with Al. When we arrived in Letheilean, we were a bit taken aback to find you, Alexandra, and Alison too. Our parents never really accepted us as children who weren't replacements for Alexa. I'm afraid we're more or less estranged from them now.'

David tried to lighten the conversation. 'What don't we miss?' Bruce said immediately, 'London traffic.' Lucy joined in, 'Politicians, particularly those in charge of the health system.' Olivia expanded on this: 'With luck there's no government at all in London, or in Edinburgh, and we can do better next time.' Deborah had a smaller scale suggestion; 'Telephone queues, surely in a re-organised world call centres will be illegal?'

***

Lucy was exercised about the sexual health of the women and girls. She approached Olivia, who suggested, 'I think we should talk to Katherine, and also Alexandra and Margaret so we can think ahead for Jessica and Julia. I know that Ruth wants a baby, if she can find a donor. While we're at it, we may as well include Deborah, for Rose in the future?'

When all the women were assembled, Lucy started. 'We're returning to an earlier era: I'm afraid childbirth is going to be more hazardous, but the younger the woman the safer it will be.' Katherine looked worried; 'How risky, how early must we start?' Lucy decided to be absolutely direct: 'Even in medieval times, the maternal death rate was only one to two percent, and we haven't forgotten all modern knowledge. Assuming the hospitals haven't been destroyed, we may be able to find drugs, scanners and other equipment which will help enormously. As for age, girls used to start in their teens, so you'll do!' She glanced apologetically at Ruth, who muttered, 'I'm twenty-seven, that used to be ideal.'

Alexandra asked, 'Talking of teenagers, what about contraception for them?' 'That's OK at the moment, but it will be difficult to achieve in due course. The pill is rated for a year, although it will probably be effective for three to five years. I don't think the data were released; With luck we won't find out! Other forms of contraception will deteriorate – perhaps on the same timescale. Most of them will be very difficult to develop in the future, but remember people weren't entirely helpless before modern medicine. Hopefully we won't return to large families, but it will be advisable to have babies young.' Margaret brought the discussion to a riotous close by observing, 'Indeed – have you seen Peter looking at Jessica?'

In a private moment Ruth took the opportunity to raise the old subject with Alice: 'If Morrie is stable when we get there, do you think I should have a baby? I'm already past the age Lucy recommends post Phraya.' Alice was sympathetic, but asked, 'How will you find a donor?' Ruth hesitated; 'What do you think of the idea of asking Alan?' She waited, and was delighted to receive a hug. 'I'll speak to him if you like? Only one condition: the name doesn't begin with…' 'Of course!'

Margaret felt she had to speak to Julia about what Lucy had said, and tried to do it very gently. Nevertheless she was shocked, and a week later she confided in Jessica: 'Mum didn't have me until she was thirty, but she says I've got to have babies much sooner.' 'Yes, my mum talked to me too. She had Bella at thirty-seven, and said that having children at that age will be really dangerous now.' Julia confessed, 'It scares me. I turned thirteen on the day of the air ban and look what happened to the world. I want to go back to being twelve.'

***

19 November was Rose's birthday. David had prepared by entering a sports shop in Port Monard and selecting a pair of dancing shoes. With the blue paint fiasco fresh in his memory, he had also visited further shops to obtain speakers and a range of music so wide that he was sure his daughter would approve at least some of it. She was delighted, and suggested, 'Can we have a disco?' 'I suppose so, you are going to be eleven and we need a celebration.' Jessica and Julia were put in charge – adults could hardly be expected to choose the correct songs – and the teenage boys were put on their best behaviour. When they had danced to exhaustion Rose asked, 'Thanks, dad. When will there be live music again?' Deborah, reluctant to promise anything, replied, 'We don't know when professional performances will start again, but we'll try to find some instruments so we can make our own.'

Rose's question was discussed later. Alexandra wondered, 'What has to be in place for a society to indulge in singing, drama, art for its own sake?' Olivia opined, 'Just enough food, warmth and safety to take minds out of emergency thinking?' Henry pointed out, 'That's right, primitive mankind had flutes made from bones.' Olivia added, 'Even slaves sang spirituals in the American south.' Alexandra groaned, 'Well, we're OK then.'

Six-hour days loomed, and Christmas wasn't far off; on the next trip to Innisdu, David insisted, they would search for more than mundane supplies. Olivia had caved in to Alexandra's request that Henry, her cultural protégé, should accompany Steven, Rory and David in the Eolia. When they arrived in the town it felt different, less threatening, though no-one could put their finger on how he knew this.

While Steven and Rory went about systematically, gathering necessities, David and Henry sought gratuitous luxuries. They found a television, some films on disc and a player; a guitar, a keyboard and some sheet music; toys; books; cosmetics; popping corn; tins of chestnuts, pineapple and condensed milk; Christmas lights and, their final triumph, a pudding from the previous year.

When they got back Margaret inspected the pudding's ingredients list and rehearsed it wistfully. 'It may be a while before we can make these. Apples – no problem. Sugar, barley wine, stout, suet, flour, breadcrumbs – in due course. Oranges, lemons, eggs, sultanas, raisins, currants, almonds – maybe eventually. Cinnamon, nutmeg – for goodness' sake!'

Alexandra wrote: "4 December. It might be worth recording how we are surviving. From a practical point of view first: the technologists are doing a great job. We have enough to eat, especially meat and fish, though fruit is in short supply and the vegetables are tedious. It seems we have sufficient food preserved for the winter, but it will be harder in future years when tins and dried staples run out. It's a mild winter, luckily for us and the sheep. By burning wood – renewables at last – we are warm, can cook and have hot water, though the shower leaves something to be desired. We can make electricity, so we have light, refrigeration – and computers, which are surprisingly useless. We can get around by car. Existing fuel will run out at some point and then, if we don't make a substitute, things will be much less pleasant."

"On the human side: no-one has been injured or seriously ill, and everyone is amazingly cheerful. For a group thrown together almost at random, we get on well. We can make music, and have some books. Looking to the future, we have expertise which gives us as good a chance as any other surviving group. What will happen in Morrie is anyone's guess, but I think we will endure. What's much less clear is the extent to which the fullness of life can be restored. How many decades before someone puts on a Shakespeare play?"

On Christmas Day feelings were mixed. The children were excited, but knew in their various ways that this time it would be different. The adults did their best, offering random presents purloined in Innisdu and Port Monard. They were proud of their efforts, but oddly guilty that they couldn't reproduce the usual jamboree. The mood improved when the feast began with Rory's smoked salmon with pizza-flour bread and pepper; continued with venison cooked with raspberry jam, and root vegetables roasted with tinned chestnuts; and ended with pudding soaked in whisky, and pineapple which the adults ruined by adding a disgusting liqueur. The highlight, everyone agreed, was popcorn smothered in caramel made by boiling tins of condensed milk. Lucy moaned rapturously and pronounced, 'Ah, cheap sugar is the crowning achievement of advanced civilisation. It's also the most dangerous; aren't we lucky that we don't have much?'

Afterwards, when Charles carped that he missed the Kings College choir, David led the singing of all the carols they could remember. In the absence of a piano, Alexandra played the keyboard. Then Margaret stunned everyone with a heart-rending a cappella rendition of a Far Isles love song, and no-one could go on.

Philip filled the silence by asking, 'What do we hope for next Christmas? I want a high-performance radio.' Olivia asked why, and he explained: 'It would receive transmissions from a huge distance, so we would be able to see if anywhere in Europe is working, and it might form the basis for future communications.' Lucy aspired to, 'A hospital, complete with equipment and drugs.' Steven, never one to miss a chance: 'A tractor, with plenty of fuel.' Everyone scoffed, but Deborah defended him, 'He's right, and I'll add seeds, fertiliser, insecticide, and the relevant tractor attachments.' At this point Alexandra chided everyone: 'Yes, but can't we be more imaginative? For example, I'd like to settle in Morrie and find a full orchestra living next door.' Henry got the idea: 'OK, a library, which magically has every book we want'. Bruce was just as unrealistic, 'Answers to all our questions.' When the ideas had dried up, Ruth whispered her own fantasy, 'A baby on the way?'

A week later the year turned; Henry quipped, 'We won't make the same mistake as the Romans, who missed out the year zero; we've just had that, so let's call the new year P1.' They didn't feel very celebratory about it, so attention shifted to the planned move to Morrie.

Alan wondered, 'Should we do one more reconnaissance? Port Monard wasn't entirely safe.' David was keen to get on with the big move: 'The last trip was ten weeks ago. I doubt the people we spotted will have made it through the winter, and if they have there will be plenty of us to deal with any trouble.' Katherine had a different concern: 'Will the people and equipment fit into our three vehicles?' Steven had thought of this. 'We can cram in for the first leg of the journey, but I think we should stop and fix another car.' Lucy objected, 'What do all the rest of us do while you mess about inside an engine?'

Rory raised another issue: 'What about our boats? I'd like to have mine at least, so I can think about fish farming on a loch.' Charles was doubtful. 'I'd love to take Eolia too, or those from Innisdu, but I doubt we can get any of the large ones out of the water. Steven, you like an engineering challenge, do you think we might devise a way for Rory's at any rate?' He replied, 'OK, maybe we do need a preliminary trip to Port Monard to get a car, a boat trailer and some lifting gear.'

***

On 17 January P1, Calum was five; it was clear what his present should be, and Alice got to work. 'Sausages, I can eat twenty-ten!' Alison put him right. 'You mean thirty, silly. Anyway, you'll be sick if you eat that many.' He made a valiant effort but was forced to give up while she was two ahead. He had his excuse ready: 'Alice makes them too big. Why can't we have skinny ones from the shop?

Lucy had noticed, when improvising in her school, how shops loomed large in the children's imagination. She decided to try to explain their absence to Calum. 'There aren't any now. I'll explain why but you'll need to listen carefully. In the old times people used to make things in factories. Lorries took them to shops, and we used to buy them there.'

She waited to see if he understood. 'So why can't we have skinny sausages?' She continued, 'This is the hard part, so keep listening. A little while ago, everything got muddled up. People stopped making things, so the shops don't have anything for us to buy.' He looked a little crestfallen. 'Don't worry, now we make things ourselves. You're lucky, because Alice has made delicious food for you.'

***

In late January mild weather permitted a last trip to Port Monard before the main event. Steven inspected the cars in the garage. 'The one nearest to working condition has a petrol engine; we'll risk the deterioration of the fuel. At least it will be easy to start in cold weather, so it will be insurance against the diesels failing to run.' He and David got to work, while Rory and Alan visited the harbour to search for the means to lift and transport boats. They also found a small rigid inflatable boat with an outboard motor, and a further trailer which was attached to the new car despite its lack of a proper tow bar. They also located more fuel. Two days later they arrived in Tirglas and triumphantly presented the latest additions to the shipping fleet.

Over the next two weeks the team prepared for the coming adventure. They managed to get Rory's boat out of the water. Charles conceded sadly, 'I think Eolia isn't going to be useful for a while. When we have time and energy for leisure activities, we'll come back for it.' By 15 February they had loaded the Landrover, van, cars and trailers with the two small boats; generators, farming equipment, food and seeds; several sheep and a grumpy ram; the crucial music system and twenty-six happy but nervous people. The convoy rolled out of Tirglas, and soon Letheilean was deserted.

On the door of the Achar Hotel there was a despairing note to the Blair family: "I am so delighted you have made it. We have gone to The Market Garden, Morrie. Lots of love – Katherine."

Part 3 Enclave

Chapter 8 Return

The roads were clear, and there was no traffic, but the four vehicles proceeded slowly and maintained a close formation. The landscape of the Highlands was oddly unaffected by the disaster, but the complete lack of human activity produced a deeper silence than normal. The lochs were undisturbed by the wakes of any boats. At the start of a lunch break Rory pointed out a thin shape in the distance, poking out of the water near the edge; the children were sure it was a stick, but as they drove away the heron flew off to shrieks of amazement.

Rose knew how her disco had been achieved, and suggested cunningly, 'Let's go into Port Monard and look at the shops. We might find blue paint for Billie's aeroplane.' David, still mortified about the earlier birthday, replied, 'That's a kind thought.' However, Deborah was suspicious: 'What are you after, young lady, more music?' Her father caught on and closed the discussion: 'Anyway, we're not going into any towns, we don't want to meet any funny people.'

A few hours later they selected a large house far from any others, checked that nothing could worry the children and stopped for the night. It was cold, so the men unloaded a wood-burning stove, a hob and bottled gas from the van. Margaret was pleased at first, but then her face clouded. 'Oh, I suppose you took them from Tirglas?' Steven left Bruce to point out, 'I don't think the owners will ever return, indeed no-one will be living in Letheilean for a long time.' Alan rigged up temporary flues, and soon the house was warmer. Margaret was as grateful for hot food as anyone else.

When the journey resumed next morning, the convoy progressed without difficulty through the mountains. The team paused before the final descent into the familiar valley of central Scotland, heavily populated before Phraya, and everyone stared apprehensively. Deborah was appalled; 'Nothing!' Olivia asked, 'What's wrong, what do you expect to see?' David explained, 'Normally there would be a checkerboard pattern of fields of various colours, depending on what's been done to them: dark brown if ploughed, greener if fallow or covered with overwintering crops. Instead they look similar, because they are all overgrown with crops out of control; there has been no farming.'

Bruce remarked: 'I can't even see the small gardens that you reported after your last visit. There must be very few people, as I suspected.' Alan pointed out, 'But they're too small to see from this far away, because each person doesn't need much space, and most of the plots are hidden for protection. There are people there, the question is what they're doing.'

The team continued into the valley; Rory observed, 'Empty roads, even down here. What bothers me is that there must be plenty of cars, so there can't be any fuel.' They stopped at a garage, tried pumping out the underground tanks and obtained only dregs. Steven had been thinking about this; 'We'll see if we can make anything from the rapeseed that we abandoned at Morrie.' As they went on Deborah became happier; 'Now we're closer we can see that people are at least growing food.'

In the afternoon of 17 February P1 the convoy reached the Tanner farm. David had prepared Deborah for the sight: crops unkempt, bolted, gone to seed; the ground infested by weeds; the fruits of their efforts fallen, mulched into the soil, or still standing, rotting in situ. He summarised as positively as he could: 'Excellent fertiliser!' She caught the mood; 'Some of the seeds look viable. I daresay there's some oil in the rape.'

Rose was excited. 'Mum, isn't that our house?' Deborah replied, 'Yes, but let dad have a look inside first. It might be a bit upsetting.' David went in, and a short while later emerged nodding tentatively. 'It has been broken into and roughed up a bit, and it's damp, but it's OK.' The others held back while the Tanners entered. The house was cold and dark, emptied of anything useful by the struggling intruders of the previous summer, but their family home persisted through the ghostly atmosphere. William was puzzled. 'Dad, will this be our home again?' Rose spoke for the whole family; 'We're going to make it lovely, Billie.'

Deborah called to the others: 'Come in, we can all fit in here tonight. What about those stoves, and some light?' Suddenly everyone was galvanised, and for the next couple of hours the vehicles were unloaded into the house and outbuildings. Soon a supper was being prepared.

When the children were asleep, Olivia asked Deborah, 'How does it feel to be back?' 'It's strange, the house is familiar but presumably it will witness a post-Phraya lifestyle utterly different from pre.' Margaret was already thinking about fundamentals: 'It will be more like Letheilean, dominated by the need for food.' David was upbeat: 'Yes, but assuming no-one disturbs us, things will get steadily better.' Steven, picking up on this, said, 'We'll check the smallholding tomorrow, and see if the farm equipment is in working order.'

Alexandra groaned at the inescapable drift into practicality in the team's conversations. 'But what do we feel' – she emphasised the last word rather too much – 'about our return to the scene of a destroyed civilisation?' There was a pause, Bruce looked uncomfortable, and Charles tried to placate her: 'None of us is pleased about any of this. We hardly knew what to expect in Morrie, so no-one can feel anything much yet. People are just trying to work out what to do next.' Olivia appealed for calm. 'I didn't mean to start a big debate on our first day. Plenty of time to work out all aspects of life, both pragmatic and deeply meaningful, in the weeks to come. Bedtime?' Alan insisted on setting a watch for the night and volunteered to take the first slot himself.

***

On the following day Steven, David and Alan accompanied Alice and Ruth to their home. It looked as if it still hadn't been discovered by survivors; all the farm equipment was undisturbed. This time Steven was not to be denied – he and David managed to start the tractor. It was all Alan could do to stop them driving it over to the farm immediately; 'We don't know if it's safe yet. We mustn't show our hand.'

Ruth was pleased to be back, and Alice too, but she admitted sadly, 'We can't keep calling it a market garden, as there aren't any customers.' David replied, 'We can hardly describe our place as a farm, either.' Alan suggested, 'Well, it had better become our main food supply soon, whatever we call it. I think we should work the smallholding as well, and keep it secret as we did last year, as insurance against invasion of the farm.'

***

Meanwhile the others were occupying a few houses near the farm, plus an extra one for the school. They made a list of equipment that was lacking: more generators, stoves and hobs; and the diesel, wood and bottled gas essential to their operation. Margaret hammered away relentlessly at the basics: 'First we'll need to grow some food to cook in these nice warm houses. We also need safe water.' Lucy stipulated, 'For the moment we must boil it, or use the tablets, or bleach – we're no longer in an uninhabited wilderness with peat filtering the streams. In due course we'll need the means to purify water in bulk.'

Over the next few days the team turned their attention to the abandoned crops. The Tanners worked with Margaret to decide what should be done, and everyone else did what they were told. Deborah deliberated, 'Obviously anything immediately edible was taken by survivors last year, but there are seeds that can be replanted, and also rape for conversion to fuel. Those parts of the crops which haven't already rotted can be fed to the sheep, and the rest ploughed in to fertilise new crops.' Alan and Rory built a smokehouse, this time with a larger facility for drying crops. Areas of the barn were set aside for storage of feed, rape and other seeds.

The children were kept busy. The older ones helped with the jobs around the farm, and Julia tried to get the younger ones to prepare the schoolroom. Alison was used to leading Calum, and Rose tried to boss William around, but this didn't work for long. He rebelled: 'Girls can't tell boys what to do, even if they're older.' Calum followed his lead. 'Boys are better than girls, even little boys.' Alison made peace: 'Alright, you boys can work together, and I'll work with Rose, and we'll see who does best.'

***

In late February David and Steven took Olivia and Alexandra on a tour of the other groups that they had met on the October reconnaissance. All had endured the winter, but with difficulty. They confirmed that almost no food remained from before Phraya, except insofar as crops planted the previous spring had managed to grow on their own. People were operating gardens by hand, organically; hunting, and gathering wild plants; and had preserved food for the winter. Wood stoves were the only form of heating. Most groups still ran generators for refrigeration and lighting, but some were reduced to candles and oil lights. A few ran cars, but people were conserving fuel. They had little use for travel in any case; they didn't care to risk entering the towns. They were aware of each other, and did not clash, but still kept their distance.

David saved Andrew Wilson's group for last. 'Hello, we have moved here as planned. You've met Steven, but may I introduce Olivia Lenton and Alexandra Eades? How has the winter been for you?' 'Delighted to meet you, ladies. We've been fine, not exactly living in the lap of luxury, but managing. Come in and have a cup of tea without milk.'

Olivia asked, 'Do you mind if we ask some questions about how things have been hereabouts? We have been out of touch in the far west, and are just beginning to appreciate the extent of the unravelling of life at the centre.' 'Yes, it's awful. I'll try to fill you in, fire away.' 'Thank you. We know the basic facts of the collapse, and understand the death toll, but we haven't seen any signs of re-organisation. People seem to be living in a subsistence manner, not cooperating much, and without overall leadership.' Andrew looked regretful. 'I'm afraid you're right. During the worst of the crisis hunger caused so much fighting that people have simply retreated into isolation.' Alexandra remarked, 'I'm glad to hear that the violence has stopped. I'm surprised muggers aren't taking what they want.' 'They did for a while, but found so little that they left for the towns and cities. I am hearing that it's still far from peaceful there.' Steven looked disappointed.

Alexandra continued, 'Is there any prospect of building links between people? I don't mean food production – perhaps it's best for each group to remain independent for the moment – but rather the beginnings of an empathetic society. I understand you're interested in this.' Andrew grew enthusiastic. 'Indeed! One of the groups broke up in disarray, and we took in those who looked unlikely to cope. They seem to have responded to a gentler approach to organising the necessary work – we recognise that without adequate food and warmth, there's no prospect of moving forwards psychically.'

Steven had been careful not to irritate Alexandra by allowing technology to dominate the conversation, but now he saw an opportunity: 'That's my angle; you may remember my desire to get engineering going again. I am sometimes accused of not caring about people' – he glanced at Alexandra – 'but my emphasis is to contribute by freeing them from labour. I think industry is the way forwards, and that means the cities such as Edinburgh. I understand that it's too soon to attempt a visit there, so I'd like to understand the opportunities around here. What are the physical resources, and can we get to them safely?'

'The smaller towns aren't too hazardous. The shops are relatively undisturbed; naturally there's nothing to eat in them, but everything else is untouched. Plenty of farm equipment, if you can find fuel in cars and garages.' 'What about workshops, for making and mending?' 'I think if you try that, you'll be the first person to do so in this area, and you'll find what you need.' 'Thanks, will do!'

Alexandra smiled: 'There's no poetry in your soul, Steven, but you'll probably end up supporting a few bards.' He shrugged and grinned at her. Olivia was pleased; 'Let's all work together. Can we stay in touch, Andrew?'

***

On 27 February P1 Samuel turned thirteen. 'I'm too old for one of those explanations of the world pre Phraya, dad. It doesn't matter anyway; it's post that's important, and you and mum don't know how it will turn out. She told Billie that there would be shops when we got home.' David defended her: 'She said she hoped they would open eventually. Anyway, part of growing up is realising that your parents don't know everything. I'm afraid the uncertainty is much worse now.'

Samuel paused, and delivered the coup de grâce. 'Maybe post won't be sorted out until you're dead. It's going to be up to me.' Deborah was shocked, but stayed calm. 'I'm sorry the future isn't looking as good for you as it was. We're doing our best. Actually, farming is going to be the most crucial job, and we would be happy to teach you what we know. Then you can play an important role in shaping the new start.' David wanted to inject some optimism: 'Actually I think people are going to bounce back from this much sooner than you think, and we have every intention of buying blue paint long before we die.' Deborah added under her breath, 'Aged ninety-five, let's say, if that industry is slow to start.'

Samuel reckoned the turn of conversation might have left his parents vulnerable to an unreasonable request: 'By the way, I don't want to grow crops. I'm a teenager now, and Benjamin and Peter are allowed to go hunting, so I should be too.' David looked at Deborah inquiringly and, thinking he glimpsed the shadow of a nod, decided to acquiesce: 'OK, but you go for lambs, with a bow and arrow; the gun is reserved for deer, and is for grown-ups only.' 'I am grown up. I'm taller than mum.'

That evening the adults pondered Samuel's prediction. Charles began with, 'It does look as if it will take a long time to get things going. I'm disappointed about the almost complete absence of collaboration between groups.' Ruth replied, 'I'm not surprised. Andrew made it clear that what they lived through around here was much worse than it was for us. They're still cowering.' Alan added, 'Judging by my experience the cities will be worse still.' Philip agreed; 'Yes, cooperation may have to start in areas that are already peaceful, and spread back towards the cities. Perhaps we can help that process. I think Andrew could be an ally.'

Rory suggested, 'On the other hand the resources are so much greater where the people used to live and work. Maybe we should explore rural towns at first? Just stick to the industrial estates; no-one will be there unless they're like-minded.' Steven, who was learning to keep his peace and wait for the others to reach his viewpoint, merely nodded.

Deborah had also been thinking about how a recovery could get going. 'It's no good people working the fields by hand; they need to use tractors, but that requires fuel. Even if there's some left it will soon run out, or spoil, so it must be made, by growing rapeseed. The trouble is no-one's going to grow something that's barely edible if there's only just enough to eat. How can society break into that circle?' Steven's mouth opened and then closed again.

Charles replied, 'That's where my ideas on economics come in. I didn't make myself clear when I first raised this. It all starts with each group growing more than enough food, with mechanical help while the fuel lasts. They preserve the excess, not only for the winter but also for barter. Then some groups need to devote a proportion of their time to making oil, selling it to others in exchange for food. Alan's download of survival information gives the method for converting it to diesel. Surely a group with the relevant expertise could accomplish this? Others with engineering knowledge would keep cars and tractors going. In each case food acts as money.'

Steven finally cracked; 'This is why I want to get to the area around the city, but we can start with the towns here.' Everyone groaned, but Rory defended him; 'That's just the beginning, we can make fertiliser, maybe weed-killer and pesticide, and grow even more efficiently.' Katherine cautioned, 'Those things need a full chemical industry, which will be challenging to re-establish.' Philip asserted, 'Not as hard as electronics.' Lucy observed, 'Medicine is difficult too.' Olivia brought the conversation to a close. 'As usual, we're getting ahead of ourselves. Let's explore nearby towns for the things we need for the first part of the sequence.'

The men took a break from the crops to investigate the area's estates. David knew the places for farming necessities, Steven wanted to explore garages and Alan needed tools. Charles came along to consider more generally the prospects for organised activity. They were surprised by the abundance of resources untapped during the calamity of the previous year. There was no shortage of equipment for engineering and agriculture, and they even found seeds and fertiliser, further highlighting the local failure to organise a large-scale supply of food.

Most significant was a fuel depot, entirely undisturbed; Steven was ecstatic, Rory puzzled. 'How can this be?' Charles rationalised, 'Suppose the workers in this business succumbed; no-one else would know the tank was here. Remember, everything was chaos because the crisis arose very quickly. Once it reached the point where only food and safety mattered, I don't imagine that anyone was exploring industrial premises for their immediate needs?' Alan, wary as always, said, 'Whatever the reason, we'll keep quiet about this.'

***

The daily work continued on the farm. Steven and David serviced the tractor as best they could, and brought it over from the smallholding. Alan insisted that they lock it away in the barn each evening. As areas of neglected crops were cleared, early seeds were planted. At

Katherine's suggestion the rapeseed recovered from the previous year's crop was divided into two batches; the healthiest was sown, but some was kept for an immediate attempt to make oil. Ruth made sure that crops were established at the smallholding.

Alice had noticed that some sheep had evaded the attentions of the hungry the previous summer. 'We should try to catch the males before they're uneatable, but keep one or two for breeding.' Benjamin and Peter, accompanied by a triumphant Samuel, set off to pursue them in the hills behind the smallholding. The last thing they heard was Deborah's instruction, 'Look after him.' 'I'm OK, mum, stop fussing.' The older boys weren't pleased to have their developing manhood hampered by the inclusion of a thirteen-year-old in their venture. They pressed on at a pace that left Samuel struggling to keep up. Benjamin was concerned; 'Shouldn't we wait for him?' 'No, he needs to show he deserves to be with us.'

Four hours later, when Deborah was beginning to worry, they re-appeared with Samuel in tears, clutching his left arm. 'My God, what have you done to him?' Peter looked stricken; 'We didn't see, we were ahead, but I think he's broken his arm, we're really sorry.' 'I fell mum, it wasn't their fault, they helped me get back.' 'Never mind those idiots, let's get you sorted out.'

Lucy was called and was immediately concerned. 'It's not too bad a break. I can set it, but what worries me is that the bone has penetrated the skin. He may get an infection.' For a short time the air was filled with Samuel's shrieks while she re-aligned the bones and splinted the arm. Once that was achieved she hesitated, explaining to Jessica, 'I'll clean the wound and close it to stop the bleeding, but I've got no idea what bugs have got in, and won't be able to test for that later. I'll give him a broad-spectrum antibiotic and see what happens.'

Peter and Benjamin were suffering too, under an inquisition conducted by Alexandra; she soon divined what had happened. She reported to Margaret, who confessed to Deborah, 'I'm really sorry, it's clear it was Peter's fault, he's a little big man.' 'No, it's my and David's fault for allowing Sam to go out in the first place.' 'I don't accept that; Steven and I intend to have words with our son about being a responsible person.' Later, when Peter visited Samuel, he whispered, 'Thanks for not blaming us. We'll stick together next time.' Benjamin was dubious: 'If we're ever allowed out again.'

***

When calm was restored, Ruth spoke to Alice. 'It seems safe here, provided we don't behave like teenagers, and I reckon we're in a team which is going to make it. The world will need people, and I sense the time is right to have a baby.' 'OK, do you still feel the same about Alan donating? Shall I ask him?' 'I do, yes please, if you're OK with that and you think he will be too.' Alice was nervous, so she sought him out immediately and dived straight in. 'Alan, I've got something serious to discuss.' 'Wow, isn't almost everything these days? What's on your mind?' 'It's about Ruth actually. She wants to have a baby,' – Alice gathered her courage – 'and we wondered if you would like to be a donor?'

He hesitated fleetingly and broke into a smile. 'I thought she'd never ask! No-one else will have me.' 'Alan, please, it wouldn't be done like that, and anyway you should give the matter some thought.' 'Of course, just teasing. My initial reaction is that it's a lovely idea. Shall I talk to her directly when I've digested this bombshell?' 'That would be great, I'll keep out of the way.'

***

Two days later, Samuel became extremely ill. Deborah was sick with worry, and David was grim. Peter and Benjamin skulked about, alarmed and chagrined by turns. Margaret and Alexandra were nervous and mortified, and the rest of the team held its breath. Lucy switched antibiotic and watched helplessly.

Rory had been studying the map for bodies of fresh water suitable for fish farming. He had selected Loch Fada, a lochan in the hills, and tried to distract Lucy from her medical concerns: 'It's out of the way, so other people won't discover it, but not so far that we'll burn a lot of fuel travelling there. The first challenge will be making a cage; I'll talk to Steven about that. What do you think about feed?' He became aware that Lucy wasn't listening and decided to leave it for another time.

Katherine confided in Philip: 'It's perturbing how a simple infection has become so threatening. Childbirth is at least as serious a trauma as a broken arm. I wonder if we should postpone having a baby until medicine has improved?' 'OK, let's see what happens in the next year or so. Maybe hospitals can be restarted?' 'Doesn't look likely here and now, but perhaps such things can happen in the cities eventually.'

***

Alexandra had been musing about what the team had found in Morrie. "We're back from the wilderness of Letheilean, only to find the centre of Scotland an emotional wasteland. Andrew Wilson is the only mentally strong person I've met here; I think he'll be important. We can repeat the work that has ensured our survival over the past year, but we all want more. It's not clear how much can be achieved with the shell-shocked locals."

***

In a week Samuel started to get better and was sent back to school. He was pleased to be out of bed, but complained, 'One little accident and I'm put back in a class with a five-year old. I should be doing jobs with the older boys.' Julia was unsympathetic; 'I'm older than you and I teach the little ones every day. At least you'll be safe here and Peter won't break your other arm.' Lucy broke in: 'Sam, why don't you read to Calum?' 'Yes please, I want the story about the cat with little ones in his hat.'

Samuel protested, but made a start. 'The sun did not shine, it was too wet to play,' – but already Calum interrupted, 'that's not right, the sun is shining,' – 'so we sat in the house all that cold, cold, wet day.' Some time later: 'Then our mother came in and she said to us two, "Did you have any fun? Tell me, what did you do?" What would you do if your mother asked you?' Alison shrieked, 'I wouldn't tell her!' Samuel smiled and Julia mocked him for enjoying himself.

Deborah asked Margaret to release some luxuries for a celebratory meal. 'We haven't got much, but I'll send Peter out with his father to learn how to stalk sheep without killing himself or anyone else. If they succeed, we can have a roast.' A few days later, with Samuel safe, the feast took place. William was allowed to turn the spit, and to hold the knife with Alice while she carved. He gave a piece to Calum, who asked, 'Is this ham?' Alison identified it: 'We're not cooking a pig, it's lamb.' William corrected her scornfully, 'No, Alice says it's mutton.' While they bickered, Deborah raised her glass; 'I propose a toast to Dr Scott, resident medical genius.' 'Lucky prescriber of random medicines, you mean.'

Chapter 9 Settling

Alan spoke to Ruth. 'Alice tells me you'd like to have a baby, and I'd love to help. She doesn't want kids, and it doesn't look as if I'm going to have any myself, so it would be a good way of carrying the Petries into the post world.' 'Thank you so much! I think it will be nice for the child to have a dad as well as two mums. Let's hope it works, and I can dodge Lucy's warnings about older mothers.' 'Old? Things have changed.'

***

Rory had another go at the conversation about fish, and this time Lucy was paying attention. 'When we first discussed this, you wondered what to feed salmon. How about rapeseed? It's oily, so that might be a good start.' 'I guess so, if they'll eat it. I daresay Steven can spare a little from his biodiesel ambitions.' She continued, 'The next question is how to get some salmon in the first place. I daresay a classy yachtsman like Charles has done some fly fishing.' 'A better idea is to visit the rivers in the spawning season, late in the year, and bring fertilised eggs here. If we can keep them alive, we can introduce the resulting fry into Loch Fada next spring.'

***

Isabella's eleventh birthday fell on 16 March P1. Bruce gave her 'Alice in Wonderland', and Alexandra 'Little Women', which they had found in the Achar Hotel. 'I know about Alice and her adventures, but who were the little women?' Her mother replied, 'They were a family of four American sisters who were very modern for their time.' 'When was it set?' 'It was the late 1860's, before women could vote.' 'Wow, that wasn't fair.' 'No, but soon afterwards girls like them started to change such injustices.'

Isabella reflected, 'On my last birthday everything was nice, but now it's all gone strange like when Alice went down the rabbit-hole. When will the world get back to normal?' Bruce replied, 'I'm afraid it might be a long time until it is fixed, but perhaps quite soon conditions will be as good as they were for the little women. They didn't have aeroplanes and the internet, but they had houses, fires, food and clothes. We've more or less got those organised.'

Reflecting on this conversation the following day, Bruce was inspired by a thought. He gathered Philip, Katherine, Steven, Deborah and Lucy. 'I was telling Bella that we are in a state roughly equivalent to the nineteenth century, but I hesitated to say how long it will take to re-establish the twenty-first. Thinking about this, I was struck by the odd mixture of shortage and abundance we're facing. We know that we lack many resources, most obviously food, electricity, heating, electronic communications, the list is endless. On the other hand, we have an almost unlimited supply of buildings, land, wood, steel. Other things are plentiful but badly compromised: cars with no fuel, motors without electricity. We need to reinstate what used to be regarded as utilities; diesel we've discussed, but we'll also need gas, pumped water, sewage, an electricity grid. We must restart fundamental industries – mechanical, chemical, pharmaceutical, electronics. Some of these are much harder than others, and many endeavours depend on others before they can even start. I'm wondering whether we can analyse all this, in order to determine what needs to be done, and when.'

Steven complained, 'Every time we try to think ahead like this, Olivia drags us back to the present.' Deborah defended her; 'Yes, and she's right because we must perform the immediately essential tasks, or we won't have a future in which to do the rest.' Katherine replied, 'Perhaps we can devote just a little of our effort to the longer term? After all, Alexandra is always urging us to indulge in cultural activities, although strictly they are unnecessary.' Lucy argued, 'I agree, and I don't think we should neglect endeavours which are impossible to achieve fully, like medicine. Let's at least make a start.' Philip suggested, 'As someone whose occupation is a long way off, I'd like to propose a compromise. You predicted the collapse of the pre-Phraya world, uncle Bruce. Why don't you try to model mathematically the regeneration of the post? The rest of us can feed you input information, and otherwise get on with Olivia's short-term tasks.'

***

Steven wanted to explore more widely, ostensibly to obtain netting for Rory's fish cage, but also to see what a larger town was like. Anticipating trouble, Olivia insisted that she and Charles would come, with David, Alan and Henry in a second vehicle. They selected a nearby market town and entered the outskirts watchfully. As they drove into the centre, they were greeted by bodies eaten away and dead rats indicating that the plague was at an end. Now it seemed to be the dogs' turn to starve.

A lone survivor came into view, saw the car, looked alarmed to see so many people and froze. Olivia decided to speak to him. 'Hello, how are things in town?' He looked surprised to be addressed civilly. 'Not too good. You have to watch out for thugs. There's still a bit of food if you know where to look and avoid being followed.' 'Perhaps you'd be better off out of town? People are growing food rather than eating their way through existing supplies. Would you like to get away from this?' 'Sure, but how do I do that?' 'I can introduce you to a group who are willing to take people on, if they agree to help with the work.' The man nervously indicated where he could be found.

When they got back Lucy raised the question of the hazard from the bodies in the coming summer. Bruce had considered this; 'I don't think there's any hope of each survivor burying some hundreds of victims. Nature will reduce them to bones, and eventually to dust.' Ruth was revolted by this, and had a suggestion: 'Couldn't we establish a burial ground – beyond the smallholding for the safety of our water supply – and treat with decency at least those we come across?' Philip observed, 'It's clear that people have no capacity to do such things. Some are barely coping. Shouldn't we have taken in the man we met in town?' Olivia resisted, 'I think we're a tight-knit group, and we can best help people by organising them. Andrew might agree to take him.'

***

The team repeated what they had done in Letheilean, on a bigger scale; food production was limited by capacity for labour rather than the availability of land. Hunting was resumed, under much closer control after Samuel's accident; the gun was locked away from those under the age of eighteen. Venison was now assured, at least while the ammunition lasted. Rory found some fish in the loch, confined them in a temporary cage and experimented with vegetarian feed. Like people, they ate what was on offer when they were deprived of what they preferred.

As more land was cleared, further crops were planted. This time they were nourished, using commercial products but also by ploughing in the previous year's waste. As the last seeds were sown, the local supply of fertiliser ran out. Deborah said, 'We need to find the regional depots before next spring.' David replied, 'Perhaps, but in the long run we must feed our plants properly: composting of residues; wood ash; animal manure, even human waste if we're careful of disease – the whole organic dream.'

***

12 April P1 fell on a Sunday, so everyone was relaxing. Margaret reminisced, 'It's a year since we landed on Salay, on the same day as Phraya hit the news.' Lucy replied, 'We heard about it too, but for me the crisis started a week later, when I had a first patient.' Deborah admitted, 'We were much slower on the uptake. Despite the air ban we didn't believe Bruce's warning when Olivia called us the next day.' He looked regretful. 'Don't be hard on yourself, the calamity unfolded

incredibly fast; it was all over in three months. The recovery seems to be proceeding more sluggishly.' Henry reacted: 'Yes, what can we do to speed it up?'

Deborah was in a reflective mood. 'The problem is that most people who were in the thick of it are wary, almost withdrawn, and who can blame them? We are in a better state of mind, because we have been comparatively safe throughout. We also have a good mix of skills for survival and leadership. Perhaps we need to get out there, galvanising other groups?' Bruce was doubtful; 'I agree with the thought, but I'm not sure the people around here are up to it intellectually. I hope that people near the city, who used to work in academia and high tech, might be more switched on.' Alexandra objected to this: 'I doubt such people are so different, except that they may be even more traumatised there. We certainly don't know if they are any better organised.' Steven poked his head above the parapet: 'Let's go and see.' Olivia took her usual role. 'We'll investigate the city eventually, perhaps when the local towns calm down. For now, let's work with the groups around us and see if we can produce some coordinated action.'

***

The ewes brought from Letheilean gave birth, but Alice insisted that all the lambs should be reserved for further breeding. Luckily, as spring progressed it became clear that the escaped sheep included young rams that the farmers hadn't got around to culling. Alice was willing to permit hunting of most of these. 'There's no beef, pork or chicken, but at least we'll have some meat.' William asked, 'Why isn't there any beef?' 'Because the cows got eaten when everyone was hungry last year, and there are none left.' 'What about pork?' 'The same I'm afraid, and the chickens too.' 'Maybe if we can find some eggs, then chicks will hatch out?' 'Even if they haven't been eaten, it's a bit late for that.' He recovered well: 'Oh … I was joking.'

Alice mentioned to David that the wild ewes from the hills needed shearing. He replied, 'I'm not a sheep farmer, nor an Australian.' 'Very amusing.' 'I don't even know how to catch them alive. Perhaps blowpipes and poison dart frogs?' After a struggle the ewes and their female lambs were caught unharmed, shorn and added to the flock on the farm.

***

Alexandra ran across Olivia and Henry. 'Well, it turns out there isn't an orchestra living next door. I don't think anyone around Morrie has the capacity even to miss music. Perhaps the technocrats are right, and we need to go to Edinburgh to find artists as well as industrialists?'

Henry pointed out, 'At the least we'll find books in libraries, and instruments even if there's no-one to play them. Perhaps we can get a cinema going, or at least find a large television to play films?' Olivia promised, 'You'll get your piano one day.' Alexandra looked gloomy; 'What worries me isn't the mechanics of the performing arts, it's whether anyone has the energy to aspire to them.' Once again Henry tried to provide encouragement from the deep past: 'Twenty thousand years ago people clambered into caves and created beautiful paintings of animals. Picasso visited, and when he came out he said that we have learned nothing.' 'I understand that's a myth.' Olivia reproved her: 'Cheer up, as soon as Steven has conquered the physical environment, we'll have fine art.'

***

Lucy gathered the ladies for a further bulletin on women's health. 'The contraceptive pills have expired, though they'll probably work for a long time. Similarly, barrier contraceptives are likely to be OK for some time past their dates.' Deborah asked, 'What about the men?' 'Condoms are certainly OK for quite some time.' 'And if they don't want to use them?' After a pause, Olivia enquired, 'Is it feasible to do vasectomies?' Lucy replied, 'It's a very simple operation; the main danger is infection, but I think that can be handled. Actually, I've been thinking about it for Rory; I'm happy with my two and I don't think it's a good idea for the only doctor to be giving birth. When the time is right, I'll discuss this with him and report back to you.' After the younger women had departed, Lucy said to Olivia and Alexandra, 'The other matter I've been considering is hormone replacement therapy; you may be alright, but by the time most of the ladies reach the menopause the tablets and creams won't be safe to use. I've no idea if we'll ever be able to make the hormones synthetically, and there are no horses!'

***

Life went on, and it was clear that the team would survive, as on Letheilean. Indeed, by June their efforts were boosted by an unearned bonus: self-seeded crops were beginning to mature in the fields around Morrie. David explained: 'Some of them will be useless, because the seeds sown by farmers last year weren't all suitable for propagation. Hybrid varieties don't produce true seed, so the next generation doesn't work properly, but heritage seeds yield plants which grow correctly; we need to concentrate on the latter.'

Charles decided that the fortuitous harvest should be discussed with other groups. He, David and Ruth went on a tour of the area, proposing that the successful crops should be shared. They also floated the idea of bartering surplus home-grown food, and introduced the possibility of a degree of specialisation. They even pointed out the feasibility of making biodiesel in order to run tractors. In most cases these suggestions were greeted as risky novelties, but Charles was happy to have made any progress at all.

Ruth also raised the subject of the burial of bodies. No-one had faced up to this, so she offered to deal with victims in exchange for whatever other groups could spare. When they mentioned it to Andrew, he volunteered to say a few words at the burials. The result was that he visited Morrie and got to know the team.

***

One day a stranger wandered into the farm and engaged the Scott children in conversation. 'Hello, dearies, are you having fun? I know a good game.' Calum was interested; 'We like games, can we play?' She replied, 'Certainly, you can be the daddy and your sister can be the mummy.' Rory watched, intrigued but wary. The woman continued, 'You lie down and stay very still, and the mummy has to look sad because the daddy is ill.' Rory was no longer amused. 'Excuse me, that's not suitable for little ones.' She ignored him; 'Why don't you give me a cuddle, dearies, I've been lonely since my husband was taken from me.' Alison was suddenly frightened and dragged Calum towards their father. He said, 'Run along to your real mummy, I'll talk to this lady.' When they were at a safe distance, he confronted the newcomer. 'I'm sorry if you've had a bad time, but you really can't do that here. Let's take you home.' 'I don't want to go there, he doesn't answer when I speak to him; actually, he hasn't moved for weeks.'

Rory began to understand, and changed plans. 'Why don't you have a rest in that barn, and I'll go and get some help.' She lay down and seemed to fall into an exhausted sleep. He ran off to find his children, and placed them in Julia's care. After a hurried discussion he took Olivia and Lucy back to the woman. They gently led her into one of the houses, away from all the youngsters, and gave her something to eat. Then Lucy sedated her. 'She'll sleep until morning; what are we going to do with her?'

Olivia gathered everyone for a discussion. Rory insisted, 'She can't stay here. Obviously she's mentally ill, and we can't know what she'll do to the kids.' Deborah nodded. Alice agreed, 'Even if we think she's safe, we mustn't take the risk.' Philip replied, 'Well we certainly can't take her back to her dead husband.' Margaret concurred: 'Yes, we've got to show a degree of compassion.' Alan was dubious; 'Perhaps, but I saw enough crazy people in Edinburgh, there's an endless supply of them.' Steven argued, 'I think having them in our camp will derail our project.' Eventually Alexandra offered, 'I'll go over to Andrew's tonight, and see if he can help. I'll promise we'll go and deal with the woman's husband.'

***

Rory had been hatching a plan, and revealed it to Lucy: 'I'm keen to get going on fish farming, but it's going to take forever to assemble the necessary kit. I wonder if a trip to the west coast is feasible?' She responded, 'Surely you don't propose to go all the way to your own place?' 'No, somewhere closer, just off the mainland.' She had been thinking of a similar journey, but with a different agenda: 'I really need to know what happened to my parents and brother. You could go to Caladion and do both things?' 'We'll have to consult the others.'

Margaret started the discussion: 'It's a good idea to get going on another source of food. Protein that doesn't run away!' Bruce objected, 'You'll need to take the van, the Landrover, a trailer and your boat, so the trip will use a lot of fuel.' Deborah was in favour; 'It's not so far to that part of the coast, and you're bound to find what you need. Definitely worth it.' Katherine raised a concern with their other aim: 'Caladion filled up with refugees from the islands; it might be dangerous?' Rory countered, 'The fish farms are out of town, so if it looks hazardous we can skip the search for Lucy's folks.' A yearning for salmon won the argument, and no-one faced up to the possible result of Lucy's quest.

On 5 July Rory set off with David, Steven and Alan. The journey to the west coast involved no significant towns, and was trouble-free. They started at the fish farm premises, where they found the equipment required for maintenance and operation. After working to get a large boat running, they spent a couple of days making trips to the cages. They cut them up and hauled the pieces into the van. Rory was pleased; 'Let's hide all this and just use the Landrover to go into Caladion.'

The harbour was crowded with craft of all sizes, but there were no cars to be seen. The town seemed deserted but bore witness to the struggles of those who had fled the islands. Hundreds of bodies littered the streets, and there were animals everywhere. Rory couldn't speak; David provided a slim hope: 'There were boatloads of people from the islands, and they had no way to move on and nowhere to stay. But Lucy's family had a car; maybe they escaped?' Alan offered, 'Let's go to their house. I'm willing to go in while you wait outside.'

***

Meanwhile, Jessica's sixteenth birthday passed without a special celebration, but Lucy took the opportunity to speak to Alexandra. 'It's obvious that she and Peter are attracted to each other. He's not sixteen yet, but are you happy for me to talk to her about contraception?' 'By all means, things are different these days.'

'I'm sure you know about these things,' – 'yes, mum talked to me ages ago, and Margaret told Julia' – 'but you need to know the details if you want to be a doctor eventually.' Lucy ran through all the methods of contraception, their expiry dates and the difficulty of manufacture in a post-Phraya world. At no stage was Peter named, but Jessica felt she had been given the go-ahead.

***

A few days later the men returned from the west, the van loaded with rusty equipment redolent of fish. Everyone admired it, and greedily anticipated the salmon it promised. Rory wanted some privacy for a difficult task: 'I'm so sorry, Lucy, here's a note from your brother.'

"Dear Lucy, I rather hope you never find this. After you called, the exodus from the Far Isles to Caladion continued until the town was dreadfully overcrowded. Everyone was desperate to travel onwards, but they didn't have cars. The crowds were extremely intimidating, and I was worried the car would be stolen. I argued that we should make an escape while it was possible, but mum and dad were reluctant. I stayed to look after them, as you requested. Then they caught the Phraya bug, and quickly became poorly. By the time they agreed to leave, they were too ill to travel, and got worse quickly. They asked me to tell you that they loved you, and I do too. Lucy, I'm afraid our parents didn't make it. I buried them in the woods behind the town."

"That was three weeks ago. Since then I've been trying to lie low, but Caladion has descended into madness. I'm going to make a run for it, but I've got no idea where to go. I hope you are managing in Mansay, and Rory, Ali and Calum are OK. I'll try to get there if and when things settle down. All the best, your loving brother, 15 June."

When Rory emerged, Alexandra said, 'I'd like to arrange a gathering, if you think that would be helpful for Lucy.' 'Yes, I think so, I'll ask her.' For the rest of the day people shared their concerns for their parents, brothers and sisters, friends and colleagues. Some clung to faintly rational hopes of recovery from disease or escape from adversity; others simply fantasised about miraculous reappearances.

The following day Alexandra opened a sombre ceremony with an expression of the thought that everyone had been suppressing: 'We are entering another phase in our discovery of what happened during the Phraya crisis. We already know that the overwhelming majority of people have died. This fact is utterly impossible to grasp, literally unimaginable. Nevertheless, each of us has been trying to face the likelihood, the practical certainty, that our loved ones are among the victims. What is new, now, is that we have proof in the case of Lucy's parents. We grieve for her and for ourselves.' Ruth said, 'We must make the best of each other, and all those who have survived.' Henry read:

'I cannot say and I will not say
that he is dead – he is just away!
With a cheery smile, and a wave of the hand,
he has wandered into an unknown land,
and left us dreaming how very fair
it needs must be, since he lingers there.
And you – o you, who the wildest yearn
for the old-time step and the glad return –
think of him faring on, as dear
in the love of there as the love of here;
and loyal still as he gave the blows
of his warrior strength to his country's foes.
Mild and gentle, as he was brave,
when the sweetest love of his life he gave
to simple things: where the violets grew
pure as the eyes they were likened to.
The touches of his hands have strayed
as reverently as his lips have prayed;
when the little brown thrush that harshly chirred
was dear to him as the mocking-bird;
and he pitied as much as a man in pain
a writhing honey-bee wet with rain.
Think of him still as the same, I say:
He is not dead – he is just away!'

***

Deborah declared, 'Time to cut timber, before we're too busy with the harvest!' She even allowed Samuel a turn with the axe, under Alan's strict supervision and with Peter and Benjamin out of the way to dull any tendency to competition. 'I'll turn you into a woodworker yet. Do you want to help me build the drying shed?'

Chapter 10 Probing

By the beginning of August, Steven was itching to fulfil his ambition of visiting Edinburgh. Margaret protested, 'It's still too dangerous.' 'How do you know? We haven't met anyone from there, and neither has Andrew in recent months.' 'Just look at Caladion.' 'What about it, we met no-one. Granted it was a scene of horror, but that reflected a past that has finished happening. The same is probably true everywhere. We're no longer seeing lone survivors wandering the towns round here.' 'At least let's have a meeting about this.'

Olivia introduced the debate: 'I doubt we can hold Steven back much longer, whatever anyone says; but I'd be interested in views, from everyone, on an exploratory trip to Edinburgh.' Charles opened, 'I think he is right, we haven't got very far with organising people hereabouts, and we need to find out if they're any more dynamic around the city.' Alice countered: 'I think it's risky, they may be livelier but perhaps crazy too; we have met too many troubled people even out here in the sticks.' Henry volunteered, 'We need to take the temperature at the centre, and I'm willing. We can be light on our feet.' David suggested, 'Yes, just one vehicle, four people. No need for the Landrover, as the roads seem to be clear now; the petrol car is fastest.' Ruth was worried, 'I don't see how a supercar is going to help when you talk to unknown people.' Deborah, balanced as usual, concluded, 'I support the trip, but it should definitely err on the side of caution.' Philip: 'Hear, hear.'

Alan volunteered, 'If it's going to happen I should go, because I know the area and was there during the troubles.' Olivia checked: 'The majority are for it. Are you OK with this, Bruce, Alexandra? Everyone happy?' Nods from the Lentons, and Margaret muttered, 'Ecstatic.' Olivia drew the debate to a close; 'OK, the decision is that four will go in the car – Steven, Alan, David and Henry – Rory had a bad enough time on the last trip, and should stay with Lucy.'

***

Steven and Alan cobbled together a cage in Loch Fada, assisted by the newly reunited team of Peter and Samuel. Benjamin and Julia demonstrated their skill at catching fish, and confined them in the cage. Margaret devised a diet for them, using rapeseed and other waste crops; she dried some for use in the winter. To their surprise the fish not only ate it but thrived and grew. Rory admitted, 'It isn't clear whether they will reproduce in situ, but we can keep catching young ones and fatten them up.' Benjamin tried to persuade Julia, 'They're being fed vegetarian food, so you can eat them?' She wasn't fooled, but enjoyed the attention.

Isabella took Rose aside and whispered, 'I think my brother is interested in Julia, and my sister certainly likes Peter. It's alright for them, but who can we be with?' 'You might end up with my big brother, but there's nobody for me.' 'I don't know, but there are other people alive, maybe we'll meet them one day?' 'Yes, if we go to Edinburgh there will be lots of lovely boys.'

***

On 10 August the Edinburgh reconnaissance team were almost ready, but Alan delayed them by insisting on fixing his bicycle to the roof. Henry ribbed him, 'Trying to avoid inner city traffic?' 'It has rescued me from thugs more than once.' Steven suggested, 'The gun might be more appropriate for that.' David replied, 'Definitely not – we want to see if the people are cooperative, not to fight them.'

They decided not to use the bridges, in case they were unsafe after more than a year without attention. Instead they drove round the estuary, using small roads to avoid towns. The situation in the countryside between them was similar to that around Morrie: no crops except those that had propagated themselves; abandoned cars, now mostly cleared off the roads; and pockets of small-scale food production. As they travelled, they introduced themselves to several groups who were growing crops, and found them capable and peaceable but not much more enterprising than the people around Morrie. Steven was disappointed, but they gathered that the situation might be more promising nearer the centre of things. They also learned that the city itself was still rather threatening. Towards nightfall they approached it with some trepidation. Alan suggested, 'Better to stay away for now, until we know more?'

The following morning they drove through an industrial estate, and saw that although it was quiet there were signs of activity. They looked a little further out and saw a small plantation with people working on crops. David approached and asked politely, 'Who's in charge here, please?' Soon a stocky man approached and introduced himself; 'Alastair Dunbar, pleased to meet you, where are you from?' We're from further north, we're just exploring the industrial areas to see what's going on. We may move to this area if it's safe.' 'Well, as you can see, we're managing to produce food for our little group. Some of us are engineers, and we're trying to get some equipment going. As for safety, it's OK here but the gangs still operate in Edinburgh itself. Steven quizzed him in a friendly way, and was impressed. 'I think you're doing the right things. Can we keep in touch?'

For the next two days they worked their way around the outskirts, meeting various groups. David probed the agricultural activities, Alan tried to find out about the city – it wasn't entirely discouraging – and Henry quietly observed the zeitgeist as Alexandra had requested. Eventually he said, 'OK, we've seen that people are managing well out here, time to go into the centre!'

On 14 August P1 Alan, heart in mouth, led the others towards his home. The place was in much the same state as when he left thirteen months earlier, except that nature had almost completed the work of recycling the victims of Phraya. They had to circumvent many blockages caused by cars, fallen trees, piles of debris – and bones. They saw nobody, and little evidence that anyone remained alive. David had anticipated this; 'There's no food, and the only safe water is rain from gutters.' Henry asked, 'In that case what are the gangsters eating and drinking?' Alan knew the answer: 'A year ago they were running around fighting for what remained in other people's houses; I suppose the winners have stockpiled what they stole from the losers.'

With much backtracking and re-routing, they reached Alan's house. His hideaway was still undiscovered, but it did not smell nice. David was impressed; 'You stayed in here for almost ten weeks, without going out?' They spent the night in the remainder of the house.

***

The next day was Alison's eighth birthday. 'Last year we had ham.' Lucy explained, 'Sorry, there are no more pigs. You had it the year before too; can you remember that?' 'Yes, I had a party at the beach with the white sand and purple water, I swam with my school friends,' – she paused – 'but they're not here. Are they still alive, mummy?' Rory took over and went further than the previous year: 'I'm afraid they probably aren't, Ali. You know the horrid bug made lots of people ill, well, quite a lot of them died. What was even worse,' – Lucy broke in, 'Rory, please,' – but he pressed on, 'was that there wasn't enough food, so people fought each other, and a lot more were killed. It's awful, but you need to know what happened.'

Lucy frowned at him and turned back to Alison. 'It's nice that you can remember the party before all that bad stuff. Actually, things are getting better now, so your next one will be as good as when you were six.' Rory had an idea; 'We can make this good, right now. Why don't we go to Loch Fada? There isn't a beach, but we can go out in the boat, jump out in the middle of the lake and swim. We can also feed my fish.' Calum, who had been listening with an increasingly doleful air, perked up; 'I can swim right across the loch.' Lucy groaned, 'Great, we can drown both of them in one trip and avoid any more awkward birthdays.'

***

Before leaving Morrie, the explorers had been given detailed instructions on the things they should seek in Edinburgh. They tried to drive further into the city but were defeated by blockages. Alan was triumphant: 'This will teach you not to tease me. We'll walk in, with me scouting ahead on the bike, ready to retreat if I run across any crazies.' They found a small supermarket, entirely empty of anything edible, but boasting a plentiful supply of everything else.

They reached the library and found that its door had never been breached. Henry was pleased, and consulted a list: 'Thank goodness books were still printed. Right, Steven, you want engineering; David, you'll look for horticulture; Alan, survival techniques. We also need to find physics and maths for Bruce, electronics for Philip, fishing for Rory, chemistry and biotechnology for Katherine, and medicine for Lucy. As for me, I've got to keep Alexandra happy with novels and poetry.' Steven remarked, 'Before Phraya we would have been hard pressed to think of a reason why four men would be marching through town with three trolleys and a bike!'

They found a musical instrument shop and emerged with a violin for Charles, a clarinet for Katherine, recorders for the children and suitable music. They kept a nervous lookout, but it seemed there was no-one around, so they spent that day and the next exploring the shops. On their way out they met further groups who reinforced the more favourable impression of the outskirts. It was time to set off for Morrie.

***

When the men returned, everyone gathered to hear their stories over a meal. Afterwards Henry, slightly drunk, provided a summary of the state of the city: 'Two vast and trunkless legs of stone stand in the desert. Near them, on the sand, half sunk a shattered visage lies, whose frown, and wrinkled lip, and sneer of cold command, tell that its sculptor well those passions read.' Olivia went with the flow and asked, 'Who are you, my boy?' 'My name is Ozymandias, king of kings; look on my works, ye mighty, and despair!' Alexandra indulged in a little mockery: 'Steven wants to know, is anything useful left?' 'Nothing beside remains. Round the decay of that colossal wreck, boundless and bare the lone and level sands stretch far away.'

In the morning Olivia called a meeting to mull over the situation. 'The question we're trying to address is whether we might move to

Edinburgh, now, later or never. The reasons for going at some point have been rehearsed often; what are the arguments against doing so immediately?' David said: 'That's easy. We are making a success of the farm and smallholding. We have enough food, and no-one is disturbing us.' Philip added, 'We know the city is threatening, so we should stay here unless a further visit indicates that things are improving there?'

Katherine questioned this: 'There are threats here too. I don't mean gangs, I'm concerned about whether we can sustain our present success. We're dependent on a freakishly lucky supply of fuel, and haven't yet demonstrated that we can make our own.' Deborah pointed out, 'There's also the question of seeds. We may run out of pre-Phraya ones, and we're not yet sure which of our crops breeds true.' Bruce argued, 'Those concerns apply wherever we are.' Charles suggested, 'We might find more seeds elsewhere. If someone else has them, we barter.' David replied, 'Well, go and fetch them in that case. No need to shift our whole operation.' Steven joined in: 'In the case of fuel, we may need help. We stand a better chance of finding it around Edinburgh, if and when it's safe.'

Ruth produced the clincher: 'That leads us back to the threat from gangs. For the moment, doesn't that trump any argument about the positive aspects of the city?' Olivia soon pushed the discussion on: 'OK, let's accept that it's too risky at the moment. I think there's a consensus that we'll move in due course, but let's check whether there are there arguments for remaining here indefinitely?' There was a pause. Alexandra said, 'Apparently we all doubt that we can make a full life here. Even if we overcome the immediate threats, staying here seems passive.' Henry agreed; 'Yes, we'd find that some kind of revival would emerge from the centre and reach us. I'd rather be in the thick of it, shaping events.'

The discussion continued but became rather aimless, so Olivia called a halt. 'OK, we stay here, making further trips to monitor the situation. We may go in early spring like last time, but no firm conclusion yet. Steven groaned, 'Yes, that's probably wise.'

***

A double harvest was under way, of self-seeded crops as well as those sown by the team. Most of the yield was preserved for consumption by people, but Steven and Katherine were processing some rape to feed engines. He had devised a contraption for extracting the oil; when it produced a disappointing yield, she suggested heating the seeds: 'No need to make fancy cold-pressed stuff.' The result was a dirty liquid which they filtered and left to separate into brown water with surprisingly pure yellow liquid above. Margaret tasted it and declared that some of it could be re-directed to humans; 'It's hardly olive oil but it will be useful for frying and in dressings.'

The next stage was to convert the extract into diesel fit for engines. Alan provided a recipe from the research in his hideaway: 'Dissolve 5 grams of potash in 200 millilitres of methanol, and blend with a litre of rapeseed oil. Separate the glycerol which settles to the bottom. God knows what that means.' Katherine replied, 'Potash is an alkali we can extract from the ashes of a wood fire; and methanol we can also get from wood.' Alan plunged back into his computer files and came up with a way of extracting the first ingredient: 'Place the ashes from a hardwood fire in a barrel with sand at the bottom; add water; reduce the liquid which drips out to half its volume; filter; boil dry; heat the resulting crystals. Good luck with that.'

Steven asked, 'What about the methanol?' Alan had found that too: 'Heat wet softwood shavings in the absence of air to 78C – we'll need a cooking thermometer – and condense the vapours. Abracadabra!' For several days the three of them laboured in their chemical laboratory, and eventually produced a few litres of pale liquid. Steven insisted on finding an old car on which to try the biodiesel. 'I'm not putting this into the tractor until I have no choice.'

The whole team turned out to witness his triumphal drive round the farmyard. It turned into an impromptu party. David felt that the children had been absorbing a rather forbidding impression of the prospective move, so at his suggestion Rose read a more optimistic view of Edinburgh:

'My tea is nearly ready
and the sun has left the sky.
It's time to take the window
to see Leerie going by;
For every night at teatime
and before you take your seat,
With lantern and with ladder
he comes posting up the street.

Now Tom would be a driver
and Maria go to sea,
And my papa's a banker
and as rich as he can be;
But I, when I am stronger
and can choose what I'm to do,
O Leerie, I'll go round at night
and light the lamps with you!

For we are very lucky,
with a lamp before the door,
And Leerie stops to light it
as he lights so many more;
And oh! before you hurry by
with ladder and with light;
O Leerie, see a little child
and nod to him to-night!'

***

Bruce had been analysing the barriers to long-term recovery, and reconvened the relevant people. 'It's not easy to predict the limiting factors. We're working on biodiesel so we can run vehicles and other internal combustion machinery. Generators provide some electricity; in the medium term solar and wind energy, and a local electricity grid, will allow people to run powerful electrical motors. These will enable industry to get started.' Katherine pointed out, 'The other fundamental input is chemicals, and we'll have to do without petroleum feedstock. It's going to be difficult to produce plastics, and biochemistry will be much delayed.' Lucy remarked regretfully, 'Medicine may have to return to using natural remedies.' Philip added, 'We won't have a mining industry either, for a long time. The materials that lie at the heart of electronics, and the high-tech equipment for making components from them, may be many decades away.' Steven concluded, 'Yes, I think we face a long period of fixing and recycling, in the manner of cars in Cuba, across many industries.'

Bruce resumed, 'There's an over-riding danger that concerns me. We're assuming that all we lack is materials and resources such as energy and machinery, but the real limitation may be knowledge.' Deborah knew what he meant; 'Yes, there may be problems for which we just can't find solutions.' Steven, being self-reliant, had trouble seeing the difficulty; 'We can work out how to solve them.' Bruce replied, 'You can, and maybe all adult survivors will be able to contribute, but what about forty years from now? Continuation of the recovery will depend on children alive now and those born in the future. Education will be crucial, and research. We will have to restart the universities.' 'Well, that's not going to happen in Morrie.'

***

On 28 Sept P1 it was William's tenth birthday. David had tried the patience of his companions in Edinburgh, but had succeeded: 'There you are, Billie, paint the colour of the sea, for your aeroplane.' 'Thanks, dad, but … the shops aren't open yet, are they?' 'No, this was made before Phraya, and it has been waiting for you in a shop that's still closed I'm afraid.' 'I thought so, now that I'm in double figures I do understand what's going on.' Samuel muttered, 'Oh look, there's a pig flying by.' Rose took the opportunity; 'Well, make him some ham, then, clever clogs.' Deborah remonstrated, 'Kids, let's not be sarcastic, it's the lowest form of wit.'

****

In October Steven and David went on another trip to Edinburgh, this time with Olivia and Alice, who wanted to take a preliminary look at possible farmland. 'We need arable of course, but sheep pasture and deer habitat would be nice. We might get other animals, if anyone has managed to keep any alive.' They identified a place on the industrial perimeter, near the hills, which hadn't been claimed by anyone else.

Next they called on the engineers, and spoke to Alastair. Steven had a present for him. 'We've made some biodiesel; here are a few litres to try.' 'Very impressive! Can we have the method too?' 'Sure, and perhaps you could let us know what it does to engines?' 'Certainly. Any progress on moving here?' 'Well, may I introduce Olivia, our leader?' She answered the question: 'One of my roles is holding Steven back, but we're gradually becoming persuaded, and meeting people like you certainly encourages us to take the risk. We are quite organised folk and are keen to influence what goes on.' She quizzed him on the potential threat from gangs in the city, and he was guarded.

They visited another group that Alastair had mentioned as potential chemists. Rhona Anderson greeted them: 'Alastair reported your last visit; you would be welcome here.' Steven repeated his explanation of oil processing, which she understood, and he apologised that he had given away his sample. Olivia was persistent about Edinburgh, and Rhona was more forthcoming: 'It's true that there are remnants of the groups who ran around making merry hell during the crisis. They beat each other up regularly, and make occasional raids out here. We have been able to buy them off with what amounts to protection money, and it's manageable.'

****

When they returned, Ruth had a surprise for Alice: 'I'm pregnant!' 'That's fabulous, congratulations, how wonderful.' 'Well, according to one of Lucy's expired tests, anyway.' 'I'm sure it will be right. Shall I tell Alan?' 'Yes, he should know as well, even if it's not yet certain.' Lucy had to be told, too, and soon Deborah guessed; in no time it was common knowledge. Ruth didn't mind; 'There are no secrets among twenty-six people.' Alice corrected her joyfully: 'Twenty-seven, I think.' 'Oh my God!'

***

There was now sufficient momentum behind the idea of moving to Edinburgh that Olivia was forced to hold another meeting. 'First let's re-address the question of whether we're going; and if we decide to do so, when.' This time Steven didn't hang back; 'We're not going to get anywhere fast by staying here. You know you want it.' Everyone laughed, and there was a pause while people assembled the counter-arguments. Ruth, feeling especially vulnerable, had a go: 'OK, what if there is real violence?' Alan joined in; 'It could happen. I saw those people up close, or at least heard them from my hideaway, and I was chased on my bike.' Alice replied, 'I don't trust them either, but there are groups dealing with them as we speak. If anything bad happens, we can always come back.' Ruth was persuaded: 'That's right. We would empty the farm and leave everything hidden at the smallholding.'

Olivia observed, 'There's poetic justice in the three prospective parents making this decision,' – she paused to see if anyone disagreed – 'so perhaps we should move on to the timing?' Henry said immediately, 'Why not soon?' Lucy argued, 'I suppose that would allow us to establish ourselves before the weather closes in and precludes the option of a retreat?' Katherine countered, 'If that's our attitude why not stay here until it's warmer, and avoid any city thugs who might spend the winter stealing other people's food?' Deborah concurred, 'Yes, not until early spring, like when we came here. Ruth will be five or six months pregnant, which is favourable.' Everyone nodded, so David said ruefully, 'I see we're planning to abandon my farm for a second time.' Everyone could tell he wasn't serious, and the decision was essentially made. However, Philip added, 'Nearer the time, we can make one last trip to check the situation hasn't worsened.'

***

Rose was twelve on 19 November. She understood the differences between life pre and post Phraya more clearly than William. Nevertheless, she was happier to be told about them than Samuel: 'Why can't we just go back to the old ways?' Deborah replied, 'There isn't enough trust yet. If a person doesn't know that he can go to a shop and buy food, he won't work on something like a film, that can't be eaten. He just wants to grow crops. Even fertiliser, which helps food production, will only be made by someone who believes that they will be fed – or paid. Money allows everything to get done, but it only works if people have faith in it.' 'So can we get all that going again?' 'Dad and I are concentrating on the food itself. Steven and others are working on equipment, like tractors and fuel, to speed up farming. Some are looking further ahead. Charles is keen to get groups of people doing different jobs. Then they can swap whatever they've made for things they need. Everyone hopes all this will work better when we move.' 'It sounds really hard.'

David added, 'I'm afraid there's another problem: although we are competent enough to ensure that we have enough to eat, with so many people missing we don't know how to do many other things. The young are going to have to learn whatever practical skills are needed.' 'I'm not sure I'm going to be good at that.' 'Don't worry, once things get going life will be more varied. People will need to be cheered up by singing and dancing, and that's your talent. You just might have to weed the crops as well.'

***

The cold weather came early, and the team were grateful that they hadn't attempted the move. In Morrie they were well prepared: the crops were in and being preserved; overwintering crops had been established just in time. The wood store was full, smoking was under way, freezers were stocked. The sheep were in the barn, also pregnant. The team was sufficiently confident to salve its collective conscience by asking Andrew whether he would accept some food in exchange for the work he was doing with those who were finding life unsustainable.

***

On 3 December Peter joined Jessica in the adult world; sixteen was old enough in the post era, and Lucy had a word with him about this and that. All four parents were pleased, and they were openly treated as a couple. His other present was permission to use the gun, under supervision. He went off with Henry and they wasted a number of bullets missing every deer they stalked. Charles was not impressed.

***

In the school, the children were making Christmas decorations. Benjamin had volunteered to help; Lucy knew this was so he could be near Julia, but thought it rather charming and accepted the offer. He had a suggestion: 'We can't keep raiding shops to get things from before Phraya. All the presents should be home-made too.' Julia said, 'That's a lovely idea. The kids can make some when they've finished decorating the tree with baubles.'

Margaret visited the schoolroom to help the youngsters make a Christmas pudding. Ever since her perusal of the label on the previous year's one, she had been trying to collect substitute ingredients. Fresh apples and carrots were available, wild fruit had been dried, spices could be found, and there was still flour from the Italians on Innisdu.

She had hidden honey specially for this purpose. Alice had produced a kind of suet from her sheep; Margaret was dubious about it, but when the kids mixed it with all the other goodies, it smelt pretty good.

A few days later, in a further display of his interest in the children's education, Benjamin showed them how he made bows and arrows. William begged, 'I'm ten now, so can I have one?' Lucy replied, 'Certainly not a full size one, but perhaps you'll get a small one at Christmas, if you're nice to him.' Julia suggested, 'You could make targets so the grownups can practice.' Rose made one for Peter, and Julia helped her draw a picture of a deer's rear end on it. Calum howled with laughter and offered, 'I can draw a poo coming out.' Lucy said, 'Aren't you getting a bit too big to talk like that?'

Alan helped Peter and Samuel make useful presents. They made Henry a crossbow, Rory a long-handled fishing net, and Bruce a steam preservation device hitherto unknown to the food industry. For the children they made flutes of square cross-section; drums and other percussion instruments; and low-powered bows and blunt arrows. When Lucy saw these, she raised her eyes to heaven; 'Now they can make enough noise to kill me and dispatch each other afterwards.'

***

The weather had been snowy, and the ground was covered in thick white drifts, but on 25 December P1 the sky was clear. The stage was set for an authentic pagan festival. Henry showed the children the Milky Way; 'It hasn't changed in thousands of years, so we're seeing the same panorama as the Neanderthals.' Samuel asked, 'Why did they die out?' Alison wondered, 'Perhaps the dinosaurs ate them all?' Benjamin understood the timescales better; 'No, they died out long ago, there weren't any humans. Probably the different kinds of people fought, and the modern ones won.' Rose observed, 'Sounds a bit like what's been happening recently.'

None of the usual commercial trimmings was available, but an unorthodox meal was relished by all except Ruth, who was nauseous. While most of the team enjoyed Peter's first success with the gun, she and the near-vegetarians favoured Rory's fish. She also managed some of the ersatz pudding. David and Margaret sang ethereal songs composed for the occasion. The children gave a concert on the do-it-yourself flutes; Alexandra's verdict was, 'You're doing a great job, but these are tuned in a manner unknown even to Indian music.' Isabella suddenly spoke up. 'You don't like this world, do you mum? Dad seems happier with it.' A frisson ran round the gathering.

After a momentary pause, Alexandra replied, 'Your father has embraced the challenge in an admirable way, but I feel that so much pre has vanished that it's sometimes hard to enjoy the positive aspects of post.' Bruce was defensive: 'I feel the loss too, but one can only spend so much time regretting, and then one has to start rebuilding the best of what has been lost. It wasn't all perfect anyway.'

Deborah asked, 'OK, let's compare. At Christmas time we used to rush around buying crappy presents made in China, cook a hideously dry turkey and gassy Brussel sprouts' – 'Alison interrupted, 'I don't like them,' – Alice sympathised, 'I'll tell you a secret, Ali, nobody does,' – 'and then lie about too stuffed to move, and watch old musicals.' Lucy responded, 'Whereas now we rush about making weird presents, trying to find the wherewithal to make a pudding, and playing square flutes for goodness' sake – sorry Alan.'

Philip suggested, 'Perhaps the most unsettling aspect of the situation is having to work out what features of the pre-Phraya world we're even trying to recreate?' Bruce responded, 'Most of it, because it worked incredibly well. I admit there were a few deficiencies: in the future we mustn't confine people in flying metal tubes with the air recycled so they can exchange bugs and deliver them to every corner of the world.' Deborah added, 'We won't store our knowledge in cyberspace. Everything was so abstract, inter-connected and vulnerable.' It was Margaret who put her finger on why the collapse was so sudden and complete: 'If only there had been a law requiring everyone to store at least a month's worth of food in their homes.'

***

It was extremely cold on 31 December P1, so the team decided not to stay up to await the arrival of the new year. As they sat down to an ordinary meal in the farmhouse, there was a knock at the door. David answered cautiously, and an exhausted man half-fell into the house. 'Do you mind if I shelter here? I'm frozen and starving – can I have something to eat please?' He seemed harmless, so he was allowed to take part in the meal and was given a bed in an unoccupied house. In the morning he explained that he had been living on his own for months, had run low on food and eventually decided that he needed to seek help. For the next few days it was impossible to take him anywhere, so he remained with the team, recovered well and did his fair share of the work.

The usual discussion took place, but this was a harder case. Rory was for taking him in; 'He seems sane, capable, worthy of being in the team? If he had walked into our lives in the islands, or even in Letheilean, we would have welcomed him.' Alice replied, 'Perhaps, but we're in a world of many people now, and we don't know them as well as each other. If we bring strangers in, we'll lose cohesion.' Philip suggested, 'We could lean on Andrew, as in the past, but offer full support this time. We're specialising in food production but avoiding distractions like this, so we could pay, if one can use that word, by feeding these unfortunate souls. Andrew's humanists can concentrate less on growing crops and more on caring and rehabilitation.'

Alexandra was heartened, and wrote: "I think we made a breakthrough today, both for others and for ourselves. We have in our team, in microcosm, what's needed for a fuller society: copers we've always had, and now carers are emerging.'

Olivia and Charles went on a private mission to see Andrew. She started, 'We're grateful that you're taking in struggling people, and are happy to feed them. We'd like to cooperate more, but it's hard going with the folks in this area.' 'I suppose that's why you are thinking of moving?' Charles continued, 'Yes, but we won't be able to work with you from Edinburgh. Here's our thought: would you like to come too?' Olivia hastened to add: 'We would operate separately but maintain our alliance.' He pressed on, 'We'd like to form many relationships down there, and have made a start on meeting other groups. You could work with them too?' Olivia held up a hand; 'Slow down, give him time to think!'

Andrew allowed their proposal to sink in, and mused, 'I think you're right; here, what most people need is to be left alone. My worry is: there, with the needy so numerous, we'll be swamped.' Olivia replied, 'We would support you, and would try to persuade others to do so.' Charles explained, 'I am thinking about the recovery in economic terms. I would like to see more specialisation. Some will raise crops, while others take on different roles, and get paid, initially in food, later with money.' Andrew laughed; 'Gosh, you are thinking ahead. Please let me reflect on all of this.'

***

When the weather improved in mid-January Steven, Rory, David and Charles went on a last trip to check out the Edinburgh environs before the move. They visited the proposed new farm and found nothing amiss. Charles insisted on looking for another patch of land in the vicinity. David was mystified; 'Secret mission? What's Olivia up to now?' 'It's Alexandra's idea, she's hoping to persuade Andrew to move here too.'

They went on a tour of the groups they had met previously, and added a new one: the chemists introduced Gregory Clark, who had settled on a rapeseed farm. Steven had a ready audience for a report on his attempts at biodiesel, and Charles tried out his ideas on division of labour. They persuaded him to keeping growing rape as well as food for subsistence.

Everyone they met said the situation in Edinburgh itself was gradually improving. Gang members were tiring of the cycle of violence, both suffered at the hands of their enemies and imposed on them in revenge; some of them had begun to wonder whether they would be better off working rather than fighting. One or two had left and joined other groups. The men returned to Morrie well satisfied.

***

On 17 January P2 Calum turned six. Rory took him to Loch Fada to watch the cage being dismantled; he had a boyish fascination with anything mechanical. 'Do you remember the really big cage in the sea at Pennay?' 'Where is that, daddy?' 'Near our old house on Mansay. You know how we used to drive across the causeway, and you were worried the car would sink into the water?' He looked blank, and when his father reported this to Lucy she said sadly, 'I'm afraid eventually he won't remember anything at all of his life before Phraya.'

Rory decided to stick to post. He showed Calum the fertilised salmon eggs he had collected from rivers, and told him they would turn into baby fish. 'Can they swim when they're little, or do they have to learn like children?' 'Let's wait until they hatch in the spring; then you can watch.' 'Will they go in your cage?' We're getting it ready to move it somewhere else.' 'Are we going back to the place with the big one?' Rory sighed; 'No, a new and even more exciting place.' 'Wow, great!'

***

Alexandra went for a last visit to Andrew. 'What do you think of Olivia's proposal? David and Charles have found a promising piece of land near where we intend to settle.' 'I've discussed it with my folks, and we're open to the move. However, do you mind if we hang back and await your reports?'

The team started to pack for the move. The last of the fuel in the depot was decanted and filtered. The sections of fish cage were brought over from Loch Fada. The old car, still running acceptably on biodiesel, was provided with yet another trailer. The vehicles were loaded with as much of the food and equipment as could be managed, and the rest was hidden at the smallholding. On 20 February P2 a convoy consisting of a tractor, assorted vehicles, trailers and a boat pulled out of Morrie and started to crawl towards the former capital of Scotland.

Part 4 Nexus

Chapter 11 Centrality

The team pulled into their new home in the crook of the hills. Deborah said, 'Here we go again, third time lucky.' Steven crowed, 'This time in the right place.' Ruth was nervous: 'I hope it proves so.' Henry was upbeat: 'Whatever is destined to happen, it will take place here; we'll make sure it's a good outcome.' Philip muttered, 'That's what we all love about you, such unjustified confidence!'

As spring emerged over the following weeks, they embarked on a practiced routine of setting up houses with heating, cooking and washing facilities; clearing ground, sowing seeds – now dominated by their own – and nurturing small plants brought from Morrie. The sheep were housed indoors for lambing, and hunting parties were sent out. Rory complained, 'We've got a good supply of water, but there aren't any lochs nearby. Does no-one care for fish?'

***

Steven visited Alastair and his engineers, and was informed, 'Your biodiesel burns, but the long-term effect on engines isn't clear yet.' 'Do you think we'd be better off making alcohol and putting it into petrol cars?' 'No, the engines will suffer much more, especially if there's no proper fuel to mix in. Besides, as you know most tractors and other heavy equipment are diesel powered.' 'OK, just checking, biodiesel it is then; what about rapeseed as the basic ingredient?' 'It's fine, and we haven't got much choice anyway. We've been talking to Gregory, who is gathering the crop planted before Phraya, and is growing it afresh. Also Rhona, and she says your recipe for converting it is fine. It's all pilot scale, though.' 'Charles has ideas on getting people working together to increase throughput, and Olivia will be talking to everyone.'

The team gathered to address the question of whether they should grow rape as well. Margaret surprised no-one: 'We should stick to food for now.' Steven was immediately roused, and almost shouted, 'We need oil for the tractor. Why else did we drive it all the way down here?' There was a pause, and Deborah argued calmly, 'Yes, we must aim to operate efficiently from the start, so we'll run it; but we may not find much fuel here, and if there is any it's deteriorating, so we've got to make it.' Charles reminded the meeting: 'Gregory is processing the seeds, and we'll buy it using the food the tractor produces, so we don't need to grow it ourselves.' Katherine was cautious: 'But what if he doesn't succeed, or bargains unreasonably?' Ruth said simply, 'We won't be very efficient if we run low on food.' People seemed exasperated by the tangled arguments, so she tried to lighten the mood: 'Some of us are eating for two, you know, so we better grow food,' – she waited for the uneasy laughter to die down – 'but on the other hand I might develop a craving for the oil itself.' Olivia suggested a compromise: 'We could stick to allowing the pre-Phraya crop to grow as best it can on its own, and urge Gregory to do it properly.'

***

16 March P2 was Isabella's twelfth birthday. Bruce, keen to steer her towards acquiring skills useful for the post world, offered a book on chemical technology. Alexandra, wanting to avoid too much realism, gave her 'A Book of Nonsense', and she was pleased. After a few hours' practice she produced a response to both gifts: 'There was an old man a bit sad. For maths and his numbers so mad. His girl took a look, a chemistry book – how nice, well thanks, what a dad!'

***

Charles proposed to Steven: 'Let's visit your contacts, to establish the supply chain for diesel.' Accordingly they started with Gregory, and gave him the hard sell: 'We survived two years ago in Letheilean, and even managed to produce a surplus of food last season, in Morrie. We are expecting to do the same here, with the help of our tractor, if we have enough fuel. If you risk growing rape, we will be happy to pay for it, in food.' 'You sound confident. You better make sure it can be converted into useable fuel.'

When Charles made a similar pitch to Rhona, she pointed out, 'Extracting and processing the oil is more complicated than growing the seeds. Gregory has no inputs other than his people's labour, and only one output.' 'For the moment, you're right. However, we hope that at some point a tractor and therefore fuel will be involved. The improved yield will produce a lot more oil than is burned by ploughing. Later fertiliser will be weaved into the operation, to improve efficiency further.' 'Fair enough, but even at the outset we need two things: seeds, and wood for the chemicals. We'll also produce things other than biodiesel.' 'Indeed, in due course both operations will become complicated, and we'll have to establish prices for all inputs and outputs. For now, it would be great if we can all work on faith that the whole will be greater than the sum of the parts.'

***

The team's new home was christened by David: 'I can't bear to call it a farm, we've left that behind. Let's call it the steading?' This was an understatement; there were several houses, outbuildings, barns, enclosed fields and rough land uphill, but the name stuck. Ruth remarked, 'It's rather bare, not many trees for timber, and it's certainly not well hidden like the smallholding. I hope we aren't disturbed.'

Alexandra admired the view over Edinburgh. "We're back where civilisation used to be, but it's conspicuous by its absence. From this eyrie we can see the sea, hills to the north and south and, closer, the whole of Edinburgh – as extinct as its volcano. This is where the recovery must, can, will take place. I wonder what's happening beyond, in England, in Europe? The USA, Asia, is Australia still there?"

Through the steading ran a stream, which Rory wanted to dam to make a small loch for fish. Bruce insisted that this was done at the lower end of their land, to ensure the purity of the water they would be using higher up. Alan co-opted the teenage boys to the task, Steven adapted the tractor for earthmoving and David taught the lads how to drive it. Calum was excited; 'Will we put the cages together again?' 'Yes, when we've made a big enough pond. If we're in time, we'll put the eggs in and they'll hatch out and make' – he was interrupted – 'alvins, flies, purrs, smellies and then salmon!' 'Well, you got the last one right.'

***

Henry had an idea for another trip into the city, and asked his mother. 'Let's find a piano for aunt Alexandra.' She replied, 'OK, but let's make the trip worthwhile in other ways, and safe.' He gathered the relevant people: David drove the Landrover, Alan navigated, and Bruce came in another car with a trailer. Katherine said, 'I'd like to see what's in the university chemistry department, perhaps someone was doing research on synthetic fuel.' Lucy came too; 'Almost certainly! I want to look at the hospital, maybe it will be fully staffed with no waiting lists.'

They made their way into the centre, using the Landrover to clear obstructions. Everything looked much the same, but Alan noticed some changes which indicated that people were still around. The scene was a shock those who hadn't already seen it; Katherine gasped, 'I suppose Glasgow will be the same?' The others knew what she was asking, and no-one dared to answer.

When they reached a piano shop, David said, 'we can't manage a grand; her ladyship must make do with an upright.' 'Alan muttered, 'Considering her comments about my flutes, she'll be lucky to have more than a keyboard.' Bruce found a set of tuning tools and an electronic aid; 'We'll have to keep her out of the way while we use these.'

Next stop was the laboratories, where Katherine collected books, apparatus and chemicals; 'I'm not sure what can be done with these, but Rhona will be pleased to hear that the labs are intact.' Finally they reached the hospital. Lucy raided the pharmacy and took basic medical gear – including obstetrical necessities – but despaired at the advanced equipment. 'Heaven knows when anyone will be able to operate the scanners here.'

***

On the second anniversary of Phraya, after dinner, Alexandra was asked to close her eyes and was led into another room. When allowed to open them she squealed, 'A piano, how heavenly, thank you so much!' With a flourish Henry produced a large pile of sheet music; as she looked through it her eyes welled up. She composed herself and played Claire de Lune, very slowly, and soon everyone else was in tears. To cover his confusion at being affected too, Steven teased her: 'Enough of that classical rubbish. Let's have some boogie woogie!' Margaret saw through this, and gave him a kiss.

David remarked, 'You know, I think we're entering a new phase. The challenges stretch ahead, but we must be reasonably confident to have wasted effort in such a way.' Rose corrected him: 'Spent it, dad, not wasted.' Henry asked, 'Where else should we invest our spare energy?' Lucy urged, 'It would be nice to have central heating,' and Deborah added, 'and underfloor heating in the bathrooms.' Steven cautioned that these weren't easy, but Alan was more ambitious: 'One of those machines that fells trees and chops them into logs.' 'That's even harder, but at least it would be useful.'

Alexandra scolded them: 'Not again! While we're enjoying the piano, we should at least remember needless luxuries, for example hairdressers, but without the compulsory chat.' Everyone spoke at once. Rory wanted to avoid the endless cooking: 'Restaurants, which accept payment in pre-Phraya money.' Ruth: 'Plants that you can't eat, like flowers.' Alice remarked, 'You would probably develop a craving.' Charles tried to raise their game: 'Stupidly fast sports cars.' Isabella got the idea: 'A heated indoor swimming pool, with a huge chute that goes outdoors and a wave making machine.' Katherine outdid them all: 'Airplanes writing lovers' names in the sky.'

***

The time for Ruth's labour was approaching. Lucy assembled the drugs and equipment from the hospital, and lectured Jessica on childbirth. Alice and the reluctant trailblazer were taught separately, and more optimistically. Alan's role was to arrange heating in an unused house, scrub it thoroughly and otherwise confine himself to a distant interest. The teenage girls awaited the coming drama with more anticipation than they would have in earlier times; the boys were indifferent; and the adults maintained a slightly strained confidence. Julia explained everything to the smaller children, but Alison was dubious as to the feasibility of the proposed method of delivery.

Julia confided to Jessica. 'I don't envy you, having to attend the labour.' 'Well, it's part of learning to be a doctor, I'm not nervous.' 'What about giving birth yourself sometime? Perhaps not so far away?' 'That's different, I hope I'll see a couple before I have to do it myself. What about you, if you're going to be with my brother you might have a baby yourself one day?' 'I can explain it to the little ones, but I'm scared! If Ruth manages OK you can tell me about it, but if it's hard I don't want to know.' 'I think you're going to find out in any case. The times when women went off to hospital, and emerged with a baby wrapped in a shawl, are gone.'

In the event, Ruth's labour was uncomplicated. It started in the evening and progressed smoothly through the night, with Alice and Jessica in attendance and Lucy resting nearby in case she was needed later. Sleepless but untroubled, Ruth gave birth to a healthy boy in the early hours of 10 May P2. She and Alice had chosen a name – Stewart Petrie Paterson – but they wanted to consult Alan. 'He's lovely, must have good genes. None of the names starts with a, and there are no l's at all.'

While the participants recovered, the rest of the team prepared a feast for the evening. During desert – Margaret had produced another surprise out of thin air – Deborah proposed a toast to her friend; 'Congratulations Ruth, the first of many for the team.' Katherine felt eyes on her. Henry read:

'I know a baby, such a baby, -
Round blue eyes and cheeks of pink,
Such an elbow furrowed with dimples,
Such a wrist where creases sink.
'Cuddle and love me, cuddle and love me,'
Crows the mouth of coral pink:
Oh, the bald head, and, oh, the sweet lips,
And, oh, the sleepy eyes that wink!'

***

David was worried: 'The crops aren't all growing correctly. I suspect some of the seed we gathered in Morrie came from hybrid plants or were cross-pollinated. At any rate they haven't grown true.' Katherine asked, 'I guess crossing is the most serious hazard? It will degrade the genetics of our plants?' 'Yes, we may have to cover plants to protect them, and hand-pollinate.' 'In the meantime, should we destroy undesirable plants?' 'Yes, otherwise we're wasting effort; we really must be more systematic about what we sow and harvest.' David and Deborah visited the other groups to warn them and compare notes. They agreed that it would be wise to swap seeds, young plants and future produce.

***

Alexandra decided it was time to try to persuade Andrew to move down from Morrie. She, Charles and Deborah went to visit him, and he reported that things were much the same: 'Everyone is still operating separately. What's it like down there? Charles replied, 'People are starting to work together, and it seems safe. Why don't you come?' Deborah disclosed that the team had taken a liberty: 'We've sown extra crops on some nearby land, to get you started, and will lend you the tractor if you like.' Andrew was persuaded, but preferred a staged approach: 'Some of us could come and make a start, while others stay put until the harvest. Then we can make a final decision and either move down completely, or retreat.' At the beginning of June the team helped him carry out the first stage of this plan.

***

Katherine was greatly encouraged by the safe delivery of Stewart; she spoke to Philip: 'Let's start trying for a baby. It might take a while, and if not we'll be following Lucy's advice to get on with it while I'm young.' 'I thought we had agreed that you would wait for the hospital to get going?' 'Yes, but everything went fine for Ruth, and we've got access to it if necessary.' 'No staff though, apart from Lucy and Jessica, but if you're game let's go for it.'

***

Steven, Deborah and Katherine went to see how Rhona was getting on with biodiesel. 'We've got rapeseed from Gregory, mostly dried out or half rotten from pre-Phraya crops, but we can get some oil out of it. The main problem at the moment is that the process uses a lot of wood.' Steven had been thinking about this since hearing Alan's fantasy at the piano party. 'We'll talk to Alastair about a logging machine. That may take some time, so in the meantime we'll cut you some timber by hand.'

On their return he urged Olivia to press-gang all the men, teenage to middle-aged, for a few days of wood-cutting. She found that this gave rise to some resistance, so she called a meeting. Deborah identified a potential difficulty: 'This team operates as a collective; we know each other, we all work hard, and share everything. Cutting timber for our own use is fine, and anyway it's the right time of the year to start stockpiling wood for winter heating. However, if we give some of it away, for biodiesel or any other purpose, we're relying on this cooperation working on a bigger scale. What if it doesn't yield any diesel, or not enough?'

Charles broke the silence. 'We shouldn't get into the kind of debate that once blighted politics, socialism versus capitalism and all that. At this stage we simply need to be sure that everyone is doing their bit. I suggest we agree with Rhona how much food corresponds to given amounts of rapeseed and wood in, and oil out. It's a bit trickier to decide the value of machinery for cutting wood, but a few days hacking with axes and saws might throw light on that.' Bruce volunteered, 'I'd like to try to calculate all those things, and then you could negotiate with the other groups?'

Chapter 12 Crimes

By the beginning of July the crops were doing well, and the earliest were ready for harvest. Early one morning Alice, taking the air as usual, saw strangers in the steading, picking crops and loading them into a van. She ran around rousing the men, and they emerged with the pumping adrenaline of suddenly broken sleep. In the chaos most of the invaders fled, but Alan and Rory managed to lay their hands on one of them. Others soon arrived and it was clear he was not going to escape. 'Let me go, damn you!' Rory thought otherwise; 'Not likely. Who are you and what are you doing here?' 'None of your business. They'll come and get me, you'll see, the westsi ...' He caught himself, but too late; Rory asked Alan, 'Is that one of the gangs you encountered?' 'Yes, the westsiders, I'm afraid; they were in charge during the fighting.'

When Olivia arrived, she had a quick word with Alan and addressed the captive calmly but ominously: 'Your name please?' 'I don't have to tell you anything.' 'Then I may have to ask the northers; I understand they don't appreciate rivals.' He looked terrified, and blurted, 'Glen Buchanan.' 'Thank you. I'm afraid we're going to have to restrain you while we decide what to do.' They tied his wrists behind his back, shackled his ankles and secured him to a chair.

Once it was clear that there was no immediate hazard, Olivia set Peter and Benjamin to watch for the return of gang members, asked Julia to entertain the children in the school, and invited Andrew over to take part in a discussion with the rest of the team. 'What are we going to do with Buchanan?' Alan wasn't well disposed; 'These are the people who trapped me for half the summer two years ago. I think we should make an example of this guy.' Deborah asked, 'Yes, but how exactly? If we hurt him, we'll start another war.' Rory pointed out, 'We can't confine him here indefinitely.' Margaret said, 'It's clear these people operate by stealing other people's food, and now they've found us. If we simply let him go that will encourage a return.'

Alexandra looked at Andrew enquiringly; he was sympathetic, but said, 'We're happy to take on peace-loving people, even if they're a bit crushed, but we haven't the capacity to handle criminals. There may have to be prisons eventually, but for now ...' He tailed off, and there was silence while everyone pondered the conundrum. Suddenly David had an idea: 'We have to release him, but not necessarily here. Let's take him by car somewhere far away, and drop him, with food, in the middle of nowhere. He'll walk back, with plenty of time to think, and warn the others.' No-one could improve on this, so it was done the next day. Alan arranged a lookout rota.

For days there was an undercurrent of uncertainty while everyone digested the consequences of the gang's invasion and the team's response to it. People were fearful, determination grew, doubts crystallised, everyone was confused. Alexandra unburdened herself to her diary, "I wonder whether we've made a mistake? We can see here both the human predisposition to cooperation, and the propensity for conflict. Should we retreat to Morrie? Most of us think we must stay the course in order to ensure that collaboration proves more important than competition."

***

Gregory had mentioned a group who were growing cereals. Charles went to visit their leader Peggy Fraser, and tried a specific instance of his usual pitch for teamwork: 'Perhaps you could grow sugar beet? People crave something sweet, and will barter for it.' David had come along to ensure that what he proposed was reasonable horticulturally. 'I know it hasn't been grown in Scotland for some decades, but it used to thrive here.' Peggy was open to the idea, but asked, 'Where would we find some roots to get started?' 'Even up here it was used as cattle feed before Phraya, so you may find some, or it will arrive from England eventually. Alternatively, we may find some of the seeds that used to be sold to enthusiasts for home growing.' Charles expanded: 'Failing that, people may value your wheat – we all miss bread – or barley – we hanker after beer too – or even oats – I suppose a few Scots might want porridge.'

***

On Alison's ninth birthday, 15 Aug P2, Lucy wanted to prompt her memory. 'You know how we used to go on the ferry from our island to the mainland?' Rory warned her: 'Is this wise?' It was too late, Alison was interested. 'It took a long time, so we always had a picnic on the boat.' 'That's right, and when we landed, we would go and see grandma and grandpa.' 'Yes, we got parma violets; the sides were hollow so you could poke your tongue into them.' Lucy was pleased; 'You see, she does remember.' Rory looked relieved. 'Perhaps leave it at that?'

That evening Lucy remarked, 'Ali is at the watershed between older children, who retain something of the world before Phraya, and younger ones and the unborn, who must be taught about it.' Ruth asked, 'What should we tell Stewart of the past, when he's older?' Bruce replied, 'We must transfer as much technology as possible, that's what matters most.' 'That's very narrow, what else?' Henry admitted, 'Maybe all human affairs came to an end with Phraya, and will start afresh, so there's no point teaching history?' Alexandra disputed this;

'Despite the hiatus, it will remain crucial if we're to avoid an eventual repetition of the disaster.' Katherine remarked, 'It's actually technology that's under threat; most advanced science will have to be re-discovered completely, following a different path.' Ruth persisted: 'So, what of our knowledge might be useful to the unborn?' Deborah suggested, 'Just about every aspect of human culture will be changed by Phraya. We can't tell the kids nothing, so we must cover it all?'

***

Alice had heard that a new group had just arrived from the far north, bringing chickens. Bruce insisted on coming with her to meet them. 'Are you sure they haven't been exposed to the Phraya virus – it came from chickens in the first place.' Raymond Barber was confident. 'Yes, we're aware of that. Both we and they were protected during the disturbance, and have been healthy throughout.' Alice tried to avert the looming inquisition. 'It's wonderful that you've been able to keep them going. Do you think there's a prospect of any other animals?' 'We saw cows gone wild on the way down, and have plans to bring them here if we can arrange transport.' 'We might be able to help with that. I suppose pigs would be too much to ask?' 'That depends on finding someone who kept them hidden during the troubles, and has managed to feed them as well as themselves since then.'

***

Lucy was aware that a group of doctors was in the area; she went to meet them, introduced herself and gave a summary of the local situation. 'Gordon Lyle, radiologist from Glasgow, nice to meet a doctor who can still practice her skills to some degree.' 'I'm sure you'll be able to make yourself useful as soon as things improve. Is the situation bad over there?' 'It's much worse than Edinburgh; the bigger population produced more conflict; the chaos persists and there's little cooperation so far. It's too dangerous to try to get the hospital going.' 'Ours is undamaged, and full of equipment for you to operate. Perhaps you should consider moving here for the moment?' 'I'll report back, and then we may do so.'

Katherine was thrown into turmoil by the news. 'When Gordon goes back, he could look for my parents.' Philip tried to dissuade her; 'You know the overall situation, and you saw what happened when Rory tried to find Lucy's parents.' 'They couldn't leave Caladion because they were so ill with the virus, and but my folks might not have caught it.' 'Gordon has told us how bad Glasgow was; perhaps they couldn't escape, maybe they did, but they certainly didn't make it to Achar and then on to Morrie. Do you really want to find out exactly what happened?' She was adamant. Philip had a sinking feeling, but gave in. 'OK, but you're not going to meet him.'

Philip knew it wasn't reasonable to ask Lucy to make the request, so he spoke to Gordon himself: 'My girlfriend made contact with her parents as the crisis developed, and they said they would leave Glasgow if it worsened. Here's their address – could you look them up?' 'That's on the outskirts; we can probably get there, but we may find something dreadful.' 'I know, I tried to tell her.'

***

By the beginning of September Andrew's group was fully established in Edinburgh, having gathered crops in Morrie and completed the move. Olivia's team was enjoying a good harvest, despite one or two misfires on the seeds, and was cooperating well with other groups. Most people were satisfied with the exchange of their previous peace, and stasis, for a more challenging but progressive life.

***

Throughout the summer Alan had insisted on maintaining a guard against further raids, but as the weeks had passed it had grown more lax. In the afternoon of 20 September P2 Alice was at the bottom of the steading, on duty, but paying more attention to the fish than the outlook. Suddenly she was aware of a man standing close by, but she wasn't alarmed. 'Hello, can I help you?' 'I think you can, if you're in the mood, my dear.' 'I'm not sure what you mean.' 'You're a pretty lady, I'm sure you do.' Now she was alert. 'Oh! I don't know you, perhaps you're thinking of someone else?' 'No, you'll do, and I think you'll enjoy it too.' Alice looked around but no-one was in sight. 'Don't think of running away, just when we're getting to know each other.' He smiled lasciviously.

Alice was thoroughly frightened, and was finding it hard to think straight. As he looked at her with obvious intent, she retreated into a dreamlike state, and heard herself make an absurd appeal: 'I'm sorry, but I prefer ladies. Nothing against you, I'm sure some girls would be pleased to go with you. Very kind of you to suggest …' 'Oh don't worry, everyone has an exciting time with me. This will change your mind.' 'I don't think so. I've never … I don't think I can …' He stepped up to her and gripped her arm tightly. She struggled to wake from the nightmare, tried to scream but nothing came out. She managed to hiss, 'Please!' 'Just relax, lie down, keep quiet and you'll be fine.' She fought but he was stronger. 'Please, no.' 'I won't hurt you if you're a good girl.'

When it was over, she was suddenly back in the waking world, and found a piece of cunning. 'You were right, that was lovely. My name is Alice Petrie, perhaps we'll meet again? Sorry, I've forgotten your name.' 'Liam Brodie, at your service.' She sighed at this small victory, fell into passivity and waited for him to leave. When he was out of sight, the tears came.

By supper time Alice was missed and Ruth, busy feeding Stewart, asked Alan to go and look for her. He found her wandering distractedly; she muttered a man's name. 'Alice, what's wrong?' She unburdened herself: 'Remember that name,' – then clammed up – 'and just take me to Ruth, please.' He guessed, and said helplessly, 'Yes, she'll be able to help.' He held out a hand, but she couldn't take it. He led her away, arm outstretched to maintain the offer of contact, and she slowly followed him up the hill. Ruth saw them coming and, somehow, by the time they were close she knew too. She handed Stewart over and the two women disappeared for the night.

Alan sought out Olivia, and was grateful to find her alone. Once he had managed to convey what he thought had happened, he could say only, 'I will kill him, I've got the name, I'll find and kill him.' 'You will stay here and help your sister, your son and his mother. Forget everything else.' She called Lucy and sent her in to attend to Alice.

***

There was no announcement, but by the following morning everyone had heard. Deborah was the first to visit Alice and Ruth. 'I'm so sorry, everyone is thinking of you. The only thing I can offer is to promise that if you want to go back to Morrie, David and I will go with you, whatever anyone else says. We could make a living on the smallholding.' 'I thought of that in the night, but I've already decided that I won't let what happened to me drive us backwards.' 'I agree, our son was born here and he's going to grow up in a peaceful capital.' 'OK, your decision, that's very brave. We won't subject you to a stream of visitors, but can you bear to see Alan? He's really upset, it might do you both good?' Alice managed a smile; 'That would be helpful, send him in.'

Although Olivia refused to hold a meeting, small discussions arose spontaneously. Margaret suggested to Steven: 'I suspect Alan will find comforting Alice insufficiently active after a while. Perhaps you could identify something technical for him to get his teeth into?' 'Any ideas?' 'If you and he can devise a really luxurious hot shower, you'll both earn the undying gratitude of everyone here, especially any women who are feeling sullied.' 'OK. Anything else?' 'Yes, stop him rushing off in pursuit of the culprit.'

Alexandra tried to express her feelings to Bruce. 'This threatens the rapport we've built with others in the area.' 'Yes, and I doubt it will help Charles's economic cooperation.' 'No, I mean the sense of community, of working together to re-build a civilised society.' 'That's what I'm talking about, people are only going to direct their efforts towards goods for barter if they believe others will give up something immediately useful, like food, in exchange.' 'This is a dialogue of the deaf, I care about confidence in others, for its own sake.' 'Sorry, we really are talking about the same thing. We used to trust strangers, but in the limited sense that we expected them not to harm us. Money was a means of extending that conviction to produce cooperation on larger scale. It's not as if we used to commune with the people in China who made the things we needed. Barter could play the same role now.' 'Rather an unlovely attitude. Couldn't we focus on the fact that the other groups round here were starting to become friends? That's going to be under threat if we fear that some of them may steal our food, or kill us.'

Alexandra gave up and went to tell Andrew, in confidence, what had happened. 'Any words of wisdom?' He replied, 'Perhaps we should think of offenders like Brodie as mentally ill? He might have been a fine person before Phraya. We don't know what he has experienced in the past couple of years, but it probably damaged him.' 'If so, shouldn't we try to treat such people?' 'Yes, sadly we may need mental hospitals, as well as prisons for those who are merely criminal.' 'Do you think you can help those who are unwell spiritually?' 'Perhaps when we're more fully settled we can try, but there's a danger that our efforts could be disrupted, either by gangsters or by broken people, more deserving of our sympathy, who nevertheless misbehave.'

Charles went to visit other groups and, without revealing the specifics, tried to discover whether they had suffered similar depredations. He dropped Brodie's name and discovered that he was a westsider who was sometimes seen raiding on his own, but no-one reported more serious misdeeds. He left it at that, and reverted to his normal conversation about what the groups were doing for each other, and how they were to be rewarded.

***

Alice, though still reeling, was determined that there should be a celebration for William's eleventh birthday on the 28th. She sent Bruce to see Raymond. 'You must apologise for quizzing him about whether his chickens harbour Phraya, and beg him to let us have some eggs.' 'Heavens knows what he'll want in exchange for them.' 'You could talk to David about what he can spare from the harvest. Pay what you have to; we'll try for a better price later.' When his day came, William took breakfast orders from twenty-five ecstatic survivors of Phraya. 'That's six soft-boiled, eight hard, five poached, three fried and three scrambled.' Julia stuck to her principles, but it was tough.

All the children understood, in their different ways, that something bad had happened; but William, particularly, stood on the threshold of comprehension. After receiving evasive answers from various people, he confronted his mother. 'Just explain, please.' Deborah drew breath. 'Well, you know how babies are made, and normally it's a pleasure shared between a woman and her husband. In Alice's case, she prefers other ladies and that's why she's with Ruth. The man from the westsiders forced Alice to make love, which is rape, a terrible crime comparable to murder. Perhaps it's even worse for a gay woman, I'm not sure, but she is being incredibly brave. It has upset everyone, and it's a threat to the peace.'

***

Alice went to see Lucy. 'I feel strange, different, but perhaps that isn't surprising?' 'When's your period?' 'It should be in a few days' time.' 'Well, I'm afraid it's possible that you're pregnant. The tests aren't sensitive enough for the earliest stages, but we can try it when you're slightly overdue. If it's negative, we won't be sure of anything, but in the unfortunate event that it's positive, we'll have to believe it.'

A week later Alice returned, in tears, and asked for a test. Ruth held her hand as she prepared for the longest two minutes of her life. She couldn't watch, but soon Ruth said, 'Oh, I think there's a line,' – Alice stiffened – 'I'm sorry.' Lucy said gently, 'It's up to you, everyone is different, and the circumstances are unusual in so many ways, but I am guessing you don't want this baby?' 'No, no, can you make it go away?' 'Yes, but it will be more risky than normal as I can't deal with infections as well as I'd like. On the other hand, it's very early and that makes it easier; we can start with a pill.'

***

The team tried to pursue normal life. The school was now operated differently: Alison, Calum, William, Rose and Isabella attended full time; and Lucy and Julia provided childcare for Stewart in the classroom. Peter, Benjamin and Jessica received part time cultural education from Alexandra; and vocational training as part of their work. Samuel hovered uncomfortably between the two groups, not properly educated in any of these ways.

The P2 harvest was on such a scale that it was impossible to preserve all the food immediately. A large number of freezers had been assembled for temporary storage, but the corresponding generators used fuel so rapidly that it was essential to process the food as quickly as possible. Bruce and his assistants had expanded and improved their repertoire of techniques to the point where food promised to be plentiful and varied even in the winter.

***

By 12 October it was clear that Alice was still pregnant, and Lucy was forced to intervene surgically. The procedure was successful, and antibiotics were administered, but within days infection set in and an emergency was under way. Once again the team was on tenterhooks, but this felt different; when Samuel had broken his arm it had been viewed as an accident, even if Peter was hauled over the coals for failing to look after him. Now there was an external culprit. Although the immediate cause was Lucy's termination of the pregnancy, the thought that she could have done better did not even arise; nor was Phraya blamed for the inadequacy of post medicine. Instead feeling swelled against Brodie and the westsiders. Olivia watched Alan carefully, and a daring idea formed in her mind.

Chapter 13 Rehabilitation

Alice slowly recovered; relief soon mutated into anger, and a clamour arose for action. Eventually Alan demanded a meeting. 'I said I would kill Brodie, but I was persuaded to help Alice instead, and was glad to do it. Now that she's OK, all we've got out of this is a better shower. Well, that's not enough to wash away the crime. Why shouldn't I go back to my first instinct?' Philip asked, 'Do we think killing him will do a good job of sorting out this mess?' Rory responded, 'I suppose it might shock the westsiders into behaving better?' Katherine disagreed: 'Or it might produce open warfare once again.'

Olivia allowed the debate to sway backwards and forwards, and then declared: 'I've got an idea, and would like you to hear me out before you shoot it down. The westsiders have endured as much violence at the hands of the northers as they've inflicted. I think we need to treat them as people who turned – under a duress at which we can only guess – to the dark side, but can be redeemed. Some of them may be ashamed of their way of life. It looks like they've lost their coherence; indeed, some have left.'

She paused and looked around as if daring anyone to speak before she had finished. 'Here's my idea. I think we can convert these people into a force for good. If we offer them food, in exchange for work rather than the use of force, they may regard that as an easier way to make a living. They could do public works, under our control, and be a kind of police force or army.' One or two people gasped audibly. 'They could start by coercing the northers to switch to constructive behaviour. They … but thanks for listening; now you can tear this to shreds.'

Deborah opened, 'Interesting, but how are you proposing even to suggest this transformation? Just walk up to them, and be laughed at?' She dropped her voice to a whisper: 'Or raped.' Rory suggested, 'A few of us men could come too, for protection.' Lucy countered, 'Or we could do the exact opposite, just women so they don't feel threatened. I don't think they would attack us.' 'I had been thinking of going alone. Perhaps two or three women?'

Katherine changed the subject: 'Assuming nothing bad happens, there's still the question of whether they'd take the idea seriously.' Alexandra was optimistic; 'I think it might just work. Andrew's theory is that they're just damaged souls.' Steven suggested mischievously, 'You could always threaten them with Alan's vengeance, even if we don't mean it.' Margaret preferred a subtler approach: 'No need to make the threat, it can just hang in the air unspoken?' Henry proposed a compromise: 'If they don't accept a full transformation immediately, we can offer them some food without the need to fight for it – give them something useful to do and try to bring them round gradually.'

Alan had remained quiet since he introduced the debate. 'I'm willing to go with this, on condition that Brodie isn't part of it. He must go far away.' All eyes turned to Alice. 'Yes, let's try it.' Olivia closed the meeting; 'Alright, I'll go tomorrow with Lucy, and the men can watch from a distant hiding place.'

***

The ladies were calm, fatalistic but determined. 'Can I meet your leader please?' After a few moments a man emerged; he was small but authoritative. 'Gavin Baird. What do you want?' 'I'm Olivia Lenton, the leader of the group which runs the steading on the hill. We caught Glen Buchanan after your unexpected visit. I hope he made it back?' 'He did, and he was pissed off. You're brave, turning up here, I'll give you that.' 'The raid is water under the bridge. The reason we're here now is because Liam Brodie raped one of us. Your man, I think,' – he nodded – 'and I guess you didn't know he'd done this?' 'No, and he didn't have my authority. We're looking for food.'

'I'm Lucy Scott, a doctor. You also won't know that the victim fell pregnant. I performed an abortion, she got an infection and nearly died.' 'I'll have words with Liam. As I said, we just want food, and we only get rough if people don't give it to us.' 'Well, people are more likely to share their food if you treat them well.' 'I'm thinking you weren't around here when it got nasty. You got food any way you could, or starved.'

Olivia saw an opportunity. 'You're right, we were out of the way during the crisis. I'm sure it was hell here, but things are changing now. People like us are growing food and trying to cooperate with others. We've got a proposal. We'd like to work with you.' 'You must be joking! Why would we do that?' 'We're willing to give your people food, in exchange for them working at things that need doing, like farming, fixing cars, maintaining roads … and maybe keeping the peace.' Baird was quiet for a moment.

Lucy tried another angle. 'We know you've been fighting the northers for years. I guess they've killed quite a few of you? Some of your people have got sick of it all, and have left. We'd like to make a deal with both groups, and then we can all stop fighting and grow food instead.'

Before he could object, Olivia drew the meeting to a close. 'Why don't you think about it? In the meantime, here are some eggs.' 'Christ, where did you get those?' 'We bartered for them, never mind where. If you steer clear of us, we'll keep the victim's brother away from you. We can talk another time?' The ladies walked away.

***

Charles had arranged a further meeting with the other groups involved in the production and use of biodiesel. They started at the rapeseed farm, and Gregory reported the harvest: 'It has grown true, and we've got a good crop.' 'How are you getting on with Steven's device for extracting the oil?' 'It works, though I suspect more could be squeezed out by using steam rather than merely pre-heating the seeds.' 'I daresay the engineers can make that advance eventually.'

They moved on to Rhona's laboratory. She demonstrated various refinements of the process. 'Of course the oil is a sine qua non, but the real challenge is the timber.' Alastair said, 'We're working to mechanise the felling of trees and cutting them up.' She continued, 'Once we've got fine chippings, it's relatively easy to make the alkali. However, it's a waste burning wood in the summer, as we can't make use of all of the heat. We need to store the ash from winter heating.' Charles asked, 'All well with the methanol?' 'No problem, and we do take advantage of some of the heat from the first process in the second.' 'Then you simply mix the three ingredients,' – he waved his hands magically and she finished his sentence – 'and you have biodiesel. As a by-product you also get glycerol, which is sweet and edible if you can purify it.'

They finished with Alastair's report on the damage caused to engines by running them on biodiesel. 'Various parts suffer, such as seals, rubber pipes and fuel filters, but for the time being they can be replaced by raiding other vehicles. Eventually we'll solve the materials compatibility problems. The other significant challenge is starting in cold weather; while we've got some petroleum-based diesel we can use it to get engines going. Later we'll have to devise fuel heaters.' Charles ended the meeting by remarking, 'It's nice to be cooperating instead of worrying about the westsiders, even if just for an afternoon. Olivia is working on them, by the way.'

***

On 19 November P2 Rose entered her teens. She had intended to play down any rite of passage, in view of Samuel's misfortune. However, on that day Katherine discovered that she was pregnant; within ten minutes the whole team knew, and spontaneous celebration broke out on both counts. Alice was delighted, 'How lovely, another baby who's wanted.' Alexandra looked at her books and announced, 'Pray silence for Rose, just entering womanhood, who is going to read a tricky poem.'

'Germ of new life, whose powers expanding slow
For many a moon their full perfection wait, –
Haste, precious pledge of happy love, to go
Auspicious born through life's mysterious gate.'

Katherine smiled; Rose blushed and continued to the end:

'Haste, little captive, burst thy prison doors!
Launch on the living world, and spring to light!
Nature for thee displays her various stores,
Opens her thousand inlets of delight
If charmed verse or muttered prayers had power,
With favouring spells to speed thee on thy way,
Anxious I'd bid my beads each passing hour,
Till thy wished smile thy mother's pangs o'erpay.'

***

The engineers had suffered another raid, and had fought back; Alastair told Olivia he was dubious about her scheme for the transformation of the westsiders. She went to meet Baird again, taking Andrew this time. 'I hope you enjoyed the eggs, Gavin. Have you had a chance to think about what we said?' 'I'm impressed that you've got plenty of food, but we can do what we like, we could just come and take it.' 'But you meet resistance when you do that. Wouldn't it be easier – and safer – to get food by working for it, instead of fighting?'

Baird hesitated, so Andrew tried his luck. 'I'm sure most of your people had ordinary lifestyles before Phraya. You led them through dreadful times, doing what was essential for survival in the city. Now you've got a chance to bring them back to normality. You don't have to give up your authority, and you can always revert to the way you live now. All I'm suggesting is that you might do some of the jobs suggested by Olivia, for everyone's good, and eat the food she gives you in return.'

'What about the northers? They fight us and everyone else.' Olivia had a ready answer. 'Until they change their ways, you can continue your battle with them – just leave everyone else in peace. I intend to talk to them too, and will offer them the same deal, along with the possibility of ending the conflict with you – if that's acceptable.' 'OK, I'll talk to my people. We'll come to your steading and see what we can do.' 'Just a few of you please, and not Brodie, he remains a problem that we'll have to deal with later.' Andrew surprised them both: 'If you come to my farm instead, and do some useful work, I may be able to help him.'

On the way back, Olivia asked Andrew, 'What did you mean about Brodie? It will be a triumph if we can get the westsiders to work on your farm, but surely he can't remain so near to Alice? Think what Alan might do.' 'I realise that. I haven't mentioned this yet, but we hedged our bets and left some of our people in Morrie. I was always planning to try to help people there, even if we don't return en masse. It's so peaceful that I was thinking of establishing a sanatorium. My thought is that Brodie could go for treatment.' 'What if he commits similar atrocities there?' 'The same applies wherever he goes, and I'd rather keep an eye on him. I hope he can be rehabilitated.'

First Olivia spoke to Alice, alone. 'You mean Brodie is going to be as close as Andrew's place?' 'Only briefly; he'll never be on his own – Gavin says he'll stay with him at all times – and you'll not meet him. At the moment he's on the loose, so this is an improvement, and soon he'll be far away.' Alan joined them and listened quietly to the proposed plan. 'What do you think, Alice?' 'I think it's as good as can be achieved.' 'Yes, I suppose we should be grateful to Andrew.'

Brodie was taken away. Winter came and there was enough food for everyone; Gavin began to believe and ensured that the remaining westsiders kept to the bargain. Olivia and Deborah visited the northers and started the process of talking them round. No-one quite had the heart to observe Christmas or New Year.

***

17 January P3 was Calum's seventh birthday. Rory showed him salmon eggs; 'I remember when you showed me them on my last birthday. Are these different ones?' 'Yes, I got some more from a river, quite far away, on the border with England.' 'What's England?' 'It probably doesn't matter any more, but it used to be another part of this country.' 'What's a country?' He sighed, and Lucy changed the subject: 'What other kind of eggs have you seen?' 'Chicken ones! Which came first, the egg or … no, the chi …' Alison explained the joke to her brother.

***

In the early spring, almost three years after Phraya had shattered communications, the first pioneers came from London. Olivia asked their leader, 'Is there a government down south?' 'I don't think so, unless there's a bunker somewhere with the prime minister still eating tins of beans. If so, he can't communicate.' 'What happened?' He drew breath. 'When the flights were stopped, things collapsed rapidly. Soon afterwards the underground stopped working, the entire city snarled up with cars, lorries couldn't deliver enough food, the shops emptied and it was chaos.' Alan asked, 'I was in Edinburgh, and it was awful. I had stockpiled food, and hid for two months. How did you survive?' 'We stayed in our workplace, where no-one came looking for food. We had to go out and fight for it; the less said the better.'

Deborah asked, 'What about the last three years?' 'After the mayhem, we escaped to farmland in a quiet part of the coast northeast of London. We grew vegetables and got good at fishing.' 'So why have you come up north?' 'Despite the enormous number of deaths, there were many survivors. They moved around the countryside, and recently reached our little sanctuary.' Henry was puzzled. 'Isn't it good to be near the old capital?' 'It's still too chaotic. Seemingly the bigger the city, the worse the fighting, and the longer before it stopped. We wanted to have space.'

Charles was interested in the interactions among survivors: 'Once the worst of the conflict was over, did people cooperate?' 'Groups stayed apart for a long time, and have only just started to work together.' Steven asked, 'What about getting technology and industry started?' Some people were trying, but a lot of the resources were around the city, where there was too much trouble, or the memory of it, to allow the necessary trust to develop.' 'What about other cities, in the industrial heart of the country?' 'We bypassed them on our way up, but as far as we could tell from those we met, the situation is much the same wherever there was a large population.'

***

Olivia and Gavin went to meet Richie Carr, the leader of the northers. 'I hear you've gone soft. Is this the new boss?' 'I'm still in charge of my people, but I'm thinking of changing the way we do things. Yeah, we're working with Olivia; her lot grows more food than you can get from raids, they're working with the engineers, fixing tractors, making fuel, they've got a doctor too. I've decided the old way has had its time.' 'We heard about Brodie. What happens when she decides to send more of your people away? Are you just going to do what you're told?'

Olivia joined in; 'I suspect you know what he did to one of our women – but never mind that, perhaps you'd like to consider how Gavin has changed? He has offered to help keep the peace around here. If you would cut some timber you might find you can exchange it for food, without anyone getting hurt. Alternatively, you can carry on stealing food and see what Gavin's people do about it.' It was obvious Carr was listening, but she took care not to press him too quickly.

***

Gordon Lyle brought his doctors over, and told Lucy, 'It's not yet possible to start up the hospital in Glasgow. We may try later, but first we'll set up in yours.' 'Great! It's becoming more peaceful here, and we can help you with food in the early stages.' 'That's helpful, thanks.' 'I hardly dare ask, did you manage to visit Katherine's parents' house?' He hesitated, and responded delicately. 'Yes, we did. Philip told me what happened when you traced your parents, and unfortunately the news is no better for Katherine. Could you give her this note from her sister?'

"Katherine, I'm sorry, I have terrible things to tell you. Mum and dad promised you that we'd get out of Glasgow if things got really bad. We were planning our escape, but they caught the bug and were too ill to travel. They recovered, but by then the city was so chaotic we didn't dare to venture out. We began to starve, and I'm afraid I had to offer myself to gangsters in exchange for food. At one point we made a run for it, but we were spotted by the same men and stopped. Dad tried to fight, and he and mum were killed. They kept me captive, but I escaped eventually. I've come back – briefly, to leave this in the house – and I'm about to set off to see if I can find you. All my love, Jocelyn."

There was no meeting, but everyone in the team finally accepted that there was nothing to be gained by further investigations of the fates of loved ones.

***

By the time Isabella became a teenager on 16 March, she had changed her mind about her parents' gifts of the previous year. 'There was an old lady, too numb to post world delights to succumb. To chemistry blind, for music she pined. How useless the pre world, dear mum.' Alexandra responded with a prediction, confined to her diary: "There was a young girl of thirteen, who vented her anger and spleen, at first on her pa, then skewered her ma. By twenty on both she'll be keen."

Isabella carried her agitation into the classroom. 'I don't see the point of learning about other countries. Airplanes won't fly in my lifetime, so we can't hope to visit faraway places. We don't even know if anyone survived.' He mother argued, 'We've already had visitors from Glasgow, the north of Scotland and London. The situation sounds the same everywhere. People will have crossed the channel to and from France, and will be moving all over Europe. We need to know their languages and culture.' 'I'd rather do something useful right now. Dad says we've got to make fertiliser, and lots of other chemicals, without relying on minerals and oil dug from underground.'

***

Olivia continued to work with the westsiders, and to talk to the northers. Charles suggested to other groups that they should trust the former as police and providers of emergency services; and argued that the latter would end up working on public utilities. In due course they managed to persuade the leaders to meet, alone, for the first time. Gavin started: 'We've definitely decided to change to Olivia's way. If you don't, you'll be on your own. We and the other groups will make best of it. It would be great if you joined us.' Richie replied, 'OK, I'm willing to try this. We'll cut wood and see if we get enough to eat. It may not be easy for our people to work together, so we better keep apart for a while.' 'If we reach agreement now, and control our people, it might work out.' After further discussion the two men ventured a handshake; to their surprise it turned into an embrace, and they parted in embarrassed silence.

Chapter 14 Emergence

The children were growing up. Calum, Alison and even William belonged entirely to the post era, and were interested only in the developments around them. They listened to explanations of the past but treated them like Greek myths. Factories, shops, televisions and the internet were tantamount to Roman ruins. Rose and Isabella were poised between pre and post, feeling the adults' pain at the lost world. Half-remembering how things had worked, they were mystified by the juxtaposition of old but advanced technology – generators and electricity – with the new but primitive – fuel from wood and rape. Samuel, though definitely a teenager, remained separated from the other boys by his lack of a girlfriend; Isabella wasn't a fit for him. He found companionship with Alan, in a similar boat despite a kind of fatherhood, and they worked together on the timber-based economy. Peter and Benjamin, now firmly in the adult world, were learning engineering from Steven and increasingly by working with Alastair. Jessica was being trained by Lucy and occasionally by Gordon at the hospital; and Julia was working with Lucy in her other capacity as a teacher. Philip and Katherine had always been in the adult camp; Henry, who had been at the threshold at the time of Phraya, wasn't sure of his role.

***

Lucy had a private conversation with Rory. 'I've been thinking about our family planning. I don't think we want another baby?' 'All being well, probably not, but what if something happens to Ali or Calum?' 'You may be surprised, but that's unlikely. Although medical care is much compromised, childhood diseases aren't going to re-appear until population density builds up, and routine travel resumes, which will take decades, maybe much more.' 'But what if one of them has an accident?' 'It could happen, but unless it's soon I wouldn't want to undertake a pregnancy even in such a scenario.' 'It's hard to imagine what we'd think. I'd certainly feel even worse if you tried and it ended in disaster.' 'So we've finished making babies?' He nodded.

She paused, and he began to realise where she was heading. 'You want to give me the snip, don't you?' 'It's the easiest operation that I'm likely to be called on to perform. Contraceptives are going to become completely ineffective, or actually dangerous, and relatively young men are going to have vasectomies, in order to protect their women from much worse hazards. What better way to demonstrate that it's safe than for the doctor to do it to her husband?' She left it at that, and in a day or two Rory realised he had no choice. It was done within a week, and Rory informed all the men that it was not to be feared.

***

At the third anniversary of Phraya, Peter nervously approached Jessica's parents. 'I don't know how these things will work post, but do you think people will still get married?' Bruce failed to put him at his ease. 'I presume you are referring to Alexandra's elder daughter?' 'Yes sir, I would be pleased to have your … er … her permission … and your blessing.' She put him out of his misery: 'We would be delighted, and I know that your parents are pleased too.' 'Thank you! Philip and Katherine didn't marry, but we would like to do so, if there's a way.' 'I think their moment passed during the aftermath of the crisis, but we should re-establish these important rituals. We can check with Olivia where she thinks the law stands, if anywhere, and if she gives the go-ahead I would be happy to conduct a ceremony.'

***

Bruce and Katherine were planning to visit Rhona to discuss what chemistry was feasible. Isabella begged to be allowed to come too, and Alexandra gave in; 'I suppose it's safe enough these days.' They were given a rundown on what could be done in the short term: 'From wood we're already making alkali and methanol for processing rapeseed oil; charcoal for use in high temperature fires; and some pitch and tar for repairing roads. The wood also yields gas; it's rather dangerous so we just burn it, but we might use it eventually.'

Bruce asked, ''Great, what can we do next?' 'If we are willing to dismantle buildings for raw materials, we can select those made of limestone. If we grind it up, it's already useful for treating acidic soil. Alternatively, we can bake it and react the resulting quicklime with water to produce the slaked version.' 'What lovely old-fashioned names. I suppose they reflect past roles?' 'Yes, the wet form is suitable for purifying water, and for making mortar. Later, we can heat the dry material with charcoal to make calcium carbide, from which we can produce acetylene gas. Then if we make oxygen by electrolysing water, we'll have an oxyacetylene torch, which will please the engineers.'

'None of that sounds easy, but we can make a start on it. What's important but completely out of reach at the moment?' 'Good question. We'd like to make ammonia, which could be converted to nitric acid and other things, including fertiliser. Unfortunately, without mining or industrial chemistry, the only sources are urine for ammonia, and dung for nitrates, both in tiny amounts.' Katherine asked, 'As you can see, I will soon be in labour; what about nitrous oxide?' 'Easy once you've got the other nitrogen compounds, hard otherwise.' 'OK, this is all basic chemistry, what about biochemistry?' 'Forget it for a few decades.' Isabella piped up, 'Don't worry, I'll do it when I'm grown up.' 'Great, you can teach my baby when he's old enough for school, to make sure our knowledge endures.'

***

On Saturday 24 June P3 the team gathered for Peter and Jessica's wedding. Alexandra started, 'We have come together to celebrate the union of two families, one capable and useful, and the other ... well, Bruce and I offer our beloved Jessica, who has helped bring new life into the world and may do so herself. I cannot better the advice given by Jane Wells to her daughter in 1886:'

'Let your love be stronger than your hate or anger.
Learn the wisdom of compromise, for it is better to bend a little than to break.
Believe the best rather than the worst.
People have a way of living up or down to your opinion of them.
Remember that true friendship is the basis for any lasting relationship.
The person you choose to marry is deserving of the courtesies and kindness you bestow on your friends.
Please hand this down to your children and your children's children.'

After a brief ceremony she declared the couple to be man and wife, and the dancing began. David sang to Katherine's clarinet: 'L is for the way you look at me, O is ...' and ended, 'Love was made for me and you.' Everyone watched entranced as Stewart toddled up to the bride and clung to her dress.

***

Philip had found a group of electronics people, and went to visit. Keith Johnston did not spare him: 'You might have to face the fact that your career is cut short before it even starts.' 'Surely there is a huge supply of components left over from before Phraya?' 'Yes, but they will wear out, and the prospect of making new ones is extremely distant. Certainly, integrated circuits are unattainable. The next smartphone is three hundred years away.'

Philip understood this but persisted. 'Perhaps so, but we can work on immediately useful things like radio communication, which was first achieved before modern circuitry. It would be a big improvement on driving cars along deteriorating roads. Telephones? Texting, reinvented?' 'Sorry, I didn't mean to say there's nothing to be done – just that the industry will be completely transformed. We've found the house of a radio ham, presumed dead, and we're broadcasting to see if anyone answers eventually.' 'My uncle will be interested in what you think can be done. He's a mathematician, and he's trying to model how technology can be restarted, what are the bottlenecks, how we can circumvent them – he argues that we don't have to re-tread the historical development path.'

***

Summer came and, with it, Katherine's time. She had decided to give birth at the steading rather than in the hospital. 'It sounds like a ghost town, despite Gordon's efforts. I'd rather be here with the team.' It was a long and difficult labour, but fortunately Lucy had gas and air. Jessica was amazed to see a labouring woman sleep between contractions, wake to howl for a minute and then snooze again. At the end, however, things were less relaxed. Lucy had to resort to forceps, which she had seen used only once during her training. She asked Philip to leave, and Katherine was too far gone to object. Jessica was alarmed to realise that even a woman of twenty-three could struggle. However, all was well in the end; late on 9 July P3 a little girl announced her health by cries loud enough to alert everyone. When Philip returned, Katherine told him, 'I'd like to call her Jocelyn, after my sister, if that's alright with you.' 'She would have been honoured, and lives on in more than one way.'

***

Raymond borrowed the group's van, and another vehicle with a trailer, and made a trip north. A few days later he reported a triumph: he had managed to capture a few feral cows, their calves and, crucially, a young bull. 'There will be no beef for a couple of years, because clearly we're not going to kill them any time soon. We hope to get milk, either from these cows or from their daughters, and we may get meat from their sons in due course.' William rehearsed what he could remember of milk: 'We can use it to make cream, cheese, butter, ice cream – and yoghurt, but that's yukky and a waste of milk.'

***

With Brodie gone, Alan was willing to supervise the northers' wood-cutting on Andrew's farm. Once he was convinced that Richie had established discipline, and that his people were peaceful, he took Samuel along. They set about constructing a large-scale facility for drying the wood. 'How are we going to cut the timber to size?' 'The engineers are working with Steven on a machine for chipping the timber small enough for Rhona's biodiesel process.' 'Don't we need to use it for heating too?' 'Yes, we'll leave some of the timber big enough to burn slowly in stoves.'

***

After a week digesting what she had witnessed, Jessica felt the need to talk to someone about it. Before Phraya she wouldn't have considered Benjamin, but things had changed and her brother had grown up. 'I was OK while I was watching Katherine in labour, but if I think of doing it myself that's different. If I have a baby Peter will be expected to attend.' 'Philip wanted to stay but was sent out; I'm sure Peter will be just as dutiful.' 'Well, if you're going to be with Julia you'll face it too one day.' 'Perhaps the hospital will get going in time for the four of us.'

***

Charles wanted the team to develop standardised parcels of preserved food, as a stepping stone between barter and currency. 'Let's settle on one day's food for one adult.' Deborah pointed out, 'But people aren't going to want to eat the same thing every day.' 'True, and they won't. They'll grow other food, or barter for it, or buy it with these … call them cels for short. All that matters is that a person could survive on a cel per day in the absence of anything else, and actually wants to eat it in combination with other food.' 'OK, I'll work with Charles and Margaret on what can be preserved, transported and transformed back into something desirable; and is balanced nutritionally, consistent, safe and trustworthy. Is that the specification?' 'I'm getting hungry already.'

***

Olivia continued to monitor the situation with the westsiders and the northers. There had been one or two clashes, quashed immediately by the respective leaders. Recently a norther who refused to cooperate with the new regime had been banished by Gavin; to Olivia's relief Richie had agreed to the removal of his man. With the help of a couple of westsider guards, Andrew took him to Morrie. After a few days of observation, he reported: 'The sanatorium is working satisfactorily. Brodie isn't causing trouble, and there is more cooperation with other groups too.'

***

Alison was ten on 15 Aug P3. As a treat Rory took her to meet the some of the other groups, starting at Raymond's place. She had a small drink of milk; 'It's warm, and silky, it's like heaven!' When she took some back to the team, Calum asked, 'Where does it come from?' His father explained, 'From the cows' udders, but they used to take half the cream out, sterilise the semi-skim, put it in bottles and sell it in the shops. I had forgotten it was so nice straight from the cow.' She added, 'There was a herd of deer too, but you can't get milk from them, just venison.'

Next Lucy took Alison to the hospital, where Gordon was trying to get the equipment going. 'Do you want to see the bones in your hands?' 'Are you sure you've got the dose low enough, I don't want to practice oncology on my own daughter.' 'It's OK, this is one of the instruments we've conquered. Let's see how many fingers you've got, young lady.' He counted backwards on the image of her hand: 'Ten, nine, eight, seven, six … plus five on the other hand … oh dear, eleven fingers, perhaps the X-rays have made you grow an extra one.' She was puzzled, and muttered numbers under her breath all the way home.

***

Local trade thrived with the help of the cels. The team was eating its own food, rapeseed oil from Gregory, cereals from Peggy; and chicken, eggs and venison from Raymond. Other groups were preparing versions of cels that had been agreed with Margaret. The growing spirit of trust was threatened, however, when in mid-September most of the team succumbed to food poisoning. Julia was OK, so meat was suspected. Imperfect memories suggested that those who had eaten venison but not chicken were unaffected, so Lucy started by assuming salmonella from the poultry, and treated it symptomatically. When some people remained ill, she turned her thinking to other bacteria and administered antibiotics, but they didn't help. She spoke to Margaret. 'We're going to have to keep a diary of who eats what, whether it makes them ill, where it came from and the health of the supplying group.' Everyone recovered eventually, as the doctor put it, 'Thanks to or in spite of the treatment.' No-one knew which food to blame, and the exchange of food supplies was cautiously resumed.

An excellent P3 harvest prompted Alexandra to optimism: "There is plenty of food, the gangs seem to have been tamed and groups are working together well. In the absence of any further crises, the question of mere survival seems to be resolved. The challenge now is to bring about a fuller revival of society, and to avoid a fading of purpose in the coming months and years."

***

William was clear about what he wanted for his twelfth birthday: to continue the theme of introducing new foods, this time ice cream. He asked Charles to negotiate with Raymond for some milk, and begged Margaret to release some precious sugar; by now eggs were almost a commodity. As 28 September approached most people were well on the way to recovery from the food poisoning, so there was an appetite for luxury food and festivity, but Lucy insisted that she and Bruce would oversee the safety of the endeavour. At the tasting Margaret lied, 'Made with the finest vanilla pods from Madagascar.' When the children asked where that was, they were forced to look it up before they got any desert. Lucy groaned, 'Ah, mankind's greatest invention, refrigeration, helping to disguise the sweetness of its main sin.'

Inspired by the ice cream, and knowing that the ingredients were too scarce to permit a repeat, David went to see whether Peggy had made any progress with beet. 'We got hold of some seed, and it came up this summer, but I'm determined to leave it in the ground. It should flower next year and then we'll have more seeds as well as a small number of beets for experimentation. I'm afraid you must wait at least another year for sugar in any quantity.'

*****

In November Ruth announced that she was pregnant again. Alice tried to explain to Stewart, 'Mummy has a new baby in her tummy. Do you want a brother or a sister?' This was too difficult for an eighteen-month-old; he merely pulled up his T-shirt and said, 'My tummy.'

Lucy reckoned that Ruth's second pregnancy was a reasonably safe proposition, and secured her permission to use it for educational purposes, both for the small children and also for the older ones. Isabella asked questions about the development of the foetus, and Rose suggested, 'Let's make models, once a month, to show the growing size of the baby.' Lucy provided the anatomical details, Julia helped them with the clay and Peter built an oven to fire the models. Benjamin, now firmly an item with Julia, paid more attention to the progress of the baby than a man in his thirties in the days before Phraya.

*****

Bruce planned to quiz Alastair on future engineering challenges. All the teenage boys wanted to go, so Steven went to make sure they listened and learned. Bruce asked the same questions that he had addressed to the chemists. 'What's happening at the moment?' 'So far we've been concentrating on keeping cars, tractors and generators running on pure biodiesel. We've also done one or two special jobs like the machine for cutting timber.' 'What next?' 'We've been working mainly with hand-held tools. We need to progress to machine tools, and get proper metalwork under way by mastering the technologies for cutting and joining.'

'What's more aspirational?' In due course we'll need to cast and forge parts, so we can make completely new things rather than simply keep old equipment running. We can work with glass, but the real difficulties start with polymers, because the chemists can't make them afresh. All we can do at present is melt existing thermoplastics and re-shape them.' 'What's a long way off?' 'Engineering on very large scale, and anything requiring serious electrical power. Micro engineering and high precision will also be hard to re-establish. These things demand a complete ecosystem of appropriate technologies.'

***

As Christmas approached, the team felt that they should make up for the fact that it had been ignored the previous year. Henry put his finger on it; 'I sense a craving for merriment; let's make another trip into the city centre to find what's needed to satisfy it.' Alexandra was keen to come; 'It must be safe by now, though unpleasant. I suppose those of us who haven't seen it should face up to the reality?' It was agreed that she, Olivia, Rory and Deborah would go in a car with a trailer, following David and Alan in the Landrover. Charles, Philip, Margaret and Alice, who hadn't seen the city, didn't want to do so; and the teenagers, who did, were dissuaded.

Edinburgh was deserted. There were no rats or dogs, but the plants thriving in the streets supported some deer. Even the bones which had proved so shocking on previous visits had disintegrated and were half-hidden by vegetation. Deborah remarked, 'All these buildings, starting to break down already. What an incredible waste! We should remove useful things before the weather gets in and destroys everything.' David replied, 'At the moment we're here to find things for Christmas, but we could come back in the spring and make a serious raid on the resources.' They entered many buildings and searched thoroughly. They were amazed to find that in some cases there were still remnants of food, hidden during the crisis under floorboards and in attics. It wasn't much, but would support a seasonal celebration.

Everyone in the team agreed that Christmas P3 was the best yet. There was good food and drink; a concert; singing; and readings. Ruth confessed, 'In Morrie I had my doubts about moving here, and I've had a few more since, especially after … you know … but I think we've done a good thing.' 'I told you so!' Alexandra growled, 'Oh shut up, Steven, we admit it, you were right.' Philip sounded a note of caution: 'We don't know the future. What do we think are the existential risks?' Bruce perked up, 'Well I hate to be the bearer of bad news, as once before, but I've been thinking about the threats as well as the opportunities.' David sighed; 'Well, lay it on us, then.' 'There could be crop failure; disease; invasion by unfriendly people; shortages of basic materials; technological challenges for which we lack the expertise.' 'On the other hand, an aeroplane could fly over and drop a lifetime supply of crème brûlée.' Lucy corrected him: 'Praline, you mean.' Margaret contradicted them both: 'Don't be daft, fresh mangoes.' Isabella had the winning idea. 'A magic potion that can turn rapeseed into whatever each person wants.'

After that, people weren't inclined to attempt serious analysis. Everyone was merry, Henry more than most, and no-one paid any attention when he wondered how things were progressing in London.

Chapter 15 Communication

Early in P4 Philip visited the electronics group; Keith said, 'I've got a late Christmas present for you: our radio ham transmissions have been answered!' 'That's wonderful – where were they received?' 'In Carlisle, almost 120 kilometres away. That's probably why it has taken so long; at that range, with modest power, conditions have to be good.' 'At last, speed of light communication, like when Marconi put carrier pigeons out of business. Perhaps a network will emerge?' 'We've set up a schedule with the recipient, and have urged him to transmit in search of people further south.'

***

On 17 January Calum declared he was now a big boy. He had been learning history and maths and wanted to combine them: 'How old was I when Phraya happened?' Rory replied, 'Four, you were too young to remember it.' 'Well, Ali can't remember it properly either, she was only six.' 'What are you trying to work out?' 'She wasn't even twice as old as me?' Alison helped him out: 'No, one a half times.' 'What about now? I'm eight, and you're ten.' Rory had to do this one for them. 'Ali is one and a quarter times older.' He thought about this, and announced triumphantly, 'So I'm catching up.' Lucy was impressed. 'Our efforts to educate these two haven't failed entirely, but I think we better get Bruce into the classroom; or perhaps Benjamin – we don't need advanced maths, and Julia would like it better.'

***

David visited Rhona to discuss fertilisers for the coming season. 'We can provide potassium from wood ash and, with help from the engineers, calcium from lime. Seaweed for sodium, and it's a good general feed. Then it gets a bit more dubious.' 'How so?' 'Well, as you know we can make small amounts of nitrogen from urine, and from other waste composted separately, if we're vigilant about disease. The main missing element is phosphorus,' – 'I suspect I know what you're thinking,' – 'which we can get from bones.' 'I suppose that would honour the victims, we can see how other people feel about it.' 'It would also give us a reason to clean up.' David concluded, 'Let the northers do it, they caused a lot of the mess.'

***

In early spring people started to arrive in numbers from various parts of the country. Some were simply escaping their experiences since Phraya. Others were seeking loved ones, however hopeless the cause.

Many recounted horror stories, but the team was inured to them. Curiously the visitors' accounts of life elsewhere were often uplifting, and suggested things were improving overall; the cooperative spirit which had emerged around Edinburgh was not unique. Steven was pleased to hear that technological efforts were under way in other places. A few of the travellers had specialist skills, no longer needed where they had come from, which they hoped to offer more widely.

One or two nomads urged wandering for its own sake. This reinforced a conviction which had been growing in Henry's mind, and now he voiced it more clearly to his mother: 'I think we should explore much more widely. I'm going to head for London.' Olivia was appalled. 'You might be waylaid, and we'd never know what happened. Can't you at least wait until we've got more information, and better communications?' 'Establishing those things is precisely the purpose of the trip.' She tried to forbid it, but he said simply, 'I'm twenty-two, mum.' 'Well, let's at least see what the rest of the family thinks.'

Bruce prioritised his nephew's ambition over his safety: 'It's a good idea, we need to find out what's going on elsewhere. I think the country is peaceful enough now.' Katherine was less sanguine; she pointed at Jocelyn, who was trying to escape from Stewart's rough play. 'If this goes wrong, she will never know her uncle.' 'I'll go carefully, asking people in each area how things are further south.' He felt the tension and made an ill-judged attempt at a joke: 'Anyway, you'll hear how I got on when you read the obituary.' Charles was not amused; 'At least take your family's concerns seriously.' Philip had an idea: Perhaps you could wait until a chain of radio hams is established?' Alexandra surprised everyone: 'I think the venture is worthy but risky. It will have my support if there's some kind of communication.'

***

Ruth was starting to show, so Alison and Calum were now more interested in the pregnancy. The models of the foetus were still small, but they looked more like a baby each month. It was quite difficult to make them realistic, but Rose and William did their best. Lucy made sure that Jessica, Peter, Julia and Benjamin understood what they would be undertaking in the future. Everyone was anxious after Katherine's experience.

***

Philip had been working with Keith on how to increase the power of radio transmissions. After a while he reported, 'As a result of our instructions to Carlisle they've made contact with someone beyond our range. We've asked travellers heading for London to look out for ham aerials, and to seek electronics people. We've handed out printed instructions on how to get a station going. Hopefully the connections will multiply.' 'The next challenges will be to send text and to forward it automatically to all stations.'

***

The news from Glasgow was getting better. There wasn't yet any kind of central authority, but cooperation between groups was improving. People were organising themselves against raids, and the gangs were dissipating as they met more resistance. This prompted Gordon to send some of his team back to reconsider the feasibility of starting up the hospital there. Lucy took advantage of Bruce and Alexandra's willingness to countenance Henry's mission southwards; she suggested that Jessica should be allowed to go to join the trip to the western hospital.

***

By early April the radio network had reached London, in several stages; and it was possible, laboriously and unreliably, to send messages by a chain of conversations. Philip suggested to Keith, 'Once we've automated the relaying of text, we might be able to set up a point-to-point communication system? A person could visit their local station and send a kind of email, to be picked up by the addressee at another station?'

When Henry heard these dreams, he convinced himself that they would fulfil his promise about keeping in touch; he started to plan his trip. Steven and the engineers prepared a car and a generous quantity of biodiesel. Bruce and Margaret supplied him with plenty of cels and additional food. On 12 April P4, the fourth anniversary of Phraya, he kissed all the women and children in the team, hugged the men and set off for Carlisle. In a bid to distract Olivia, Katherine set her the task of providing a finger for Jocelyn to clutch as she learned to walk. Stewart, holding her other hand, walked rather too fast and dragged her, half-falling, to her mother.

The next day Philip went to the radio station and was told that Henry had dutifully sent the first experimental text of the post era: "There you are, mum, nothing to worry about. The wolves weren't too fierce, and I was able to fight off the first few attacks by rebel forces. Your loving son." Philip sent a reply: "When you hit genuine trouble, as you surely will, kindly suppress news of it for the sake of our mother's sanity. Substitute stories about how kind everyone is in England." The weather was not cooperative, and by the time this reached Carlisle, Henry had moved on.

***

Back in Scotland, David heard that Peggy's sugar beet seeds had germinated. When he told the team, Lucy closed her eyes and luxuriated in a glorious vision: 'Just a few months, and we'll have meringues … fudge ... cakes with icing … maybe Steven can devise a spinner for making candyfloss for the kids.' Margaret told her off: 'Remember you're the dentist as well as the doctor. Who's going to fix your teeth when they rot?'

***

Over the next few days Henry drove southwards, initially through countryside resembling that of Scotland. The land was sparsely populated; vast areas of wilderness separated tiny oases of food production, and cooperation between groups was local and limited in scope. Further south the cities hosted more people and greater activity, but the surrounding industrial areas were still silent, ghostly reminders of the capacities of the past. He approached people cautiously, and found that although outright hostility had dwindled, people scarcely trusted one another; instead an exhausted truce had descended everywhere. Engineers were trying to restart equipment, but in some cases they had no fuel for engines, no electricity and therefore made little progress. Henry passed on the method for making biodiesel.

At each radio station he gave details of those he had visited earlier, and was instructed on where to find the next one. In every case he sent a message to the north and asked that replies be forwarded southwards. However, he was always moving away from the responses, and received none during his journey. He was not concerned, as he could see that the grasp of technology was insecure even locally, let alone across distance. However, he was slightly guilty that each additional station added to the problem.

***

The initial flow of missives reaching Edinburgh grew more sporadic, Olivia's questions went unanswered and she became extremely concerned. Philip explained, 'The radios are far apart, and when a link is broken the chain fails. When it's working, I imagine the operators are swamped by messages from concerned people all over the country. Over time more stations will join in, producing a network which can withstand the loss of individual connections – like the internet.' She was not encouraged by this analogy. 'Look how that collapsed.' 'Yes, but people were abandoning it, whereas now the system is improving all the time. Once communications are by text rather than voice, it can be automated. Then Henry will be in touch, as charming and tactless as ever.'

***

Life had to go on. Stewart would be two soon, and Ruth was determined: 'We ignored his first birthday, because he couldn't understand, but this year we'll put on a show.' Julia suggested, 'Let's make toys for toddlers; we haven't needed any yet, and we shouldn't simply take them from shops.' Alan and Samuel visited the schoolroom and helped Rose and Isabella make wooden trains. William, Alison and Calum decorated them with paints previously rejected by William for his airplane.

On the day, 10 May, Calum showed Stewart how to make the train engine pull several carriages. 'Let me, it's mine.' He tried to push them from the back, they soon broke apart, and he cried. When he was shown how to do it from the front, he insisted, 'Let me, my can do it self!' Now it worked better; 'See, my am doing it.' Lucy looked wistful, and Alison asked, 'What's wrong, mum?' 'Do you remember explaining to Calum that cars can't pull many carriages, but trains can?' 'Oh yes, he was a very silly boy then.'

***

'My name is Henry Lenton, and I am delighted to meet you!' 'Patricia Carter, call me Trish; the feeling is mutual. Where are you from?' 'I've come from Edinburgh.' Wow, that's quite a journey – how are things up there?' 'We're a group of twenty-six – and two new babies – growing food and making diesel fuel from rapeseed. We have started to work with other people: engineers, chemists, cereal farmers. We had trouble with gangsters but my mother, who seems to have emerged as leader, turned them into worthy citizens.'

'That's very impressive. We're not quite so far ahead, but we're growing enough food. We've tried running engines on raw rape oil, and it doesn't seem to do them much good.' 'I've got some instructions on how to convert it to something better. Are people cooperating here?' 'Yes, it's peaceful now and folks are helping each other, but there are so many gaps in our knowledge. I'm not much use, as I was studying history and art at school.' 'Even worse, just history. The things I'm describing were achieved by technologists.' 'Everything sounds so well organised in Edinburgh. Why have you come down here?' 'I thought we should find out what's going on in the rest of the country. I'm especially interested in trying to re-build the world culturally.'

***

Jessica returned from Glasgow and reported to Lucy: 'The city is calm enough, so some of the doctors stayed to get the hospital started.' 'Let's go and see how Edinburgh's is progressing.' They took Alison, who wanted revenge for Gordon's finger-counting. He analysed the feasibility of getting the hospital running properly. 'There's a huge amount of equipment, but much of it is challenging; we lack mains electrical power, consumables and expertise. It might be possible to do simple operations, but general anaesthesia is a serious undertaking. There are drugs, which will probably last years, but doing tests to back up their use won't be possible for a long time.'

***

Within a few days of meeting, Henry and Patricia had got to know each other very well. She said, 'I suppose we have to cover the usual question. How did you survive Phraya?' 'My family was lucky; we were on a boat in the Far Isles, and kept away from everyone. When the worst was over, we met others in the islands and in a remote part of the Highlands called Letheilean. After a year we moved to a farm in central Scotland and then, in spring two years ago, to Edinburgh. What about you?'

'It wasn't as serene as your experience. I was in school just outside London. My parents got the virus,' – she hesitated – 'and I'm afraid they died quite quickly.' 'Oh, I'm so sorry to hear that. What on earth did you do?' 'I retreated to a shed, and moved the huge amount of food that they always kept in the house. I stayed there for a long time, seeing no-one. I couldn't face going back to deal with ....' 'I understand, please don't dwell on it. What about later?' 'People came to raid, but soon went away again. Eventually, when things calmed down, I escaped and came here – my mother knew the farmers, so they looked after me. Later we returned and gave her and my father a proper burial.'

***

Olivia pestered Philip and Keith constantly for progress on the radio. In early June the first message came along the whole chain from London, but it had taken many days – and it wasn't from Henry. She sought Andrew's wisdom. 'He's a boy, away on the adventure he was about to enjoy when Phraya struck.' 'Yes, but he might at least report that he's OK.' 'He's fine, enjoying himself; he'll be embarrassed later at the distress caused.'

An unknown software engineer devised an automatic procedure for forwarding text, and everyone installed it, but the limiting factors continued to be transmission power, gaps between stations and the weather. Olivia gave Keith no rest: 'Are you sending something every day? Damn it, perhaps we should start training pigeons.'

***

Patricia had taken Henry on a tour of the immediate area. He remarked, 'This isn't so different from Edinburgh. I want to see London itself. Would you like to come?' 'Yes, why wouldn't I accompany a crazed adventurer to the scene of the worst Phraya violence?' 'You sound like my mother. I can hear her now, telling me that we should take our time, and talk to people as we go in, to get an impression how safe it is. I really must get a message to her, and there's one more radio station nearer the centre.' 'What will you tell her?' 'We can't be bothered pussyfooting,' – she interrupted – 'we're just going to drive straight up to the machine gun emplacements and challenge the guerrillas to shoot us.' 'At last, someone who's madder than me.'

***

Alice had spoken to a traveller who had spotted pigs, apparently gone wild, in a remote forest in northern England. She mentioned this to Raymond, who was keen to add pork to his repertoire; they hatched a plan to go and capture some sows and a boar. Olivia was dubious. 'Another team member wandering off into the unknown, never to be seen again.' 'With all due respect to your son, I'm older and wiser; I'll be with others; we're not going far; and it's not an open-ended trip.'

When they were alone Charles pointed out to Olivia, 'I know you're anxious about Henry, and so am I, but from now on we won't be sticking together as closely as we did in Letheilean. Even when we were in Morrie, we mounted various expeditions. Now that we're established here, working safely with other groups, the team will keep breaking up and re-forming. Perhaps the best attitude is that it is expanding to include the whole Edinburgh community? You're effectively in charge of the enlarged operation.' 'Perhaps, and I welcome all that. I admit I was wrong about Alice's plan, and I'll apologise. Henry's doing something altogether different, and I reserve the right to worry about him.'

***

Henry and Patricia set off towards the former capital of the United Kingdom. As they advanced they consulted the locals, and found that for the most part a spirit of collaboration had won the victory for which Alexandra had hoped, overcoming a tendency to clash. On the other hand, they saw little evidence of organisation across the region, and no leadership; his parents would be crestfallen.

They reached the radio station, and met Adam Middleton, the leader of the local electronics effort. 'Hi, I've come from Edinburgh, and am keen to inform my mother that I'm still alive. I've sent many messages, but have heard nothing; could I please send yet another?' 'Sure, but the connections are still flaky; quite a few intermediate stations have to receive, send onwards and be heard all along the line.'

They continued into the centre of the city and found it more comprehensively ruined than Edinburgh. Widespread wreckage was mute witness to conflict on a greater scale. Nevertheless it was curiously unthreatening: reclamation by nature was well advanced, so it was leafy, almost pleasant; and it seemed to be deserted. 'It was the same in Edinburgh. Too far from arable land, no clean water, possible danger from remaining gangs.' 'We used to go into town for the museums, galleries and theatres, without thinking about the practicalities.' 'Yes, a city was a miracle, an artifice, wholly dependent on resources from outside.' 'Well, it's pretty useless now.'

***

Philip approached his mother, waving a piece of paper. 'I've got a disappointing text from London.' She sat down to avoid collapsing. Seeing that he had inadvertently alarmed her, he smiled, and she knew immediately that all was well.

"I have reached London, and it's a bit of an anti-climax. There's no-one in the centre, nothing going on, not even gangs. The outskirts are similar to Edinburgh, peaceful and cooperative, except that there's much less structure to the activity. Definitely no sign of a government."

"It hasn't been a fruitless journey: I have met a girl, Trish, who has aims similar to mine. She's gorgeous, too, blonde, big … blue eyes, perhaps you will meet her one day. In the meantime, it would be nice to know that you're getting these messages."

Olivia groaned, 'A girl, now he'll never come back.' Charles looked at the note more closely. 'Meet her one day – fine – but when and where? He doesn't spare our feelings.' Philip was dispatched to send a reply, along with yet another plea to Keith to improve communications.

***

Gordon had made progress at the hospital, at least for routine medical procedures. Ruth went for an ultrasound scan, which indicated that all was well with her baby. Nevertheless, influenced by Katherine's labour, she decided that this time she would give birth in comparative safety of the maternity ward. When the time came, Alice, Lucy and

Jessica accompanied her there, and found it strangely quiet. Without much intervention, and with little noise to fill the silence, Flora Paterson was born at dawn on 26 July P4. Ruth decided she would like to learn midwifery.

***

Henry and Patricia made a further trip to the London station. "Dear Henry, after a long pause – damn the radio – I got your letter about Trish. How lovely, we are looking forward to meeting her soon, up here I hope. London sounds deeply discouraging – perhaps we should concentrate on Scotland first? However, I have embraced the need for wider exploration, and you are forgiven. You missed Ruth's Flora, all well with mother and daughter. Did I mention soon, and here? Your loving mother."

After this, the radio network improved rapidly. News began to flow from all over the country. The operators automated the text system so that communication delays didn't stop messages in their tracks. A station in Dover established contact with France, and there were reports of boat trips across the channel. The situation seemed to be much the same on the continent.

***

Alice and Raymond set off to look for the pigs. She was concerned about catching them. 'It won't be easy to get hold of a boar; they're usually solitary and are unlikely to climb voluntarily into our vehicle.' 'I'm sure your team has come up with a solution.' 'I hesitate even to mention it, but I've got some sedative from Lucy, which we might be able to deliver with a bow and arrow.' 'Oh great, we have the latest technology, no problem.' 'Well, have you got a laser beam?' He had a better idea: 'If your solution fails, there's always nature. Sows come into heat every three weeks, and won't be synchronised in the wild. If we can capture a few by offering food, the boar will soon be attracted to one of them.'

***

Henry asked Patricia, 'Would you like to come with me to Edinburgh? You don't have family here, and I'm sure mine would welcome you.' 'Yes, that would be lovely, but might a new person upset the established equilibrium?' 'No, although you would be the first adult to join the team, everyone is bound to love you as much as I do.' 'Such sincerity, keep talking!' 'Seriously, I'm sure there is going to be more and more mixing of the groups in any case. At the least you would be welcomed by Alexandra to balance the technocrats.'

***

Gordon's colleagues reported such good progress in the Glasgow hospital that he decided to split the team permanently. He persuaded Philip and Keith to move a radio station to allow communication between the two sites. With this set up, Olivia and Alexandra were much more relaxed that Jessica wanted to spend time at both places. Lucy said, "This is hardly different from Peter working with the engineers, it's just a bit further afield. The children are growing up faster than before Phraya. William will probably end up at Raymond's farm.'

***

In early August P4 there was an exchange of messages which took only three days: "Henry is heading back to Edinburgh, and I'm coming with him if that's OK with you. Love Patricia." "Everyone is delighted! If you make it by the 15th, you'll catch Alison's eleventh birthday. Olivia." "Thank you for making Trish feel welcome. Prepare a feast; you can tell Margaret that peaches will be available. See you soon – Henry."

When he arrived on 12 August, Olivia hugged him so tightly that Patricia joked, 'Hey, he may be your boy but he's my man.' 'Sorry, he's put us through the wringer – along with the insufferable radio.' Henry put his mother in her place: 'OK, enough, it's Flora I really want to see anyway.' Stewart had the last laugh: 'No, she's my sister. You can't have her.' Ruth remonstrated, 'Remember to be gentle, she's very tiny and Henry wants to meet her before you hug her to death.'

Over the next couple of days Patricia got to know everyone. She had already memorised their names and roles, and just had to put faces to them. She spent much of her time apologising for the uselessness of her skills. Alexandra wouldn't have it; 'Nonsense, it's people like you and Henry that are going to shape society now that the technologists have conquered the immediate necessities.' Philip's verdict on Patricia was simple. 'Not an entirely wasted trip then, Henry?'

By the time of Alison's party the team, now thirty strong, had embraced its newest member. She surprised everyone by joining Alexandra at the piano, and they played an impromptu four-handed version of 'Happy birthday to you.' Alison asked suddenly, 'Didn't my friends play this once, on recorders?' Lucy's eyes welled up; 'That's right; shall I tell you about the earlier occasions?' 'Yes, please.' 'When you were one, you were more amused by the packaging than the presents. You had a bit more understanding at two; you neglected an expensive electronic music box in favour of a colourful wooden car.'

'Like Stewart's train a few months ago?' 'Yes, the simplest toys are the best. At three you knew the event was for you, and cried when you didn't win pass the parcel. You planned every detail of your fourth bash, avoiding games with winners and losers, and did a drama performance instead. It was on the fifth that the recorders were played, and I know you remember your sixth.' 'Remind me, what did we do?' You swam in the sea.' 'Oh yes, that was brilliant.' Patricia said, 'Funny, every aspect of those birthdays can be achieved now.'

***

As the harvest progressed, Charles negotiated with other groups to standardise the prices, expressed in cels, of animal products: lamb, venison, chicken and eggs, beef and milk. There was no pork yet. It was the same with cereals: wheat, oats and barley had their cel equivalents, but sugar still wasn't a commodity. The basic economy was determined by the availability of these foods, various seeds, fertilisers, rapeseed, wood and biodiesel. Everything else was a luxury made or bought by whoever desired it sufficiently to sacrifice something more ordinary.

***

On 28 September P4 William turned thirteen, but he followed the teenage tradition of disdaining any ceremonial. Instead he extracted from Alice and his parents a promise of an eventual apprenticeship in animal husbandry. In the meantime, his birthday present was a trip to see Raymond's pigs. 'Most of the sows are already pregnant. This means piglets in winter, but we can keep them warm and fed, so we're getting on with it. Pork in the spring with luck.'

In the late autumn Peggy allowed a limited number of beets to be harvested. Katherine consulted Rhona on the extraction of sucrose, and they produced some dubious-looking brown crystals. Charles suggested a very high price. 'We've got to inhibit Lucy somehow.' Bruce remarked, 'I remember Alexandra citing it as an example of the vulnerability of the world to entirely artificial shortages.' Margaret replied, 'It's a curious thing: it would have been easy to store a few basic foods – flour, rice and oats as well as sugar; beans, dried fruit, nuts and seeds; dried meat; chocolate; powdered milk; salt, herbs and spices; oil, vinegar and water – and yet no-one did. At any rate, not in sufficient quantity to prevent the Phraya panic.'

***

Bruce had been working on his model of the regeneration of industry, and wanted a chance to air his conclusions. Olivia gathered a reluctant team and he launched into a detailed lecture. 'We're in a very strange situation. At first sight one might think we're thrown back to the early eighteenth century, before the industrial revolution. However, we're in a better position in many respects: modern science, twenty-first century technology. On the other hand, we're also stymied by lack of personnel and knowhow; and by the fact that all mining resources are hopelessly deep underground.' Steven interrupted, 'Yes, we know all this; no oil or minerals, no chemical industry; little chance of biochemistry or electronics.'

Bruce continued, 'We can overcome some of these difficulties eventually: wood and other renewable energy; substitute source materials for chemical engineering; and slow buildup of the relevant industries. What worries me is certain obstinate bottlenecks: things that can only be obtained elsewhere, perhaps in other countries; and crucial skills for which we must search widely enough until we find a survivor. Otherwise we have to pursue a much longer path of re-invention from scratch.' Henry reminded everyone, 'Where are these skills? I went to London and found it less advanced than here.'

'I think the metropolis is still emerging from an even worse experience than Edinburgh. There must be many experts, awaiting their opportunity to shine. Given that the majority of the pre-Phraya population was concentrated in the southeast, presumably the survivors are too, so London must be important once it emerges fully from Phraya? In the long run the entire country has to pool its resources. If we don't, we face the most serious danger of all: we will die off before the post generation has been kindled. Then mankind might descend into a primitive state.'

Alexandra told her diary: "I thought we were making excellent progress, but Bruce insists that fundamental problems threaten to limit the recovery. We must scour the country, maybe the whole world, for the people who can vault the barriers. I'm happy with this, as it will re-unify the various cultures that made a melting pot out of the globe. These processes will go on for decades."

Part 5 Province

Chapter 16 Influence

"30 March P6. The situation on communications has improved vastly over the past year or so. Philip tells me that the radio network has become more branched and denser, so it withstands breakdowns better and the weather matters less. There are stations at the steading, and at the sites of other leaders all over the UK, but not at every house. When texts are sent out, they usually get through and are read on the same day. Adam Middleton is very useful at the London end, coordinating the entire system."

"Olivia and the team form the de facto government of the Edinburgh area. The westsiders are accepted as the police, armed and ready for emergencies; and the northers are viewed as providers of public utilities. Similar governments are gradually emerging in Aberdeen and other small cities, but Glasgow is still functioning as several separate communities. It's much the same down south; large cities are aren't yet cohering, and London is a long way behind. Disparate areas need to be unified; there is no government of Scotland, nor of England, and certainly not the UK."

"Peace is almost universal, as everyone has enough food if they work; idleness and stealing aren't tolerated among those capable of the effort. There is regular travel and trade, at least locally. Cels, or their equivalent, are trusted wherever they exist. Services as well as goods are being exchanged locally or paid for in cels. Education is organised, not only in essential practical matters but also in history and the arts; at last progress is being made culturally."

***

Samuel was at Andrew's farm, helping Alan enlarge the timber drying shed. While the boss was busy checking what was needed, his shy apprentice at last took the chance to talk to a girl he had noticed in recent months; it had taken him this long to pluck up the courage. He started clumsily: 'I don't think you've been here long? Where have you been all my life?' She laughed, 'I came from way up north, last autumn.' 'Sorry about that, I'm Sam Tanner, and I'm not as daft as you probably think.' 'Shona Macfarlane, don't worry, I thought your question was charmingly direct.' He relaxed a little; 'I think you came on your own, haven't you got a family?' 'Yes, I was with my parents, on a remote sheep farm, when Phraya happened. Everyone disappeared, so we decided to stay put, and we were OK because we had meat and could grow other food.' 'So why did you leave?' The atmosphere was tense with my parents, so when it was safe I came down here and Peggy took me in. What about you?' 'We were on a farm, but there were too many people around, so we went to the middle of nowhere and met some friends of my mother's …'

***

The children of Phraya had been transformed; post adulthood started at sixteen, or sooner in practice. Peter was working with his father and Alastair's engineers, and proved very inventive at practical tasks. Jessica helped at the Edinburgh hospital and also, for periods, at the Glasgow one. Benjamin was studying physics, mathematics and engineering with his father, and picking up electronics with Philip and Keith's people. Julia was teaching the children of several Edinburgh groups as well as the team's remaining pre-Phraya kids. Samuel did joinery with Alan full time, when he wasn't honing his social skills on Shona. Isabella was learning on the job too, with Katherine and Rhona's chemists. Rose looked after the team's post children. William, now fourteen and aspiring to join the others in employment, spent some of his time with Alice and Raymond's animals. Unwilling to be entirely bound by the classroom, Alison was exposed to some medicine by Lucy. Even Calum, by his interest in the radio system, hinted at a future role. Stewart, Jocelyn and Flora ran around evading attempts to instil civilisation into them.

The new adults were busy with the task of repopulating the world. Jessica was full term and preparing for her labour. Like his brother – for whom Phraya had intervened – Henry hadn't bothered to marry; and now Patricia announced that she was pregnant. Planning was under way for Benjamin and Julia's wedding. When Margaret declared, 'I'm much too young for all this, I'm not even fifty,' Alexandra replied, 'What about me, about to become a grandmother,' and Olivia muttered, 'Thanks for reminding me.'

Deborah was particularly struck by the transformation of her offspring. 'When the world changed, our three were definitely kids. Even now they would still have been children emotionally, even if they had shot ahead physically. As it is, they've grown up mentally and are keen to make their mark.' David replied, 'Yes, and I shudder to think what may be coming soon.' 'I know, like the others of a certain age, I'm not sure I'm ready for it.'

***

On the sixth anniversary of Phraya, Alexandra opened the ceremony: 'Once again two families are united in a wonderful cross-marriage. It will be fascinating, but it ain't gonna be easy, as Langston Hughes might have put it:'

'Well, son, I'll tell you:
Life for me ain't been no crystal stair.
It's had tacks in it,
And splinters,
And boards torn up,
And places with no carpet on the floor –
Bare.
But all the time
I'se been a-climbin' on,
And reachin' landin's,
And turnin' corners,
And sometimes goin' in the dark
Where there ain't been no light.
So boy, don't you turn back.
Don't you set down on the steps
'Cause you finds it's kinder hard.
Don't you fall now –
For I'se still goin', honey,
I'se still climbin',
And life for me ain't been no crystal stair.'

At the party after the wedding, Isabella couldn't resist: 'There was a young boy, name of Ben, for Julia fell, as ye ken. To them I express my joy in excess, at being a bridesmaid again.' Margaret replied, 'I don't mind the English stealing our girls and poking fun at the Scottish language – but I am imposing an embargo on mother-in-law jokes.'

***

During the wedding Jessica had experienced her first contractions, but they led nowhere and were dismissed as false ones. A few days later she started a long and slow labour, and moaned piteously, but Lucy was firm: 'You're hardly dilated, I'm afraid. No need to go anywhere yet.' Stewart heard her wailing, and asked, 'What's that, mummy?' Ruth replied, 'She is having her baby.' 'Why is she crying?' 'It hurts a bit, but it's OK, that's what always happens.' He informed Jocelyn, 'She's got a baby in her tummy. You're a girl, you can have one.' 'I like babies. I look after Flora.' The toddler heard her name mentioned, and insisted, 'Me big girl.'

Eventually Lucy agreed it was time to take poor Jessica to the hospital. Gordon greeted her cheerfully, 'Ah, come to practice what you preach?' She waited for a contraction to subside; 'Very amusing, I hope you've made some advances in obstetrics.' On the following day,

18 April P6, she gave birth at last; little Thomas made almost as much noise as his mother.

The next day Isabella sought out her best friend. 'When we were in Morrie we hoped there would be boys in Edinburgh, and there are, but I can see where this will lead.' Rose was puzzled; 'Yes, it's lovely. What's wrong?' 'Childbirth! I've spoken to my sister, and it doesn't sound painless.' 'She's exhausted, check in a couple of days and she'll tell you how worthwhile it is, and easy too.' 'The post world doesn't seem to allow us much time to grow up.'

***

Olivia and the team were beginning to influence a wider area than Edinburgh. All over Scotland other regions, with less effective leadership, recognised that the city's recovery was ahead of theirs. Advice on technology emanated from the city, and others tried to replicate its success on practical matters. The team also became a more general clearing house for the dissemination of information, radiating optimism and leading the way on social renewal. Charles saw that progress in many disparate areas of life could be unified; he urged other leaders to adopt the cel as a lubricant for trade.

***

On 10 May Stewart was four. He loved to climb, so Alan took him up onto some scaffolding he was using to mend a roof. His son saw a gap and said, 'The rain can go in there.' 'No one is living in this house at the moment, but we want to use it, so I'm fixing the slates.' 'Why isn't there anyone here?' 'Well, before Phraya there were a lot more people, but they've gone away, so their houses are empty.' He was interrogated further: 'What's Phraya?' He decided against further explanation. 'You'll hear about it when you're older. If you hold on, you can watch me block the hole.'

***

For the past year Charles and Philip had been talking to Keith about the possibility of re-establishing the mains grid. 'The idea is to run a large diesel generator at a substation, reduce the resulting thirty-three kilovolt electricity to eleven, distribute that to local transformers, and we'll have mains.' Charles asked, 'That doesn't sound easy. For a start, will the generator run on rapeseed diesel?' 'I think so, we'll involve Alastair and Steven.' 'OK, but assuming you can achieve that and the rest, the consumption of electricity will rise hugely. We'll need to grow a lot more rapeseed – I'll talk to Gregory – and cut additional wood –

I'll get Richie onto that. Finally, Rhona needs to scale up the conversion of seed oil to biodiesel.'

***

On 9 July Jocelyn boasted, 'I'm three years old! How many is that?' Stewart showed off: 'I know: one, two, three, it's easy.' When she spouted this without comprehension, Philip intervened, 'I'll show you how to explain it to her properly.' He assembled a tower by piling up wooden blocks, intoning the numbers up to ten. She tried, counting too quickly, but omitted some numbers, and ended up with the right answer. The children were triumphant, and Ruth was amused, 'Good grief, brilliant teaching.'

***

Lucy gathered people to consider the prospects for making condoms. 'We don't want to have to revert to cecum.' Katherine asked, 'What's that?' 'The membrane inside animal intestines.' She wrinkled her nose and began to question Rhona about rubber. 'For the time being it's impossible to make the synthetic types, which used to be based on petroleum. The natural version, which starts with latex from plants, is a more reasonable aim.' They looked enquiringly at Peggy: 'This won't be difficult for survivors in hot wet countries, where the proper rubber tree grows; I suppose we might succeed in greenhouses. Otherwise,' – she consulted a book – 'we'll have to make do with alternative species, such as poppies, milkweed, thistles and dandelions.' She agreed to milk them for their sap and deliver it to the chemists for experimentation. David remarked, 'We really are out of our comfort zone, growing weeds on purpose.' Lucy pointed out: 'On the question of comfort, the poppies will also produce opium, which will be useful for pain when the pre-Phraya drugs give out; and I can give some to Steven to slow him down.'

***

On 26 July it was Flora's turn to have a birthday. She remembered Jocelyn's and declared, 'I'm three.' Stewart put her right; 'You're only two. That means you've been alive for two years.' 'What's a year?' 'It's … a long time …' He ground to a halt, so Ruth had a go: 'When the weather is hot like this, it's called summer. It gets cool – in the autumn – and then there's snow – winter. Luckily it warms up – in the spring – and then it's lovely summer again. These are called seasons, and they happen slowly, and take a whole year. You've done all that twice already.' Flora looked blank, but Jocelyn half understood; 'I've done it one more time.' Stewart explained, 'So you're three.' Flora was completely confused; 'What's three?' Ruth sighed and asked, 'Does anyone want cake?' 'I like cake.' 'Yes, I'm allowed three pieces.' 'Well, then I should get four.'

The burst of birthdays ended with Alison's thirteenth. 'I don't want any presents, but I should be allowed to study to become a doctor.' Lucy had a brainwave; 'Why don't you learn to be a dentist? There aren't any around here, and we might find some books and equipment.' Rory interrupted; 'But first you could finish your childhood?' 'Dad, that doesn't last so long these days. Don't worry, I'm not going to get pregnant for a long time.' Her parents shuddered, and she continued, 'I just want to make a contribution. Pulling teeth sounds like fun.' Her mother compromised: 'You need to stay in school most of the time, but we can add some gnashing and grinding so you can be a useful citizen eventually.'

***

Bruce and Steven reviewed the state of engineering with Alastair. 'We're conducting experiments on running cars on alcohol. Rhona is already making methanol from wood, and everyone knows that ethanol can be obtained by fermentation followed by distillation – booze essentially, but for a worthier purpose. There are quite a few cars designed to run on a mixture with up to 85% alcohol, but they won't run without any petrol.' Steven asked, 'Is there a substitute for it?' 'Probably not, at least not for now, but engines can be adapted for pure alcohol. Various components have to be stronger to withstand higher pressures, and the fuel injectors have to change; they've had all this in Brazil for years.' 'Well, let's nip over and get the necessary parts. Failing that, can you make them?' 'We're starting to make metal components from scratch, by casting and machining. We may get to that level eventually.'

***

Samuel and Shona got together, but she made one thing clear: 'I'd love to be with you, but I won't want to get married.' 'It doesn't have to be any time soon. But eventually? Why not, aren't you sure about me?' 'I think I am, it's just that my parents weren't really at peace with each other and shouldn't have stayed together. The upheaval didn't help, and afterwards I couldn't stand it; that's why I left as soon as I could. I hope you understand, they weren't a very encouraging example of marital harmony.' 'Well, Phraya has changed everything anyway; the Lenton brothers are doing OK without weddings.'

***

In September P6 the team hosted a meeting of the leaders of all the Scottish communities. Olivia explained her approach to building an informal regional government; the others were keen to emulate it. The cel was standardised to foster trust and cooperation. Personnel were exchanged to fill gaps in skills, and to build a sense of a province. The idea of Scottish nationhood seemed premature; for the time being the regions remained separately administrated. However, it was clear that Edinburgh was moving towards its previous position as the capital.

***

In the early morning of 4 December, Patricia went into labour; and by mid-afternoon Marcus was born, pink and healthy, and was feeding greedily. Katherine complained, 'That's not fair, she didn't do any work at all!' Rose told Isabella, 'I don't know what you were worried about. I told you it was easy.'

When Henry's parents visited, their daughter-in-law was a little tearful. 'I'll never be able to show my parents their grandson, but I'd love to show him to the people who took me in after Phraya. When that will be possible, I wonder?' Henry replied, 'I'm sure there will be a trip south one day, to your home and maybe beyond.'

Chapter 17 Authority

In early December P6 Olivia sent a message to Adam Middleton at the London radio station: "Bruce would like to send out a targeted call for expertise, and offers to coordinate the results in a database. Do we have the means to reach the right people, other than by simply firing text in all directions, like a blunderbuss?" Two days later she received a reply. "I've located the mystery software engineer who achieved the automatic forwarding of text. He might be able to aim them more intelligently." "Splendid, in the meantime let's just accept indiscriminate broadcasting; the aim is to identify survivors who have skills in the specific areas listed below."

***

At Christmas Samuel made an announcement which he intended to be jocular, but it misfired: 'Shona and I are engaged, but to be unmarried.' Deborah remarked stiffly, 'I know everything is different these days, but that's a strange way of putting it.' David reacted better; 'That's fine, we understand. We think it's lovely that you have found each other, and we welcome you warmly as a daughter-not-in-law.' Realising she hadn't spoken very delicately, Deborah also made a corrective attempt at humour; 'Yes of course, let's have a non-celebration right now.' Samuel had another surprise; 'We thought we might live over at Andrew's farm. Shona wants to help people come to terms with Phraya.' This time David got his reply in more quickly. 'That's fine, we're all moving around a bit these days.'

***

New Year was a jollier affair, and everyone was a little drunk on Rhona's hooch. With things running smoothly around Edinburgh, the team mused in an ill-focussed manner on the state of affairs elsewhere. Philip reported, 'The radio messaging shoft – er, software – is improving, so uncle Bruce's call for help is reaching the right people.' Alexandra interjected, 'Cry for help, more like.' Her husband ignored this; 'I've made a start on my database of key problems. The responses confirm our impression that things aren't so advanced in the south, especially in London and other big cities, but now we're hearing from people with expertise who don't have the means to use it locally.'

The team struggled to sober up; Deborah wondered, 'How frustrating for them, can we help?' Benjamin replied, 'We could write papers on how we do important things like biodiesel, and send them to anyone who's interested?' Peter added, 'Yes, and how to keep tractors running on it?' David suggested, 'Also it's crucial to grow true crops; we could take photos of defective plants.' As the suggestions flowed, the team began to realise how much progress had been made, and an enthusiasm for supporting others grew. Then Isabella made an awkward observation: 'Ideally these reports would include pictures and graphics, but unfortunately we're limited to text.'

After a pause, Steven remarked, 'Instead of helping other cities by sending instructions, perhaps we should actually be there?' Charles asked simply, 'But where?' Samuel answered, 'We could be useful all over the country.' Rory objected, 'Precisely, we can't go everywhere.' Henry glanced at his mother, and stuck his neck out: 'Just London then?' Everyone laughed.

***

On Calum's eleventh birthday, 17 January, he was given an electronics set found in a toy shop. 'I've noticed that buildings are full of computers that aren't doing anything. I know that they were much more useful before Phraya, but for what?' Philip tried to explain: 'Back then, the internet combined them all to make a much more powerful system.' 'I've heard of it, but how did it work?' 'Homes and offices had links to servers which downloaded information to the computers and uploaded it from them.' What were servers, and how did they do that?' 'The servers were special, more powerful machines, connected into a worldwide network. The result was that a person could sit at home and type on his keyboard "What's the population of Edinburgh?" The question would go to the nearest server, then to another one which knew the answer, and within a fraction of a second the person would read on his screen, "500,000." It was incredible.' This was an unfortunate example; Calum was numerate enough to be shocked, and that led the discussion into murkier waters.

***

Keith and Adam, who had never met or spoken, had organised further improvements to the radio network. Bruce's initiative had flushed out individuals who were able to help this process, producing further advances, and progress snowballed. More stations were brought into play, ensuring that messages could reach their destinations by multiple routes, very rapidly. The sender could restrict the readership to a single person, select a group or broadcast to anyone who visited a radio station. A system for attaching documents to the text was devised, though there were strict limits to the amount of data that could be transferred.

The first fruit of the new ability to send images was entirely frivolous. Rose had broadcast a request for sheet music to musicals and had heard nothing. Adam found 'Guys and Dolls' in a music shop in London, and used it as a test case for the new system. Alexandra was so pleased that she turned it into an excuse for a concert. On the coldest day of the winter the team gathered to hear Rose as Miss Adelaide, David as Nathan Detroit, Margaret as Sarah Brown and Henry as Sky Masterson, with Alexandra on piano. A great deal of hilarity arose from the players' inappropriate ages and relationships in real life.

Experts started to tackle problems identified by Bruce and Steven. One group worked on restarting high power radio transmitters, with the aim of enabling the human voice to be broadcast to anyone with an old AM set in their house. Philip explained to his mother, 'This would be the first means of communication directly to ordinary houses rather than to ham radio stations.' Others were emptying septic tanks and processing the waste to make safe fertiliser. Someone was producing methane by anaerobic digestion of biomass; and engineers were trying to compress it sufficiently to produce a fuel suitable for petrol engines. All this activity increased the team's importance over a wider area.

***

In spring P7 Rose went on a tour of the other groups, to identify toddlers who could play with Stewart, Jocelyn and Flora under her care. At the rapeseed farm she met an unfamiliar young man. 'Hello, I'm Rose Tanner. I haven't seen you here before. Where have you come from?' 'From the far west.' 'Oh, we went to Letheilean to escape Phraya, then we returned to our farm, and in due course we moved down here. What's your name?' 'Fergus Sutherland.' He paused, as if unsure what to say next, so she filled the silence. 'That's an interesting name, I've never heard it before. What work are you doing for Gregory?' 'I helped with the rapeseed harvest when I arrived last autumn, and then separated the seeds ...' 'I look after the smallest children at our steading, and might take on some of the little ones here.' He seemed unable to say any more, so she let him off; 'I expect I'll see you around, goodbye.' When she reported this meagre conversation, Isabella said, 'He's only just arrived from the wilderness, so he's shy, give him time.'

***

Olivia had a word with Philip. 'The radio messaging system is wonderful these days, especially compared with driving around the country, but it has its limitations. When will it be possible to have voice conversations, beyond the nearest station?' 'I can see three ways. The obvious possibility is to resurrect the landline telephone, but in recent decades it didn't operate by copper wire all the way. Instead most of the distance was covered by fibre optics, with local digital exchanges, and those will be hard to re-establish.' 'Gobbledygook! Are these options going to get even tougher?' 'I'm afraid so. The next possibility is to fire up the cellular network; very challenging I think, even assuming the old smartphones continue to work. Finally, you could wait a hundred years for the web to reappear and enjoy voice over internet, with moving pictures.' 'Can't we make the ham radio system do it?' He thought for a while. 'You're a genius, mum. We may be able to forward analogue voice from station to station, in real time, or at least with a small enough delay that it doesn't make conversation awkward. I'll talk to Keith.' 'Double Dutch, but it sounds promising.'

As the team's authority increased, transport and trade continued to improve within central Scotland. Progress was slower both to the north and for some distance southwards, because there were no easily accessible cities of adequate size. Olivia called a meeting to consider, more soberly than at New Year, ways of extending the team's reach. Charles started: 'I think Steven was right; if we want to help the recovery more widely, we need to have a physical presence elsewhere.' Deborah argued, 'It doesn't make much difference where we are – what matters is organising people, whether in person or remotely. If we're scattered, we won't be able to talk properly amongst ourselves, and we'll offer less effective guidance to others.' Henry remarked, 'If we were all in London, we'd be together but in a more relevant place. It must be the heart of the country eventually?' This time no-one laughed; instead many separate conversations erupted simultaneously. Olivia decided not to bring the meeting to order, but rather to give people time to think about this radical idea.

***

Rose tried again; this time, following a suggestion from Isabella, she was determined to do less of the talking. 'Hello, Fergus.' 'Rose, nice to see you.' He paused, so she simply said, 'If it's not too awful, I'd like to hear about your experience of Phraya.' 'OK. I lived with my parents and little sister on a remote farm in the Near Isles. Everyone left when the ferries stopped bringing food,' – he paused, so she prompted, 'yes, it was the same in the Far Isles' – 'but we decided to stay. Ever since then we've lived on our own.' 'How did you manage?' 'We were growing enough food, and fishing, and there were sheep.' 'So the four of you were there for six years?' 'Yes, and it was a bit lonely for us kids, with no friends within reach. I suggested that we move but my parents wouldn't consider it.' 'We've done a lot of moving, but there were more of us to egg each other on.' 'When I grew up I decided to leave, and they didn't resist. After a few adventures I found my way here. 'Well, I'm glad you did.'

***

Thomas was a year old on 18 April P7. Peter and Jessica weren't planning to make anything of the occasion, but there was a celebratory mood for another reason; the radio network had bridged the channel, and for the first time text had reached the UK from another country. Alexandra leapt on this. 'See, we must keep international culture going. Tom will learn French!' Jessica had been on an exchange the summer before Phraya, and tried to remember; 'Mais oui, d'accord, maman.' Bruce asked, 'I'll add languages to my database of skills. What are they saying over there?' Alexandra had studied the messages; 'The situation is comparable. Paris is a little ahead of London, and they've done something similar with ham radio.' 'I bet their system is incompatible. We'll have to unify "le software" if possible.'

***

Olivia asked Andrew about his sanatorium in Morrie. 'How do you handle people for whom the world is just too much?' 'Our approach has been to give them food whether or not they are able to help grow it.' 'What about those who cope, but in a way that damages others?' 'We make it clear that we'd rather they avoided doing certain things, but they are supported anyway. Almost all carrot and as little stick as is compatible with good order.' 'What about people who are crazy?' 'Our regime seems to be helpful for everyone, whether sad, bad or mad. Brodie and the banned norther – I don't know to which category they belong – have calmed down and are fitting in. Actually, they're good for discipline. I've heard about rough treatment of difficult people elsewhere, and would like to try our method in other places.'

***

Keith reported success on electricity. 'Alastair helped us get the big generator running at the substation, and mains emerged at the far end. It's not easy to balance supply and demand, so don't expect reliability.' Bruce asked, 'Is there a smaller scale approach?' 'Yes, we've also managed to hook up wind turbines to produce power without the danger of kilovolts. It's even safer to use solar panels to charge twelve-volt batteries, and then inverters to give 230 volts, but this is much lower power.'

Alexandra wrote: "Our wonderful wizards are well on the way to mains electricity, the first utility of the post era. Who knows, perhaps eventually we'll have pumped water in and drainage out? Gas for cooking and central heating? Chilled champagne piped into every house? If we artistic types can lay on an arts festival, we'll have achieved nirvana."

***

In late April leaders from all over Scotland met again. This time there was a sense of togetherness, and it was agreed that the Edinburgh community would be regarded as the central authority of the province – nobody was ready yet to claim it was the capital of a nation. The question of choosing a leader arose; the selection process was scarcely an election, and as there were no candidates other than Olivia, so her position was confirmed without a formal vote.

***

The idea that the recovery of London was crucial to that of the UK had taken hold, and Olivia held a further meeting. Alice asked, 'Do we know what it's really like there?' Bruce replied, 'I think I have a handle on this. People are trying to apply our methods, and are succeeding in some places but not others.' Steven wanted to know, 'What's holding them back?' Samuel argued, 'We can't really know without being on the spot.' Margaret objected, 'We've already decided we can't be everywhere.' Deborah suggested, 'Perhaps we need to go on a tour, all the way to London and back, and then offer advice appropriate to each place?'

Olivia turned to the question of who should go on the trip. 'I'm sure, Steven, that you would like to evaluate engineering progress. Ideally Philip would check the radio stations, but new parents shouldn't leave their small children.' Henry groaned, but she ignored him. 'However, I would like give the next generation a chance. Benjamin, perhaps you can handle electronics?' Alexandra jumped in; 'In that case Bruce and I could go to cover logistics and culture?' 'We should stick to one car, so that's enough people?'

On 10 May P7 the expedition set out. Stewart, five years old that day, asked, 'Where have the others gone?' Ruth tried to answer: 'They're exploring.' 'Why?' 'To see how other people are getting on.' 'Are they going a long way?' Alan thought he knew how to explain; 'You know we can see a volcano from the steading? That's four miles away. When we climb to the top of the hill behind us, we can see much further – it's forty miles to the big mountains, ten times more. Well, Bruce and the others are going ten times as far as that – four hundred miles.' He paused to see if he had been understood. 'Wow, won't the car get tired?'

As they progressed southwards, Benjamin asked about progress with radio and Bruce proselytised about the cel. In northern England, where Henry had observed little more than subsistence, tractors were running but people were still cooperating largely through barter. Further on, around the previously bustling cities, there was rather more industrial activity and trade, but they were disorganised. Alexandra suspected that the arrival of rapid communication over long distances was acting as a stimulant, but it produced cacophony rather than symphony. There was a sense of shared destiny, and everyone thought they knew the best way forward, but the recovery lacked focus.

***

David was dissatisfied with the situation on fertiliser, so he spoke to Katherine and Rhona. 'There's no decent source of nitrogen. Naturally we do what people did in pre-industrial times – rotate crops, and grow legumes, which fix nitrogen from the atmosphere. Now that we've got a reliable surplus of food, we can afford to leave fields fallow, and sow clover. All so nineteenth century; in order to advance into twentieth, we need to do more.' 'That's why we've been worrying about ammonia. Bruce tells me that the worldwide production of ammonium nitrate in pre-Phraya times was almost two hundred million tonnes per year, nearly all for fertiliser. Scaling for the present UK population, he reckons that corresponds to two thousand tons a year.' Katherine was aghast; 'How are we going to make that much?' 'I've heard of someone in the Midlands who's trying to produce the required chemicals without the high pressures needed by the processes before Phraya.'

***

The missionaries arrived in London and went to Adam's radio station. 'Hello, I'm Benjamin Lenton, you've been talking to my cousin Philip. My dad Bruce and mum Alexandra Eades, and Steven Lynn, our engineer.' 'Great to meet you all, face to face at last. Olivia has been asking for voice communication, and we're on the case.' When they had covered technical matters, Alexandra asked, 'Tell us about how things feel down here.' 'We are emerging at last, from a worse state than other parts of the country, I think. The example of Edinburgh has been inspiring, but there is no overall direction down here.' 'How can we best help?' 'I suspect we need organisation, discipline, and a sense of belonging to something that will succeed – in a word, leadership.'

***

Jessica updated the team on the hospitals. 'Gordon is doing simple operations, and has got some of the scanning equipment going. Certain blood tests can be done. He's worried that things will go backwards when consumables run out or stop working – they all passed their expiry dates long ago. A few of his people are working on traditional remedies, but it's all a bit "Eye of newt, and toe of frog," and you can't get all the plants mentioned in the books.'

Chapter 18 Southwards?

On 2 June P7 the expedition returned. Olivia allowed everyone a day to hear what had been discovered, and then called a meeting. 'It's clear that many of us believe that a fully recovered UK can only be led from London. For this reason, some argue that we should move there. We seem to be ahead of everyone else in the UK, and we've acquired some practical authority. On the other hand, we don't have to be the leaders; and even if we want to be, it's not obvious that we must move now, later or at all. Can we start with whether we want to move at any stage?'

Charles set the ball rolling. 'To save Olivia the embarrassment of taking sides, I should say that the she and I want to go. We think Scotland is in a good state, but England isn't yet. If there's to be a United Kingdom again, London will have to be brought up to scratch.' David replied, 'I think it will rise naturally to a position of leadership. It's taking longer because of the depths to which it, and all major cities, sank during the crisis. Perhaps we helped speed things up around here.' Steven argued, 'In which case we might help in London too.' Deborah developed her point from the previous discussion; 'Indeed, but we can do that from our present base, if communications keep on improving as they have.' Philip warned, 'Don't assume we're going to be seeing people's faces on our smartphones soon.' Bruce had been developing an idea on how best to enable progress. 'I have identified certain fundamental problems which, if unsolved, threaten to bring progress to a halt. In order to address these, we need to set up centres of excellence – call them universities – from which solutions will emanate. Most of these will have to be in the south, where the majority of the people survive.'

Margaret dragged the meeting back to immediate fundamentals. 'Numerous people might be a problem as well as an asset. Up here there's plenty of land, relative to the population, so we grow enough food without clashing over resources.' Patricia was unconcerned; 'There's plenty of room even in England. Before Phraya there were millions of people, and when the dust settled the survivors were just that – they were able to eke out an existence. I was there.' Alice argued, 'But the population will rise.' Samuel countered, 'That will take years. We'll keep up easily.' Lucy wasn't so sure; 'Numbers may not rise rapidly but the movement of people will, and then we might be threatened by diseases. The south is more vulnerable, and medicine is still extremely primitive.'

Jessica raised a different concern. 'I'm not sure we should subject the new generation of children to the upheaval.' Peter was dutiful; 'Although I'm tempted by engineering challenges, I agree for the moment.' Katherine seemed to agree: 'I understand your concern, and I was nervous when Jocelyn was tiny,' – Henry interjected, 'You always are!' – and then surprised everyone: 'but I think it's safe everywhere now. The little ones will grow up and should have a chance to be at the leading edge of innovation.' Ruth wanted a quiet life for her kids. 'Stewart is already used to being here, and I'm reluctant to disturb him.' Benjamin added, 'We're trying for a baby, and if we succeed it wouldn't be helpful to move at a delicate time.' Julia blushed; 'Thanks for that, but I guess you're right.'

Rose pointed out, 'No-one is talking about whether we actually want to go, for our own sake; well, I do.' Everyone laughed when Henry said, "You all know my preference.' Alan replied, 'No thanks, I'm happy to stay in my own country.' Isabella said, 'Nothing against yours, but I'd like to go back to what used to be mine.' Rory admitted, 'The truth is I'd like to get back to the islands, the sea and proper fishing.' Shona remarked regretfully, 'I've never been to England, but I don't feel at home in Scotland any more, so I don't know what I think.' Alexandra complained, 'I don't think we're showing enough vision. We've got to re-build a world in which people come to the UK because London is the most cosmopolitan city in the world. International musicians will beat a path to our door.' Olivia counted and declared, 'Well that's a balance of opinion, a dozen people on each side. We'll have to cogitate and return to the debate.'

***

Jocelyn was four on 9 July. She sang 'Happy birthday to me' so well that Katherine asked Rose, 'Heavens, she's in tune, and in time – will you teach her music?' 'Certainly. Perhaps one day she'll start the opera company that Alexandra hankers after.' 'Why does she need hankies? I don't want anyone to cry at my party.' Stewart, always happy to instruct his friend, explained, 'No, a hand kiss; you blow it to the person who's sad.' Ruth was amused by the game into which they had stumbled. 'You didn't listen properly, she said ham, kids I think we better have the party food.'

***

Olivia went to seek Andrew's opinion on London. 'I'm quite attracted by the idea of going there to help the people worst affected by Phraya. I could establish a central sanatorium, train people and send them out to set up others. It's about time we addressed the psychic health of survivors everywhere. If we rebuild society correctly, I think we can avoid prisons and mental hospitals altogether.' 'I don't mean to be disrespectful, but is this a new kind of religion?' 'Much more useful, I think. Nothing to believe in except the wellbeing of humans, no gods to muddy the waters.'

***

Steven went to talk to Rhona. 'The roads are beginning to suffer. Even without enormous lorries to hammer them, they are damaged by ice in cold weather and then ordinary cars displace the loosened tarmac.' She replied, 'Bruce has mentioned this. The problem is that asphalt is yet another petroleum product, and we haven't been able to make enough tar. We have been trying to make a substitute, by heat-treating rapeseed and other waste biomass, and mixing it with the broken material from wrecked roads. Richie's people have fixed a few potholes and we're keeping an eye on them. So far so good, only the winter will tell.'

***

At her party on 26 July, Flora had a go at 'Happy birthday'. Alexandra winced, 'Ah, not a musical talent to challenge Jocelyn. I may not be able to accommodate her in the London Conservatoire.' Ruth wasn't amused; 'She's only three, for God's sake. We're not going there anyway.' 'Oh, I think we will in the end. Scotland's emptiness may have saved us when we were in Letheilean and Morrie, and has helped since then in Edinburgh. London, with so many more people, was a scene of horror during Phraya, and been slow to recover. In the end, however, England will rise to a position of dominance once again.'

A frisson ran round the room. Olivia suggested, 'Shall we go for a walk, Alexandra?' She directed a significant glance at her old friend; 'Can you help here please?' As they left Deborah said carefully, 'I hope the debate on London isn't going to polarise into the two nations. I, for one, came from one of them, moved to the other and love them both.' Margaret was tight-lipped; 'That was certainly pretty arrogant, and fairly absurd considering the current wreckage of the UK capital.' Her loyalties divided, Jessica offered an immediate apology to her mother-in-law: 'I'm sorry, I'll go and talk to mum.'

Meanwhile Bruce attempted an explanation: 'I think all she meant to do was to reflect something I've been saying. If there were ten times as many people in England as in Scotland before Phraya, the same is probably true of the survivors in the two countries. If so, once the south has recovered from its worse starting point, it will be critical for the future shape of the UK.' Margaret conceded, 'Steven has made the same point. It's quite a long way from what she actually said, but it's a reasonable argument, and does suggest a move.'

***

Alastair had machined some moulds, and Peggy had harvested some latex. Rhona filtered it, added acid and squeezed the excess water from the coagulated material. She pushed the rubber into the mould and heated it until it was dry. The results were dubious, but practice made perfect; in due course Lucy presented the best of a bad bunch to Jessica and said, 'Give these to Peter and see if you can get him and the other lads to try them out.'

***

Alexandra gathered her family. 'I have decided I should be more honest. It's not about population; your father and I lived in England, so naturally we want to go back. You passed most of your childhoods there; why don't you?' Jessica replied, 'We grew up fast when we drove up north, and associate Scotland with adulthood.' Benjamin confessed, 'If we're going to tell the truth, we've fallen for a couple of Scots and don't feel we should drag them away from their homeland.' Isabella joined in: 'Well I haven't, so I'm happy to go and look for an Englishman.' Bruce intervened; 'It's all very well acknowledging our emotions, but there are actually good reasons for moving. There are real problems lurking ahead, technological challenges which can't be addressed with the resources up here. Most of the answers are likely to be down there; it's not a matter of nationality.' Jessica conceded, 'You may be right, we should continue to analyse the arguments. In the meantime, mum, perhaps a word with Ruth would help?' Later, Alexandra approached her with, 'I'm sorry, I didn't explain myself at all well, I apologise,' and they hugged.

***

By the end of October, Jessica was pregnant again. She was the first to hear Shona's news: 'Me too; we'll have our babies about the same time. Let's hope we don't decide to move any time soon. Sam has been working on persuading his family, and Alan too; he says there must be lots of joinery to be done in the south.' They showed the children the baby models, and Jocelyn said, 'I've got a baby in my tummy too.' She stuffed a doll under her jumper, and Flora insisted, 'Me too, it's not fair.' Stewart wasn't graceful in defeat; 'Well, boys can't have babies, but I don't want one anyway.' Thomas and Marcus tried to grab the models but couldn't reach the shelf where they were stored.

***

Electricity was almost becoming a commodity in some Scottish cities and was appearing elsewhere. Charles was concerned about excessive use; he wanted to introduce charging by means of the meters in the houses. Keith pointed out, 'The difficulty is that people can use the power anywhere; even if we could read all the meters, we can't know who has used it.' Charles raised the subject in a team meeting. 'This is part of a more general problem, whereby some people in society don't pull their weight. With most other resources they don't get it if they don't make or buy it, but electricity is more abstract. The same will apply to any other utilities we manage to restore, and some of them aren't even metered.' Alan suggested, 'Perhaps the westsiders can knock some sense into people.' Deborah was more thoughtful, 'The question is whether we're trying to re-build capitalism.' Charles looked exercised; 'Yes, we don't want a centrally controlled economy; we need incentives, but we may create an underclass and have to set up a welfare state. Hmm.'

***

Margaret had a word with her children. 'Your father and others are trying to persuade me that we should move to London. I know you want to really, Peter, but are inhibited by concerns about Tom.' He replied, 'Yes, and I suspect Benjamin is the same. You're not even expecting, Julia, but the possibility is holding him back.' Margaret concluded, 'So if I were to decide I want to move, and Jessica were convinced that her son will be OK, all four of you would probably agree, and both families could move together?' Julia looked surprised, but conceded, 'Yes, perhaps so.'

***

One day late in the year, when Isabella was at Rhona's place, she was approached by a young man. 'Hello, I'm Donald Grant, what's your name?' 'Isabella Lenton. I don't think you've been here long?' 'No, my parents and I live with Peggy, and I've just started working over here. I'd like to become a biochemist, if it's possible these days.' 'I fancy chemical engineering, but I'm not sure that it's much more feasible. Katherine Blair, one of our team at the steading, was a student at Strathclyde when Phraya struck; same subject, a little ahead of you.' 'Maybe I can meet her, but first I'd like to get to know you better.' She liked him already.

***

The leaders of most communities in England were well aware of the team's role in diesel, radio, electricity and other industries. They were beginning to be influenced by Olivia's leadership. Charles managed to get the cel adopted and standardised. Bruce provided a quietly structured approach to further technological advances. Alexandra probed how society was developing, discussed the results with Andrew and fed his suggestions back. From the London radio station, Adam reported that some were suggesting that the team might form a government there.

On Christmas Day everyone remembered the awkwardness of the previous one, and of the debate about London, and stuck to straightforward festivity. At New Year, however, tongues were loosened. As the AM radio broadcast announced midnight, Henry greeted it with, 'Ah, P8, the year we move south.' Rory, who had located a bottle of 25-year old Scotch and was correspondingly merry, replied, 'Oh no it isn't!' Steven and Philip shouted, 'Oh yes it is,' and soon there was a uproarious competition. Olivia smiled and declared, 'Using our sophisticated new voting system, I judge that there's an increasing consensus in favour of the move.' When the objections had died down, she asked, 'Now, where's my drink?' There was an immediate chorus: 'It's behind you.'

***

Calum was twelve on 17 Jan P8, and his treat was to be taken on a tour of the radio stations. At the engineers the Scotts ran across Graeme and Anthea Melville, who wanted to speak to Lucy. They indicated their daughter; 'We had Kyla three years before Phraya, and afterwards the moment was never right. Now we're wondering about the snip.' 'We'd already had two, our daughter Alison and Calum here, when I performed the operation on Rory; it was very easy.' Kyla asked, 'What's the snip?' Calum explained self-importantly, "It's to stop a couple having any more babies.' As the families parted, boy watched girl, she turned for a moment and their gazes met.

***

The team had decided that another survey of the south was needed, and on 24 March Olivia, Philip, David and Alan set off. She wanted to meet other leaders, and to see to what extent the cities were gelling. Philip was keen to speak directly with Adam, at last. David was looking for suitable sites for a settlement, in the event that the team decided to move; and Alan was going specifically to represent the sceptical members of the team.

***

Although Isabella and Donald had got to know each other, they hadn't been through the ritual exchange of Phraya stories. She started; 'We got out of London when dad predicted the full effects of the virus, and went via Edinburgh to Letheilean.' 'Yes, I know it, very beautiful.' 'We kept out of the way for a year, then went to Morrie,' – 'where's that?' – 'at the northern edge of the farmland in central Scotland. After another year we came here, and now we may go back down south! What about you?' He gave his potted history: 'My parents lived in a remote part of Estra.' 'I've been told about it – everyone left, I think?' 'Yes, except us, so we had it to ourselves. We found some supplies left behind in the panic, fished and eventually grew enough food.' 'When did you come here?' 'In P3 we joined Peggy's group.' 'I can't believe we didn't meet until recently.' 'Better late than never.' 'If we go to London, I hope your family will come.'

***

Adam greeted Olivia warmly: 'I'm very pleased to see you. When are you coming down here for good?' 'We're having an ongoing debate about that. It would help if we could see evidence of local leadership; if we're to make cloth there need to be threads to weave together.' 'I think that is finally happening. I'll take you on a tour to get to know some of the relevant people.' Over the next few days she was introduced to groups running farms, engineering workshops and rudimentary chemical engineering plant. Philip met Adam's group, and it became clear that the communities were cooperating, at least locally. They were aware of similar alliances around the former capital; Alan gained confidence in the state of English affairs. On the way back, David identified pieces of land which might be suitable for an enlarged version of the team's farming operation.

On their return, Julia announced that she was also pregnant. Allowing a day for celebration and rest, Olivia called a meeting for the eighth anniversary of Phraya. 'My feeling is that if we're going to move south, the right time is after the harvest this year. We would spend the interim preparing ourselves and the target communities. However, the purpose of this discussion is to see if we can decide whether to go at all. I also feel that we should all go, or none of us, though I can envisage halfway houses, temporary arrangements and the like. Ideally we will agree unanimously, or by a large majority, and come to a firm conclusion.'

Complete silence. Philip said, 'A decision like this is a bit frightening, but what the hell, let's just start talking and see where it takes us.' David drew breath; 'Perhaps I should start, for a couple of reasons: I think we should stay here, but I'm English so I can't be accused of Scottish bias. Also I've just been down south, and I admit that it's ready to be helped. It's just that I believe in local leadership. London should rise to dominance – sorry, Alexandra – by its own efforts. Perhaps the UK will be rebuilt with Edinburgh as its capital?' Alexandra winced, and then smiled. 'I deserve that! But this sounds a bit like letting nature take its course, however red in tooth and claw. Couldn't we help, without declaring in advance where the government of the UK will be?' Rory objected, 'By moving south, aren't we effectively throwing our authority behind the conclusion that it will be there? Henry cut across all this: 'I reckon London will be capital in the end, with or without us. I'd just like to be there when it happens.'

Alice insisted, 'I just don't want to leave the country I've always lived in, just because of a stupid virus.' Margaret replied, 'Neither do I, but Phraya has utterly changed everything; Scotland ceased to exist on this very day eight years ago. It was mine too, and realising that it has gone changed my mind about moving.' Lucy pointed out, 'England also vanished, and we don't need to recreate it in the ruin called London.' Bruce argued, 'You're both right, and now we have to think from first principles. The people and the equipment are in the south, so that's where a new country – just one – must be created. The fact that it seems to have got going up here is an accident.'

Olivia interrupted the debate; 'I know we haven't reached agreement, but it might be worth having a show of hands to see if any consensus is emerging. First, those for moving,' – many hands went up – 'and now those who want to stay.' Rory, Alice and David raised their hands; Lucy and Deborah wavered. Suddenly Ruth made an appeal: 'All this nation-building is very high-minded. Let's remember we're also deciding what a group of people is going to do. If we're not careful we're going to splinter the team into two shattered memories of years of intimacy. Please,' – she was close to tears – 'please, let's find a way to stay together, even if some aren't getting what they want.' Deborah looked at David pleadingly. Rory watched Lucy's half-raised hand slowly sinking to her side. Alan said, 'Give in, Alice.'

Part 6 Nation

Chapter 19 Money

"12 April P10. A significant anniversary – time for a survey of the past few years. Firstly, the children have grown up and made more! Our reciprocal link with the Lynns has been fecund: first Jessica and Peter gave us Tom and Sarah, then Benjamin and Julia produced Victoria; both couples are expecting again."

"The inseparable girls concocted a double wedding – Isabella to Donald and Rose to Fergus – on Flora's fourth birthday, with her and Jocelyn as flower girls, which made up for my faux pas the previous year. Rose was so anxious about conceiving that she insisted that her man be tested, and she was right. Samuel found a secret donor and she is now pregnant. Isabella is trying more patiently."

"Henry and Trish delivered Marcus and Eleanor; lastly, Sam and Shona had Craig and recently Fiona. So, ten new children and rising!"

"We've got around quite a lot. After meeting on Letheilean and returning to Morrie, we established ourselves in Edinburgh and found, to our surprise, that we were leading the recovery. In October P8 the team transferred to an area just north of central London. It's semi-rural, so we can farm, but industrial enough to enable engineering activity, and close enough to the city to allow us to regenerate it as a capital."

"We had tried to persuade other leaders to come with us, and some did. Gregory started a new rapeseed operation nearby, with Ruth helping. Rhona brought some of her chemists; Katherine and Isabella work with her. Keith came to pursue electronics with Philip and Benjamin, and they've started to train Calum. Gavin brought most of his westsiders and Richie the northers; it's a pity they're still known by their gang names. Andrew continues his humanitarian work in the south, with Shona as a caregiver."

"Alastair didn't want to leave, so Graeme Melville is leading the engineers, working with Peter, Alan and Sam. Peggy stayed up north too, so David is in overall charge of food crops. Rose and Fergus work on cereals, and Rory handles fish farming, with help from Donald on the feed. Raymond didn't come either, so Alice runs animal husbandry in his place, and trains William. Gordon would have moved, but Olivia asked him to remain in Scotland as leader there, and his deputy Ramsay Macrae came to run a London hospital. Jessica works with him; so does Lucy part time, and Ruth acts as a midwife when required."

"Food production is still at the heart of things, Margaret insists, but these days it requires only about half the available man hours. Olivia has expanded some people's roles beyond the team's premises: Deborah is trying to coordinate farming efforts across the nation. Bruce identifies technological challenges to be addressed, Steven organises tasks and Charles gets everyone cooperating on them. Other groups are willing but not yet fully organised; sixty thousand or so survivors require central and local governance, and that is taking time. In order to ensure that we advance culturally I try, with help from Henry, Trish, Julia and Rose, to coordinate our efforts on economics, the law, education, the arts and mental health."

***

Charles had been working with Andrew on a new idea, which he explained to the team: 'I think we should get coins minted, with values tied to food; in fact they could be called cels, to emphasise a link to the standard parcel.' Alan remarked, 'Sounds confusing; proper money can be used to buy other things.' 'Indeed, but at first the currency would represent only food, and be exchangeable for it. Already this would be a convenience, because it wouldn't be necessary to carry parcels about and barter them for other things.' Philip asked, 'Will people trust the coins?' 'I think so, precisely because they will be so closely associated with having enough to eat.' Rory was dubious; 'Perhaps, but it doesn't sound all that useful.'

Charles continued, 'Over time, the currency would be used more widely. The suppliers of biodiesel, for example, would be happy to be paid in coin cels, knowing that they can always exchange them for food ones. Pretty soon they'd realise that they, in turn, can use the currency to buy yet other things, neither food nor biodiesel, but whatever they need. So gradually the coins become money.'

Deborah changed the subject. 'How do we introduce the currency? If we just hand it out, it won't be valued.' Andrew replied, 'This is where I had a thought; if people have to earn the coins they'll be respected. I propose one is issued whenever someone gives away a food parcel or provides a comparable public service. This will establish the fact that the coin really is worth a food cel. This social security initiative will gradually increase the amount of currency in circulation.' Ruth exclaimed, 'Very clever, and worthy too.'

Charles resumed, 'Over time the word cel will transfer itself from the parcel to the coin, and eventually the food version won't even be made; instead people will buy whatever they actually want to eat. The value of the currency won't drift as it did in the days of the gold standard whenever anyone found a new vein of ore.'

Benjamin suggested, 'For small purchases we could have other denominations, perhaps a cent worth a hundredth of a cel, along with two, five, ten, twenty and fifty cent coins? Also bigger ones, two, five, ten cels,' – here Charles interrupted – 'but no bigger, or we'll have a problem with counterfeiting.' Alice asked, 'Yes, what about that?' 'The westsiders will discourage it, best not to ask how.'

***

London had brought Alison into contact with trained dentists, so at last she was able to start her training properly. At Ramsay's hospital she ran across his son Cameron, and recognised him; 'Hello, I think we might have met in Edinburgh, but perhaps I was too young for you to notice?' He had a twinkle in his eye: 'I saw you before the move, but thought I better wait; there might have been even more beautiful girls in the land of the Angles.' She pretended to mishear: 'But angels come from the land of the Scotts.' 'Well, now that I consider the matter more closely …'

They were interrupted by Ruth; 'Cameron, where's your father? Alison, go and get Lucy. There's some kind of complication with Julia's labour.' She was bent over double, clutching the back of a chair and holding her breath. 'What's happening? It wasn't like this with Victoria. My waters were a bit pink, not as red as this. It didn't hurt like this early on, either.' Benjamin, looking worried, was trying to comfort her, but he was dismissed and she was taken away for an ultrasonic scan.

When Lucy arrived, she conferred with Ramsay and gave Julia their diagnosis: 'It looks like a small placental abruption; that means part of it has detached from the wall of your uterus. It sometimes happens much earlier in the pregnancy, and it's more serious then. For the moment we'll carry on as normal.' She allowed Benjamin back in, to keep his wife calm, but refused to let Jessica take part; 'It's your brother's baby, you're pregnant yourself, and I'm not sure how it will end.'

As the labour progressed the doctors grew more concerned. The scans showed the baby moving less, and Julia began to be extremely alarmed. 'Can't we do a Caesarean?' Lucy was firm; 'That would be much too dangerous for you, given the present state of medicine.' 'I'll do it, I want to save the baby.' After further whispering, Ramsay confirmed the decision: 'I'm sorry, it isn't appropriate to risk your life, and we hope the baby will be alright in any case.'

Within a few hours half the team was waiting outside the hospital. Eventually Benjamin emerged, white-faced, hugged his sisters, kissed his daughter and spoke in a low voice, 'Julia is OK, but has delivered a stillborn boy. It's incredible: she is already saying that we will try again.'

Margaret hurried in to her daughter. 'You poor thing, the doctors did what they could; you were brave, but it wasn't to be. I'm so sorry.' Steven wasn't far behind; 'You've done it once, so you will be luckier next time.' 'For God's sake, give her time!' 'But Benjamin told us she was determined.' Julia managed a strained smile; 'It's OK, dad's right, onwards and upwards as always.' Her mother acquiesced; 'Perhaps, but we should allow ourselves a moment in the present first.' Peter, who had been hovering in the background while his parents bickered, came forward, said nothing and simply hugged his sister. 'Thanks, go and give my husband one too. Dammit, Jessica will soon put you ahead by three to one.'

Benjamin was having trouble matching his wife's courage, and Bruce felt a pressure to say something. 'I'm sorry, son. Lucy warned us that childbirth was difficult without modern medicine, and it looks as if Julia was the victim of statistics. There's a high probability that it will be fine next time.' He wandered off to see if his mother could offer a more human perspective. 'We should have a funeral, and I've found something lovely for the ceremony.' The next day Jocelyn read:

'The world may never notice
If a snowdrop doesn't bloom,
Or even pause to wonder
If the petals fall too soon.

But every life that ever forms,
Or ever comes to be,
Touches the world in some small way
For all eternity.

The little one we longed for
Was swiftly here and gone.
But the love that was then planted
Is a light that still shines on.

And though our arms are empty,
Our hearts know what to do.
For every beating of our hearts
Says that we love you.'

On 18 April Thomas was four, but his parents hadn't the heart for merriment. 'Why can't I have a party?' Peter tried to explain; 'Everyone is a bit sad because aunty Julia's baby wasn't alive when it was born. We'll have a party a bit later, and it will be even better than one today.' 'Was the baby alive, and then dead?' Jessica took over: 'Yes, it was moving about in her tummy, like mine is,' – she pointed to her developing bump – 'but then it stopped moving, and…' Sarah, almost two, sensed the mood, and burst into tears. 'I want a baby to play with.'

***

Travellers were beginning to make trips, almost routinely, to and from Europe. Although messages had been passing back and forth for some years, and pioneers had been seen much earlier, the arrival of people in significant numbers gave a better sense of how other countries were progressing. They had city governments, but these still operated rather separately; national governance was developing only slowly despite good radio communication. Technology advanced, but without overall coordination. Trading was still by barter; Charles was determined to improve this. Alexandra urged that more languages should be added to the school curriculum. Henry was interested in the wider world, and wondered how he might help.

***

In early May Ruth spoke to her son. 'People are still a bit too sad to celebrate your eighth birthday, Stewart, but I've got an idea. By the summer everyone will feel better; you could be in charge of a party, combining your special day with Flora's sixth and Jocelyn's seventh. Tom will have the fourth he missed, and Sarah and Craig will be two.' 'What about the others?' 'Well, Marcus, Victoria, Eleanor and Fiona don't have birthdays in the summer, but we'll let them come too?' 'Great, can I organise the games?'

Isabella had good news for Donald; 'I'm not absolutely sure yet, but I think you're going to be a father.' His face lit up – 'that's wonderful,' – and immediately clouded – 'but I'm not sure the team is ready for an announcement.' 'Yes, it's not fair on Julia and my brother.' 'Your mother is good on this kind of thing; let's ask her what she thinks.' Alexandra was pleased, but after pondering for a while she suggested, 'Why not wait until the summer birthday party, and see if it raises the mood?'

***

Steven had a request for Rhona. 'When we do building work we're still forced to use lime mortar; I think it isn't the same as real cement?' 'You're right, lime doesn't adhere well, and it's weak and porous so it weathers badly. Proper Portland cement, once it has set, is more like rock, especially when mixed with stones to make concrete. However, producing it is quite complicated. It involves a variable mix of limestone, sandstone, marl, shale, iron, clay, and fly ash; the process requires close control. We'll do some experiments and creep on the full recipe.' 'Well, I did ask! Something a bit stronger would be appreciated.'

***

Alexandra had decided that a little healing of the national psyche wouldn't go amiss. She sent out messages encouraging people to submit their stories of Phraya survival and also, if they were willing, what they had discovered about the fates of their loved ones. When she circulated a few responses, this emboldened others and soon the trickle grew to a flood. Henry was intrigued; 'Why don't we distribute them properly, and indeed any other writings that people are producing?' 'Yes, we should be making new literature as well as preserving the old.' She had a word with Philip about digital publishing, and with Steven about getting printing equipment going again.

***

Contraception was becoming more troublesome, as Lucy had feared. She was worried about pre-Phraya intimate products, and would only use drugs in emergencies. The sole achievement of the post era was condoms of doubtful efficacy. She asked Rory to speak to the men, once again, about the snip; this soon had a surprising effect. Katherine, having had a hard labour, was spooked by the stillbirth of Julia's baby. Philip offered, 'I'm willing to have a vasectomy, then you could stop worrying.' 'But you're only thirty.' 'Yes, but Jocelyn is coming up to seven, so we're not going to have more kids.' 'What if I'm not around in the future, and you find someone else?' 'It's more likely that you'll get pregnant, and childbirth might have serious consequences.' They consulted Lucy, and she dutifully pointed out, 'In the old days I would have strongly advised a man as young as you against this.' 'Things have changed, please let's get on with it before there's another disaster.'

***

Over the past few years casual marketplaces had come into being, for the sale of food grown or goods manufactured by the proprietors. Initially payment was made by barter, or with food cels. Now, with the gradual appearance of coins, they developed into proper shops with permanently staffed premises. Old stores continued their ghostly existence, progressively emptying of all but the most useless items.

Children who had been born after Phraya had been taught how a real shop worked, but it was novel to encounter one, and the contrast with the old relics was confusing. William could just remember, and he explained to the kids: 'When I was your age you could walk round any town getting sweets, or toys, in exchange for coins your parents had given you.' Rose, who recalled rather more, added, 'Or if you were a grownup you could wave a piece of plastic and be given food, or clothes, or cars.'

The kids were flummoxed; Stewart asked, 'How did that work?' Samuel, who had understood even then, replied, 'Your money was stored in a place called a bank, and the plastic could transfer money to the shop to pay for what it sold you. But don't worry, it will be ages until it's like that again.' Jocelyn wanted to know, 'What about now?' William kept it simple enough for them to grasp; 'If you want some diesel for your car, you give the shop-keeper cel coins, and he can use those to buy food in another shop.' Flora complained, 'I still don't understand.'

***

Time nursed the team, and it was healed by the summer birthday festival. When the children had played games and stuffed themselves to a standstill, Isabella finally had a chance to make her announcement. 'What do you think I've got in my tummy?' Marcus piped up, 'Is it cake?' Flora corrected him: 'No, it's a baby.' Sarah clapped her hands excitedly; 'I like babies.' Thomas announced importantly, 'My mummy has a baby in her tummy too.' Isabella confirmed, 'You're both right, I do have cake in there, because it's a party; but I also have a baby in another part of me.' Rose muttered, 'At last, Jessica and I are already showing.'

***

Bruce had been arguing for years that technological capability was the key to the future, and now he fulfilled his longstanding ambition to found a university. He explained to the team, 'The aim is to secure the theoretical and practical knowledge that was once taken for granted. This will involve re-discovery and fresh invention in the countless specialties where there is no expertise among the survivors. Basic science is well represented in books – which we must conserve – and on the internet – parts of which we may be able to recover. Unfortunately, applied knowledge was more scattered: knowhow was often proprietary, embodied in the minds of lost practitioners, or was never captured in a form we can access.'

Philip and Benjamin joined him full time, considering long-term priorities and feeding research requirements to Steven, Katherine, Lucy and David. They in turn coordinated the required efforts all over the UK, starting with a systematic search for information uploaded pre Phraya. Software engineers hacked into home computers and business servers, established a database of recoverable knowledge and identified the gaps to be filled. Olivia, Charles, Margaret and Deborah administered the more routine work that was needed to keep the country running day by day.

***

On 22 August P10 Jessica went into the maternity ward of the hospital. Although Sarah had come more easily than Thomas, Peter was anxious after his sister's experience, and rightly so; this was hard once again. Gas and air failed to provide much respite, and the scene was reminiscent of a lying-in hospital. The doctors were chagrined as their patient – having no choice, like her eighteenth-century forebears – laboured on. Two days later Mary was delivered, crying robustly, and her father gave way to tears too. Julia was the first to visit, and was so generously joyful that it paved the way for the team to breath a collective sigh. Benjamin, still struggling with his feelings, hid them by taking Victoria in to meet her new cousin. Isabella, morning sickness assuaged by relief, went to hug her sister.

In the aftermath Lucy expressed concern: 'It really won't do that we can't perform sections because pre-Phraya anaesthetics are out of date, and post ones are inadequate.' Rhona reported the experimental production of ether. 'We've made it from alcohol and sulphuric acid, which is available from car batteries but is in short supply. It's a good anaesthetic, but it's hideously flammable so we'll have to be extremely careful.' Lucy asked, 'Anything safer?' 'We have also synthesised chloroform, which doesn't burn.' 'But it's more hazardous biologically, despite Queen Victoria's enthusiastic use of it in childbirth.'

Lucy continued, 'What about painkillers?' Katherine replied, 'They're all difficult to make, so we must fall back on aspirin, opium and other drugs which can be extracted from naturally occurring sources.' 'Even if we could do the Caesarean itself safely and without pain, we dare not because of the risk of infection. What can be done about that?' 'Penicillin may have been discovered by accident, but the production of a pure strain was a sophisticated business. We've made it by treating the blueish green mould on bread with citric acid, but I'm concerned that this simplified process yields a mixture of the desired species and other less benign ones.' Tests on animals showed that it worked, and did no harm, so it was tried in the manner of the mushrooms years earlier.

Cameron had toothache; he decided to trust the devil he knew – Alison – but not any of Rhona's nineteenth century sedatives. She removed a tooth with the help of nitrous oxide, and they discovered why it had been given its nickname. He didn't quite laugh under the gas, but was very relaxed, and grateful to have the pain extinguished. The experience did their relationship no harm, and soon they were a couple.

***

On 24 October Rose went into a trouble-free labour, and soon gave birth to a girl, Rachel. Shona brought Craig to hold his cousin. 'She's very little. My sister is bigger.' His mother explained, 'That's because she has been growing since she came out of my bump. This baby will get bigger too.' Watching the fuss, and observing David's and Deborah's delight, Fergus was a little detached from it all. 'My folks are far away, and there still isn't very good communication with the islands. Maybe they will visit one day, or we can take Rachel to see them.' Shona sympathised: 'My parents too, I'm barely in contact with them; I'm not even certain they're still together. I don't think they care about my kids at all. I'm sure yours will, even if they can't see their grandchild soon.'

Fergus still felt odd, and wandered off to talk to Alice. 'How does it feel to be a non-birth mother?' 'It's fine, after a short time it makes no difference.' 'Yes, but my position is different. Alan was the donor, he's your brother and is involved as an extra parent. I don't even know who Rose's donor is, he's a ghost, a rival father.' 'Nonsense, he's just a supplier of genetics.' 'Seems quite important.' 'I don't think so, nurture will win out over nature.' Seeing that he wasn't reassured, Ruth tried something much simpler: 'You'll just be a parent to a child who loves you.'

***

Julia had recovered and was determined to mark Victoria's second birthday on the 2nd of December. Patricia suggested that the task could be eased by bringing Marcus's fourth birthday forward two days. He was keen on the idea of a party; 'Yes, we can have games. I can do them. Sarah and Craig can play, and Victoria and Eleanor.' 'Why not Fiona, Mary and Rachel?' 'They're just babies. They can't do anything properly.' 'We'll let the little ones run around thinking they're taking part?'

On the day, however, the older children muscled in. Jocelyn sang for the musical chairs, and at first it all went swimmingly. At one of the pauses Marcus missed out on a seat, but was brave about it for a while. When Flora took over the singing Stewart suggested, none too delicately, that it would have been better if she hadn't; she cried. Marcus claimed that a new singer meant a new musical round had started, and Tom, who had been the last to sit down, objected to this. The argument made Victoria burst into tears at the dissolution of her party, and soon Julia was upset too. Patricia brought it to an end: 'OK, enough games; next time a grownup will be in charge. Time for food.'

***

William noticed a girl newly arrived in the animal group. 'Welcome, my name is William – Tanner, if you can believe that in this line of work – but call me Billie.' She matched his corniness: 'Thank you, I'm Anne Holmes. I've left one home to make another here, hence the plural.' He laughed, 'Well I suppose I asked for that. Where was the first one?' 'I've been living in the north, with my parents and younger brother, and have come down here to get to the meat of the matter!' 'OK, I give up, you win. I'm from Scotland, is that where you meant?' 'No, England, but not far from the border.' 'Ah, topside!' Alice had been watching; 'OK, you two, time to chuck it. Haven't you got any work to do?'

Chapter 20 Taxes

The winter of P10/11 was the most severe since Phraya, and Steven raised once again the question of the roads. 'The volume of goods being moved around is growing, so there are more lorries and, more seriously, heavier ones – they do disproportionate damage. When the snow and ice thaw, we're going to find that the tarmac has been wrecked.' Olivia asked, 'What can we do about it?' 'We're trying to get diesel-electric trains going to take heavy goods in the future; but for the moment they're not going to replace trucks locally.' 'Well, ships won't either, and aeroplanes … forget it?' He nodded. 'What about better maintenance of the roads?' 'In the absence of petroleum, asphalt is expensive, but Rhona has perfected a replacement for it.'

Charles had been listening quietly. 'I've been thinking about public services generally. At the moment we identify activities required for the common good, such as preserving the tarmac, and pay the people who carry them out. We use resources, ad hoc, across the whole of what used to be called the public sector. For example, Gavin and Richie are running semi-official operations which ought to be incorporated into the state. It's not sustainable; I reckon we're going to have to introduce organised taxes and a properly funded civil service.' Deborah remarked, 'Death certainly wasn't abolished by Phraya, but taxes were; now they've come back.' He continued, 'Then we can pay government workers from revenue rather than continuing to mint new cels, which threatens to become inflationary.' Olivia mused, 'If we have taxation, we must have representation as well; we should formalise the business of government, and eventually hold elections?'

*****

The winter blasted on through January, and the team waited to see if Isabella would produce a sixth successive girl – memories of Julia's stillborn boy had been quietly suppressed. On the 26th Isabella surprised everyone by giving birth, quite easily, to a son. Her first words to Donald were, 'Let's call him Douglas, as a tribute to the country where we met.' 'OK, that's a nice thought.'

When the grandparents visited, the Grants reminisced about survival on Estra. Their son remarked, 'I don't suppose you expected ever to see a grandchild. Bruce interjected, 'Neither did we, when we were making bows and arrows on Letheilean. Now we've got several, but Dougie is our first mutual grandchild.' Alexandra's faced contorted as she tried simultaneously to smile at the diminutive name and grimace at the needlessly revealed personal detail.

When Julia and Benjamin went to see the new baby, she whispered to him, 'Don't tell anyone yet, because I haven't even missed a period yet, but I feel pregnant again. I'm a bit scared.' Suddenly his courage returned. 'Don't be, that's wonderful news, I know it will be OK.' 'Dougie was the thirteenth post baby, so perhaps you're right.'

***

Technology marched on. Agriculture was highly mechanised, and the threat of hunger had receded entirely. In some areas purified water was being pumped locally. Sewage treatment was not yet established as a utility, but the contents of septic tanks were being composted to make fertiliser. Vehicles were serviced, diesel and ethanol fuels produced, and roads conserved. The mains grid was well established in many areas. Communications had been extended to many houses, using a strange mixture of analogue radio and repurposed digital technology. Recently voice communication had become possible, though not widespread or convenient. Bruce declared, 'We're approaching the standards of the early twentieth century. What's not so easy is to reproduce the progress after the Second World War.'

The cel coin was working well. It was trusted, and as a result people were willing to exchange them for goods unrelated to food or its production, and even for services. As anticipated the parcels were no longer made, except to ease travel. In the absence of significant trade with other climates, the preservation of food remained crucial, to handle winter. Phraya had taught people to lay in sufficient reserves for crop failures or shortages of funds; the threat of conflict, never far from their minds, was mitigated by this precaution. Charles had been urging Europeans to adopt the cel, or at least the idea of equivalence to food. They minted their own currency, called the nuro, but to his alarm it had no definitive link with anything of current economic value.

***

As always, the team held a gathering on the anniversary of Phraya. It wasn't a meeting, but a discussion arose when Jessica remarked, 'I'm keen to make up for the lateness of Tom's party last year.' Isabella pointed out, 'That would be nice, but thirteen children is just too many for all of them to celebrate each other's birthdays.' Julia surprised everyone: 'Despite the fiasco of the games for Marcus and Victoria, I think we should combine the parties into, say, two big ones each year.' Henry was enthusiastic; 'Yes, observe the solstices like the ancients. Sacrifices!' William suggested, 'Perhaps not human, maybe a hog roast?' Rose added, 'Dances round standing stones?' Patricia insisted, 'Fine, incantations to forgotten gods, but the games must be organised by adults.'

***

There was an impressive response to Alexandra's request for experiences of Phraya. Countless emails and voice messages were reconstructed from imperfect memories of the early stages of the calamity; while notes, often written at moments of complete uncertainty, provided objective evidence of later horrors. Tales of survival, escape and heroism mingled with sagas of broken communication, failed rendezvous, hints of abandonment and betrayal. Thousands described how they had avoided the virus, or caught it and recovered; but most heart-breaking were last words by victims, and farewells to the departed. Henry wondered about writing a formal history. 'We need to capture all this before records are lost, memories fade and survivors pass away.'

***

Plans were afoot for the summer party on 21 June, to mark birthdays falling from March to August. As it happened this meant all the older children – Stewart was nine, Jocelyn eight and Flora seven – so sophisticated activities would be needed. Simpler games were required for Thomas, five years old, and Sarah and Craig, both three. Those born September to February would be granted half birthdays, with special dispensations to allow Marcus, Victoria and Eleanor to play games. Little Fiona and Mary, despite having spring and summer birthdays, would merely look on with Rachel and Douglas, the autumn and winter babies. It had been decided that it would be best if none of the parents or grandparents was involved in running the party, so William, Alison and Calum were put in charge. Lucy remarked, 'It's lovely, there are youngsters of every age, with Phraya responsible for a hiatus of only six years between Calum and Stewart.' Shona told her privately, 'Well I'm think I'm going to add yet another.'

***

Olivia had decided that it was necessary to clarify property law. There was no parliament or established legal profession, so the government, such as it was, simply declared the new state of affairs: everyone could still help themselves to most resources outside their homes – land, unused buildings, vehicles, equipment, roads, utilities – but there was an ever-growing list of exceptions. Groups would own everything at their sites, and whatever they had made; the distribution of wealth to individuals was left for them to determine. Companies barely existed and were considered unworthy of property rights; but the government itself was a growing economic force.

***

William and Anne had conducted a whirlwind romance and were planning to marry. She went on a tour of the pre-Phraya shops with his mother and sister, but couldn't find a dress that she fancied. 'I don't think I can wear any of these confections in this day and age. We should make our own candyfloss.' Deborah reflected, 'Although there are plenty of clothes left, they're beginning to suffer, physically as well as stylistically. That's another industry we'll need to restart.' Rose, her interest aroused, volunteered, 'I've been considering the need for theatrical costumes; I'll see what I can do.'

On 3 September P11 William stepped onto the stage dressed as Theseus, Duke of Athens:

'Now, fair Hippolyta, our nuptial hour
Draws on apace; four happy days bring in
Another moon: but, O, methinks, how slow
This old moon wanes! she lingers my desires,
Like to a step-dame or a dowager
Long withering out a young man revenue.'

Anne, a resplendent Hippolyta, replied:

'Four days will quickly steep themselves in night;
Four nights will quickly dream away the time;
And then the moon, like to a silver bow
New-bent in heaven, shall behold the night
Of our solemnities.'

Stewart, playing Puck, picked Cupid's flower and David, as Oberon, declared, 'The juice of it on sleeping eye-lids laid will make or man or woman madly dote upon the next live creature that it sees.' Thomas had great fun as Bottom, donning an ass's head; but looked confused when Deborah's Titania fell in love with him.

The comedy continued as Peter, in the role of Lysander accidentally drugged, fell in love with his sister playing Helena. All was well: he ended up with Jessica, as Hermia; and Julia ended up hitched to Benjamin, playing Demetrius. The climax was the entrance of William and Anne to Mendelssohn's wedding march, performed by Patricia on piano, Katherine on clarinet and Charles, very rusty on violin.

Afterwards Anne used the nascent radio telephony system to speak to her parents and brother in the north, ending a broken conversation: 'I'm hoping to bring my excessively large new family to see you sometime.' The newlyweds went to live on Alice's livestock farm. Alexandra wrote, "The team is scattering geographically, but it still exists as a social and emotional unit rather than a living arrangement."

***

Julia went into labour early on 20 October. Lucy, Ruth and Jessica all insisted on being present despite Benjamin's assurances that he knew everything would be fine this time. The rest of the team pretended to do useful work while they waited. All this neurosis was needless, however, and by mid-afternoon another healthy boy, Robert, slipped silently into the world. When the proud father emerged with the news, Alexandra embraced him, Bruce shook his hand self-consciously, Margaret burst into tears and Steven whooped. Peter, embarrassed once again by his parents, went in to hug his sister the same way as last time – but for such different reasons!

***

Katherine reported progress on making biogas: 'Waste material from crops is being treated in anaerobic digesters, producing significant quantities of methane. Jocelyn describes it, rather accurately, as turning slime into farts.' Olivia laughed; 'Excellent, what can we do with it?' Steven outlined the options: 'The current approach, easiest and safest, is to store it just above atmospheric pressure, in bags, for cooking and heating houses; but it's a nuisance to transport at such low density.' 'Can we pump it along the existing pipes to houses?' 'Yes, but there would inevitably be leaks.' Katherine agreed; 'The resulting whoopee cushions might amuse Jocelyn and Flora, but they would be flammable – quite a public hazard.'

Steven continued, 'The obvious alternative is to bottle and transport it, and then use regulators to reduce the pressure on site. However, the required compression isn't easy or safe, and would use a significant amount of biodiesel. On the other hand, the gas could then be used as fuel in adapted petrol cars.' Katherine pointed out, 'Another use for methane is as a substitute for petroleum, or rapeseed oil, as a feedstock for a chemical industry. Then we have a chance of making plastics, and one fine day we can do biochemistry.'

***

The next big party was held at Christmas rather than the solstice. Nevertheless, the team made an effort to repeat for the new generation the pagan theme of a decade earlier. The winter birthday children were younger, so they were entertained by a yuletide play put on by the summer kids. Marcus loved it all; Victoria and Eleanor were frightened by some parts, but they liked the fire, the kissing bough and the buttermilk bread. Rachel and Douglas, around a year old, watched without understanding or fear; she toddled and he tried to imitate her.

***

On 28 February P12 Philip took Calum to Graeme Melville's place; 'The mechanical engineers will broaden your electronics education.' The reluctant student spied the boss's daughter, now grown up, and remarked earnestly, 'Yes, these motors are very interesting, I need to learn some electro-mechanical engineering.' This didn't fool his teacher: 'For goodness' sake! Take a ten-minute break.'

Kyla recognised Calum; 'Hello, I think we met briefly in Edinburgh?' 'Yes, you've grown,' – here he realised he was looking in the wrong direction, and made things worse – 'upwards, I mean.' She tried to hide a smile, and changed the subject to spare his embarrassment; 'Have you heard the news from your group?' 'No, I don't think so.' 'Shona has just produced her third, another boy, called Roy.' 'That's great, how come you're well informed?' 'I'm training as a nurse, and Jessica told me.' He made one more mistake: 'Well, you don't have to worry about babies yet.'

***

Keith and Adam had been helping other countries to improve their radio networks. As a result of the improved communications, and the increasingly regular movement of people, the first trade with Europe had started. Exotic fruits and vegetables, not easy to grow in the UK, were transported across the channel in small boats; and exchanged for goods, mostly technological, which weren't yet available in France. The main limitation was the different currencies; there was no exchange mechanism, and the value of the nuro drifted just as Charles had feared. Increasingly his attention was directed southwards.

***

Life went on, and there was time for frivolity. By the summer of P12 the party involved so many children that nobody really cared who had a birthday and who didn't. Alan counted; 'I want to go back to my hideaway – fifteen kids!' This led to competitive grandparenthood; Bruce boasted, 'They're central to the recovery post Phraya. I might say that Alexandra and I have been responsible for six of them.' Steven replied, 'Yes, but five of those are ours too. We've only got two children, so if you consider babies per child we score two-and-a-half whereas you're only a miserable two.' Alexandra shot Margaret a glance, but the men didn't see it; David offered, 'We may only have four at the moment, but Rose and Anne are pregnant, so we'll soon have six with more to come. Eventually we might win on both ways of reckoning.' Deborah sighed, and all three ladies laughed. Alan tried another approach: 'We donors don't even know how many descendants we've got, might be dozens.' Ruth observed, 'Men are so puerile.' Rory objected, 'I say nothing, not because I can't compete, but out of maturity.'

***

Alexandra had extended the request for Phraya experiences; as the months rolled by, she received replies in many languages including, tantalisingly, some from Asia. In the autumn Henry started writing his history. He began with the UK, but already harboured ambitions to enlarge the scope, eventually to the whole world. He mentioned to his mother, 'I'd like to visit Europe.' 'Oh no, not again!' 'Dad wants to influence the people there, perhaps I could help?' 'Your kids are too small, wait a few years perhaps?'

***

Donald and Isabella were working on feed for Rory's salmon. As always, they used rapeseed residue from Gregory's farm, mixed with various cereals provided by Rose and Fergus. Experiments with soya, squash and other ingredients led to a breakthrough; but they didn't have the analytical techniques to determine what caused the fish to thrive. Katherine suggested 'It might be the omega-3 content of the soy.' Margaret wasn't interested; she merely noted, 'This is a new stage in our food economy. We're now using eatable crops, that could have fed people directly, to produce more desirable foods.' Steven replied, 'I think that's acceptable now that we can so easily produce enough to eat.'

***

Lucy had been thinking about how Henry's history could be presented to children. 'Phraya is a bit like the facts of life; you have to explain it to kids many times, at increasingly sophisticated levels as they grow up, until they feel they've always known.' Alexandra pointed out, 'But we can't explain the crisis unless they understand what it was that collapsed. We've got to bring the previous era to life for them.' Rose suggested that those who were children at the time should prepare simple vignettes for the winter party. 'Let's see if we can manage an explanation without help from the older generation.'

At Christmas Rose spoke first; she was due soon and wanted to get her part done. 'In the olden days, people could go to watch a show. There might be a singer and musicians, with loudspeakers so everyone could hear the songs easily. Sometimes dancers swayed in time with the music. Instead actors might put on a play, telling a story about kings and queens, or ordinary people. Sometimes they did all these things at once.' Jocelyn was torn: 'Mum tells me I should be a scientist, but I want to be a singer in musicals.' Katherine demurred; 'You can do what you like, but there may not be any openings for full-time performers. Why not study something useful for the progress of technology, do music as a hobby and see how it goes? Rose does a mixture of things.'

Next Benjamin tried to explain the internet. 'If you were planning a holiday, perhaps in Australia, you could go on your computer and look up fun things to do there.' Sarah asked, 'Where is it?' Jessica replied, 'On the other side of the world.' 'Did people live there? Did they have children?' 'Yes, they did, and perhaps they still do.' Marcus wondered, 'Do they speak like us?' Patricia answered, 'Good question; in some countries they speak other languages, but it's English in this case.' Benjamin continued, 'We used to be able to talk to them whenever we wanted; we can't any more but perhaps we will again one day.' Thomas objected, 'But it would be night-time there. They would be asleep.' Everyone smiled at his logic. 'That's right, but you could find out from the news what they had done the day before.'

When it was his turn, Samuel showed a picture of a commercial jet. 'The world is huge, so if you wanted to go to another country you usually flew in an airplane.' Craig was awestruck; 'How did they get into the sky?' 'The wings held them up, but they didn't flap like a bird's. Instead those round parts spewed out fire, and that made the airplane go very fast.' 'Wow, when can I go in one?' He regretted raising his son's hopes; 'I'm sorry, maybe not in your lifetime. For now, we must keep our feet on the ground.'

Julia simply described her own childhood. 'I lived with my mum and dad in a city called Aberdeen. I went to a very old school with a thousand children.' Flora was amazed; 'I didn't know there were so many people then.' Ruth didn't want to upset the little ones; 'Yes, remember I explained about Phraya? I'm afraid there is a much lower population now.' Julia hurried on: 'We were in classes of thirty kids, and we had to sit still and be quiet.' Stewart admitted, 'I wouldn't like that; our school is much better.' Alan laughed out loud; 'I know; you're only happy if you're balancing on the top of your chair with your feet in the air.'

William did his best. 'I can hardly remember how things worked before, but I recall going to a zoo.' Victoria piped up; 'What was that?' 'It was a place where they kept animals from other countries, so you could see what they were like.' 'What did they eat?' 'The zookeepers brought the food they liked, sometimes from a great distance.' Thomas wondered, 'Why didn't the animals run away?' Anne explained, 'There were cages around them; and for the animals that could fly or climb, they had roofs.' Eleanor volunteered, 'I've seen sheep, and cows, and birds. I don't like creepy-crawlies.' Fiona agreed; 'Yuk!'

Isabella could remember more; she painted a picture of London before Phraya. 'We lived around the edge, in places like this. In the centre there were shops, theatres and museums; people travelled from their homes to visit or work in them.' Craig wondered, 'Did they go in cars?' She remembered the traffic; 'Sometimes, but mostly they travelled in trains in tunnels under the ground.' 'Wow!' Marcus asked, 'What was in the museums?' 'They were full of old things,' – she dried up and Henry helped out – 'which showed what life was like even earlier in history.'

Peter outlined the former conquest of the physical world: 'In this country most people were lucky. Homes were warm, dry and full of things to make life comfortable; there was plenty of food of all kinds; travel was easy; the work wasn't tiring; there were games for spare time; and we were sure of all of this.' Thomas asked simply, 'How did it work so well?' 'The world was one big factory, using machines to make all the things people wanted. Diggers extracted the necessary stuff from the ground.' Flora asked, 'What about other places?' Jessica took over: 'It wasn't quite so good everywhere. Some people were poor, or had to struggle, but at least part of the world worked pretty well until Phraya.' Alison, unable to contribute, interjected: 'Let's talk about that another time. Shall we have something nice to eat?'

***

On 7 January P13 Rose went into labour, and made good progress at first. Given the ease of Rachel's birth, nobody expected any difficulty, but the dilation stalled. All day and night Fergus breathed with his wife; Ruth, Jessica and Kyla took turns to allow him some rest – but there was none for the patient. The next day Deborah went to talk to Ramsay for the umpteenth time. 'I know what you're going to ask. Since Julia's misfortune the state of the art has advanced, and there have been two Caesareans, both successful.' Lucy, who had come along to provide support, went straight to the point: 'When?' 'I suggest first thing tomorrow if there's no change.' 'I agree, let's get ready.'

Ramsay insisted on explaining to the exhausted couple: 'You need to understand the balance of risks. It's a serious procedure. The anaesthetic is unsophisticated, and we don't have the right instrumentation, testing and backup. Infection is likely, and we lack proper antibiotics. I can't guarantee the outcome, but it's the baby's only chance.' Fergus was worried about Rose, but she was past caring and the operation went ahead. She kissed him and her family, grabbed the mask and went under. The team gravitated towards the hospital, but Olivia calmly sent them away to distract themselves with their work.

Fortunately, the operation went well; mother and daughter Celia came through it unscathed. The team was delighted, and grateful to Ramsay for his handling of the emergency. The trouble came a fortnight later, and it wasn't medical in nature. Fergus went to see Olivia. 'I've had a bill for the operation.' 'Well as you know, in this team we share all costs.' 'Yes, and we appreciate the support, but it's a huge amount.' She was startled; 'Goodness, it is, I'll talk to the relevant people.'

Lucy spoke first; 'I really object to this. He did a good job, but the fee is unreasonable. In this team we all work for the common good, and ask only for a sufficiency, but Ramsay seems to be on the make.' David was torn; 'It's hard for us to judge, because it was our daughter who was in danger, and he almost certainly saved her life.' Deborah added, 'Celia's too, she deserves a chance at life. Perhaps I'll have a word with Andrew; he might be able to influence Ramsay.' Olivia mused, 'This is capitalism again, and not very pretty.' Charles pursed his lips; 'Perhaps we need to re-invent the national health system, funded by the state, free at the point of use but limited in scope. I'm afraid we would still have to reward the doctors and nurses according to supply and demand.'

Alison spoke to her husband: 'I need to raise an awkward subject, Cameron. My mother has been discussing with me what I should charge for dentistry, but I'm afraid I think she's really talking about your father's invoice for the Caesarean.' 'Yes, I've sensed some tension about this, and I'm not comfortable with the situation. I'll have a word with him.'

***

Rhona reported a breakthrough on basic chemistry. 'As you know, nitrogen compounds have always been problematic. For several years we've been able to make acid by heating air in an electric arc, and reacting the resulting nitrogen oxide with steam.' Bruce butted in, 'But this is so inefficient that it consumes more rapeseed, to make the electricity, than the extra that can be grown by using the resulting nitrate fertiliser.' 'True, this is only acceptable as a way of making laughing gas, but now there's another approach.' 'Excellent, let's have it.'

Rhona continued, 'There are several stages. We start by making ammonia, using wood as the energy source, as follows: calcium carbide, from lime, is heated in air to make cyanamide, which is reacted with water.' 'I'm a mathematician, but I think I follow. Is the process easy?' 'You have to burn charcoal to ensure the temperature is high enough to avoid the production of cyanide, so it is quite dangerous.'

Katherine asked, 'What about conversion to nitric acid?' 'The ammonia is oxidised, at a more modest temperature, ideally using pure oxygen and a platinum catalyst, but air and copper will do. The point of all this complexity is that it produces nitrogen oxides, but without using electricity, and then nitric acid is easy. Finally you can make ammonium nitrate, a holy grail for food production.'

***

Bruce had noticed changes to one of his testicles, and went to see Ramsay, who gave it to him straight: 'It's probably cancer, but it's not easy to diagnose accurately in the present state of the art. We'll do the tests that are available.' 'What's the best case?' 'We operate on one side and you never know the difference.' 'And the worst?' 'Well, if it has spread, we might not be able to handle it surgically. We would have to try chemotherapy, with expired drugs I'm afraid. In some scenarios there is also the possibility of using certain kinds of radiotherapy that don't need isotope sources. We'll probably start with the simplest surgery and see what happens.' Over the next few days Bruce was sufficiently worried that he sealed in an envelope some thoughts that he wanted to survive him:

"I would like to sound a warning to future generations. The world before Phraya was much more fragile than people realised. Food, fuel, electricity and other crucial resources were provided only just in time; they came from all over the globe; and very little was stored locally. Production and transport depended on an industrial complex of inputs, outputs, equipment and services, with a high degree of inter-dependence between them. The energy and minerals required to feed the system came from non-renewable sources, sometimes concentrated in politically unstable areas of the world, and often deep underground. The result was that the satisfaction of fundamental human needs was vulnerable to collapse at the slightest stress."

"The human side of the pre-Phraya world was as unstable as the physical. Law and order, and even civilisation itself, were thin veneers over the animal origins of mankind. People were driven by greed, companies by the profit motive, nations by a drive to dominance. Inequality was extreme; the abandonment of redistributive tax policies, and even of any kind of socialistic instinct, was a failure of the left. Instead the right dominated, fuelling fear, irrationality and racism, and organised religions hindered rather than helped. Those in power didn't have the interests of the masses at heart, and served only themselves. How the world worked was kept secret by governments, corporations and shadowy cabals. Even public knowledge was stored in a delicate web, prone to corruption and loss."

"I would urge that as the post-Phraya world emerges, it is constructed to be robust against the vulnerabilities demonstrated by Phraya. The essentials for a calm and collaborative atmosphere must be stockpiled everywhere – food, fuel, medicines. As far as possible basic resources should be renewable, sourced locally and shared equitably. Economics should be meritocratic yet egalitarian; the dominance of individuals, firms and nations limited; and education must be emphasised, especially in science."

***

In the morning of 8 March P13 Anne went into hospital, assuring her mother-in-law, 'Don't worry, with luck I won't need a Caesarean.' Deborah replied, 'Indeed, although Rose was fine, they're not yet safe.' 'I didn't mean that, I just don't want to cause further expense.' 'Heavens, you are confident, and funny!' Bruce, in for his operation, hid his nerves behind a veneer of rationality. 'I've found some pre-Phraya statistics; only a quarter of births were by section, and many of those were elective, so you'll be OK. My cancer used to be even more favourable, but I'm not convinced that post oncology is very good.' 'You'll be fine too.' Her optimism was justified; by the evening, as she put it, 'With the arrival of Dylan I've become twice the person I was, whereas Bruce is only half.'

More bills arrived, and Lucy went to see Ramsay. 'Olivia is disappointed at the cost of medical care.' 'I know, Cameron mentioned that Alison had raised this, but we're working hard and I feel we should be rewarded.' 'So does everyone else, including those doing less glamorous work for the public good.' 'I think doctors are a special case.' 'Well, we don't, the government's approach is that we're all in this together. You may get nationalised – and by the way, your son supports the idea.' Andrew, who had agreed to come, spoke softly; 'One way to look at this is to ask whether we're merely trying to reproduce the world that was lost to Phraya. We have an opportunity to create something new and more fully human.'

After his operation, Bruce was relieved to discover that no further treatment was required. He immersed himself once again in the task of organising the world according to his unpublished mission statement. He knew this would need a healthy population, so he was pleased when he and Alexandra raced into the lead on the grandchildren front: on 17 May Isabella produced James, at home, with no need for medical intervention.

Calum had recovered from his poor start with Kyla and, with advice from Alison, had pursued her more subtly. The girls got on well, and through Cameron they helped move Ramsay towards the idea of a public health service.

***

The market economy marched on. There were now shops selling a wide range of goods, bought in from manufacturers and growers rather than produced by the proprietors themselves. Some provided luxuries like two-way radio communications to houses and exotic foods grown under glass. Those who could afford it had central heating and enough fuel to run second cars. Olivia wanted to know how the team felt about all this, but it was no longer feasible to gather everyone for a meeting on every subject; instead she spoke to people in two groups.

First she approached those who remembered the pre-Phraya ways. Ruth started: 'I welcome the new economics; if we want grapes, for example, someone will have to see a profit in them.' Margaret cautioned, 'It's known that they can be grown here, so it's fine to allow gardeners to plant them in sheltered places, or repair greenhouses, and get on with it. In other cases, such as avocados, it's best to investigate before effort is wasted; that would be best coordinated centrally.'

Steven went further: 'In many areas of engineering, the feasibility of an endeavour has to be established by a considerable effort up front, paid for by the government; only then is it appropriate to encourage people to set up a manufacturing facility.' Deborah agreed, 'This argues for a mixed economy. The state can direct pure and applied research in the university's laboratories, place contracts for production, and finally throw the opportunity open to businessmen.' Lucy pointed out, 'Don't forget utilities, roads, law enforcement and health; they should be publicly funded.'

Rory drew the conversation back a little. 'Many goods and services are self-evidently desirable and feasible, and all that's needed is a financial and legal basis for entrepreneurs to pursue them.' Charles jumped at this; 'Yes, we need to re-establish the company as an economic entity; and limited liability as a mechanism for risk-taking and investment.' Alan was keen; 'Yes, I'd be happy to return to working for myself, or perhaps with Sam.' David had a far-away look in his eye: 'Oh, my farm,' – Alice sighed – 'and my market garden.'

Alexandra asked, What about cultural life? A gallery or museum doesn't turn a profit, and doesn't need research either, so it isn't in either of the categories we've been discussing. Even a concert or a play will be hard to provide on a purely commercial basis for a long time to come.' Bruce surprised her: 'I suppose those things will have to be financed from taxation, like the university.' She was about to celebrate his openness to the unquantifiable benefits of the arts, when he added, 'But we're a long way from such an advanced civilisation.' Olivia drew the inevitable conclusion, 'It looks as if we must establish the state as a major economic entity, raising significant amounts of money by taxation and spending it in all these ways. The government must also act as an administration; and as a legal institution, passing laws.'

Next Olivia sought opinions from members of the team born before Phraya, but with limited memories of it, and found them just as divided. Philip, Katherine and Benjamin were researchers who required funding; while Julia, Jessica, Peter, Alison and Cameron all worked for the government in more immediate ways. Several young people were aligned to the private sector: Henry, Patricia and Rose were artistic; and Fergus, William and Anne showed entrepreneurial tendencies. Some couples looked both ways: Isabella, Shona and Kyla worked for the state, while their partners Donald, Samuel and Calum wanted to start businesses. Their leader was bewildered.

***

Bruce had resumed his analysis of the future development of technology; he spoke to senior team members. 'Many of the fundamental bottlenecks involve resources from other countries.' Charles replied, 'Yes, and I'm concerned that international trade is seriously inhibited by the mess over coins – each currency works locally but is untrusted in other countries.' 'Well, it's essential that a solution is found.' 'I have been working on an idea: a government-controlled international "bank" that will exchange cels for nuros at a variable rate.'

Olivia asked, 'How will this help trade?' 'When we buy goods from Europe, we have to pay in the local money; the bank will make this easier by converting cels into nuros. At the moment, if we want to sell abroad, we often have to accept payment in foreign currency. This will be acceptable because the bank will transform it back into cels. With me so far?' 'Just about.'

'The bank will help just as much if the trades are conducted in cels: Europeans selling to us should be willing to be paid in them, knowing that the bank will turn them into nuros; and if they are forced to buy in cels, they can get them from the bank.' Bruce was pleased; 'Very elegant, all four cases work.' Alexandra's eyes rolled; 'It's a mathematical certainty. What do you want to happen next, Charles?' 'Even unilateral action would help trade, but I hope the Europeans will set up a similar bank.'

Chapter 21 Capitalism

At the gathering on the sixteenth anniversary of Phraya all the talk was of the imminent wedding of Calum and Kyla. The senior members of the team thought it appropriate that the marriage of the youngest Phraya child should be conducted entirely by the older ones.

Rose undertook to stage a performance of 'Brigadoon' just before the ceremony. 'This time we'll have the right people marrying; Calum will play Tommy Albright, and will wander into the village and fall in love with Kyla, as Fiona MacLaren. I'll play her sister Jean, who marries Charlie Dalrymple.' Fergus interrupted; 'Does that mean I have to appear in the musical?' 'Yes, you'll be fine. William can be Tommy's friend Jeff Douglas, because Anne will be hilarious as Meg Brockie chasing him.'

Benjamin asked, 'Can I be in it?' 'By all means, thanks for volunteering! You can be Harry Beaton, who dies.' 'Oh, great.' 'You'll be hopelessly in love with me, and Shona can be Maggie Anderson yearning for you.' Cameron played the sisters' father, and Samuel was Harry's; Isabella drew the short straw as Jane Ashton, Tommy's rejected fiancé.

On 25 April P16 the happy couple sang 'Almost like being in love.' The play ended with Calum returning to find Brigadoon vanished, but his marriage to Kyla was heralded by the theme tune. Peter, having married Rose and Fergus as Mr Lundie in the play, conducted the ceremony for real. Anthea Melville walked out with Rory, and Graeme with Lucy, happy that the world was safe in their children's hands.

***

"Well, there hadn't been a wedding since Alison's in autumn P13, and a lot has happened since then."

"The team is now of three generations. Those of us who were adults at the time of Phraya have always worked hard to ensure that our children would eventually be able to take over from us. This has begun to happen: science and technology, the caring professions, business and the arts are all well represented by people in their prime. I'm a bit worried about Sam; although he works well with Alan, he doesn't show much interest in preparing for the future."

"The grandchildren are also beginning to show their tendencies: Alan is turning Stewart into a roofer, Rose is training Jocelyn as a singer and Charles is shaping Flora to be an economist or businesswoman. Tom might be an engineer and Marcus is showing a talent for languages. With the younger ones it's harder to predict: Sarah is keen on babies; Craig is wild but he's interested in geography; Victoria likes plants, and Eleanor enjoys drawing. Then Fiona, Mary, Rachel, Dougie, Robert and Roy are still young children; Celia, Dylan and James are toddlers; and the latest babies are Anne's Louise and Alison's Jeannie. What a crew!"

"National government is firmly established in London, and local administrations have been formalised in Edinburgh and other regional centres. A mixed economy has emerged, based on centrally planned utilities – mains water and basic drainage have now been achieved in some areas – combined with capitalism based on the cel. Shortages of crucial equipment such as tractors, previously plentiful, have begun to arise; so the 'commons' have been taken into government ownership. Licensed 'taking' of what remains plentiful is still permitted, but charges made for things which aren't."

"Trade with Europe is beginning to thrive, thanks to Charles's bank, but it's still at the level of individuals or groups – there are no large companies, let alone international ones; and no trading between the governments of different countries."

***

Andrew had a private word with Olivia. 'I need to discuss something potentially awkward: I want to bring Liam Brodie down from Morrie. I thought I better ask you first.' 'Thanks for telling me. May I ask why?' I want him to run a sanatorium here. Don't be alarmed, he's a completely different person.' 'If you say so, but it's bound to stir up old feelings. Is it really essential that he works near here?' 'That's specifically part of my purpose, although it may sound as if it amplifies the wrong done originally. I feel that there are two parts to a rehabilitation: the amelioration of the culprit, and the acceptance by others of his redemption.' 'I understand. Can I have a few days to sound people out?'

Olivia started with Alexandra. 'You've always had a high opinion of Andrew. He has done wonderful work, but I wonder if this is a step too far?' 'It's daring, but perhaps we should give it a chance? I suspect the real barrier is Alan; you could start with him, approach Alice next and only then others?' 'Do you think I should ask Andrew to come with me?' 'No, better to have a one to one clearing of the air.'

Alan listened to Olivia's nervous preamble, and bristled as soon as he saw where she was heading. 'Dammit, why should Alice be put through this?' 'I agree it's a big thing to ask. Actually I think she will be up to it, and it might be best, if you're willing, if you could put it to her?' He was silent. 'I know Andrew isn't quite your type, but you have to admit he has achieved some remarkable things. Please think about it.' He knew that he had no rights in the matter, so he approached Alice immediately, and she surprised him. 'I've been expecting something like this for years, and decided long ago that I would cooperate.' 'I wish I was as worthy as you or Andrew or, it seems, Brodie himself!'

***

Rory spoke to Lucy tentatively: 'I'm thinking of doing fish farming on a bigger scale, running the operation as a proper business.' She didn't hold back: 'I don't think it's a good idea.' 'Why not, Donald and Fergus are interested, it could work.' 'What does that mean, feed more people or make a profit?' 'Both. The whole point of a business is to make money, but we'll only do that if we provide food at a price that people are happy to pay.' 'I just don't think it fits with the team ethos.'

At the same time Donald was having a similar conversation with Isabella. 'Higher turnover would advance the biochemistry.' She was also probing for motivation; 'I suppose so, but is that the sole purpose?' He sensed that she objected to the venture, hesitated and tuned his line of argument: 'The main aim would be to let us optimise our operation; better feed, healthier fish, more food for our customers, a contribution to the recovery.' She looked at him enquiringly, and he cracked; 'I suppose the money would help us bring up our children too?'

Alexandra disapproved too, and bent Charles's ear. 'In the past few years you've re-created private companies, and they're playing their part in the recovery. We need to offer would-be tycoons goals other than the pursuit of lucre. How about publicly owned corporations?' 'State-run industries didn't work terribly well in the pre-Phraya climate.' 'People are more public-spirited now.' He paused to consider. 'I suppose these bodies don't have to be monopolies. Maybe some kind of department, fisheries in this case, could provide state-regulated oversight of a collection of private suppliers?' 'That might keep Rory motivated.'

***

By the P16 summer party, Jocelyn was joining Stewart as a teenager disdaining the celebration. That still left nine birthday kids and as many half-birthdays, so the occasion was chaotic. In the biannual grandchild count, the Tanners had drawn level with Bruce and Alexandra. Alison said, 'I think I'm pregnant again, but that's hardly going to help my parents compete.' Deborah wasn't satisfied. 'You've all your in-laws to hand, but Shona, Fergus and Anne all have parents far away.'

***

Bruce had good news: 'You'll recall that six years ago we started searching all the computers in the country for information stored before Phraya. We've combed through hundreds of thousands of them, and have already found out a lot, but now we've really struck gold. A prepper left a readme file on his desktop.'

"To whom it may concern. Congratulations on surviving the apocalypse. Presumably I didn't, or you wouldn't be reading this. Perhaps Phraya got me, or the mayhem that's developing everywhere. Sad, but I would like to dedicate my collection of data to whichever survivors are capable of absorbing it. I hope you use it wisely and rebuild a better world than the one which is just ending."

'He sounds a bit cracked,' – Alexandra muttered, 'it takes one to know one' – 'but he was knowledgeable about technology. He was interested in what would be applicable after a collapse; he had already been collecting material for years, and redoubled his efforts in the early stages of the crisis. He filled multiple drives with a vast repository of downloaded books, articles and technical manuals. We can use it to organise new efforts in many spheres.' Philip added, 'We've made a start on it all. He couldn't store all the documents he could access, and he knew the internet wouldn't be working afterwards, so he listed an enormous amount of further information. He also attempted to locate the servers where it was stored; we can try to find them.'

Calum asked, 'What sort of knowledge did he capture? What can we do with it?' Steven replied, 'I'll give one example from hundreds. Magnets are crucial in electric motors and many other devices. The strongest ones use iron and boron – no problem – and also neodymium which is found mainly in China but also in Sweden. Ideally they contain a small amount of dysprosium, also found in China but in Norway too.' Henry picked up on this; 'At least they can both be found in Europe.' 'Yes, but it's not just a matter of getting the ingredients, though it's not trivial to dig and crush rock; the processing of dysprosium needs ion exchange equipment, which in turn will need other things, and the magnet itself takes some making.'

Peter could see where this was going. 'Every technology depends on so many others. Doesn't this mean we're going to have to be more international?' His mother remarked, 'Sounds hopeless. Shouldn't we concentrate on aims that can be achieved sooner? If we're going to branch out, why not get olive oil, and do without magnets?' 'Eventually the existing stock of motors will fail, so we must conquer the necessary technologies.' 'Are you related to my husband by any chance?'

Katherine intervened; 'OK, here's a more immediately relevant example, related to your highest priority, Margaret: food production. David has been warning for years that we have no decent source of phosphorus fertiliser, now that the bones have been used or crumbled away. Luckily the trove of knowledge told us where to find the required phosphate rocks.' Henry groaned; 'OK, don't keep us in suspense, it's found in China I suppose?' 'It used to be mined in the desert in Morocco, – 'oh, great,' – but it also occurs in France, – 'oui, pas de problème!' – 'and Spain.' 'Sí, no hay problema!'

Charles moved the conversation on. 'It's clear there will be many examples of needs which can only be met abroad. We now have very good communications with Europe and beyond, goods are being imported privately, and there is some migration to and from the continent. The question is how to scale up international trade. Henry was serious now: 'I'd like to go on a tour of Europe, with my family.'

***

Improvements to the radio system had helped Anne and Fergus establish better communication with their families; and Shona had even managed to talk directly to her parents in the far north. The Tanner family decided to go on a trip to show the in-laws the grandchildren. Deborah pointed out, 'We'll need a bus, literally.' David was about to ask why, but he stopped himself and counted on his fingers. 'You're right, there are fifteen of us.' She continued, 'Yes, and they range from the middle-aged,' – 'speak for yourself' – 'to Louise, barely walking.' 'OK, I'll see about a suitable vehicle and child seats.' 'We better take plenty of supplies. We don't really know what the north of Scotland is like, let alone the Near Isles.' He and Samuel assembled a generous supply of biodiesel, and stocked up with food cels as insurance against possible difficulties with the coins.

In July they set off and made their way through the Midlands to the wilder country beyond. Craig was pleased to escape school and indulge his curiosity about other places. He consulted a compass: 'We're going northwards; will it be icy when we get near the pole?' Fiona was more concerned with the people; 'Who lives there? If it's cold, why don't they move somewhere warmer?' Rachel retorted, 'It's quite hot here, the sun is cooking us like meat.' David was impressed; 'Heavens, they are curious, if only partly educated!'

Eventually they reached Anne's original home near the Scottish border. Her parents and her brother – who had grown up in the intervening years – were pleased to see her and to meet her new family.

David and Deborah were surprised to observe that they seemed overawed to be in the presence of members of Olivia's mythical team. The children were fascinated by the Holmes dog; William explained, 'People used to keep them as working animals, for example to herd sheep, and as pets. After Phraya no-one could spare the food, and they're still rare.' Roy, Dylan and Celia chased it and Louise vainly tried to follow.

After a couple of days, the crew moved on to Edinburgh and sought out the people who had stayed behind when the team moved to London. They started with Alastair and his engineers; 'Hello Sam, are you still working with Alan? How's Steven, pursuing the next big thing as usual?' 'Yes, and yes. I stick to practical work and let others grapple with the technical material unearthed by Bruce.' 'They've already sent me some tasks to attack.'

William introduced Anne to Raymond, and they discussed the latest on animal husbandry. Craig admired the brindled cattle; 'Where do they come from?' Shona replied, 'The Highlands.' 'When will we start going uphill?' 'You'll see when we go to see my family.' Fiona wondered, 'How can the cows see when their hair covers their eyes?' Rachel replied, 'They don't need to see far, they just keep their heads down and eat the grass.' Fiona wasn't satisfied, and produced a complicated theory: 'If they get angry, they shake their heads. That moves the hair, and then they can see the person who's annoyed them. They charge and spike you with their horns.' Celia squealed in fright, and Roy reassured her; 'No they don't, she's just joking.'

Next they went to see Peggy. Fergus enquired about the production of animal feed from sugar beet waste, but he had another purpose for the visit: fish feed. He described progress with rapeseed and soya, and then asked about corn, seaweed, and algae. She was confused; 'What do these have to do with feeding salmon?' 'We found a pre-Phraya research paper on producing the chemicals needed by carnivorous fish from plant sources, and these were mentioned.' 'OK, always happy to think outside the box, indeed outside the farm altogether. I suspect algae aren't even plants – how do I grow them?'

Finally, they called on Gordon for an overall view of how Scotland was progressing. Deborah enquired, 'First of all, how is Edinburgh?' 'Much better; cleaned up and partly occupied. We're maintaining buildings, or at least the most important ones. Other cities are springing into life too.' Shona asked, 'Has the full recovery reached the northernmost parts of the country?' 'There are still groups living independently, but they are harmless; most of the population has embraced the project.' Fergus added, 'And the islands?' 'Progress is patchy, and transport is tricky, but they're taking part.' 'Well, we hope to go there to see my folks.'

****

As Phraya receded into recent history some people, especially the younger generation, undermined the sense of common cause. Each individual tended to look to his own advantage, and the result was more misbehaviour of all sorts. The westsiders had been keeping the peace for more than twelve years: meeting violence with superior force, or the threat of it; and handling theft by simply recovering the stolen goods and discouraging a repeat offence. Recently, however, some of their members had begun to abuse their positions; punishment became heavy-handed, and fines began to look like protection rackets.

The older generation was worried about this. Alexandra remarked, 'The influence of the previous civilisation is waning. Those whose formative years were interrupted are finding it difficult to take on the responsibilities of parenthood.' Olivia replied, 'Well, in this team we've been careful with our offspring, and theirs are turning out alright.' 'Not in every case. Sorry to criticise your old friend, and to speak ill of those who are absent, but ...' She hesitated, and decided to say it: 'David and Deborah have done OK with their younger ones, but Sam ...' Charles defended him; 'He's a good worker, not everyone can be a leader of men.' Bruce joined in; 'Yes, but he isn't ensuring that his children share his ethic. Craig isn't interested in school, and his father is insufficiently focussed on education to insist that he attends.'

Olivia decided that it was time to put in place a formal process for passing laws and enforcing them. She intended to handle legislation herself, but planned to ask Deborah to devise a trial system for serious crimes and magistrates for more trivial cases. Enforcement would still be carried out by the westsiders, rebranded as the police and more closely controlled; but the actual punishments would be jail for the worst offences and official fines for the rest. Andrew, who had argued for his sanatorium system, was disappointed but agreed to work with the prison service.

****

The Tanners continued to Morrie and visited the old farm. Someone emerged; 'Hello, can I help you?' David replied, 'Sorry to be skulking about. You see, this was our farm before Phraya ... and for a while afterwards ... but don't worry, we don't want it back.' 'I understand, it must feel odd. Would you like to come in?' As they entered the farmhouse, William said, 'When we came back after Letheilean, it was so cold.' Deborah's eyes were misty; 'That was fifteen years ago, I'm glad you remember.' The place felt all wrong, and they soon left.

David had promised they would check up on the smallholding too. It was deserted, and a small tree was poking through a hole in the roof; they wandered about aimlessly, wondering what they would tell Alice and Ruth. Suddenly Samuel pointed to a nearby hill; 'That's where I broke my arm.' Fiona said solicitously; 'Poor daddy, did it hurt? 'Yes, I could see my bones poking out.' Roy was impressed; 'They should be on the inside.' Craig asked, 'Did you have to go to hospital? 'They weren't working so soon after Phraya.' Shona remarked, 'You've never told me about this, you're a canny one.'

Olivia had asked the Tanners to assess Brodie's character, so they moved on to the original sanatorium. David recalled his earliest visit. 'It was during the reconnaissance from Letheilean. Everyone was suspicious of strangers, but Andrew made an immediate impression.' They found that his good works had continued in the years since he had moved; the team he left in place had treated rejected gangsters, people broken by their experiences of Phraya and many other lost souls. As they left, Deborah concluded, 'I'm reassured about Liam coming south.'

***

Methane was now being compressed routinely and used for cooking. Steven was running a project to adapt petrol cars to run on it. When the prototype was ready, he drove it around triumphantly as he had done when biodiesel was first produced. 'Who needs to pump oil from under the ground?' Thomas asked, 'How did it get there anyway?' Peter wracked his brains. 'Plants and animals fell to the bottom of the sea millions of years ago, were covered by sediment and gradually turned into oil.' 'How did people get it out?' 'They drilled into the rock and "black gold" came squirting out; they processed it to make diesel, and petrol, and chemicals for plastics.' His father smiled; 'Excellent! Three generations of engineers, there's hope for the world yet.'

***

The bus picked its way slowly through northern Scotland. Industrial activity had not resumed so far from centres of population, and the roads were deteriorating. On single carriageways they had to pick their way through the patches of vegetation between their wheels. At one point they had to clear a landslip, but they reached their destination eventually.

The Macfarlanes greeted their daughter a little stiffly, welcomed Samuel rather formally, and were only slightly warmer with the children. Fiona asked, 'Are you mummy's mummy?' 'Yes, my dear.' Craig enquired, 'Have you been here since Phraya? Why didn't you come to England with her?' There was a pause. 'This is where we've always lived, and we had to look after our sheep. During the troubles people weren't very nice, and we decided we'd rather be on our own.' He sensed that this wasn't a welcome enquiry and changed the subject. 'What do you eat apart from lamb?' 'Heavens, what a lot of questions! We catch fish and grow crops.' Roy volunteered, 'I like oranges best.' Shona tried to relieve her mother; 'I'm afraid they don't grow up here, and no-one brings any this far.'

When the Tanners reached the port closest to the Near Isles, they discovered there was no boat large enough to transport the bus. A few cels secured a loan of a car, and they had to travel in relays on the island. Fergus's parents and sister were delighted to see him, and embraced Rose and their grandchildren. Rachel had learned from Fiona's enquiry on the mainland: 'I know who you are! You're daddy's daddy.' 'You are clever.' Celia insisted, 'I am too.' 'Well, can you count all the people here?' 'Yes, there are one, two, three, five, ten.' When the children had quietened down sufficiently to permit conversation, the Sutherlands were fascinated by the team's progress and had many questions about life in the wider world.

As the family drove south, Craig expressed dismay at the prospect of a return to normal life. 'I don't want to go back to school, it's boring learning about the world before Phraya.' Shona did her best: 'It was much better, so everyone is trying to re-create the comfort and security that they enjoyed. It's important that you learn how they were achieved, not just the technology but also how people were organised for the good of everyone.' 'I don't want to go back to old ways. Why can't we do new things?' She looked at Samuel for support, but none was forthcoming; he was more sympathetic to his son's viewpoint than he cared to admit.

Part 7 World

Chapter 22 Europe

The first pioneers had begun to arrive from further afield. Communications had been good across Europe for some years, but patchy beyond the Middle East; so first-hand information was welcome. The picture of the Phraya catastrophe painted by the new arrivals was much as expected: it had produced a similar outcome in most places. While there were few survivors in deserts and mountains – and not many in humid areas where secondary diseases had proved most serious – everywhere else the population had stabilised at a low level. Poor countries had reverted to a subsistence lifestyle, and rich democracies had started to rebuild in the UK manner. Some countries were still held back by the original descent into violence and chaos, but there was progress everywhere. Henry was shamed into action by the adventurous spirit of the people he met from afar, and he started to plan his European trip in earnest.

***

Anne confessed to William: 'You probably thought we were showing my parents all their grandchildren?' 'Yes … oh, has your brother…?' 'No, he hasn't sown any wild oats. I think we've had an accident.' His reaction was immediate; 'That's lovely, I'm pleased. These things happened even with pre-Phraya condoms.' 'I'm glad you're OK with it. I'll have a word with Rhona about quality control. My family can do the travelling to see little Venus, or Mars, as the case may be.'

***

At the beginning of August P16 Henry and Patricia set off for France, with a very excited Marcus and an apprehensive Eleanor. The idea was that they would visit the major cities of Europe, seeking to promote international relations and trade. They would be supported by the governments they visited, in exchange for reciprocal arrangements for foreign diplomats. Charles had set his son the task of ensuring that the nuro and other currencies were tied to food, or to the cel. Craig complained, 'It's not fair, why can't I go, I'm older than Eleanor.'

They started with Paris, which they found in good order; unlike London, which still had a void at its heart, the French capital was compact enough that the problem of transporting the necessities of life into the centre wasn't prohibitive. The city had already become a true centre of government, and Patricia was heartened to observe that there were even art galleries open.

***

Isabella was worried about her cousin. 'Henry has always had the wanderlust. I hope he hasn't bitten off more than he can chew.' Jessica reassured her, 'He'll be fine. Steven is the same, and Peter reckons they're both more in control than they seem to be.' Benjamin remarked, 'It's easy for you, he isn't your blood relation.' Alexandra was shocked; 'Don't say that, we're a family, nurture trumps nature every time.' Donald added, 'I agree. None of you is my kin, but I care, and not just for my wife.' Everyone laughed. 'I'm sure Trish feels the same, and will keep Henry on a leash.'

***

Jocelyn and Flora asked if they could run the games for the winter party. Ruth said, 'The last time we tried this, it reduced all the kids, and Julia, to tears.' Stewart argued, 'That was years ago, mum, we're grown up now.' 'OK, I suppose you'll have to run the whole world one day. But it's not your party, or Tom's; Marcus is the oldest winter kid, so let him onto the organising committee.' They fetched him, and were impressed by his suggestion: 'Let's do a quiz about the whole world. We can use a globe.'

The Christmas festivities began with Stewart's musical chairs; he had constructed special high stools, with help from Samuel. Jocelyn explained, 'When I stop singing, you have to climb all the way to the top and sit down properly. Children over five mustn't use their hands. The last one is out of the game but gets a treat.' When the song ended, most of the kids scrambled for seats but Rachel headed straight for the sweeties. Flora laughed; 'I think we need to clarify the rules. The next slowcoach won't get anything sugary; instead he'll have to eat a Brussels sprout.'

Marcus had designed his questions carefully. 'The first question is for the over-fives. Where do those tiny cabbages come from?' Everyone looked blank, so Craig provided a hint: 'It's in Belgium; it has already been mentioned.' Victoria got there first and pointed at the capital. 'Here's where they grow, but they taste funny.' Lucy muttered, 'Oh, for some Leonidas chocolates.'

'The next one is for those who are five or younger. If you dig straight through the earth from there, where do you come out on the other side?' The little ones were puzzled, and this time Thomas came to the rescue; 'Of course you can't really dig through the earth, and we mustn't actually poke a hole in the globe, but where would you arrive?' The kids crowded round the globe, and Robert asked, 'Is it Australia?' Eleanor replied, 'I think it's nearer New Zealand, but you were close.'

Alexandra muttered, 'Henry was going to travel there in his gap year. I wonder if Europe is as far as he'll get?'

***

Significant companies were now coming into existence, complete with shareholders, investors, employees, salaries, profit – and loss. A major limitation was the lack of an infrastructure of other companies providing intermediate goods and services: in many cases making a technological product involved working through its entire list of inputs, improvising those that did not yet exist. Reaching customers was a challenge, too; marketing was in the early stages of reinvention for a less connected age. Even if you had orders and could manufacture, transport was a problem; large lorries were forbidden, but the first trains were running, and sizeable boats were being used to move cargo.

Stewart and Flora were growing up, and were interested in commerce. He asked Alan, 'How did you get paid for your work as a joiner in the old days?' 'When people needed things built, I planned the task and calculated how much to charge. If they accepted my quotation, I did the job.' 'So you didn't work for someone else?' 'No, I was a self-employed individual.' 'Couldn't you have made more money by getting others to do the labour?' 'I could have set up a business, taken on staff and become a manager, but I liked to keep things simple.'

Flora conducted a similar interrogation: 'What about the market garden?' Ruth explained, 'We had to buy the land and equipment, so we set up a company, and borrowed the funds.' 'Did you do the farming yourselves?' Alice replied, 'Yes, but we paid for extra help at certain times of the year.' 'I think I'd like to have a proper company, and get other people to do all the chores. I'd just take it easy and let the profits roll in.' Ruth laughed; 'Yes, I had that idea too, but it would have been risky financially. What if costs had exceeded income? Then we'd have lost everything.' 'Oh, that doesn't sound so good.'

***

Liam Brodie came into the room and stood some distance from Alice, trembling; 'I don't know how to say this …' He was smaller than she remembered, and was crying. 'Don't be afraid. Just say it?' 'I am sorry that you had to endure the worst thing I ever did. I am ashamed …' She nodded to indicate that he should go on. 'I have spent the past decade working with others who went astray during the crunch, or afterwards. It's the only way I can make amends.' She took a step forward and held out her hand. 'I had forgiven you, and still feel the same in your presence.' He shook hands tentatively, and she held on until she felt a firm grip. 'Welcome to England, and good luck with your work.'

Alan met him too, and went through the motions, but found it difficult. He asked his sister, 'How did you manage?' 'It wasn't hard, because I have genuinely come to see him as a sufferer.' After struggling for a few days, he went to see Andrew. 'I think that, deep down, I haven't really accepted Brodie. Despite the fact that Alice has, I'm struggling to follow her example.' 'Like him, you had a terrible time during Phraya. I think you're still trapped in a mental hideaway.'

***

"February P17. Report from Istanbul. I have crossed Europe and am now standing in Thrace, looking over the Bosporus to Anatolia, with Asia beyond. Everywhere trade has been limited and local, involving food and other immediate desirables rather than the fundamentals of chemistry and mechanical engineering urged by Bruce. The currency problem is more serious than we thought: in eastern Europe many coins other than the nuro have been minted, all with floating values. I have been urging that in order to get international trade going we must tie all money to food, and establish currency exchange backed by banks. Only then will uneatable minerals be traded across long distances."

"The way ahead is blocked by deserts and mountains, but people are penetrating to India and China by the old silk roads. It is clear that all lands that meet the requirements of food production are home to thriving societies that are rebuilding the future. Henry."

Olivia, in her reply, said among much else: "Your father is ill with suspected motor neurone disease. It's hard to diagnose without tests to eliminate other possibilities, but in any case it was barely treatable even before Phraya. At this stage he only has muscle weakness, so don't be alarmed, and certainly continue your trip – but no further away?"

***

Alexandra was working on a programme of news and drama to be broadcast on the radio. On 18 March P17, while Alison was in what she thought was false labour, a play by Rose was transmitted. When it finished Cameron remarked, 'I wonder how long until we can see as well as hear plays?' Calum replied, 'Moving pictures involve so much more data than stills, or sound, that it's going to be a major challenge. We can't do it by AM radio; it has to be higher frequency, even if we stick to analogue, and it would be much better to go digital. I'm afraid television is still some way off.' His sister interrupted; 'Very interesting, but I'm in proper labour now, can we go to the hospital?' 'On the other hand, we can certainly do video if we don't try to transmit it. We can show it in cinemas.' 'Never mind that, you idiots!' Her urgency was justified; Una was born later that day.

***

Bruce reported his latest analysis of the resourcing of food production. 'We now devote only 20% of available manpower to food production, even including the growing of rapeseed for the biodiesel used by tractors.' Peter enquired, 'Can that be improved further?' Steven replied, 'Actually I'm worried about it getting worse eventually, as the tractors wear out.' His son was on the case: 'Well, we're working on the manufacture of the parts that fail first.' Katherine raised a more immediate concern: 'David has now observed plants suffering from phosphorus deficiency.'

Bruce concluded, 'I daresay there are many other threats, too. It sounds as if we're in a state of pseudo-equilibrium, and we'll only be safe when we mobilise international resources.' Philip wondered, 'On the other hand the globalised world before Phraya wasn't very stable either?' Benjamin argued, 'We need to take its best features and avoid its excesses: secure crucial resources, preferably in a sustainable way, and distribute them fairly, but don't transport consumer tat from China.' Bruce wondered, 'But can we run large ships around the world, even for worthy purposes, on renewable energy resources?' Philip said, 'Well, my father is working towards international trade, or at least the possibility of it, and has sent my brother off to help.'

***

On 25 April P17 Anne gave birth to a boy; Ruth did a slight double take and went off to fetch a doctor. When William showed their older children the baby, Dylan said innocently, 'He looks funny.' Lucy came, and spoke gently: 'I'm afraid he looks as if he may have Down's syndrome. We can't do the blood tests, so we just have to wait and see how he develops. At least he will be a happy lad.' Anne was determined to be positive; 'We were thinking of calling him Max, and we'll make the most of him.' Louise, as if to confirm the family attitude, chirped, 'He's nice. Can I cuddle him?'

The arrival of a compromised baby prompted Olivia to a debate she had intended to hold anyway. 'We need to support those who can't take a normal role in society – whether through incapacity, illness or injury – and deal with those who won't – the lazy, rebellious or lawless. Andrew said regretfully, 'The natural dispersion of the original groups of survivors has broken up the social fabric. We've already set up prisons for criminals; let's not give up on care in the community for the other categories at least.' Shona argued, 'Yes, but we should fund welfare for worthy people as well as coping with the undeserving.' Kyla added, 'Nursing in hospitals could move outwards, and expand to all kinds of social work.' Olivia warned, 'Sounds expensive if all this has to be funded by the state.' Andrew replied, 'If we can keep the old spirit going, a lot of care could be provided by volunteers at little cost.' Rose suggested, 'The arts can play a role.' Patricia pointed out, 'Painting is known to be therapeutic.' 'Singing too, and drama.' William offered, 'Also the care of animals; bring back pets!'

***

"2 July P17. Report from Kiev. It's interesting how the political structures of countries before Phraya are almost irrelevant to their development after it; what matters is the strength of the pre-existing economy and the underlying culture of the people. Various forms of society, economy and leadership have arisen. They share a willingness for international cooperation, but it's not always matched by readiness." A postscript suggested a theme for the summer gathering: "The children have been writing pieces aimed at entertaining and informing the kids back home. Henry."

At the party Jocelyn displayed some paintings and read: "There are wide plains with crops waving in the wind. The most amazing are the sunflowers, five metres tall, with enormous heads that follow the sun through the day. The seeds are arranged in rows that spiral outwards both ways. Van Gogh used to paint them, but he was ignored during his lifetime, and he got so fed up that he cut off his ear! Eleanor."

"There are so many languages in Europe to learn, but I'm trying to say a few words in each place. For example, 'Tu es très belle', 'Sei bellissima' and 'Du bist wunderschön' are useful in Europe. I'd like to use 'Nǐ fēicháng piàoliang' but it's some way to China. Marcus."

"Eleanor's art history isn't all that accurate, and her brother's languages aren't up to much. He enjoys embarrassing her, and I think Henry has been egging him on. Trish."

***

One day in late summer Rory was gathering cobnuts, and while he was eating them a filling fell out. Alison asked, 'How did you do that on such soft food?' 'I was cracking the shells with my teeth.' Lucy tutted, 'Good grief, how daft, old men like you can't afford to be so careless with your gnashers.' After the hole was fixed, he remarked, 'Now I've had one piece of me cut out by my wife and another put in by my daughter!' Cameron replied, 'I can match that. I allowed her to render me unconscious with noxious gas and take out a whole tooth, even before she became my wife.' Calum laughed; 'I think Kyla and I would have been better off staying in Brigadoon.'

***

The range of available comforts grew constantly, but this served only to remind people of others still out of reach. The P17 Christmas party took place in a house heated by methane pumped through the street, and the older generation wore spectacles ground to their prescriptions, but these things were scarcely noticed. The real highlight of the occasion was a pudding made with freshly ground cloves. Victoria had read about them; 'They come from the Spice Islands.' Craig boasted, 'I know where they are, near Indonesia.' Margaret remarked, 'I'm afraid they haven't come that far; they're the real thing, but they were actually grown in Majorca.' Olivia had a far-away look on her face; 'Talking of luxuries, I remember a remark of yours, Alexandra, long ago, about good teeth and Mozart. We haven't achieved either yet.' Alison objected, 'I'm working on the former,' – and Rose joined in – 'and I'm on the latter.'

***

Henry's immediate task was complete; fiscal reform was under way across Europe. Currencies were being aligned with food and could be exchanged efficiently through banks. Trade was growing, and long-distance road transport was becoming feasible. The family was tired, and Henry was acutely aware that his father's health was deteriorating, so they came home in time for the eighteenth anniversary of Phraya. Charles had lost weight and walked with difficulty, but they found that he was still himself and mentally capable.

Victoria was pleased to see Eleanor. 'Tell me about the food.' 'It was wonderful: almonds, pistachios, figs, pomegranates, apricots and citrus fruits!' Robert asked, 'What about animals?' Marcus replied, 'Wild boars, wolves, bear … lions, alligators, dinosaurs.' Patricia interrupted, 'Don't tease him.' 'I knew he was joking!' Victoria giggled: 'No you didn't, you believed him until the dinosaurs.' Julia remonstrated, 'Leave him be.'

Craig was still jealous. 'Next time there's an adventure, it's my turn.' Shona replied, 'I know you'd love to travel, but Fiona and Roy are too young, and so are you actually.' I'm ten next birthday, I'd rather be working than go to school.' Samuel remarked unhelpfully, 'I suppose if teenagers are almost adults in the post world, then ten-year-olds are almost thirteen. On your birthday we'll start teaching you some useful practical skills.' From then on, he was even more unhappy and disruptive in the classroom.

Chapter 23 Globalise?

By spring P18 long range radio had brought news of much of the world. Asia was a mixed story: areas with manageable growing conditions were thriving, but places which suffered from dry seasons were still extremely underpopulated. It was the same in Africa, where the Sahara was impenetrable. As a result a band of the temperate north, where a living could be made, was separated by deserts from the equatorial regions which also sustained life. In the Americas different considerations applied. Canada and South America were isolated by another kind of barrier: the USA, with its gun culture and prepper mentality, had suffered a much worse collapse than the rest of the west, but it was slowly recovering. Australia supported people only on the coast; New Zealand and smaller islands were entirely isolated.

***

Patricia wanted to start an art school. Andrew lobbied for it to be an adjunct to his central sanatorium, and was successful in securing modest government funding. Henry wanted to establish an institute for the study of languages, and Alexandra saw an opportunity: she argued that it should be part of the university. 'We'll sneak the humanities in, starting with those most demonstrably relevant to the scientific-industrial complex.' Rose wanted to do the same in the performing arts, but it was deemed that this needed to stand on its own as a commercial enterprise.

***

The first brave souls arrived from the USA, and provided more detail than had been available through radio communications. The government had disappeared early in the crisis, along with any trace of a disciplined military. Although the former was being rebuilt by cooperation among the majority, the latter had splintered into heavily armed groups who preferred to help themselves to the resources of others. Their transition to good works, while under way, had been much slower than that of the westsiders. Ever since the radio had revealed a better state of affairs in Europe, the pioneers' aim had been simply to escape; an unknown future seemed preferable to the threatening atmosphere that they faced daily. They had overhauled boats of adequate size and braved the Atlantic.

***

It was impossible to maintain all the pre-Phraya buildings, despite the efforts of people like Alan, Samuel and more recently Stewart. In London, especially, leaks were appearing in the roofs of museums, galleries and other public buildings. Bruce urged, 'We need to conserve institutions that house precious information. I'm especially worried about libraries; even if we prevent water getting in, they're cold and damp in winter, so books will rot. We need to digitise them and store the data in the millions of discs that will be available to us for the next few decades. After that my descendants will have to reinvent storage media.'

***

The summer party was left entirely in the hands of the teenagers, so their parents and grandparents were free to chat. Benjamin was intrigued by the influx of foreigners. 'They're coming from all the continents except Antarctica. Furthermore, most of those who leave the UK choose to come back. Does that mean that we're ahead of everywhere else?' Patricia answered, 'Europe certainly wasn't very advanced.'

Deborah reflected, 'The USA sounds even worse – the people arriving seem desperate.' Margaret joked, 'I don't suppose we looked that great when we landed on Mansay.' Steven pretended to miss the point. 'We'd only travelled twelve kilometres,' – she gave him a withering look – 'but seriously, that was eighteen years ago, and look at what we've achieved. What have the Americans been doing meanwhile?' Philip cautioned, 'We don't know much about what's going on there. Our information is mostly from those who chose to leave; perhaps the situation is better than it seems. Are they an opportunity or a threat?' Charles said, 'I knew American businessmen, and they had a can-do attitude.' Henry had a look in his eye, and Olivia caught it. 'Don't even think it.' 'Certainly not. Don't you think I've got any sense?' 'No, and Trish is no better.'

***

Isabella reported further progress in the rough art of chemistry: 'We mix ammonium nitrate with biodiesel and a few secret ingredients. With detonators based on airbags, we have explosives!' Olivia was bemused; 'Splendid, what will we do with them?' Peter explained, 'Bring down unstable buildings, mine rock, drill for oil, make ammunition,' – 'I'd rather leave guns out of it,' – 'industrial chemistry, earthworks, cutting metal, welding, forming materials, fireworks, fishing ... terrorism?' 'OK, I can see you have a few sensible ideas among the others.'

Thomas was intrigued by the loud bangs that could now be made by his aunt; Steven produced some prototype bullets and his grandson was allowed to fire the gun under supervision. Peter encouraged this interest, but Jessica disapproved: 'Can't we get him involved in more constructive engineering?' 'If he gets hurt, it will provide work for you doctors to do.' 'Very droll. Can't he read like Mary?' 'Good idea, the noise is disturbing me.' Or look after the babies, like Sarah?' 'Yes, it's making them cry.'

***

Olivia made a private confession to Charles: 'I'm not getting any younger, and nor are you, your brother and Alexandra; we'll all be seventy soon, and even the Lynns and Tanners are either side of sixty. We should be thinking about succession planning; let the next generation take responsibility.' Charles noted that she hadn't mentioned his health, but it hung in the air. 'We should also widen governance; it's no longer just about this team.' 'Yes, we've been a benign dictatorship, but it's time to reintroduce democracy.' At the subsequent meeting she suggested, 'I want to allow plenty of time for others to emerge as leaders, perhaps through organised parties. In the meantime, with a reasonably trustworthy ex-gang-leader running the police force, we shouldn't suffer from a coup by other strong men.' It was agreed that there should be an immediate announcement of elections to come in two years' time.

***

In the late autumn Alison told Calum that she was expecting again. 'Kyla and I are trying too. Bruce will be pleased; he reckons it's crucial for the emerging civilisation that population grows quickly while there's continuity from pre-Phraya times. Of course he has produced a model, showing the numbers doubling from an assumed three million worldwide in P0, to five million at P20 and twenty million, dominated by the young, at P50.' She pondered, 'I suppose some of us might see that.' 'He wants it to stabilise at half a billion after three centuries.' 'If Alexandra has her way, they'll all be cultured souls with just enough engineers to make things work!'

Bruce was concerned with quality as well as quantity. He spoke to the Tanners: 'I'm really worried about Sam, and how he handles Craig.' David bristled; 'What do you mean?' 'He lets the boy do as he pleases. We need the young to be disciplined, and focussed on propagating the same virtue to the next generation. If the world doesn't improve, it could so easily slip into decline.' 'He's unconventional and he's allowing his son to be a free spirit.' Deborah said nothing, but she was inclined to agree with the taskmaster; later she had a quiet word with Shona about her son's parenting.

***

Andrew spoke to the older members of the team. 'I've been thinking about Olivia's decision to hand over the burden of leadership. You have all earned the right to retire, but so have many others. I believe we should extend state provision to include pensions.' Bruce objected, 'Perhaps, but the demographics are against us; so many children, insufficient manpower for essential projects, skills shortages … we can't afford to release healthy people from work until seventy.' Charles, despite his own diminishing capacity, concurred; 'That sounds about right. We could start with government support, gradually export the burden to companies and self-employed individuals, and eventually bring down the retirement age as resources permit.'

Mary had seen Charles stumbling, and asked, 'Why does he walk in a funny way?' Jessica replied, 'He's got a disease which prevents his brain from controlling his muscles properly.' Thomas observed, 'He has lost weight too. Are his muscles wasting away because he can't use them?' Sarah pointed out, 'Babies can't walk, and their legs don't get smaller.' Their mother answered, 'They are born with tiny limbs which grow when used, starting with the arms. They get taller when they start toddling. It's different with adults; their muscles are fully developed, and only shrink when they aren't exercised. Unfortunately, this process will spread around Charles's body until it's quite difficult for him to do essential things like breathe and swallow.' Mary reflected, 'It's sad when people get old.'

***

At Christmas the entertainment of the younger children was again delegated to the growing army of older ones; the theme was the wider world. Thomas described how cars used get to France without getting wet, and showed them models of car ferries and the railway tunnel. Flora explained how olives taste bitter from the tree, but can be treated to make them edible. Victoria and Sarah showed drawings of the flora and fauna indigenous to the Mediterranean region. Craig had selected suitable European songs – 'Stille Nacht, heilige Nacht' and 'Il est né le divin enfant' – Marcus translated – 'Silent night' and 'He is born, the heav'nly child' – and Jocelyn sang. Stewart was too taken up with a new belle to contribute.

At New Year P19 the parents of the older girls gathered to discuss their daughters' sexual health. Katherine was worried; 'Jocelyn will be sixteen next summer. Given my experience, I want her to be able to control her reproduction. We still can't make contraceptives.' Ruth was also concerned; 'Flora will be fifteen at the same time, and Stewart is probably already active.' Julia groaned, 'Victoria is already pubescent,' – Patricia added 'Eleanor too,' – 'and the tampons are running out.' Jessica replied, 'Well, we can make them, perhaps in time for Sarah, or at least Mary.' Shona remarked, 'Don't forget Fiona; unfortunately, we've produced a lot more girls than boys.' Katherine concluded, 'The pill is some way off, because the biochemistry is tricky; I'll talk to Bruce to see if he's found anyone with the required expertise.'

In March Kyla announced that she was pregnant. Ruth remarked, 'There wasn't much of an interlude between Calum's birth and Stewart's. The way he's chasing that girl, I don't think there will be much of a gap between their children either.'

***

The first Australians arrived, and even one person who had made it all the way back from a seriously interrupted holiday in New Zealand. Only the Pacific islands and a few other remote outposts remained uncontacted, even by radio. The latest arrivals confirmed the picture that Bruce had built up: of a world recovering everywhere, but with a patchwork of differing resources and deficiencies. He spoke to Olivia; 'I'd like you to call a meeting of the whole team, to discuss whether we should try to create a globalised economy.' 'It's certainly an issue worth discussing, but such a large meeting will be unwieldy.' 'Indeed, it won't be possible to for everyone to speak, but at least they can all listen?'

Olivia introduced the topic: 'The British have re-established themselves as a nation, and many other countries are in the process of doing so. The question is whether they should unite to form an international entity. This could mean anything from a network of local trade and cultural links to a global economy and world government, with many possibilities in between.' She looked at Bruce and he began. 'We have identified a number of limitations to our development which can only be circumvented by means of inputs from other countries: food, fuel and minerals. As I've mentioned before, the most important requirement is knowledge; and there's a time limit, perhaps another thirty years, after which we have to be self-sustaining. From then on direct memories of how things worked before Phraya will fade. The wider the pool of pre-Phraya expertise now, the further we will get before we're cast adrift.'

Deborah argued, 'I think we should distinguish physical and intellectual resources and discuss them separately. The risks and benefits may be different. Similarly, we should consider technology first, and move on to culture later.' Steven launched in: 'If we want physical mastery, we'll have to acquire chemicals wherever they occur,' – Charles interposed – 'which in turn demands trading relationships, so perhaps we can't disentangle the cultural aspects of the debate.' Everyone laughed and Alexandra caught Henry's eye. Katherine suggested, 'Let's assume for this part of the discussion that we can secure the necessary cooperation with other countries. The question is whether we want to move goods around the world, in order to satisfy all possible desires, everywhere?'

Alan provided one possible answer. 'I think we should keep to ourselves. I'm not arguing that we Scots should go home; I accept that we've created a United Kingdom, but let's leave it at that?' Peter objected, 'But our present way of life would collapse eventually. We can make do and mend, perhaps for a few decades, but then we'll need to manufacture advanced equipment afresh. We won't be able to do this if we don't secure the necessary basics.' Benjamin added, 'If we leave this until some emergency arises, it won't be possible to re-start the industrial world at all quickly.'

Margaret introduced a new concern: 'Nowhere else seems to be as advanced as we are. There are already signs that people from all over the world would like to come here. If we increase trade, there will be an increased flow of people in all directions. There's a possibility of invasion, either by stealth or suddenly, and perhaps not peacefully.' Patricia pointed out, 'That's precisely the reason for fostering cultural links. We weren't attacked when we toured Europe. We need to embrace everyone.'

Philip suggested, 'Perhaps we should identify crucial goods, and also expertise, that we need to exchange with other countries. We don't have to create a fully global economy, at least not as an immediate aim. We could manage international relations, and control the movement of people, to make sure everything runs smoothly.' Olivia remarked, 'You were always able to see both sides of an argument. You should have been a lawyer.'

***

For years Rose had wanted to set up a theatre for live performances. Meanwhile Alexandra had been pressing the argument that the university should expand the humanities well beyond Henry's linguistic institute. Eventually they obtained funding for a drama school; it was neither commercial nor academic, but it did teach those who wanted to prepare for the possibility of making a living by acting, singing and dancing. It also broadened the nation's cultural life and prepared the way for resumed study of the human condition.

This was the trigger for a long-expected rebellion by Jocelyn; she declared to her parents: 'I'll be an adult this summer, so I can choose what I'm going to do: join Rose's school. I'm sorry but I'm not cut out to be a scientist, like you two.' Philip accepted it immediately; 'That's fine, whatever makes you happy. A more connected world will need to be knitted together culturally as well as conquered technologically.' Katherine fought a half-hearted rearguard action: 'Schoolkids will need to be taught all subjects, so perhaps you can pass on a little of what we've taught you as well as providing entertainment.' 'Mum, the arts aren't mere amusement; they're the real purpose of life, once physical survival has been guaranteed by the likes of you.'

***

In the UK new electronic devices were being manufactured once more, using pre-Phraya components cannibalised from other equipment. Now Philip reported a more significant development: 'Radio communications have now leapfrogged the deserts of the Middle East, so we're getting more information on what's going on in China. They are casting silicon wafers,' – he waited, but Olivia merely looked at him quizzically – 'which means they are on their way to making chips. Electronics can get going again properly.' 'So it's now only two hundred years until we have smartphones?' 'Who knows, Calum's forthcoming child may get to see them in old age, when the Americans get going.'

***

The inconclusive debate on the question of whether to globalise proved irrelevant: people everywhere aspired to the restitution of a semi-mythical world that half of them couldn't remember or had never known in the first place. Charles, in a wheelchair and with his speech starting to slur, involved himself in the coordination of world trade. Initially this was by road, and local, but to an increasing extent goods were shifted across regions. Benjamin, under Bruce's direction, analysed the costs and benefits of sea transport; he drew the expected conclusion that over long distances it only made sense, for the moment, to shift selected commodities. Soon small ships were crossing oceans with high value merchandise and people; larger vessels were simply too challenging and expensive. The economics did not permit the exchange of frivolities across the world. Modelling showed that a full industrial ecosystem was still a long way off, but a start could be made and there was a clear path for its development.

Rory was energised by the resurgence of shipping, and discussed the possibility of trawling the sea once more. 'We could give our long-suffering salmon some proper food.' Donald replied, 'Also the people might like to eat other species?' 'Good idea, we don't want the problem of nineteenth century Scottish summers, when the servants refused to eat oily fish more than twice a week.' 'Let them eat lobsters, eh?' James asked, 'What's that?' Douglas supplied the answer; 'It's a crustacean, with enormous claws.' Rory sighed, 'Delicious, Margaret will be thrilled.'

***

The team had agreed that there would be a fortnight's holiday in the summer and a week in the winter. At the party in June P19 Craig asked, 'Can we go to Europe next year? The weather is warmer.' Marcus was keen; 'Yes, I want to try out my French.' Thomas had been watching transport developments: 'Let's go on the train through the tunnel; they've pumped out the water.' Stewart had seen pictures of the Alps; 'I'd like to climb Mont Blanc.' Eleanor was lyrical, 'The glaciers look like heaven on earth.'

The adults didn't rise to this, so the kids added to the pressure. Victoria said, 'They have delicious melons there.' Flora brushed aside a potential objection: 'We can buy them with nuros.' Rachel jumped on the bandwagon, 'It's not fair, I've never tasted olives.' Some of the older generation were tempted, but Charles pointed out, 'It would be very expensive to take everyone all the way, but perhaps there could be trips with serious purposes like Henry and Trish's?'

***

The children could no longer understand Charles's speech, so Philip undertook to provide him with a computer synthesised voice. Shona set Craig the task of working with the old man, and the provision of care proved to be the making of the boy; but it didn't cure him of his desire to travel.

***

Cultural life was developing beyond the amateur efforts of individual groups. A publishing industry had sprung up following the burst of survival stories and Henry's history. In major cities small theatres were putting on performances; any play or musical which threw light on life before Phraya was popular with those so young that they had only their parents' or even grandparents' stories to go on. Painting and sculpture filled a yearning for dreams. People had spare energy; competitive sports were reborn. The children's plea for travel was supported by a constant flow of visitors from abroad.

***

Alexandrea wrote, "I had my doubts about Craig, and Bruce can't stand the way Sam is raising him, but perhaps he'll prove to be the next Henry – Europe, Japan, next stop Hawaii."

***

On 29 July P19 Alison went into the newly re-opened maternity hospital, and was attended by a nurse with a foreign accent. The labour went quickly, and Lucy arrived just as the baby was born; she asked the midwife, 'Where do you come from? 'The Philippines. I was born there soon after Phraya, and have just come here.' She put the infant to his mother's breast. 'Well I'm glad you did, you have been so helpful to me, thank you. What are boys called at home?' 'Some of the names would be unfamiliar to you, but one of the most common ones is James.' 'That would be lovely, but we've got one already.' Lucy suggested, 'That doesn't matter. It's Scottish, and biblical, and international, so appropriate for the way the world is going.'

***

One day in the autumn, there was a noise in the air, quiet initially but getting steadily louder. Isabella heard it first, and took the children outside. The elder James pointed to the sky, and shrieked, 'What's that?' Douglas thought he knew; 'Is it an aeroplane?' Their father replied, 'It must be. I can hardly remember them; there weren't any on Estra, but we used to see them on Iseala, and when we went to the mainland.' Their mother laughed, 'You were such a country boy, Donald! I heard them fly over London every day.'

After the sighting a spontaneous celebration broke out. Julia showed the children how to make paper gliders. Samuel made a wooden plane, and Peter tried to demonstrate powered flight using elastic bands, but they had all perished. Jessica substituted strips of latex rubber, and the children were mystified by the hilarity.

Meanwhile the older generation reminisced. Steven said regretfully, 'We're such a long way from achieving air travel for real.' Bruce pointed out, 'It was business and tourist flights that spread Phraya.' Margaret nodded; 'True, but international shipping also brought us pineapples, bananas, real vanilla pods.' Charles gestured for them to wait, and he typed, 'Working on it.' Deborah, systematic as always, complained, 'We don't have full utilities, real telephones, TV, internet, proper email.' Lucy continued, 'Nor advanced medical tests, major operations, drugs.'

The mood had slipped a little, so David listed some achievements. 'We've got plentiful food, heating, local transport, basic communications, money, trade,' – Alexandra continued – 'peace, empathy for the unfortunate, law, education, culture.' Ruth asked, 'Won't that do?' There was a chorus: 'No!' Steven said, 'Onwards,' – Bruce interrupted – 'and upwards, into the sky.'

****

On 5 Nov P19 Kyla gave birth to a girl. The team celebrated with fireworks, secreted long ago by Lucy for this occasion. Calum, the last of the pre-Phraya children, put the baby into Charles's lap. He wrapped his arms around her, and silence fell while he tapped slowly on his keyboard: "Welcome little one! I wonder: what are you going to make of this world?"

www.ingramcontent.com/pod-product-compliance
Lightning Source LLC
Chambersburg PA
CBHW051050050726
47592CB00002B/467